THROUGH *the* SMOKE

ALSO BY BRENDA NOVAK

HISTORICAL ROMANCE

Of Noble Birth
Honor Bound (originally available as *The Bastard*)

CONTEMPORARY ROMANCE

Whiskey Creek Series: The Heart of Gold Country
When We Touch (prequel novella)
When Lightning Strikes
When Snow Falls
When Summer Comes
Home to Whiskey Creek
Take Me Home for Christmas (forthcoming)
Come Home to Me (forthcoming)

Dundee, Idaho Series
A Baby of Her Own
A Husband of Her Own
A Family of Her Own
A Home of Her Own
Stranger in Town
Big Girls Don't Cry
The Other Woman
Coulda Been a Cowboy

Sanctuary
Shooting the Moon
We Saw Mommy Kissing Santa Claus
Dear Maggie
Baby Business
Snow Baby
Expectations

ROMANTIC SUSPENSE

The Bulletproof Series
Inside
In Seconds
In Close

The Hired Gun Series
White Heat
Killer Heat
Body Heat

The Last Stand Series
Trust Me
Stop Me
Watch Me
The Perfect Couple
The Perfect Liar
The Perfect Murder

The Stillwater Trilogy
Dead Silence
Dead Giveaway
Dead Right

Every Waking Moment

Cold Feet

Taking the Heat

THROUGH *the* SMOKE

A NOVEL

BRENDA NOVAK

NEW YORK TIMES BESTSELLING AUTHOR

Montlake
Romance

Copyright © 2013 Brenda Novak
All rights reserved.

Printed in the United States of America.

Published by Montlake Romance

ISBN-13: 978-1-477-80876-4
ISBN-10: 1-477-80876-0

Library of Congress Control Number: 2013906526

To Uncle Jim.
Thanks for all your support.
You have been a wonderful example of love
and kindness.

Dear Reader:

I'm so excited to bring you this historical romance! *Jane Eyre* was one of my favorite books when I was a girl (it's still one of my favorites). I love the gothic feel of it, the air of mystery and, most of all, the heart-pounding romance. So when I first started writing, I set out to create stories in a similar vein. Then my career took a different turn and I ended up writing contemporary romance. After forty-something books, I'm finally returning to my first love. I hope you will enjoy reading this story as much as I enjoyed writing it.

In case you're interested, I also have two other historical romances that have been published so far, *Honor Bound* and *Of Noble Birth*. And for those who are willing to read another genre, I'm currently writing a smalltown contemporary romance series. Come meet the longtime friends who've made Whiskey Creek the "Heart of Gold Country" with *When Lightning Strikes*, *When Snow Falls* (nominated by *RT Book Reviews* magazine for Book of the Year), *When Summer Comes* and *Home to Whiskey Creek* (with more on the way). Information about these and my other works can be found on my website at BrendaNovak.com. There, you can also enter to win my monthly drawings, sign up for my newsletter, contact me with comments or questions or join my fight to find a cure for diabetes. My youngest son suffers from this disease. So far, thanks to my generous supporters, my annual online auctions (held every May at BrendaNovak.com) have raised more than $2 million.

Here's wishing you many hours of reading pleasure!

Brenda Novak

Homines quod volunt credunt.
MEN BELIEVE WHAT THEY WISH TO BELIEVE.

PROLOGUE

Northeastern Coast of England
January 1838

He'd kill her. Just as soon as he could get his hands around her delicate neck, he'd stop the black heart that beat beneath all that misleading beauty and put an end to his own misery. Although Truman Stanhope, the Earl of Druridge, had come all the way from London to Newcastle-Upon-Tyne and had a bit farther north to go before he reached his home, blind fury caused his pulse to pound as fast as the hooves of the horses that were pulling his coach. His driver had been pushing the poor beasts so hard it'd been necessary to stop and change them out at every opportunity. But he was determined to reach Blackmoor Hall in record time, to confront his wife as soon as possible.

"How dare you?" he muttered over and over. It wasn't enough that he'd lost his beloved parents to a terrible carriage accident shortly after he'd married Katherine? That the child she bore him had lived only six months—and died under mysterious circumstances, circumstances that made him suspect she might have had something to do with it?

He glared down at the letter she'd sent him, at all the lies written in her perfect penmanship. Did she *really* think he was so addle-brained? So terribly gullible as to believe the child from this new pregnancy could be his?

My Dearest Husband,

I am pleased to share this good news with you, so pleased, in fact, that I dare not wait until your business has concluded in Town and you have returned home. Knowing how eager you have been to have a child—

He noticed that she did not refer to their firstborn. She never did, never had. Since the moment little Jeremy entered the world, she'd ignored him, and Truman feared it was *his* love for the child that had given her the incentive to do what he believed she did. She'd seemed singularly determined to destroy him, no matter how far she had to go.

Think of it, she wrote. *Now, if God grants us a son, you will have an heir to your lands and title. At last our prayers have been answered.*

"Prayers," he growled, feeling the rage boil up again. *"Prayers?"* He'd long since quit asking God for any type of a child—boy or girl—with Lady Katherine. He didn't think she was stable enough to be a mother. There was something wrong with her, something vital that was missing. He'd seen it time and time again in that odd, blank stare of hers. In her spiteful, cutting words. In the way she laughed at anything that brought him misery.

The letter went on to say she must have gotten pregnant that night nearly three months ago, when he was intoxicated and, although she'd represented it differently, desperate enough that he nearly took her back into his bed. He'd started to kiss her, to touch her—his body had demanded a release after the many months he'd remained celibate—but he hadn't finished the act. He'd thought of Jeremy and been unable to finish. As drunk as he was, he had not been so drunk that she could rewrite history.

So what was this *really* about?

He wished he couldn't answer that question, but it was all too obvious. He'd left her alone long enough that she'd grown desperate for a way to cover her betrayal. After three months, or maybe longer, she was probably beginning to show and knew she had to explain the pregnancy to him somehow. Waiting until he returned and found her big with child would look too suspicious. So she'd penned this letter full of false excitement, hoping to disarm him with her "good news" and hope of an heir.

Instead her words had brought all the hate he'd begun to feel for her rushing to the surface.

"Are you well, m'lord?"

It was his driver, calling out to him from the box on top. Truman had been so silent on the trip that William kept checking on him.

"Fine," he responded, but his mind wasn't focused on his answer. He was wondering who the father of this child could be. The way Katherine flirted and fawned over every man she met left him with so many possibilities. She'd spent a great deal of time in London, both with and without him, and loved nothing more than inciting him to jealousy. . . .

He crushed the letter in his hand. "Damn her!"

"Did you say something, m'lord?"

He hadn't realized he'd spoken out loud. But he didn't bother to explain. They were already passing through the black-iron filigree gate and charging up the drive to Blackmoor Hall. It was Sunday morning. With any luck, the servants would still be at church and he'd have the chance to speak to his wife alone. Katherine had mentioned that she had "taken to her bed lest she risk the well-being of *their* child."

The irony of her being so careful, after what he believed she'd done to little Jeremy, made his muscles bunch. Heaven help him. He was finished, he promised himself, and he'd tell her so. He would get a divorce, no matter the consequences to either of them. He would not live with her another day. Or maybe once the baby was born, he'd have her committed to Bedlam.

Jumping out the moment the horses came to a stop, he ran into the house and shouted her name.

Chapter 1

Creswell, England
February 1840

Something tickled. Rachel McTavish squirmed, trying to reach the spot just beneath her left breast that itched so mercilessly, but the layers of her shift, corset and wool dress nullified the efforts of her fingers.

Perched on a ladder propped against the shelves of her mother's bookshop, she glanced around the empty shop and through the front windows. It was early yet. No carts or carriages rumbled past.

Plunging one hand down the neck of her dress, she closed her eyes and scratched. *Ahhh . . . blessed relief!*

The bell tinkled over the door. Rachel's eyelids flew open to find a man standing just inside the entrance, staring up at her with a mocking smile on his lips. Only it wasn't just any man—it was the Earl of Druridge. Although Rachel had never seen him at such close proximity before, she would have recognized him anywhere. She had feared he might come to call. His solicitor had visited her thrice already.

Her scalp tingled with apprehension and embarrassment as she extricated her hand from inside her bodice.

"I'm sorry to interrupt, Miss McTavish." His voice was a deep baritone, thicker and richer than honey. "I can see you are quite busy, but I think you know why I am here."

Ignoring the subtle taunt, Rachel descended the ladder, half-wishing she could stay where she was, well out of his reach. She felt like a bird unwisely abandoning the safety of its cage to flit about the nose of a cat.

But she knew the relative security of the ladder was an illusion. The earl was nothing like his small, bespectacled solicitor, in looks or in manner, and would not be so easily routed.

"I have nothing to say to you, sir. I've told Mr. Lewis and your butler, Linley, so before, and on more than one occasion."

"So you have." He smiled but no kindness entered his amber-colored eyes. "Perhaps they didn't mention that I am willing to make your cooperation well worth the effort."

Lord Druridge possessed a full head of dark, wavy hair and stood several inches taller than most men. Once on an equal footing with him, Rachel had to tilt her head back to look into his face, a visage hard and lean enough to remind her of the hungry wolves fabled to have roamed the countryside. Although he had probably just shaved, the shadow of a heavy beard darkened his jaw. And he was wearing gloves, but she'd heard that scars from the fire at Blackmoor Hall two years ago marked his left hand, extending as far up his sleeve as one could see.

"Your man mentioned a large purse, but I am not interested. My father is dead. I have nothing to say to you."

"Your father may be dead, but by the narrowest of margins, I am not." The earl took a step toward her, his face losing all pretense of civility. "I won't rest until I learn what happened the day the fire killed my wife and the child she carried—"

"Someone else's babe, by all reports." Rachel uttered the words before she could check them, but once they were out, she refused to feel the least penitent, despite the sudden clenching of Lord Druridge's jaw. Most likely no one had ever dared say such a thing to his face, although the villagers, even his own servants, gossiped about his late wife's many dalliances and anything else that had to do with him or his family.

"Already I see you know more than you led my solicitor to believe," he said, catching her in her own words. "Please, continue to speak freely."

"I know nothing. Only that you had as much reason to set the fire at Blackmoor Hall as anyone," she said. "Mr. Lewis told me what Linley claims to have found, but I don't believe it. And I am not so impressed with your power or your money as some might be. I will not let you intimidate me."

The earl's hand snaked out to grab her elbow. "If you are not intimidated, you should be," he said. "I hold the lease on this building as well as your home. I could turn you and your family out, and will do so if I must. I will have my answers, one way or another."

Fear raised the hair on Rachel's arms as she tried, unsuccessfully, to pull away. She wanted to put some distance between them, to escape the subtle smell of soap that clung to his body. "Isn't it enough that you had my father sacked when you knew—had to know—he was dying?"

He released her, but his body remained taut, like a tightly coiled spring. "I sent your father away from the colliery because he was a blustering drunk with a penchant for starting trouble. He'd been warned before." The earl made an impatient gesture with his hand. "But I haven't come to justify my actions. Believe what you will of me, Miss McTavish, only speak the truth. What do you know about the fire at Blackmoor Hall?"

"My father had nothing to do with it."

"More than one man has pointed me in his direction."

"Because Lewis and Linley go around plying various miners with their insidious questions, and my father is a likely scapegoat. He had just lost his job; he was angry. He said some things he shouldn't have, but that doesn't make him a murderer."

The earl's eyes seemed to glow with an inner light. "Neither does it give him much to lose."

Rachel lifted her chin. "He had his family. He wouldn't have wanted us to suffer because of his actions—"

"From what I know of Jack McTavish, he rarely took the suffering of others into consideration," he broke in. "Regardless, I am not looking to falsely accuse anyone, even a ghost."

"Then look elsewhere for your murderer, my lord."

"I will go where my questions lead me. Unfortunately for both of us, they have brought me here."

"A waste of your time, surely."

"Not if you hope to retain your home."

She swallowed hard. "More threats, my lord? Well, consider this: If you turn us out, you will never get your answers."

Rachel looked past him through the window, hoping someone would enter the shop so she wouldn't have to be alone with him any longer. But she saw, for the first time, that a liveried footman stood outside. No doubt he worked for Druridge and had been set there to ensure his master's privacy, as if the presence of the Druridge carriage wasn't enough to discourage all but the boldest of souls from entering.

"It would seem we have reached an impasse," he said.

Feeling helpless in the face of his persistence, Rachel eyed him. The earl could send his solicitor or his trusted butler to press her or appear any number of times himself, and he could stay as long as he liked. She could do nothing about it. To make matters worse, her mother was bedridden with a raging fever. If he turned them out, they'd have nowhere to go.

"Please, let us be," she said, lowering her voice. "My mother is ill, I have a young brother to care for, and I have much to do here. I cannot help you."

He skewered her with a pointed stare. "Believe me when I say I am sorry for your misfortune, Miss McTavish. But I think you can help me, and if you know what is good for you, you will. You may have no interest in money, although it appears you sorely need it"—his gaze ranged over her simple dress, making her doubly aware of its threadbare state—"but I have something of much greater value to offer."

"I don't care what you have, my lord. You can evict us if you want, but my answer will not change." *Brave words, for a coward.*

"Even for a competent physician to attend your mother?"

Rachel's breath caught and held. A physician? Besides an old drunk called Smedlin, Creswell had no expert in the healing arts. And thanks to the terrible weather over the previous two weeks, she had been unable to convince anyone more capable to traverse the long road from Newcastle.

"I doubt a doctor could do anything more than I have—"

"You don't know that, do you?"

She'd been bluffing when she'd thumbed her nose at his threat to toss them into the street. She could never allow him to do that. The promise of a doctor baited the hook better still. . . .

"Dr. Jacobsen is a fine physician," the earl continued as though sensing her weakness. "He is staying at Blackmoor Hall this very instant. I need only send my carriage to bring him to your cottage." He raised his eyebrows while absently massaging his left hand—his scarred hand.

Fleetingly, Rachel wondered if it pained him. Any scarring would be a pity, considering it blemished a manly form as close to perfection as she had ever seen. Maybe Druridge's face was a bit too exaggerated in its planes and angles, a bit too hard-edged to be considered handsome. But a woman could never complain about the rest of him. Thanks to his broad shoulders, lean waist and long legs, she couldn't help feeling a bit . . . dazzled in spite of her feelings where he was concerned. It didn't help that he wore his expensive clothing—a calf-length, green cape, beige trousers and a black coat with matching waistcoat—with an indifferent air that suggested he'd just as soon be garbed in something simple as something so obviously rich. His physique, and how fluidly he moved, set him apart from any other man she'd ever met, especially when she compared him to the stooped miners that comprised the better part of the village.

"No." Ignoring the raw magnetism that emanated from him like steam rising from a lake, she crossed her arms in a decisive manner. "My mother will be fine. She merely needs her rest."

"Certainly the three of you will rest easier once Dr. Jacobsen has taken a look at her. . . ."

Not if Jillian knew what she had to trade for the visit. And her mother would guess at first sight of a gentleman doctor. Accepting help from the earl, the one man Jillian blamed for the death of her eldest son and, less directly, her husband, would be enough to send her to the grave. Besides, after all Rachel had secretly done to unite the coal workers against Druridge, her sense of honor wouldn't tolerate any kind of alliance with him.

"You have received my answer. She will recover," she said and prayed she spoke the truth.

The earl studied her for several seconds. Then he said, "I will allow you some time to think about my offer. I ask only that you answer a few questions in exchange for Dr. Jacobsen's visit." He gave her a stiff, mocking bow. "I hope you will reconsider before it's too late," he added. Then he strode through the door and disappeared into the dark interior of his large coach.

Rachel hovered over her mother's bed. "How do you feel?" she whispered.

The wasted figure that was Jillian McTavish nodded weakly. Her skin was as waxy and pale as a yellow moon; her eyes looked like huge pits in her sunken face. "Well enough, daughter."

"I'll see ye in the mornin'," called a soft feminine voice from the other room, and Rachel realized that she hadn't said good-bye to Mrs. Tate, the neighbor who sat with her mother and younger brother while she minded the shop.

She caught the older woman as she was stepping outside. "Thank you. I know it's not an easy thing," she said, her voice faltering.

"'Tis better me watchin' it than ye," Mrs. Tate responded. "You're sufferin' right along with 'er, that ye are."

A tear trickled down Rachel's face, but she swiped at it. "We cannot always choose what happens to us. But we can choose how we handle what does." She echoed her mother's oft-repeated words with more conviction than she felt. At the moment, she wondered if she could bear to be alone with Jillian. Surely it was only a matter of time. How much longer could her mother cling to that gossamer strand of life that kept her among the living?

Mrs. Tate lowered her voice as she clasped Rachel's hands in her own. "She will likely pass tonight. Ye need to be prepared, luv. She's been like this for nearly a week."

"Part of me prays that she can be released from the pain," Rachel whispered. "Watching her suffer is . . . it's so terrible. But the other part . . ." She hesitated, and Mrs. Tate spared her the effort of continuing.

"I know. We'll all miss 'er. She's been a pillar of strength to this village for years, teachin' so many of us our letters." The rotund woman shook her head and, with a squeeze of Rachel's hands, let go. "You should know that Geordie tried to wait up for ye, but sleep got the better of 'im, poor lad."

She'd seen her brother curled up in his bed by the far wall; they all slept in the same room. "I had some accounts I had to go over at the shop. My mother has always taken care of the books, and I'm having a devil of a time trying to figure out what she's done."

"Ye can't be everywhere at once."

"Rachel? Is that you?" her mother called from the other room.

"Go to 'er before she wakes Geordie," Mrs. Tate said.

Rachel felt little concern that she'd disturb Geordie. He slept too deeply. But she didn't want to put her mother to a lot of effort. "I'm on my way."

"Let me know if ye need anythin', child," Mrs. Tate said as she left.

Rachel forced a brief smile before closing the door and hurrying to the bedroom. Dipping her hands into the bowl of cool water on the washstand, she brought up the rag that floated inside and wrung it out so she could dab away the beads of sweat that glistened on her mother's forehead.

"I can't take much more." As Jillian tossed on the sweat-soaked sheets, a spasm gripped her frail frame, and Rachel held a bowl while she vomited a clear liquid flecked with blood.

The Earl of Druridge and the physician he'd offered came immediately to mind. Could this Jacobsen help? Or was Rachel, tired of carrying the heavy burden of her mother's illness alone, turning coward?

Eventually Jillian sank back on the bed and lay without moving, leaving Rachel to stew in frightened indecision. Was Mrs. Tate right? Would her mother die this night? Or was the worst of it over?

She glanced at Geordie, sleeping peacefully in his bed. Maybe their mother would begin to improve. . . .

Rachel embraced that last glimmer of hope as the long hand of the mantel clock swept inexorably toward midnight. The welcome respite of sleep washed over her soon after, but she dreamed of her father's funeral: the wooden coffin, the overpowering scent of roses, the aging church, the weed-strewn graveyard.

The clock chimed one, waking her with a start. The wind had come up. Outside, tree branches clawed at the house, creating an eerie sound. A flurry of snowflakes fell, those close enough to the window luminescent in the light of the tallow candle that sat, flickering, on the pane.

Rachel shivered. Tomorrow all the world would be white and cold . . . but hopefully not so cold as now. She rose to draw the drapes and stir the dying embers of the fire in the hearth. She had been raised in this small, two-room, wooden house. Still, late at night it could be a foreboding, lonely place.

Her mother groaned, and Rachel whirled to face her bed.

"Come sit with me, dear. I don't have long." Jillian's voice cracked as she struggled to sit up.

A lump congealed in Rachel's throat as she rushed to prop a pillow behind her mother's back. "Don't talk. Rest. You need to conserve your strength."

Jillian's hand clutched at Rachel's. "You have been a good girl and made me proud. We might be poor since my father died, but no one could tell it from your carriage or your speech." She gasped for breath, winded by the effort of communicating. "There isn't a man around, even a gentleman, with a better head for numbers and letters. You would have made your grandfather proud."

The foreboding Rachel had felt all day grew stronger. Her mother's words sounded suspiciously like a farewell. "Mum, listen to me. The Earl of Druridge came to the shop today—"

"*What?*" Her eyes flew wide, shining with the false luster of sickness. "Oh Rachel, you mustn't speak to him. Promise me you won't—" A bout of coughing rendered her speechless, and Rachel took advantage of the opportunity to interrupt.

"He only wants the truth, Mum. Perhaps he has a right to know, at least as much as we can tell him—"

"No!" Her mother's fingers curled into the flesh of Rachel's arm. "You don't understand . . . I have feared this day"—she swallowed hard—"tried to protect you, all of us, against it—"

"Hush." Feeling guilty for having broached the subject, Rachel patted her mother's hand. She had hoped to achieve release from a promise made years ago, but she now feared her mother wasn't strong enough to withstand such a flood of emotion. "Forget I brought it up. We can discuss it in the morning, when you're feeling better. For now, you should rest."

Jillian ignored her protests. "If Lord Druridge has turned his attention on you, he will not leave things as they lie," she wheezed. "He is a determined devil, that one. But you mustn't tell him, Rachel."

"Mother—"

"No! It was wrong of Jack to leave us with such burdens, but I will not betray him.... What was a woman to do?... Whoever thought it would come to what it did?... Such nasty business... I told him, but he wouldn't listen.... wouldn't light the fire in this cold house..."

Rachel grew more worried as her mother's words became unintelligible. When she merely grunted and moaned, tossing in agitation, Rachel feared Jillian was losing her mind. She gripped her mother's hand with a ferocity that belied her calm demeanor.

"Don't leave me, Mum." The howl of the wind echoed the wail of pain in her heart. "I don't want Geordie and me to be alone. First Tommy, then Father, now you... *Please* try to relax. Forget I said anything about the earl. I can take care of things; you know I can."

She fell silent. Her mother's eyelashes rested on her paper-thin cheeks as Rachel watched the barely perceptible rise and fall of her chest, waiting, hoping and praying that she would survive. But then the truth crystallized in her mind, lending her fresh determination, and she accepted what she had known deep inside from the beginning. So long as there existed the smallest chance to save her mother's life, she would do anything, sacrifice anything, promise or no.

Releasing her mother's hand, Rachel rushed to the coat rack to retrieve a heavy, wool cape.

"Rachel...?"

Reluctantly, Rachel retraced her steps as far as the door to the bedroom.

"Where are you going? We must discuss this." Jillian gasped for breath. "Just give me a chance to recover my strength."

"We will have all the time we want in the morning, Mother," Rachel gently insisted, steady now that the decision had been made. "I am going out, but I will get Mrs. Tate. She will be here if you or Geordie need anything."

"Wait," her mother called.

But Rachel had no time to spare. She had wasted far too many days and hours already, holding herself to a promise she could not keep. "I love you, Mum. Just rest. I will be back shortly." She tossed the last of her words over her shoulder as she rushed to the front door, where she raised her hood and plunged outside, into the biting cold.

The fire in Truman's study popped and crackled, a singularly comforting sound as he bowed over the ledgers strewn across his desk. The servants had long since gone to bed. Even Linley had retired. Only Wythe was up; at least, Truman assumed he was up. He wasn't home. Although his cousin never said how he spent his evenings, Truman had heard enough to know he frequented Elspeth's, the village brothel, on a regular basis. He guessed Wythe was there now. Newcastle was too far away to visit more than once a fortnight, and country society offered little by way of late-night entertainment.

Setting his quill in its brass and marble holder, Truman flexed his fingers and stretched his neck. He was exhausted but he fought the weariness that threatened to overtake him. Sleep had become his own personal hell, fraught with memories and contortions of events he would rather not revisit.

Almost involuntarily, his gaze strayed to the painting of Katherine hanging on the wall in front of him. It was one of the few pieces of art, of anything, the villagers had salvaged from the cinders of Blackmoor Hall and, ironically, the only item that hadn't sustained considerable damage. The blaze that had claimed Katherine's life had left her portrait untouched to haunt him in its perfect likeness—as if he could ever forget her. And he was just stubborn enough to hang her picture where he would see it most, an unspoken challenge to unmask her murderer, even if the face behind that mask turned out to be his own.

He pulled his gaze away from her beauty and forced his mind back to the colliery accounts. Another twenty minutes passed before he finished checking his bookkeeper's work. Then, shoving the heavy ledger away, he stared into the small flame that danced atop the candle on his desk. What other business awaited his attention?

The grandfather clock in the hall beyond his closed door chimed one thirty. He scrubbed his face with his hand. Nothing remained pressing enough to keep sleep at bay for long, he feared, riffling through the papers at his elbow.

The engraved, mahogany box sitting on the corner of the desk sheltered his personal correspondence. He opened it and set aside the ugly, accusatory letters from Katherine's parents. The Abbotts were growing angrier as time passed. At first he'd questioned whether the fire could have happened accidentally. But with all the servants at church and the fires well banked, there was little chance of that. The fire had broken out in the empty room next to the library, a room that was hardly ever used and hadn't seen a fire in the grate for months. The timing worked against him too, considering that he'd just learned of her infidelity. The Abbotts pointed to all these things, over and over, but he wouldn't deal with his in-laws now, not until he could say with some certainty how their daughter had lost her life.

Tonight he craved a simpler diversion, like sorting through the myriad social invitations he had failed to answer over the previous months.

The first of the rose-scented cards received his attention, but his chin soon bumped his chest.

Sliding his chair back so he could lay his head on his arms, he decided to let himself rest for a few moments. But as soon as his eyelids closed, he was riding through the streets of Creswell when an old woman harangued his coach, sounding as though she stood at his side. "Murderer!"

He twitched but couldn't wake as her rotten apple thumped his coach, followed by another and another until the sky seemed to be raining refuse. Calling to his driver to stop, he got out and opened his mouth to deny her words. But the instant he laid eyes on the old lady, her straggly hair turned into bright, golden tresses, her eyes into icy, blue pools and her rotting teeth into Katherine's accusing lips.

"Murderer!" Her fingers grabbed for him, clawing the air in desperation—and suddenly they were in the library together at Blackmoor Hall, surrounded by fire.

Smoke filled Truman's vision and burned his nose and throat. Despite the pain that seared his left hand as if he had thrust it into a cauldron of boiling water, he could think of nothing besides Katherine's betrayal. The baby. Someone else's child.

I'll kill her for this. He uttered the words over and over until they sounded like an incantation. Katherine screamed, as if in answer, and Truman jerked again. She wasn't far; he could hear her panicked movements not two feet away.

Strangely, her suffering brought him no pleasure. He reached out, but whether to pull her to him or push her away, he didn't know. Before he could touch her, everything went black and he didn't come to until his cousin Wythe hefted him over one shoulder.

"M'lord?"

With a start, Truman raised his head and blinked at the wood paneling of his study, the dying embers of the fire and, finally, the small pointy face of Susanna, one of his maids.

Shaking his head to clear his mind of the sounds that echoed there, he forced himself to return to the present. It had only been a dream, a slight variation of the nightmare that constantly plagued him. No doubt the storm raging outside, making the trees knock against the windows at his back, had been the apples that thundered upon his carriage.

If only that knowledge could ease the torment inside him.

"Can I bring ye anythin' before I retire, m'lord?" the maid asked, bobbing in a curtsy.

Truman took a deep, cleansing breath. "You're still up, Susanna?"

"Aye, m'lord."

"I told Mrs. Poulson not to have anyone wait up for me. I certainly cannot expect my servants to keep such hours."

"She didn't charge me ter wait, m'lord. I"—Susanna glanced at her feet— "well, ye seem a bit troubled of late. An' I thought per'aps ye might 'ave need of"—her gaze lifted, then darted away the moment her eyes met his—"some female companionship, m'lord."

Was this shy, young maid offering herself to him for the night? He had taken no one to his bed since Katherine. For all his wife's accusations, he had remained loyal to her for fidelity's sake alone. Since her death, the fear that he would wake in a cold sweat, as he had just done, kept him from letting anyone get too close—that and the doubt he saw in so many women's eyes, the doubt that mirrored his own.

But this girl seemed so unassuming, so eager and so safe he was almost tempted.

"Master Wythe says I can ease a man like no other," she added.

Her words were meant to entice, but they doused any desire her initial offer had kindled.

"He would know."

"Beg yer pardon, m'lord?"

"Nothing." He raked his fingers through his hair. "Thank you for your kind offer, Susanna. Please forgive me if I say I am too tired . . . tonight," he added to soften his refusal.

Looking like a child whose bedtime kiss had been rejected by a parent, she nodded and turned to go.

"Susanna?"

"Aye, m'lord?"

"For your own sake, I would let Wythe ease himself somewhere else. A babe is no small burden for a woman alone."

"Aye, m'lord." She flushed to the roots of her dark hair and quietly shut the door.

When she was gone, Truman dropped his head into his hands. He had to speak to Wythe about dabbling with the servants. But with his cousin still out he couldn't do it now.

It wasn't long before his mind returned, inevitably, to his most recent dream. Why couldn't he remember what happened the day Katherine died? He could recall, in minute detail, the events leading up to the fire: Katherine's letter informing him of the babe she carried, his mad dash from London, the frightened look on his wife's face when he confronted her in his anger.

But what, exactly, had followed their first heated words?

Closing his eyes, he grappled with the remaining wisps of his dream, opening himself up to all sensation, anything that might have made an imprint on his brain, both real and imagined. And suddenly, almost too simply, too easily, it was there: a slight but important detail he had never noticed before.

The realization of what his discovery could mean brought him to his feet. "My God! Could it be true?"

He rounded his desk to pace in front of the fire, examining the vision in his head until he felt quite certain of it. Then he penned a letter to an acquaintance in London.

When he finished, he looked at Katherine's portrait again, only this time he smiled. He wouldn't let her win. In life, she had tried to destroy him, had hated him for knowing the leprous character beneath her pretty face. In death, she was more vengeful still. But he would persist, and when he could eventually see through the smoke that clouded the truth, he would know, at last, whether his soul had been worth the fight.

Chapter 2

Blackmoor Hall was a daunting edifice. Built in the Strawberry Hill Gothic style, with a little Palladian thrown in, its gray stone walls rose several stories high, extending along cliffs that fronted the ocean. Although most of the structure had been rebuilt after the fire, nothing looked new. Large, diamond-cut windows spaced symmetrically on two long wings collected snow in the cradle of their thick panes. At least half a dozen chimneys rose from the roof. And an elaborate portico sheltered the entrance. Ancient and overwhelming, the manse resembled something out of a history book, with tall columns, expansive gardens, fountains and Greek statues. Now, late as it was, the estate was dark and rather forbidding.

Leaning into the wind, Rachel prodded Mrs. Tate's donkey forward while clinging tenaciously to the lantern she carried. Cold down to her bones in spite of her cloak, she shivered like someone with a palsy. Traversing the five hilly miles from the village to Blackmoor Hall seemed to take forever. But Rachel was so intent on her purpose she scarcely acknowledged the wet or the cold, except to wipe the clinging flakes of snow out of her face.

Amid the growling of the sky and the howling of the wind, Rachel could hear the surf not far away. Under normal circumstances, she loved the ocean, thought its rhythmic *hush . . . hush* the best of lullabies.

Tonight it proved a lonely sound.

As soon as she reached the portico, she lowered herself from the donkey's back and ducked inside its half-shelter. Many of the villagers believed Lord Druridge set the blaze that had destroyed his ancestral home to kill his unfaithful wife and the unwanted child she carried. But why would a man like the earl risk his own life and property? If he was bent on murder, there were easier ways to rid himself of both wife and child—and Rachel's imagination readily supplied them: poison, strangulation, an unfortunate incident on a horse. Any number of possible accidents, really ...

Unless he acted out of rage.

Rachel remembered the clenched muscles of his jaw at her thoughtless words, "Someone else's child," and wondered if the temper she had glimpsed could provoke him to murder. Perhaps she wasn't wise to arrive at his house alone in the dark with no one to say where she was. But she was determined. Her mother was dying. The earl had won. Only he possessed the trump card.

Stamping her feet to rid her skirts of the snow that clung to her hem, Rachel raised her lantern to reveal the door. Although she put all her energy into pounding on the thick, wooden panel, she could scarcely hear the impact of her fist above the storm.

"Let me in!" she called. "Please!"

Her efforts conjured nothing. No light. No sound.

After setting down her lantern, she raised hands as cold and unwieldy as blocks of ice to knock again.

Several minutes passed during which only the wind answered her pleas. The gale shrieked and moaned as it whipped about her. In that instant, Rachel could imagine the voice of the woman who had been murdered in the fire, crying out for vengeance....

The door creaked inward, and a single candle lit an older woman's seamed face. Deep-set eyes peered at her above a hawkish but proud nose. "Who goes here?"

In her panic, Rachel took no thought of the spectacle she made. She pressed forward with a desperation that caused the other woman to shrink back. "I need to speak to Lord Dru—"

A man moved out from behind the woman, leveling a pistol at her. "That's far enough, Miss. We'll 'ave yer name an' yer purpose for besettin' this 'ouse in the middle of the night before ye take another step."

The barrel of his pistol glinted in the candlelight. Hugging herself in an effort to control the shaking of her limbs, Rachel said, "I-I need to speak to Lord Druridge."

"Why?" The woman addressed her again. Rachel guessed, from her age and autocratic manner, she was the earl's housekeeper. Dressed in a linen nightgown with cambric frill edging, she wore a mobcap on her head, testifying to the fact that Rachel had indeed summoned her from bed, which, of course, came as no surprise.

"My mother is dying."

"And what has our master to do with that?"

Rachel eyed the pistol, checking her emotions. Evidently a commoner's life wasn't sufficient reason to disturb a peer of the realm's slumber. "Lord Druridge offered me a trade today. I have come to accept it."

The woman gaped at her. "And who might *you* be?"

"Rachel McTavish. My mother owns the bookshop in the village."

"Well, you're daft if you think I'll drag Lord Druridge from his bed at this hour. I'll tell him you were here. Perhaps he'll send a few shillings to help with your mother's burial."

"I'm not after money!" Rachel heard her voice rise to a shrill note. "Lord Druridge will want to see me, I assure you. Just rouse him."

The woman propped her fists on her hips. "I'm supposed to wake him on your word, am I? As if you have the right to come barging into this house?"

"Is the doctor here?" Rachel tried to circumvent the two servants, despite the pistol. "Doctor?" she called into the vast reaches of the house. "Is there a doctor here?"

Hurrying to bar her way, the housekeeper nodded to the man, who waved her toward the door with his gun. "Get out or I'll shoot."

Rachel turned back to the woman. "*Please . . .*"

The light of the candle expunged the color from the housekeeper's face, leaving it as bleak and empty as the snow-covered hills. "Do you think for one second that—?"

"For God's sake, it's only a woman." A deep voice boomed through the cathedral-like entrance. "Arthur, put that gun away."

Rachel stared at the spiral staircase where the Earl of Druridge descended, a mere shadow in the darkness.

"But m'lord, she might not be alone," Arthur argued. "Thieves can be right tricky, they can, and—"

"There is no need for this little incident to disturb your sleep, my lord," the housekeeper cut in. "Everything is under control. I told this young woman that you would see to her in the morning."

"By morning she might not have need of me." Ignoring his housekeeper's tacit disapproval, the earl moved toward them with the same sure-footed grace Rachel had noticed earlier at the shop. "Perhaps, Mrs. Poulson, you will be so kind as to put on some tea. I believe our guest could use a spot to hearten her nerves."

"I haven't come for tea." Rachel's eyes attempted to pierce the darkness, to latch onto the man she had come to see, but it wasn't until he stepped into the circle of light shed by Poulson's candle that she could make him out. There was no sleep lingering about his face, but he was wearing a close-fitting pair of dark trousers and a single-breasted dressing gown open down the front, as if he'd donned it in haste.

The sight of his chest, covered with a light matting of hair that tapered down a flat stomach, caught Rachel unaware. For a moment, she couldn't help but stare. He looked so different from her father, so firm and muscular....

Her cheeks flushing hot despite the chill, she forced her eyes up as he captured and tied the ends of the belt dragging behind him. The scars on his left hand could not extend far, she realized. His torso appeared unblemished.

"Come in, Miss McTavish."

Rachel shook her head. "No. I have to get back. I only came—"

"I know why you came. But I offered you a trade, remember?"

The wind swirled through the open door behind her, blowing his hair. "I haven't forgotten."

"Then surely you won't mind indulging my curiosity."

Rachel gathered her cloak more tightly about her. The moment had come, yet the thought of breaking her promise to her mother was no more palatable for its expediency. She would answer his questions, but she would volunteer nothing of her own accord. "I have every intention of keeping my word, my lord. Ask me what you will, and let us be on our way."

Druridge nodded at the icy flakes falling from a black sky. "I intend to do just that, Miss McTavish, but must we do so here?"

"I dare not dally."

"I will be brief."

It seemed she had no choice. "If it pleases you."

"It pleases me."

Held fast by the chains of hope, Rachel hovered at the portal while the man the earl had called Arthur tucked his pistol away and Mrs. Poulson lit several lamps. Blackmoor Hall was beginning to look more hospitable, but Rachel could not escape her anxiety.

"We must hurry—"

"You will lose no time, I assure you." The earl took her by the elbow and guided her farther inside. "I will send Arthur to alert Dr. Jacobsen, so that when we are finished with our little chat, he will be ready to accompany us to your home."

He also told Arthur to have his coach prepared. Then he led her into a room situated off the large, vaulted entry. Furnished with a pianoforte, velvet drapes, polished mahogany tables, Louis XIV settees and Turkish rugs, the room's rich textures immediately cocooned Rachel against the blustering storm outside.

The earl strode to the marble fireplace and stirred the golden embers that smoldered there, bringing them back to a semblance of life. As he added more kindling and coal from a brass bucket, Rachel struggled to keep her teeth from chattering. What would he ask her? Would he be satisfied with her answers? Would he follow through with his end of the bargain as quickly as he'd indicated?

She pretended to study the high ceilings and paneling of the room while she tried to stop shivering. The hand-carved, arched double doors at the entry were beautiful, as was the detail above the windows. On the ceiling she saw a painting of clouds and angels and harps.

"Your mother has taken a turn for the worse?" Lord Druridge broke the silence as he pulled a chair closer to the fire and motioned her into it.

Eager to bathe in the warmth of the flames that were beginning to lick at their new fodder, Rachel moved forward, surprised when the earl reached out to take her cloak.

"I will keep it, thank you. As soon as we are finished here, I will start out and wait for you at home—"

"What good will it do for you to go ahead of us? Doubtless we would pass you on the road. The doctor will need a moment, so you might as well relax."

"But I have my neighbor's donkey—"

"Which we will tie behind."

The thought of riding in a carriage, protected from the elements, was certainly more inviting than fighting Mrs. Tate's stubborn ass. . . .

He reached for her cloak again, and this time Rachel relinquished it into his hands so she wouldn't continue to drip on the rug.

The rattle of a tea service came from the direction of the door. Mrs. Poulson entered, laden with a silver tray filled with tea, cakes, scones, fresh butter and clotted cream.

Rachel hadn't realized until that moment how terribly hungry she was. She had been so exhausted when she left the bookshop, and so concerned for her mother, that fatigue had overwhelmed her before she could eat any supper.

The housekeeper seemed to sense her interest in the food. Mrs. Poulson gave her a sidelong, piercing gaze that made it quite apparent she resented having to serve a commoner, someone no better than herself. But when the earl turned, she lowered her eyes to the floor. "Will that be all, my lord?"

"Yes. Please bring me word the moment the doctor is ready."

She curtsied. "As you say."

The door thudded shut behind the bony woman, and Rachel swallowed, trying to ease the dryness of her throat.

"Won't you have something to eat, Miss McTavish?" The earl indicated the food at her elbow. "You look as though you might faint."

The smell of the freshly heated scones rose to Rachel's nostrils, causing her mutinous stomach to clamor for sustenance, despite her preoccupation and worry. Careful not to reveal her near starvation by cramming it into her mouth, she took a cranberry scone.

The earl touched nothing on the tray but watched her intently. Rachel couldn't raise her gaze without encountering his thoughtful golden eyes, eyes that held the promise of the interrogation to come.

A twinge of conscience caused her to push the tray away long before she had satisfied her hunger. Betraying her mother's most heartfelt wishes, and the memory of her poor dead father, didn't come easily. Like Persephone, she was making a deal with the devil. She was warming herself at his fire, dining on his food—

He cleared his throat, and she glanced up.

"Who set the fire that killed my wife, Miss McTavish?" On the surface, his voice remained unchanged, dispassionate, but a strong undercurrent revealed his eagerness for her answer.

"If you think I can tell you that, my lord, you are sure to be disappointed."

"Someone knows what happened that day." The flames cast moving shadows on the side of his face. "According to my sources, your father received a large sum of money two weeks before the fire. I would like to know where it came from."

This was the question Rachel had expected, yet defensiveness, in place of honest answers, rose to her lips. "Would it be too difficult to believe he received some sort of inheritance? My grandfather's patronage is, after all, how my mother came into possession of the bookshop, is it not?"

"Did he?" The earl's eyes glowed with the same tawny light as the fire.

Rachel wondered if he could see right through her. "Receiving a large sum of money doesn't necessarily make him guilty of anything."

"Especially if you can prove its origins."

The hiss of the fire grew louder. Suddenly, Rachel felt scorched by its heat. Her father had hated the earl as far back as she could remember, even before Tommy's death.

She hated him, too—or, rather, she didn't know him well enough to hate him personally, but she hated what he stood for. He was responsible for the miners' terrible lot. Underpaid and overworked, they suffered too many accidents like the one that had claimed Tommy's life. The long hours of crouching and crawling in narrow tunnels had stunted the growth of some and distorted their bodies. Others had miner's lung, the disease that had killed her father. Yet the earl lived in luxury, apparently indifferent to their difficult existence.

"Miss McTavish?" he prompted when she didn't speak.

"Someone paid my father to fire Blackmoor Hall." She stated it baldly and then looked away to avoid seeing the satisfaction on his face. "He took the money . . . but he could not go through with the agreement." She faced him, hoping to convince him of something she was no longer sure of herself. "He did *not* set the fire."

"And how can you be so sure?" The tension in Lord Druridge's body reminded Rachel of a hound straining at the end of a leash, only he was, at the same time, master, holding himself in check.

"Because he told me so."

"Would he readily admit to murder, Miss McTavish?"

"Why would he deny it? He knew he wasn't long for this earth."

"To protect you from the taint of his deeds, perhaps?"

"No. He told me about the money so he could die with a clear conscience. Why admit only half the truth? Leave something far worse to harrow up his soul?"

Druridge seemed skeptical, but didn't press the point. "Who gave him the money?"

"He wouldn't say, so for all I know"—Rachel clenched her hands in her lap—"the money could have come from you."

The earl gave an incredulous laugh. "You think I tried to hire your father to fire my home and kill my wife and, when he refused, did it myself?"

Superstitiously fearing the earl's hypnotic eyes, Rachel once again dropped her gaze to the floor. "That is one possibility."

He moved toward her, his deliberate steps reminding Rachel that she was completely at his mercy. She doubted whether any of the servants sleeping in the nether regions of the manse would hear her should she cry out. There was only Mrs. Poulson, and she was no ally.

"Except that I did not hire your father," he breathed, now only inches away. "That much I know, despite my fickle memory. If I tried to pay a man to kill my wife, I would be more prudent than to let him live long enough to die of miner's lung. Or to tell someone like you, someone who could conceivably prattle the tale about town."

His words caused the short hairs to rise on Rachel's nape. Half-expecting him to reach for her, to encircle her neck with his powerful hands, she shrank into the chair as he towered over her.

"Have you no answer to that?" he asked.

She dragged to her lips the words flying around in her head. "Perhaps you thought the money sufficient to buy his silence."

"So my bothering you is just a way to see if he kept his end of the bargain?"

"I don't know you, my lord," she said, scrambling to hide her fear. "I can only judge according to instinct, and my instincts tell me that you are indeed capable of such a thing."

"Capable of murder?" He laughed. "Perhaps. But then, under the right circumstances, I think we are all capable of murder."

Rachel said nothing. She wanted to leave and never see this man again, but he leaned over, propping his hands on the arms of her chair and pinning her to her seat.

"Your attitude raises another question," he said. "Believing, as you do, that I tried to finance the commission of this crime, I cannot help but wonder why you haven't contacted the authorities. Was it because you were so eager to keep the money? Is that why you closed your eyes to the probable truth? Were you hoping the deed would simply fade into the past? That no one would come looking for the money or for answers?"

Rachel dared not move lest she come into contact with him. She tilted her head back to look in his face and saw a steely determination that frightened her even more than his words. "My mother insisted we say nothing. We needed the money to stock the shop"—she cringed at the mercenary light in which her words painted Jillian—"and we did not know who to return it to. If you had indeed paid my father to set the fire, we felt safe as long as we said nothing. Our shop serves a great purpose. It is the only outpost for books this far north. Many of the country homes in the surrounding counties rely on us to stock their libraries, seeing that we are much closer than London."

"Justification, surely."

"Not only that but my mother was trying to protect against—"

"My turning you out." His breath, smelling faintly of brandy, fanned her cheeks, and Rachel nodded.

"Funny how you suffered no qualms about keeping money that was not your own. That was, according to your knowledge, given in trade for a woman's life. Yet you dare censure *me*?" His voice sharpened. "You would let the mystery of a murder go unsolved while holding a piece of the puzzle, and for money and security's sake never come forward? Tell me, have you no respect for truth and honesty?"

Rachel stiffened at his condescending tone. The question of whether or not it had been honest to keep the money and hold her silence had troubled her from the beginning, but she'd used her belief in her father's innocence to justify her behavior. In the beginning, no one had connected Jack McTavish with the fire. So why cast any aspersion on his name? Her father hadn't killed Lady Katherine. Someone else did, and it could have been Lord Druridge as easily as not.

She summoned the last of her courage. "That's an easy thing for you to say," she replied. "Forgive me for not shouting what I know from the rooftops, but I felt the money well spent. It is not as though we have lived like you do." She waved a contemptuous hand around her. "We used the money to keep the shop open and to buy books—for our wealthy clients, yes, but also so that we could teach the villagers how to read and write. On some level I considered it your contribution to the community, if you will. Besides, what I know would not have helped anyone, you least of all. So forgive me for letting you run the gauntlet alone. You, who are virtually untouchable by the law and, by comparison, have known so little of need or loss or difficulty. Even the fire rid you of a wife you no longer wanted!"

The muscles of the earl's face tensed until he looked as though he had been carved and polished out of marble. With a haughty glare, he pushed himself away. "Are you certain my life is so much better?"

"At least you don't have to worry about hunger or deprivation."

"I didn't know that affluence, or possessing a title, for that matter, made me any less human, any less capable of feeling than other men."

"My lord, if you had a heart beneath that fine dressing gown, you would not have forced me to betray my father's memory to save my dying mother—"

Her voice broke, causing Rachel to draw a shuddering breath that sounded more like a sob. Standing, she shoved past him and headed for the door, eager to make good her escape before she lost any more of her dignity. "I am going back, with or without your precious physician. So if you plan to kill me as you did your wife, you had better do it quickly."

Catching her by the elbow, he spun her around before she could reach the door. "Kill you? You little idiot! If I were the monster you accuse me of being, you would have been dead long before now. Instead, you are alive and well enough to make damning judgments on matters you know nothing about. Do you think I felt no betrayal when my wife slept with other men? Do you think it wasn't painful to be taunted by the knowledge of it? To receive the bland smiles of those I considered my friends, who had taken my wife into their beds? That I could not feel—that I still do not feel—the loss of my son, a life I valued more than my own?" His fingers tightened almost painfully on her arm.

"Stop, you're hurting me," she said, but he wasn't hurting her. Not yet. She was just afraid he would. The pressure of his grip eased, but still Rachel could not twist out of his grasp.

"Not until you answer me. Do only the poor feel pain, Miss McTavish, while the rich know nothing but peace and happiness? By your own admission, you are an educated woman. Please, do not try to sell me that bag of rot."

Rachel didn't know what to say. She couldn't think when he was so close. She blinked up at him, her heart pounding.

A slight flaring of his nostrils revealed the degree of his anger. "If you espouse such a philosophy then perhaps I am not the only one walking numbly through life."

She didn't feel numb now. She felt vitally aware of him, more aware of this man than any she'd ever met before, and it came as a total shock that he seemed to be having the same reaction to her.

His gaze dropped to her lips, which she instinctively parted. But then someone knocked, and he shoved her away.

The housekeeper entered, stopping midstride to glance curiously at them both. "Doctor Jacobsen is ready."

The earl pivoted toward the fire. "Thank you, Mrs. Poulson." He sounded calm and in control again. And when he finally turned to Rachel, his face was shuttered, revealing none of the heated passion that had played upon it a heartbeat earlier. "I will go change. But first, I have one more question."

Rachel scarcely heard his words. The emotional storm that had gripped them both seemed to have passed as quickly as it had broken, but the earl's touch had left her shaken, burning with a memory she already knew she'd never forget.

"Can you give me the names of any of those at the colliery who were involved in this with your father?"

Rachel opened her mouth to speak, but no sound came out. Clearing her throat, she tried again. "No."

"Because you don't know or because you won't tell?"

"I don't know."

Sharp movements revealed the fact that he wasn't as calm as he pretended to be when he retrieved the poker and stabbed the logs of the fire. "Very well, Miss McTavish." He tossed the implement against its brass stand with a resounding *clang*. "You shall have your doctor. If you will excuse me, we will soon be on our way."

The earl swept past her, leaving Rachel in a tangled web of half-thoughts and sensation. Had he really looked at her as if . . . as if he might *kiss* her?

Mrs. Poulson followed him out. When the door closed behind them, Rachel touched her lips, realizing with a flash of guilty insight that some small part of her had reacted to the passion inside him. Despite his role as a titled gentleman, there seemed to be a facet inside him that society could not tame, something stimulating yet dangerous, like standing at the edge of a cliff and feeling the mysterious, subtle pull to jump.

Overwhelmed, she dropped her hand. Her mother required a physician. The rest was madness and should be ignored. For better or for worse, she had fulfilled her half of the bargain with Lord Druridge. Now it was time for him to make good.

Staring into the fire, she waited for the housekeeper or Lord Druridge to return and escort her out. But no one came. The mantel clock ticked loudly above the fire, mocking the passage of time and drawing out Rachel's nerves until she thought she might scream. When would they leave? Her mother needed her!

Finally, she could take no more. Regardless of the earl, or his doctor, or the storm that raged against the house, she was going home. Grabbing her cloak, she marched across the room, flung open the door, and stalked into the hall.

But there a sudden jolt knocked her to the floor.

Chapter 3

Rachel blinked up at the earl in surprise.

"Do you always charge from a room with such force?" he asked.

Having donned a white shirt and stock with his stirrup trousers, as well as a green brocade waistcoat with a knee-length overcoat and top hat, he reached down to help her up. He appeared unruffled and remote, while Rachel felt as though she had just barreled into the stone wall surrounding the manse.

"I am sorry. I didn't know you were there," she muttered as she regained her feet.

Ignoring her apology, he turned to Mrs. Poulson. "Has Wythe returned?"

"Aye, m'lord. He is asleep in his chambers."

"Tell him I won't be able to accompany him to the mine in the morning. I will meet him at the offices midafternoon."

When Poulson nodded, Lord Druridge shook out a heavy cloak and lifted it to the level of Rachel's eyes. Obviously, he expected her to turn so he could drape it around her shoulders.

Rachel clung to her own wet cape, which she'd folded over her arms, even though she knew such obstinacy could offer nothing but extreme discomfort.

"Miss McTavish?" The earl cocked an impatient eyebrow and, in the interest of time, Rachel turned. The weight of the garment settled around her, its length falling past her feet to drag on the ground.

Druridge took her cloak and handed it to Poulson. "See that this gets dried."

Sandalwood and soap, mixed with a subtle, male scent, rose to Rachel's nostrils. It identified the cloak he'd provided as one of his own and reminded her of the look on his face when he'd taken hold of her. . . .

Shoving that memory out of her head, she fastened the garment at the throat and gathered handfuls of the expensive fabric to hold so she could walk.

"Shall we go?" Lord Druridge opened the door and motioned her out. "The doctor is waiting in the carriage."

With a nod, Rachel grabbed the lantern she'd left on the doorstep and hurried out ahead of him.

Dr. Jacobsen was an older gentleman with snowy white hair that also covered most of his jaw. Dressed similarly to the earl, in close-fitting stirrup pants and ankle boots, he wore a double-breasted black cloth coat with velvet collar. A frown lingered on his face but, judging from the many lines around his mouth, Rachel guessed it was no more than his customary expression.

He dipped his head as Lord Druridge handed her into the fancy black coach she had noted so many times on the streets of Creswell—the same conveyance that had so recently waited in front of her own shop.

When the earl introduced them, Rachel returned the doctor's greeting and slid across the tan leather bench opposite him.

Lord Druridge climbed in last, took a seat next to her and they started off.

"You're looking fit despite the ungodly hour, my lord." The doctor had to raise his voice over the storm. Instead of blowing itself out since her arrival at Blackmoor Hall, it had gathered in strength.

"I fear you've got a formidable challenge tonight, my friend," Lord Druridge responded.

Rachel's lantern had gone out, but in the dim light of the coach's lamps, the doctor's frown deepened. "Fever, eh? Fevers can be nasty business. I have seen cholera ravage the strongest of men. This recent outbreak has been growing at an unprecedented rate." He eyed Rachel. "How long has your mother been ill, my dear?"

"Almost a week."

The earl disrupted the conversation long enough to retrieve a fur pelt from beneath the seat, which he settled over Rachel's lap.

Already too conscious of the cloak she wore and his large, manly form seated next to her, she accepted the covering with some reluctance.

Outside, the coachman cracked his whip, drawing Rachel's attention to the frozen landscape beyond her window. Snowdrifts were piled high on either side of them and more whirling flakes fell to join those on the ground. The earl's driver shouted to the horses, urging them on, but the wind swallowed most of his words.

Travel proved slow and arduous. Less than a mile from the estate, the carriage ground to a halt and the coachman appeared at the door.

"Sorry, m'lord," he shouted above the gale. "The roads are impassable. I am afraid we cannot get through to the village."

Rachel's stomach muscles tightened.

"We won't if you leave us sitting here very long," the earl responded.

"You want to continue?" His coachman straightened, obviously amazed.

"Take us as far as you can."

"Aye, m'lord." The door slammed shut, and the carriage swayed as the driver climbed back on top.

They moved forward, but Rachel could feel a marked difference in their progress as the horses struggled to pull the carriage, seemingly by inches, through the snow. Frightened that they wouldn't reach her mother after all, she peered at the earl's face. Would he give up? Turn back?

He stared out at the black night, his expression grim.

"What if we can't get through?" Rachel asked, her nails curling into her palms.

"Then I will come first thing in the morning," Dr. Jacobsen replied. "Just as soon as this bloody storm passes."

The earl glanced at him. "Morning might be too late," he said. "We will get through."

The stubborn set of his jaw brought Rachel a degree of comfort. At least the earl was a man of his word. At least he meant to uphold his end of the bargain despite the difficulty of doing so.

Hold on, Mum. We're coming. We're coming. . . .

Twice the carriage became stuck, and Lord Druridge climbed out to help free the wheels. The third time, he told his driver to unharness the horses.

"Are ye certain, m'lord?" Rachel heard the man say from her seat inside the carriage.

"We will take the horses and go on. You take the donkey tethered behind and go back."

"But m'lord, ye 'aven't the tack. An' ye know these 'orses are rarely ridden in such a manner."

"I believe I can handle my own animals, Timothy. It won't be the first time I have managed without a saddle."

Rachel looked out as the liveried servant nodded dumbly.

The doctor, still seated across from her beneath a lap blanket of his own, gaped in surprise. "See here, my lord," he said as soon as Druridge appeared at the door. "You say we are going on? We will never make it in this—"

"A woman is ill," the earl interrupted. "And you are a physician. You tell me, where does your duty lie?"

The doctor mumbled something about Lord Druridge being too young and reckless for his own good, but he complied by heaving his considerable bulk out into the storm and trudging through the snow to help the driver free the horses. Rachel followed.

"Let's go before the drifts are up to our necks," Jacobsen grumbled, taking hold of the reins of one horse and stepping into the driver's laced fingertips to climb up.

Rachel's dress became sodden and heavy in the few minutes it took for the earl to untie Mrs. Tate's beast and exchange him for the horse the driver held. She felt the weighty fabric pulling her back, making her movements awkward as she hurried to help.

Lord Druridge jumped astride the second animal, a chestnut-colored gelding. The horse snorted and tossed its head, its huge body steaming from the exertion of having pulled the carriage. Obviously, it wasn't happy about this latest change, but Druridge brought the animal under control and turned it so he could say farewell to his coachman. "Safe journey, Timothy."

The donkey brayed pitiably and Timothy sent them a forlorn glance. "Aye, m'lord. The same to you."

Rachel wondered how *she* would travel. She was perfectly willing to ride Mrs. Tate's donkey, but the earl had just given Gilly to the coachman.

"Are you coming?" Lord Druridge asked.

She blinked against the snow clinging to her eyelashes as he extended his hand to her. She hesitated, but she seemed to have little choice in traveling companions—unless she wanted to ride with the corpulent doctor, who was having a devil of a time controlling his mount.

Raising a tentative hand, she allowed the earl to pull her up in front of him.

"Don't worry about Timothy," he said, following her backward glance. "He'll manage."

"I am more worried about us," she admitted and leaned to one side to stare at the ground, which seemed too far away for comfort. "I have never ridden such a large horse and certainly not one that is more accustomed to pulling a carriage than bearing riders."

The earl's voice came as a low rumble in her ear. "It is far more comfortable than riding astride a donkey. You have nothing to fear."

Except, possibly, the man behind me.

Rachel tucked her face into the thickness of her borrowed cloak as they started out. Progress was slow even without the carriage. In places, they had to plow through drifts up to their thighs, and although the earl's horses were fine animals, they had minds of their own. The stable was the other way, and well they knew it.

Fortunately, Druridge wasn't a man to have his actions dictated to him by man or beast. Rachel could feel the muscles of his thighs bunch as he squeezed the gelding's heaving sides and spoke to it in a low but firm voice.

The doctor didn't fare quite as well. Jacobsen followed in their wake, his journey a bit less difficult because of the path they forged, except that his own mount tried to bolt several times.

"Damn this animal!" he cursed when it lowered its head as though it would buck.

The earl turned back and shouted out instructions to the doctor on how to control his mount. Then they had only the storm to delay them.

The wind played havoc with their clothes, pressing against them like an invisible hand until Rachel began to wonder why the earl *didn't* give up and turn back. Grudgingly she had to admit that she had, in some ways, misjudged him. He was honest, so far as keeping his commitment to her, and, obviously, capable and confident, especially when it came to pursuing his goals.

She studied his gloved hands as they worked the reins in front of her. *He will never give in to the miners' demands, not if they are contrary to his own will.* In that moment, Rachel knew it as surely as she felt the heat of the earl behind her. Mr. Cutberth and the other unionizers didn't fully realize what they were contending with. They thought, if they could only unite, they could press Druridge to their advantage. But Rachel finally understood just how much the earl would resist any type of coercion. He wouldn't allow himself to be overpowered by anyone.

The minutes passed with Druridge's hard, unyielding chest brushing against Rachel's back and one sinewy arm encircling her waist. He was touching her for a very practical purpose—if he didn't hold her she might fall—but he was also making her inescapably aware of him.

Despite her misgivings about that intoxicating moment in his drawing room, it wasn't long before she was tempted to sink against the support of his body. She'd gotten little sleep since her mother's illness and so was incredibly tired.

But Lord Druridge was her enemy, and not an enemy to esteem lightly. She held her body rigid until his arm tightened, and he murmured, "Relax."

Much too cold to fight him, she allowed herself to lean back, a little, and immediately felt the added warmth and comfort his body could provide.

The snow stopped falling about a mile outside the village, but the wind kept up, plastering their clothes against them and making Rachel's ears ache. Even the earl's cloak couldn't ward off the chill that had invaded every part of her body.

"Have you survived the journey?" he asked when they emerged from the moors and could see the rooftops in the valley not far below.

Rachel managed to mumble a reply, but she had never been so exhausted in her life, physically or emotionally. Only the thought of her mother, waiting for them, kept her heavy eyelids from closing.

Dr. Jacobsen had long since fallen silent. He sat as rigid as a statue, a scarf wrapped around the lower part of his face, until they began the gradual descent into town. Then the colorful grumbling and cursing that had punctuated the beginning of their venture from the carriage started up again. "Damn winters. I don't know why I traipse so far north. I won't do it again."

Lord Druridge twisted around to look at him. The earl had turned up the collar of his coat to keep his neck warm, but he wore no scarf, and Rachel could see tiny, frozen crystals clinging to the shadow of a day's beard growth. "I believe you said that last winter, Clive."

"I should have listened to myself. If you had any idea what you were missing, you would leave this godforsaken place and come to London with me, lands or not. But look who I am preaching to! You haven't the slightest inclination to visit the city these days. Forget the Season. You won't even come for business." The doctor's scarf muffled his words, but the wind had changed course and was now at their backs, easily carrying his voice to them.

"It's my good sense that keeps me away," the earl shouted.

Rachel listened to their banter, feeling the shift in their moods, the gradual lessening of the tension that had stifled their progress as surely as the blizzard. The worst was over. She would soon be back with her mother. But . . . what would she find?

As if sensing the cause of her reticence, the earl covered her frozen hands with one of his, surprising her with his gentleness. "Just a few minutes more," he said.

At last, dawn began to streak across the sky. The storm was now little more than a few drops of rain, but the McTavish cottage remained shuttered and dark. For a moment, Rachel squeezed her eyes closed. She was almost afraid to look for fear she would see some sign of her mother's death.

Eventually, she opened her eyes to find all as it normally was—not that "normal" gave anything away. *I won't last long.* Had Jillian lasted long enough for Rachel's efforts to make any difference?

Lord Druridge slid off the horse and helped her down, at which point she forced her frozen feet to lead them through the small, fenced garden she tended for her family.

At the door, she stood aside and waved them in. Her unsteady legs wouldn't carry her beyond the threshold for fear of what she might find.

Not quite yet . . .

The horses snorted and swished their tails, their breath misting in the morning air. That ugly storm had preceded one of the most beautiful dawns Rachel had ever seen. She watched the long yellow fingers of the sun crawl over the rooftops to the east, and murmured a silent prayer for her mother.

The village awakened as Rachel watched. She could smell bread baking not far away, hear the creak of wagon wheels, see vendors pushing their carts down the wet street.

Strange how life goes on even when the world is falling apart. . . .

She was about to turn and head inside when the door opened and the earl stepped out. He watched her for a few moments without speaking before glancing into the distance as if searching for what she saw.

Rachel didn't break the silence until he met her eyes. Then she squared her shoulders. She sensed he had something to say. "Is she dead?"

He looked behind them as though wishing someone else would come through the door. When no one emerged, he said, "I'm sorry, Miss McTavish. She died moments before we arrived. There was nothing Jacobsen could do."

Pain stabbed Rachel in the chest, feeling like a shard of broken glass. Unwilling to let the man she blamed for all three deaths in her family witness her grief or delight in her suffering, she sucked in a gulp of air to help her bear it. If only he had sent the doctor earlier, instead of forcing her to bargain for her mother's life, perhaps her mum would have been spared.

If only she had capitulated earlier . . .

Damming such thoughts, Rachel forced back the questions and accusations that whirled in her brain like the eddies of a deep pool. She wouldn't think of "what if" now. There would be time enough for regret in all the long years she would live without her mother's comforting presence.

She felt the earl's hand on her arm and jerked away. "You can take your doctor home, my lord," she said, amazed by the formal, steely quality of her own voice. "I will not trouble you further."

Numbly, she removed his cloak and held it out. When he hesitated, she dropped it in the snow and turned, walking past him to meet her eight-year-old brother at the door.

"Rachel, she's gone," Geordie cried, his young shoulders shaking under the weight of his grief.

Rachel stooped and took him into her arms. "I know, love, but there's always me. I'm not going anywhere, now am I? I will take good care of you; see if I don't."

Mrs. Tate came to the door, her face a vision of weary sadness. "Rachel, child! It's sorry I am. But she's better off now. She's finally at peace."

Faced with Mrs. Tate's sympathy, Rachel feared she would succumb to the tears that burned behind her eyes. She longed to release them, to let her grief escape before she simply blew apart. But she felt the earl watching and could still picture the inscrutable expression he wore.

"Thank you for tending her," she heard herself say. "I will dress her for burial." Keeping one arm around Geordie, she straightened and led him into the house, past Mrs. Tate to where their mother lay, white as the chalky cliffs of Dover.

Dr. Jacobsen was washing his hands at the basin. "You have my condolences, Miss McTavish. And, if it makes you feel any better, I doubt I could have saved her even if I had nursed her from the beginning." He gave her a kind smile. "I'm afraid little can be done for cholera victims. You must burn her clothes and her bedding to minimize the risk to you and the young lad here. And I suggest you have the burial as soon as possible, today if you can and no later than tomorrow."

Cholera. So it was as Rachel had feared.

"Thank you for coming," she murmured mechanically. "I will take care of her. I will take care of everything."

Dr. Jacobsen shot Rachel a curious look. "Where is your father?"

"Dead."

"Have you no other family?"

Rachel ruffled little Geordie's hair. "We have only each other now. But that is all we need. I will see to it."

The scrape of Lord Druridge's boots sounded on the floor behind her. She didn't turn. She continued to study Jillian's serene face, to gaze upon the loveliness of her good mother for the last time.

The earl spoke quietly to Mrs. Tate, who said something amid her tears that Rachel couldn't make out. Then he left, and Rachel didn't know how much longer it was before Dr. Jacobsen followed. She knew only the quiet sobs of her brother, and the silent screams that were entirely her own.

Chapter 4

The next day was one of the longest and most painful of Rachel's life. Having buried two members of her family in the previous three years, she stumbled through the motions all over again, feeling as empty as a hollow log and just as separated from her life's sustenance. This time, the person she laid to rest was her mother—her strength, her wisdom, her support.

Standing in the church graveyard less than a mile from her home, she stared down at the top of Geordie's head while the village blacksmith and Mrs. Tate's son shoveled frozen clods of dirt over her mother's coffin. Besides the twenty or so mourners, friends and neighbors and fellow church members, headstones surrounded them like a second audience, a congregation of the deceased gathered to welcome a new soul into their ranks.

As the metal of each shovel struck and scraped the ground, Rachel wondered how she and her brother would survive. Her mother had tried to persuade her to marry. Now she almost wished she'd taken Jillian's advice and accepted the blacksmith's apprentice. A clean-cut, sturdy young man only a few years older than herself, he had a vocation, one far less humble than her own father's, and would certainly have helped her finish raising Geordie.

But she couldn't stomach the thought of marrying someone she didn't love, any more than she could fathom sharing his bed. Somehow she and Geordie would get through the ensuing years, and they would do it without trading her freedom for bread on their table. The bookshop earned a modest living when her mother stood at the helm. Rachel had much to learn about making it a success, but she was more prepared after helping out as much as she had. She would not fail her brother, or her mother's memory, by letting go of the shop and their dream of educating the miners.

The blacksmith's apprentice was one of the first to clasp her hand after the funeral. Shy and rather awkward, he mumbled some words of consolation.

Rachel nodded, but she couldn't help noticing that his touch struck no chord in her. He was a fine, upstanding member of the community—honest, hardworking and not unhandsome. And he had professed his love for her on more than one occasion. Her mother had called him besotted. Yet it was Lord Druridge's touch, the touch of her *enemy*, that had warmed Rachel's blood and caused an odd awakening.

Rachel sighed. Surely she was the most perverse girl ever to walk the streets of Creswell. But that realization came as no surprise. She had always been different. While the other miners' daughters had cooked and cleaned or worked in the mine, she'd had her nose in a book. Instead of plying her needle, she was teaching herself French or penmanship. Instead of gossiping with the village girls, she was gossiped about. Too educated for a poor miner's daughter and too poor to be anything else, she had never felt more like a misfit than now, when the one person who had understood her best and loved her most was gone.

While the other mourners gathered in small, murmuring clumps, Mrs. Tate put her arm around Rachel. There was so much difference in their respective heights that her arm curled around Rachel's waist instead of her shoulders, but Rachel was grateful for the comfort all the same.

The ground had been too hard to dig very deep. As a result, filling her mother's grave had taken little time. But what Rachel noticed, more than anything else, was the lack of color. Black on white predominated: the clothing of the mourners against the snow that covered everything else, except the gray, marble headstones that peeked through the crusty mantle.

Her mother deserved flowers—a bouquet of the red roses that were her favorite, Rachel thought. Instead, a wreath of evergreen boughs adorned Jillian's grave, along with a few dried flowers from Mrs. Tate's cellar.

The last of those who lingered filed past, squeezing Rachel's hand as she stood in the clean, wintry air, smiling and nodding and fighting to keep her composure. Life would go on. For Geordie's sake she had to be strong.

The sun slipped behind the roof of the church, throwing her in the shadow of the building's ancient stone walls and causing her to shiver against the sudden chill. Geordie cried softly at her side, but now that she felt free to express her own grief, she couldn't shed a tear. She just wanted to go home. Her mother wasn't the cold, lifeless corpse they had just buried. Jillian was gone. No more would—

The sight of two riders on horseback caught Rachel's eye, jerking her from her thoughts. They were well beyond the church, among the elm trees that lined the property, but they seemed to be watching her. Both figures were tall and broad-shouldered and rode fine, mahogany-colored horses. The proud bearing of one gave his identity away even though, at such a distance, Rachel couldn't make out his features.

It was the Earl of Druridge. Why had he come? And where was his fancy carriage?

The villagers hadn't noticed him, or Rachel would have heard their rumblings. Had he, and whoever was with him, just arrived?

She glanced at the retreating backs of the last of her friends and acquaintances as they wandered off toward their homes or businesses, some on foot, others on horseback. Mrs. Tate patted her waist, making cooing noises, and Geordie clung to her. The moment seemed frozen in time as she stared across the distance toward the man who appeared to regard her as openly as she did him.

"Shall I stay with ye tonight, luv?"

Mrs. Tate's question hung in the air with the mist from her breath. She gave Rachel's arm a shake, but even then Rachel was too preoccupied to answer.

"Who are they?" Mrs. Tate asked, following her gaze. "Do we know them?"

Rachel forced herself to look away from the earl and his companion and down at Geordie. "Let's go home."

"No!" Geordie's bottom lip trembled anew. "I won't go. I won't leave Mum. *I won't!*"

Kneeling, Rachel groomed her voice into a caress. "Mum's not here, Geordie. She will live forever in our hearts, but she's not here."

A quick glance told Rachel the earl hadn't moved. Mrs. Tate was eyeing him curiously. "It's cold, and time to go," she insisted.

"I don't care. I want Mum, Rachel. I don't want you!"

For the first time since the service ended, Rachel thought she might cry. "I know I am a poor substitute, little Geordie. But it will be all right. I promise you that. You will be safe with me. Now, be a good lad."

She began to drag her brother away, but he resisted every step, digging his heels into the snow and refusing to make the journey easy. Mrs. Tate tried to entice him with the promise of a slice of hot custard once they reached home, but eventually she buried her face in her hands and cried with him. Only Rachel remained steadfast in her purpose. She couldn't bear to think of her mother beneath the cold dirt and didn't want to see the grave any longer. Not only that but she longed to get as far away as possible from the earl and his uncanny, all-seeing eyes. He had no right to witness her pain or to make a mockery of her mother's funeral.

With gritted teeth, she fought her own emotions as much as Geordie's obstinacy. "We *are* going home, and we are doing it *right now!*"

Mrs. Tate blinked in surprise, took Geordie's other hand, and began to pull him along. "Come on, lad," she sniffed. "A nice 'ot meal an' we will all feel better, that I warrant ye. There is nothin' more to be done 'ere, nothin' at all."

Feeling the earl's eyes on her back like two hot coals, Rachel dared not look his way again as they moved through the cemetery and cleared the tall gates that faced the street. She'd told Lord Druridge all she knew about her father's involvement in the fire. He had no more claim on her, and she wanted nothing more to do with him. Her family, or the remnants of it, no longer depended on the mine for their weekly pay. Like everyone else, she owed her rents to the earl's solicitor, but other than that she was one of the rare, blessed individuals in Creswell who could pass each day without thought of him—and she planned to do exactly that. Geordie would never work in Lord Druridge's hideous colliery. She would see the bookshop make sufficient profit that he would never need to resort to such work. "Just see if I don't," she muttered.

"What?" A winded Mrs. Tate paused to look up at her.

"Nothing." Unable to stop herself, Rachel checked over her shoulder. She half-expected the earl to be gone, but he wasn't. He'd moved forward, alone, and dismounted at her mother's grave. While she watched, he took a single yellow rose from inside his coat and laid it on the small mound.

The sight caused something to snap inside of Rachel. Dropping Geordie's hand, she left him with Mrs. Tate and, lifting her skirts, ran back.

By the time she reached Lord Druridge, she was breathing hard beneath Mrs. Tate's old cloak, but she scarcely noticed her exertion amid the flood of emotion swamping her head and her heart. Snatching the rose off her mother's grave, she shoved it at him.

"I have fulfilled my end of the bargain with you, my lord, and you have fulfilled yours," she said. "There is nothing more between your family and mine, no reason for you to be here."

He ignored the flower in her outstretched hand. "You may not believe this, but I am sincerely sorry." His eyes flicked Geordie's way. "For you and the lad."

The pain in Rachel's chest intensified. This man had caused her to break her promise, and for what? For nothing! Because of him, she had left her mother, and her mother had died in her absence. The physician Lord Druridge had held out as a carrot in front of her nose hadn't been worth her time in fetching him.

Her throat constricted, her eyes burned, and her hands began to shake with the effort of holding her emotions inside. "Go. The last thing I need from you is your pity."

He acknowledged her words with a slight nod. Then he reached behind his saddle to retrieve the cloak she had left at Blackmoor Hall. "Later, if there is anything I can do—"

"I'm sorry, my lord," she broke in, grabbing it. "Our business is done. You see, I have nothing left to trade."

He blanched but made no reply. Climbing back onto his horse, he dipped his head in farewell, wheeled around, and galloped toward the man who waited for him.

Rachel collapsed to her knees, at last letting the tears run, unheeded, down her cheeks.

"What is it, child? Was that Lord Druridge?" Mrs. Tate's breathless voice rose behind her as she trudged back into the cemetery.

Turning, Rachel saw that Geordie accompanied her and had quit crying, his surprise and interest in what had just occurred momentarily supplanting his grief.

"Was that really the earl?" he asked, sounding more than a trifle awestruck.

Rachel nodded. Draping her old cloak over one arm, she stifled her sobs and gazed down at the flower Lord Druridge had brought to her mother's grave. The bloom, a perfect yellow bud, was in its first blush of life. All thorns had been stripped from its stem.

"Where would 'e have gotten a fresh rose at this time of year?" Mrs. Tate asked.

"From his greenhouse," Rachel answered absently. "He could have brought her an entire spring garden, but all she needed was a doctor."

"'E brought the doctor, didn't 'e? Which reminds me, lass. 'E left ye some money yesterday, just before 'e took that doctor fellow 'ome. 'E asked me to wait until after the funeral and then see that ye got what ye needed." She reached inside her skirt and handed Rachel a ten-pound note.

Fresh anger made Rachel's blood boil. Ten pounds was more than most miners made in two months. She could never accept such a sum, especially from him. She refused to owe him anything but her monthly rent, not even a kind thought or a thank-you. Neither would she let Lord Druridge make her feel as though she had sold her own mother out for money. She had traded information for a physician, nothing more, nothing less.

"—kind of 'im, wouldn't you agree?" Mrs. Tate was saying. "To be so generous? I think the villagers are wrong about 'im. 'E 'as a sober appearance perhaps, but there must be a soft 'eart beneath that 'ard shell. Only a good man would trouble 'imself to bring a doctor to the bed of a dyin' stranger in the middle of—"

"That was no favor," Rachel interrupted.

"What?"

"Nothing." She handed the rose to her neighbor because she could no longer bear the sight of it. "Mrs. Tate?"

"Aye?"

"Can I borrow Gilly?"

Her neighbor's face creased into a worried frown. "Aye. A man brought 'im 'ome from Blackmoor Hall just this mornin' lookin' fat as butter. But what's the matter, lass? Don't ye feel well? Of course ye don't. Who would, at their dear mother's funeral? Forgive me for prattlin' on. We need to get ye 'ome, like ye said. Ye don't need to go anywhere on old Gilly. I will take care of ye. Come on."

"Gilly! You're not going to leave me, are you, Rachel?" Geordie gaped at her. The donkey's name had managed to draw his attention away from the departing earl. "I'm sorry I was bad," he said, his hands clutching at her skirt. "I'll be a good lad now, I promise. Don't go anywhere. Don't leave me, Rachel."

"I won't leave you, Geordie." Rachel rubbed his back and allowed Mrs. Tate to cluck over them as they made their way to the cottage. But she knew, come Geordie's bedtime, she had a delivery to make.

"You're not much for conversation today."

Truman looked up to see Wythe squinting at him, once again trying to break the silence that had engulfed them throughout the thirty-minute ride to Blackmoor Hall. "I'm a little preoccupied; that's all."

"You've been sullen as hell."

Truman peered through the trees to view the southern wall of his home. He loved this part of the journey from the village. He could hear the surf crashing on the rocks below, smell the rich earth, despite its winter slumber. Today, with the sun glistening off the snow, he admired, for the millionth time, the beauty of the black, craggy rocks that broke up the wintry scene, and the tall, leafless trees that swayed with the salt-laden wind blowing in from the sea. Blackmoor Hall soothed him in so many ways. He'd grown up here, with good parents who had given him happiness and love.

But all the pleasant memories of his youth couldn't erase the image of Rachel, pale and drawn, at her mother's funeral. She looked so forlorn, so completely lost, as if the weight of the world now rested on her shoulders.

Would Mrs. McTavish have lived if he had brought the doctor sooner?

The thought Truman had been avoiding since leaving Rachel at her cottage yesterday crept in, demanding an audience. He'd been so determined to win his personal battle with the past that he'd taken the gamble, but it was Rachel who had lost.

Living with that knowledge would be difficult. Especially because he had gleaned so little information about Jack McTavish. Rachel had merely confirmed what Truman had already suspected, which left him with the same short list of possible murderers: a group of disgruntled miners, the father of Katherine's unborn babe, or Wythe.

Truman watched as his cousin rode ahead, picking his way through the trees. Wythe stood to inherit Blackmoor Hall as long as Truman had no heir.

But if Wythe had set the fire, why did he pull Truman from the flames? And why would Wythe destroy so much of what he hoped to inherit?

With a grimace, Truman studied his scarred hand, currently gloved. After two years, he was no closer to solving the mystery of his wife's death than he'd been when it happened. Yet the stakes in his fight with Katherine's parents were growing higher by the day. The Abbotts insisted Truman confess and turn himself in, but he'd sooner die than blacken his family name and relinquish his lands and title without first having some kind of proof that he deserved such retribution.

He had made *some* progress, at least. Learning that Jack McTavish had been offered a significant amount of money about the time of the fire suggested the killer wasn't one of Katherine's lovers come from London, which made sense since the most likely culprits had solid alibis. That had narrowed his search the past six months to the area in which he lived—and it suggested that he was not to blame.

"What was all that about?" Wythe asked after halting his horse to wait for him.

"What was all *what* about?" Truman drew even with him but was still reluctant to allow the silence to be broken.

"That funeral business. Why did you want to go there?"

The indifferent tone of Wythe's voice caused Truman's hands to tighten on the reins. "I told you. The village bookseller died yesterday."

"What was she to you? It isn't as though you attend all the village funerals. You didn't even make your presence known until the very end."

"I wasn't making a political statement."

The stablemaster's hounds came bounding from the manse to welcome him home.

"Did you even know the woman who died?" Wythe persisted.

Exasperated, Truman reined in and spoke over the yapping of the dogs. "Is it so unbelievable that I might have gained the acquaintance of a poor village bookseller?"

"I thought perhaps it was the bookseller's daughter you were interested in." Wythe once again slowed his horse to a stop, a knowing smile stretched across his face. "Rachel McTavish is one of the prettiest wenches I have ever seen."

Truman stared past his cousin, seeing Miss McTavish's face in his mind's eye instead of the lacy branches and boughs of the trees surrounding them. She *was* a beauty, with her wide green eyes and thick blond hair. But she was no porcelain doll, like Katherine. Vibrant and full of life, Rachel's face reflected emotion at all times, courage and determination chief among them.

"Well?"

Rousing himself, Truman focused on Wythe as Rachel's image faded from his mind. "Well what?"

Wythe grinned. "Do you want me to send Anthony to fetch her and bring her to your bed?"

Irritation rose like bile in Truman's throat. "She has just buried her mother," he said. "Besides, I have never had anyone *bring* me a woman before. What makes you think I'll start now?"

Wythe hardly looked penitent. "Don't get self-righteous with me, cousin. Just because someone has never tasted a strawberry doesn't mean they won't enjoy that first sweet bite." He arched his eyebrows in temptation. "A good lay is just what you need. You've been living like a shade, sullen and withdrawn, haunting the manse by night. If you're afraid the McTavish wench will prove unwilling, don't be. I have seen her a time or two at Elspeth's."

This statement bothered Truman, although he didn't know why. Rachel was nothing to him. She hated him. He told himself not to dignify Wythe's words with a response but couldn't help himself. "What are you saying? She's not one of Elspeth's girls. . . ."

"All women are of the same ilk, if the price is high enough. How else do you think Rachel has contributed to her family's coffers? It's not as if they could live on what they make from that bloody bookshop."

Truman scowled. "Before the roads improved, that bookshop was an important outpost. I'm sure many from the surrounding counties remain good clients. Anyway, what Miss McTavish does is her own business. See that you leave her alone." He started his horse walking toward the end of the thicket where soft, rolling hills marked the beginning of his gardens.

Wythe trotted up to him. "You would be doing her a favor, don't you see? What's a quick stint on her back to pay the rent compared to walking the floor of that musty bookshop for endless hours? I'd say she is ripe for the picking. Just picture her silky hair spilling over your pillow, her legs spread to welcome you as you plow into that supple body—"

Wheeling his horse around, Truman threw his fist into Wythe's jaw before he even knew what he was going to do.

The blow knocked his cousin down. Wythe landed with a thud, sprawled in the crunchy snow like a discarded cloak. Truman had never struck him before. He didn't know what had come over him now, but he couldn't bring himself to regret it.

"Have you no decency? Don't ever speak of Miss McTavish in such a light again. And concerning the collection of my rents, see that Mr. Lewis manages to overlook stopping by her shop for the next few months."

With a glower, Wythe rubbed his jaw, obviously as shocked as Truman was. "She's no lady, my lord," he said tightly. "Just a village wench."

"I don't care. Stay away from Miss McTavish, as well as the maids at Blackmoor Hall. Do I make myself clear?"

Wythe glared up at him without answering. It was only when Truman stepped his horse closer that he finally nodded.

"Good." The earl watched his cousin stand on shaky legs before offering a hand to help him mount his horse.

Wythe muttered under his breath, but Truman couldn't make out what he said and didn't care to try. His poverty-stricken cousin had been raised in

London by a part of the family about whom Truman had only heard his parents whisper. He knew Wythe hadn't been in a good situation, that his aunt and uncle had been different in many ways and that his own parents hadn't approved of them. But his mother and father had taken Wythe in when Uncle John died a few years after Aunt Margaret. Problem was, by the time Wythe had come to live at Blackmoor Hall, he was already a youth of thirteen. Although that was two full years younger than Truman, who'd been fifteen at the time, Wythe hadn't been taught to curb the wild, reckless blood that ran in his veins, and nothing they did seemed capable of overcoming those early years.

Covering the last quarter mile at a gallop, Truman left Wythe behind. As much as he wanted to believe his dead father's prediction that his cousin would eventually govern himself as befit a Stanhope, Truman had always had his doubts. Except for that day . . .

Again he felt Wythe's shoulder lodged in his gut as his cousin carried him out of the burning hall. Remembered Wythe dropping him to the ground then gasping for breath as they both watched the flames shimmer against the cloudy sky overhead. In that surreal moment, Truman had been so grateful for his cousin's bravery, he'd decided he'd misjudged him during all the years before.

But his opinion had reversed itself again since then. These days Truman worried less about Wythe's heavy drinking and gaming and more about the possibility that he was responsible for Katherine's murder. Maybe he was even the father of her baby. There were moments when he'd put nothing past him.

Chapter 5

Hooves pounded the frozen swath of road behind her, causing Rachel to turn in apprehension. The night she'd visited Blackmoor Hall to summon Druridge's physician, the storm had left her alone in the forest, and worry for her mother had numbed her to all other concerns. Tonight she wasn't so preoccupied and felt much more uneasy about her safety.

'Tis no one I need worry about, she told herself, pressing forward. But whoever it was could be a thief . . . or worse.

The moon glistened on the blanketed ground, lighting her way beyond the circle of her lantern. She easily followed the rutted path left by the bevy of servants and merchants who traipsed to and from the manse each day. But whoever approached on horseback grew steadily closer.

Deeming it prudent to get off the road, she eased Gilly into the trees and slid to the ground, where she covered her lantern with her cloak.

A dark shape, almost purple in the moonlight, rounded the bend as a lone rider—a man, judging from his size—came into view. He rode at a rapid pace for carrying no light. Bent over his animal, with his cloak flying behind, he looked more like a specter than anything of this earth.

Rachel peered through the branches, hoping to remain hidden. But as the rider advanced, he slowed his mount to a walk and began to study the landscape on either side. His voice, muddled from drink, rose on the night air. *"And o'er the hills, and far away, beyond their utmost purple rim, Beyond the night, across the day, Thro' all the world she follow'd him."*

With a laugh, he bent so close to the trees that he nearly toppled from his horse. "A poet I am not, but come, do not hide. Let me see who *I* have been following on this cold night."

Rachel's hands gripped Gilly's reins more tightly. Whoever it was must've spotted her light before she could douse it. He knew she was close, but she dared not give away her exact location. Not only was this man potentially dangerous, he was drunk. Certainly he would pass on if he didn't find her soon.

"I have trailed you for over a mile. I know you're here . . . somewhere." He batted at the trees. "Are you a highwayman, perchance?"

He seemed to be weighing the odds. "No, I doubt that. A highwayman would not light his path so clearly nor ride upon such a slow beast. Who then? A servant? A merchant? Neither," he said, answering his own questions. "Who among such would have business on this road after dark? Merchants are sleeping, dreaming of how to line their pockets with the earl's gold come morning. And servants are too exhausted by bedtime to venture out."

Rachel held her breath as whomever it was dismounted and began to search in earnest, not ten steps away.

"Come now!" he barked out. "Answer me the riddle of your identity. I hope you are a woman, for I have no respect for a man who cowers in the woods."

His overloud voice, combined with his uncoordinated movements, caused Gilly to start. Braying loudly, the donkey jerked so hard on his rope that he nearly dragged Rachel into the road. She stumbled before she managed to halt the ass, and that was enough to give her away. Footsteps crunched through the snow with greater purpose and a hand grabbed her arm, pulling her out of her hiding place.

Without the cover of her cloak, the yellow glow of Rachel's lantern burst upon them, illuminating the stranger's lean face and dark eyes, which peered at her beneath a shock of hair as black as ink.

"You are—you are the earl's cousin," she stammered, recognizing Wythe despite his overall dishevelment. An inch or two shorter than Druridge, he possessed the same dark hair. But his eyes were more brown than gold, and his features, though well sculpted, seemed to lack a certain congruity, throwing his good looks slightly off-balance.

He released her but stayed close enough that he could grab her again if he had a mind to. "Wythe Stanhope, at your service. And you are Miss Rachel McTavish, if I am not mistaken. I remember you, too, from Elspeth's."

Rachel winced at his allusion to Elspeth Soward's. A decent girl never went near a brothel, but Madame Soward had become a friend, of sorts, and Rachel had never been one to worry overmuch about appearances—a rebellious trait her mother had said she'd live to regret. She had a feeling that prophecy was about to be fulfilled. She had seen Wythe Stanhope about the streets of Creswell or at the colliery many times, and most recently at her mother's funeral, yet he mentioned Elspeth's. Was he trying to belittle her?

"Elspeth has determined to read, and I tutor her," she said by way of explanation. "We usually do it at my shop but, on occasion, she has bid me come to her . . . er . . . place of business."

"Of course. Every whore should learn to read. As for myself, I was there to learn how to use a thimble and needle."

Annoyed by his sarcasm, Rachel stepped away. "Are you insinuating that I am lying, sir?"

"I am not insinuating anything. Rather, I am making it *clear* that I do not believe you." He lifted a hand before she could protest. "But I don't care what you tell my cousin of your time at Elspeth's. Make him believe that there have been no others before him, if you like, and charge him a virgin's rates. He deserves to be duped for taking my suggestion after nearly breaking my jaw for making it."

"*What?*" Rachel shook her head. "You are drunk, sir." She could smell him from where she stood, even though he was now more than an arm's length away, and he was making no sense. "Believe what you will about Elspeth's. I know my dealings with her are innocent enough."

After stooping to retrieve her lantern, she tried to lead Gilly onto the road, but the stubborn animal merely threw its head, almost yanking her arm out of its socket in the process.

"Come on, Gilly. Let us be about our errand. Blackmoor Hall isn't far, but it's getting late." Rachel gave the rope another tug—all to no avail. Gilly continued to nibble at the patch of dead grass he had uncovered at the foot of a tree.

"It *is* getting late," Wythe agreed. "And you wouldn't want to keep the mighty earl waiting. I will even escort you, since he did not deem you worthy enough to send his carriage." The earl's cousin stood next to his horse, watching her struggle with her own animal without moving to help. "Better yet"— he stepped forward, his hand closing over hers where she grasped the donkey's lead—"perhaps you will give me the first toss. We could slip into my room, where it will be warm and dry. I would ride you easy and pay you well since I can think of no better revenge than sending you to my dear cousin with the smell of me still on you."

The crudity of Wythe's words hit Rachel like a fist to the stomach. "Let go!"

His expression grew more purposeful instead of less, and his fingers tightened. "Surely you can afford me a few minutes of your precious time," he said and leaned in as though he'd kiss her.

Rachel didn't wait to find out whether that was his intent. Swinging her lantern in a great arc, she brought it crashing down on his head.

The sound of breaking glass grated on the air.

A second later, he collapsed and the light winked out.

Shocked by what she'd done, as well as by the results of it, she blinked until her eyes grew accustomed to the sudden darkness. It wasn't easy to see, but soon she could make out the twinkle of broken glass and the darker shape of Wythe, who was beginning to moan and rub his temples.

He wasn't dead.

Thank God.

But what would he do to her when he recovered?

Moving quickly, she found Gilly's rope and attempted to lead him out of the trees but, once again, the ass refused to budge.

What was she going to do? If she couldn't get the donkey to cooperate, she'd have to flee on foot. But that would be futile. Wythe had a horse. He'd catch her in a matter of minutes, even with a head start.

Spouting one curse after another, the earl's cousin tried to stand, but he was unsteady enough that Rachel was able to push him back into the snow.

After that, she captured the reins of his horse and, mumbling some soothing words that were more of a prayer for her own safety, led the spooked animal to a fallen tree.

As Wythe staggered to his feet, she wedged her foot into the stirrup and used the saddle to pull herself off the ground. But she wasn't encouraged by the results. She hung suspended for what felt like an eternity before managing to settle astride the beast.

"Don't even *think* about taking my mount," Wythe warned, but she was committed to her escape. Squeezing her eyes shut, she gave the animal a panicked kick.

The horse reared up and launched into a full run. As the ground rushed past her, she could hear Wythe's voice echoing through the trees behind her: "You bloody whore. You'll pay for this!"

Rachel hung on for dear life, but it wasn't long before her knuckles hurt too badly to grip the horse's mane. She'd lost the reins the moment she climbed into the saddle. They dragged on the ground, hopelessly out of reach.

In an effort to ease the terrible cramp in her hands, she adjusted her hold and looked ahead.

Between the indistinct scenery flying past her, the rush of wind that brought tears to her eyes and the patches of deep darkness, where the towering trees blocked even the moon's light, everything was a blur. But she didn't have to see much to know that she was perilously close to the edge of the cliff. As the animal surged on, she could hear the surf below. . . .

Dear God . . . She tried to steer Wythe's horse away from land's end, but the spooked animal had had enough of human intervention. It charged heedlessly on, sending frozen dirt clods tumbling over the edge.

Rachel's pulse pounded as rapidly, though far less rhythmically, than the animal's hooves. *What have I done?*

Using her thighs, her hands, anything she could to hang on, she looked behind her but saw no sign of Wythe. Her plan had worked far too well. There was no one to check the horse's wild flight, or to get help.

Blackmoor Hall materialized in front of her like a giant falcon with wings spread. As overwhelming as it could be, the house was a welcome sight tonight—offering, as it did, a modicum of hope that the horse would merely return to its stable. There was a moment when Rachel thought she might be fine, but that hope disappeared when her mount cut away from the road to jump the stone fence.

Rachel screamed as she came out of the saddle. She could feel the mane slipping through her fingers. . . . Once it was gone, the exhilaration of free fall lifted her stomach into her throat and the ground caught her with a solid and unyielding *thump*.

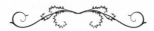

The door to Truman's bedroom was always shut late at night to hold in the heat of the fire the maids lit before hurrying to their beds.

He entered the welcoming comfort of that warmth and removed his stock and shirt before leaning one hand against the mantel and staring into the fire smoldering in the grate.

I'm getting closer, he thought, *closer to the truth.* And Linley would help him uncover the rest of it.

At the side table in the corner of the room, Truman poured himself a brandy. Holding the first swallow in his mouth to savor the rich taste, he stood with his back to the black night beyond his window, once again contemplating the flames and what his dream two nights ago had revealed.

Everyone was gone that Sunday when the fire broke out—except Katherine. He'd found his wife wearing nothing but a delicate wrap and sitting in front of her boudoir, brushing her hair. He remembered thinking it was so typical of her. The mirror and the image it projected were all-important to her. Even pregnant and ill, she worked to protect her vanity.

But he'd grown to expect nothing more. He'd told her he wanted a divorce. She'd gone hysterical and followed him into the library, threatening, pleading, cajoling. It was there that she swore she still loved him. That she told him her family would do everything possible to stop him from obtaining the Act of Parliament a divorce would require.

That had caused such an upwelling of emotion he'd never realized his father's favorite painting, *Landscape with the Fall of Icarus*, was not on the wall where it had hung for years—not until that detail had surfaced from somewhere deep in his subconscious.

An original by Pieter Bruegel, the painting was part of a much larger collection that had been on display throughout the manor. The place where it normally hung should have jumped out at him the moment he entered the room.

Maybe it had. Maybe he'd lost that detail in the haze of darkness that soon followed.

Or perhaps he was dreaming up the missing painting.

Truman sighed. He hoped he would soon find out. He was sending Linley to London in the morning to visit another avid collector. If he had to, he would have Linley visit every art expert in England, his mission to discover any piece of the collection supposedly destroyed in the fire. If he could find just one—

A groan drew his eyes to the bed, but the rich, burgundy draperies that hung there concealed who or what might have made the sound.

What the devil? Assuming it was Susanna, that she had come to his bed despite his earlier refusal, he crossed the floor and yanked the draperies back. But it wasn't his maid. It was Rachel McTavish! She lay with her eyelashes resting against her cheeks, her long blond hair unfurled on his pillow like a flag—as beautiful as any of the fine ladies he'd known.

Evidently Wythe hadn't been content to tempt him with mere words. He'd sent for her. And she'd come, just like his cousin predicted she would.

Where the sheet gaped, Truman could see one bare breast and realized she was naked beneath the quilts. How long had she been waiting for him? Why hadn't someone informed him she was here?

How like his cousin to taunt him with the knowledge that, despite his noble words, he wouldn't be able to refuse her. . . .

With that thought, he almost stepped away from the bed. He could make a considerable dent in Wythe's smugness by sending her home straightaway.

If only he didn't long to touch her, to erase the vision of her sadness from his mind . . . a sadness he was partly responsible for causing.

How much had Wythe paid her?

It had to be a vast sum, to bring her to *him*. But he couldn't find it in him to fault her. Not now, when he so badly wanted what she was willing to trade.

He remembered how courageously she'd defended her family. When he'd watched her at her mother's funeral, standing there desolate yet strong, he'd known she was nothing like her father. She was rare and beautiful and, heaven help him, he could not stifle the desire that slammed into him with the force of the ocean battering the cliffs outside. It caused his hand to shake as he reached out to slide a finger down her pale, slim arm.

"Rachel?"

She whimpered in her sleep but turned toward him, seeking his voice, making herself more accessible to his touch.

Send her home, his mind urged. *For honor's sake, send her home. Her mother's funeral was today.*

But the demands of his body spoke louder still.

The bed dipped, creating a pool of warmth where there hadn't been one before. Rachel snuggled closer and found a hard, lean body reaching for her, a glorious body with smooth skin covering powerful muscle.

Other sensations began to seep into her consciousness as well. The light caress of a man's fingers moving over her cheek and down her throat. The soft fan of his breath against her skin. Steel-like arms gathering her close.

Who was it?

Strangely, Rachel wasn't alarmed. She breathed in the unique scent of brandy, horses and cologne and immediately recognized the Earl of Druridge. It had to be him, for there was no other like him, and she remembered his scent all too well. The same scent had clung to the cloak he'd loaned her.

Pressing her face into his neck, she acknowledged his identity without thought of resistance. She didn't know where he had come from, or how he had suddenly appeared in her bed, so he could only be a dream.

And, although she hated to admit it, she'd had this dream before....

Sensing rather than seeing the dim glow of a fire in the background, Rachel tried to open her eyes, but her lids were far too heavy. Her mind seemed to be floating somewhere above her, above them both. But she could feel the earl's hands on her breasts, touching and teasing them as he coaxed her to respond to him and distantly wondered at her own inability to refuse.

She hated him. Didn't she?

No, not at the moment. She wasn't capable of feeling any such negative emotion, not when her thoughts were so befuddled and her head ached. Briefly, she conjured snippets of a memory—of Wythe bending over her and hefting her into his arms—but that image didn't make sense. And, thankfully, the loathsome Wythe was gone. It was the earl who was playing her body as expertly as a master cellist draws only the sweetest notes from his instrument's strings.

"How the mere thought of you has haunted me," he murmured, sliding his fingers down her stomach as though he could hardly believe he'd gained access to her body.

She smiled. Evidently her subconscious had conjured a much more solicitous earl than the one she knew. This man was all that was gentle and good as he kissed her neck, her jaw and finally her mouth.

Rachel parted her lips for him, instinctively knowing what he craved and wanting the same. That simple act of submission seemed to quicken something inside him. He groaned before deepening the kiss, at which point Rachel's thoughts began to splinter. More memories surfaced—a horse accident, that vision of Wythe looming over her while she lay on the ground, staring into the starry sky as he carried her . . . somewhere. But her mind could make no sense of the long nothingness that followed. And now she seemed to be viewing things from afar, disconnected, yet somehow on fire.

The earl's hands were everywhere, strong and sure as they found the hidden treasures they sought. Even the hand with the scars felt like heaven on her body, once she insisted he remove the glove he always wore. He seemed to like that she wasn't put off by his scars, that she wanted him to touch her with nothing in between, and his mouth followed his hands, nibbling first at her ear, her neck and finally licking one nipple.

She heard her own small cry at the pleasure he gave her, felt all her nerves draw up tight just below her belly. Someplace deep inside her had begun to pulse with warmth and readiness, causing her to strain for the release she craved but didn't know how to achieve.

"Soon, sweet Rachel, soon," he assured her, his voice hoarse with his own need as she tried to pull him on top of her. "There's no hurry. Let me savor the taste and feel of you." The muscles in his back and arms bunched beneath her touch, telling her he felt the same urgency but was holding back.

She clung to him as his fingers moved lower still, below her belly button around the curve of one hip to the apex of her thighs, sweeping her away in a storm of desire so intense she couldn't catch her breath. Arching toward him, she insisted he give her that mysterious something as soon as possible.

"Now," she urged. "I need . . . I need you."

He couldn't seem to wait any longer either. But as soon as he settled her beneath him and pressed inside her, a white, hot pain lanced up from between her thighs, shocking her as badly as her startled reaction seemed to surprise him.

Stiffening, she tried to recoil from whatever he'd stabbed her with. But he wouldn't move; neither would he let her go.

"Rachel, I didn't know," he murmured. "Why didn't you tell me?"

Rachel's tongue felt too numb to speak. Tears gathered in her eyes and began to roll into her hair. She could feel her body start to quiver as the physical pain joined the heartache of remembering her mother.

Druridge smoothed her hair off her forehead and kissed her tears away. "Shh," he whispered. "Don't cry. I'm sorry." He pulled back in an unspoken plea for her to look up at him, and finally Rachel managed to open her eyes.

The fire outlined his dark head and the broad width of his shoulders as he leaned on his elbows above her. *He's beautiful,* she thought. But he was no dream. She didn't know how it had happened. At this point, she couldn't even guess. But she was in the earl's large, soft bed.

And he had just taken her virginity.

Chapter 6

That night Truman didn't dream. Once he was able to coax Rachel into letting him touch her again, he'd obtained one of the most powerful climaxes he'd ever experienced, and then he'd slept like the dead—comfortable, relaxed, content at last.

When morning came, he reluctantly roused himself. He wasn't sure how long the sun had been boring through the crack in the draperies, but he could see the light behind his closed lids and knew dawn was several hours past. He'd slept in. He'd probably missed a whole slew of appointments at the colliery but, oddly enough, he couldn't find it in him to care. Katherine's restless ghost wasn't hovering over him at the moment. It was almost as if Rachel's innocence had banished the past long enough to let him sleep deeply for the first time in two years.

Instinctively, he reached for her, searching the bed with his hands before opening his eyes. But she was gone.

"Damn," he muttered, feeling a surprising sense of loss. He tried to shake off his disappointment, but the scent of her lingered, tantalizing him with the memory of how it had been to bed the strong-willed beauty he'd admired since their first meeting at the bookshop. Better, and worse, was the knowledge that only he had possessed her. Better because it somehow branded her as his own—and worse for the same reason.

Pulling back the bedding, he gazed at the slight smear of blood that proved last night had not been fantasy. Part of him felt like he owed her something more than money, even though she'd obviously agreed to whatever Wythe had arranged.

He'd pay a handsome stipend, Truman decided. She needed financial wherewithal, so that was the best way to help her. Then he'd stay away. Soon the memory of last night would fade in her mind, and the good his money would do her and young Geordie would absolve his conscience for having behaved no better than Wythe.

With a fresh burst of energy, he pulled the linens off his bed and piled them on the floor for the maids to wash. The sooner he rid his room of any reminder of the bookseller's daughter, the sooner he could forget the confusing emotions she inspired: the regret, the tenderness, the obligation, the longing.

"There," he said aloud and rang for his valet so he could dress. But when he turned toward the bureau, he spotted something wadded up on top.

Closer examination revealed it to be a ten-pound note. For a moment, he pretended a servant had found it in the laundry or that he'd left it there himself. But deep down he knew.

It had come from Rachel. The only thing he didn't understand was why.

Rachel, ye 'ad me good an' frightened last night; that ye did.

The words Mrs. Tate had spoken early this morning when Rachel returned from Blackmoor Hall still rang in Rachel's ears as she moved pensively around the bookshop, battling a thundering headache and a pair of blistered feet. Last night, after finding her clothes piled haphazardly on a chair in the earl's room, she'd dressed and walked home. She'd hoped to sneak into bed unnoticed, but she'd found Mrs. Tate keeping an all-night vigil, pacing and worrying and craving the reason for her long absence.

Rachel had blundered her way through several lies, eventually tying them into a neat package that centered on Gilly bolting while she tried to hide in the trees from a late-night passerby. Unfortunately, she'd gone on to apologize for losing Gilly, only to find out that the donkey had been fully restored and was munching hay in the small pen behind Mrs. Tate's house. For that, she could offer no explanation. Wythe had seen to it that he was returned, of course. Who else could have done it? She'd pieced together enough to know that he had found her, likely drugged her and taken her to the earl's bed. She guessed it was his revenge for hitting him with the lantern. But she wasn't about to mention the earl's cousin to Mrs. Tate, for fear of the questions it would raise. Neither did she plan to admit to another living soul what had happened to her at Blackmoor Hall. That was her secret, and she was determined to carry it to her grave. The accident, and probably a good draught of laudanum or something else, had stolen her wits, or she would've escaped the moment she realized it wasn't a dream. Instead, she'd clung to Druridge, somehow craving what he offered despite that brief flash of pain. There'd been something so satisfying about the way his body joined with hers—that delicious stretch, that sense of fullness. But she couldn't hold herself accountable for something she didn't rightly know was happening, even if, in her more honest moments, she had to admit she'd enjoyed all but a few seconds.

The bell rang over the door and Rachel felt herself blush, as if others could read her thoughts.

"Mistress?"

Hoping for a patron—money would indeed be short this month—Rachel pasted a polite smile on her lips and rounded a table piled high with books. But it was only a servant, a tall, young man of no more than eighteen. He wore the blue livery of the Earl of Druridge, which made her more than a little apprehensive. What now?

"Mistress, my master bid me bring ye this," the boy said as soon as he saw her.

Rachel stared at the envelope he extended toward her. Its wax seal bore the earl's insignia.

"What is it?" she asked numbly.

"Sorry, mum?" The boy looked surprised, even confused by her question because, of course, he wouldn't know. He wouldn't presume to involve himself in the earl's business.

Rachel accepted the envelope but asked the footman to wait. He hovered at the door as she broke the seal.

Inside she found twenty pounds and the deed to her cottage, along with a note written in what appeared to be the earl's own hand.

Dear Rachel,

You must have forgotten your money. The balance please accept as my gift.

Sincerely,
Truman Stanhope

So now she knew the price a low-born woman like herself had to pay to get on a first-name basis with an earl.

The knowledge of it, the guilt, turned her stomach. If only she'd had the presence of mind to spurn him . . .

Shoving the money, and the deed, back into the envelope, Rachel handed the lot of it to Druridge's servant. "Please return this to your master. Tell him I do not want his money. Tell him"—she took a deep breath, wondering what she could say that would keep the earl from involving himself in her life again—"tell him there is no debt between us and no need to contact me again."

The servant's eyes rounded. "That's a lot of money yer 'andin' back."

It *was* a lot of money, but the deed to the cottage tempted her more. To know Geordie would always have a roof over his head . . . But her self-respect wouldn't allow her to compromise her principles, at least not to that degree. She might have made a mistake, might've succumbed to a moment of wanton desire. But she wasn't a whore. "It doesn't belong to me. See that your master gets it."

"Yes, mum." Slipping the envelope inside his coat, the servant gave her a slight bow and left.

"Looks like you have been making friends in high places, Miss McTavish."

Startled, Rachel whirled around to see Jonas Cutberth standing next to her desk. She didn't have to ask how he'd gotten there—for her sake as much as his own the union organizer never used the front door. He came and went through the back, by way of the alley.

"Is something wrong, Mr. Cutberth?" she asked. "I wasn't expecting you."

His delicate eyebrows—delicate enough to belong to a woman—arched above black, bird-like eyes that rarely blinked. He had a neatly trimmed mustache and dark hair that fell, unkempt, across his brow. At forty, his once muscular build was going soft, but he wasn't unhandsome. Not more than a year ago, Rachel had secretly fancied herself in love with him—at least she'd been in love with his ideals.

"Nothing too serious. Have I come at a bad time?"

Rachel rubbed the knot on the back of her head—her souvenir from Blackmoor Hall—and drew a deep breath against the unremitting pain. "No. It has been a difficult week is all. In case you haven't heard, my mother passed away."

His mustache twitched as he offered her a brief, sad smile, but his eyes remained as watchful as ever. "I heard, and I am terribly sorry. Jillian was a good woman, always true to the cause."

That was how Mr. Cutberth measured people, according to their passion for the working class. Normally it didn't bother Rachel. But this morning she felt as though her own loyalty was somehow in question—a symptom, no doubt, of a guilty conscience.

"Wasn't that Lord Druridge's footman here just now?" He picked up a compilation of eighteenth-century poetry and leafed through its yellowed pages.

"It was."

"I thought I recognized him. Come to collect rent, has he?"

Mr. Cutberth was in charge of the accounting at the mine and knew Lord Druridge's business better than Rachel did, which meant he also knew the earl's solicitor took care of his rents. He wanted to know why a servant of the earl's would visit the bookshop.

To stop him from further inquiry, Rachel said, "The earl sent him to offer me money in exchange for what I know about the fire at Blackmoor Hall. He has made the offer before, remember?"

"I do. You told me you turned him down. Have you changed your mind?"

"Of course not. I know nothing that could help Lord Druridge."

Cutberth set the book aside. "Your mother never spoke of the tragedy?"

"Only to say my father was innocent."

He offered her a smile too obviously engineered to placate her. "Of course he was. But have you thought what it could mean to you and your young brother if you told the earl your father set the blaze? Jack's been in his grave for what . . . eighteen months? You no longer have to worry about your mother, God rest her soul. Druridge would have his answers. And you, my dear, would have a sizeable purse."

Rachel propped one hand on her hip. "And what would you get out of it, Mr. Cutberth?"

He grimaced at her demand for honesty. "I would get nothing, directly. But if I must spell out *all* the advantages, you would be doing our labor efforts a great service. Given the way the earl keeps nosing around, asking questions and hiring investigators, he is sure to discover the identity of some, if not all, of our supporters. If that happens, a lot of good men stand to lose their jobs."

"Including you."

He inclined his head. "Including me. I am rather fond of my wife and five children. I would like to be able to continue to support them."

Rachel waved him off. "I can't lie or tarnish my father's reputation in exchange for money. What would that make me?"

"A brave girl who is doing all she can to improve the miners' lot. Think of your poor, deceased brother. With a few precautions, accidents like the one that took his life could be avoided in future. But only if the workers unite, come together more powerfully than ever before, and demand the earl and his Fore-Overman make drastic changes."

The ache in her head escalated until it felt like her brain was trying to escape her skull. So much, too much, was riding on her shoulders. She felt herself bending under the weight of it all, even as she fought to carry the burden. "The wrong thing for the right reasons," she said, more to herself than to him.

"If you like."

Rachel rubbed her eyes. She needed sleep. She wanted to curl up in her bed while her mother moved around in the kitchen. She wanted to smell the aroma of roast chicken and homemade bread, hear Jillian humming softly to herself. But that was a luxury she would never know again. "Is that all?"

"No. There has been another accident, in Derbyshire. A nine-year-old boy was running the engine that raises and lowers the miners into the pit and was distracted by a mouse. Four older boys traveling in the cage were killed when he failed to stop its descent in time."

Rachel clasped her hands together to keep them from shaking. A cave-in had taken Tommy's life, but any tale of an accident in the mines made her blood run cold.

Cutberth said nothing to ease her distress. He paused, letting the full force of his words sink in. "How many deaths will it take, Miss McTavish, before we rally and stop the earl and others like him? The men who are getting rich off the labor of the working class? Surely public outcry over this latest accident will be enough to persuade the villagers to band together and create a formal chapter of the union." He ran a finger and thumb over his mustache. "That is, if you will do *your* part."

"Why me?" she asked. "Anyone can go to the earl and claim my father was the guilty party. They could even drum up some sort of proof, if they wanted."

"No. Druridge will believe you. I feel confident of it. You have held out just long enough to make your story convincing, and what with your mother's death and your current situation . . . Can you not see how perfect it is?"

She *could* see. That was the problem. She wanted to help the miners. She wanted the accidents to stop, which was why she'd supported Cutberth thus far. But for some reason that she wasn't willing to examine, she didn't want to lie to the earl about the death of his wife. Not after seeing how much the truth meant to him. Even after last night.

Especially after last night.

"I'm not feeling well," she told Cutberth. "Give me some time. I have to think about it."

"We don't have long. We need to ride the crest of this cage incident."

For the first time, Rachel felt a healthy dislike for the accountant. After all his professed distress over such incidents, he acted almost gleeful about this one. "I said I will think about it."

He studied her. "Fine. But do not forget Tommy. He is counting on you. We all are."

Something disturbed Rachel's sleep. Her head snapped up from the table, and she rubbed her face, trying to come to her senses enough to place her surroundings. She was at the bookshop, where she'd been trying to get a true picture of her financial situation. But a sixth sense told her she was no longer alone.

Was it Mrs. Tate coming to check on her progress? A mouse, like the one that had distracted that young trapper? Some other small animal?

Swiveling in her chair, Rachel looked behind her, squinting into the dark recesses of the shop, but the candle she'd left burning began to gutter out. Its small flame flickered and disappeared into a wisp of smoke, plunging her into blackness.

"Hello?" Her spine tingled as she stood. She kept very little money in the till, but her inventory was worth a great deal to the right people. She felt confident no one in Creswell would bother her or her business. But there were bands of thieves that roamed the northern counties. Perhaps they'd grown weary of sacking the big houses. Perhaps they were looking for an easier target. . . . "Who is it?"

"It's freezing in here. Why are you not at home?" The earl's voice, deep and resonant, carried across the room, providing Rachel with the focal point she needed. Now that her eyes had adjusted to the dark, she could make out her visitor, but just barely. Most of his body appeared as a murky shadow draped against the far wall.

"What are you doing here?" she asked, without bothering to answer his question.

"I saw the light burning."

In an effort to regulate her pulse, she took slow, even breaths, but the earl made her almost as nervous as the prospect of facing a band of thieves. What was he doing here in the middle of the night? Especially after what had previously passed between them? "You didn't bother to knock?"

She thought she saw his teeth flash in a smile. "I own the place, remember? And you were sleeping so peacefully."

"Most people are asleep at this hour, my lord. Is it your usual wont to haunt the village by night? No wonder everyone is so frightened of the great Lord Druridge."

He struck a match and, for a moment, his face glowed orange as he lit a pipe. "Not everyone is afraid of me, Miss McTavish." The smell of expensive tobacco wafted across the room. "Take you, for instance."

Her every nerve seemed taut and attuned to the man who'd made passionate, then incredibly tender, love to her less than twenty-four hours ago. Somehow the memory of their time together didn't seem congruous with the person who stood before her now. This was the old Earl of Druridge. The imperious mine owner. The peer of the realm. The privileged man her parents had hated. "I'm not sure what I think of you, my lord. My opinion doesn't matter anyway. I have enough to worry about with the shop and Geordie. What brings you here?"

"I want to know why," he said.

Rachel pulled her tattered cloak tighter around her shoulders. "Why what?"

"Why you agreed to come to me last night."

"Why I *agreed* to come to you?" Rachel tried to inject her voice with sufficient disdain. "You flatter yourself, my lord."

As he smoked his pipe, she felt his eyes cutting the darkness between them. "Perhaps, but for all your maidenly airs, I know a willing woman when I've got one beneath me."

Heat suffused Rachel's cheeks. She was glad he couldn't see her plainly. "Don't. I don't want to talk about it. I would rather we forget last night ever happened. It was all a big . . . misunderstanding."

"A misunderstanding? I find a naked woman in my bed, and she is warm and willing and more responsive than I could ever have dreamed she would be, and you tell me—"

"Please, stop!"

He chuckled softly. "Does it bother you so badly to admit that you wanted what I wanted? Are you above the appetites of the flesh, Miss McTavish?"

"That is hardly a fair question when you know I have little experience with such things—"

"Which is exactly why I am confused. Pray, enlighten me. Last night you leave ten pounds on my bureau, money I fear you can scarce live without. But when I try to return it, along with a significant amount for your . . . shall we say, discomfort, you send my servant away with every pound."

"Because I am not what you think. You wish to excuse yourself by tossing me a few pounds, to consider me better off for having given myself to you. But I won't have it. Live with yourself if you can. I want nothing from you. I was merely trying to return the money you gave Mrs. Tate when your cousin came upon me on the road."

She sensed the earl shifting, no longer leaning on the bookshelves. "Wythe said he merely extended you the invitation." His voice was soft on the outside but hard underneath, velvet over steel.

"He did a lot more than that."

"Such as . . . ?"

She waved a hand. "He said some nonsensical things about you taking him up on his idea after hitting him for making the suggestion. I told him I didn't know what he was talking about and tried to get away on his horse, but the silly beast threw me. The next thing I knew I found myself beneath your coverlet and you were there. . . ."

"Touching you." He stepped into the moonlight streaming through the front windows. "And you were telling me in ways as old as time that you wanted me to."

Yes. Even his scarred hand had not put her off. The thought of it brought her no revulsion now, as much as she wished otherwise. "No," she started but he cut her off.

"Then why didn't you say something? Let me know there had been a mistake?"

"Because I had just hit my head!" She almost mentioned that she might've been drugged, too. But that was a serious accusation and she had no proof of it. It wasn't necessary, anyway. The bump was enough. "I was too befuddled to think. I didn't even know who you were," she lied.

His laugh this time was bitter. "Of course not. You would never willingly give yourself to *me*, not for money, not for anything. I almost forgot. I am your nemesis. God forbid you might actually find yourself attracted to me." While he spoke, he moved closer, stopping only inches away. Towering over her the way he was, limed in silver, his cloak swirling around his knees, he looked darkly mysterious. "But you know who is touching you now, don't you, Rachel?" he asked, removing the glove on his good hand so he could run a finger down her cheek.

Rachel's brain screamed for her to move away, but her legs wouldn't carry her. She stood staring up into eyes that glittered with challenge and desire.

He lowered his head until his breath fanned her cheek and his lips hovered a hairbreadth above hers. What she felt in that moment reminded Rachel of a line from one of Tennyson's poems: "Once he drew with one long kiss my whole soul thro' my lips, as sunlight drinketh dew."

Closing her eyes, she swayed expectantly toward him, but he didn't kiss her. "I think you knew it was me all along," he said, and when Rachel opened her eyes again, he was gone.

Chapter 7

"Very interesting." Chuckling softly, a figure stood in the shadow of the building, watching as the earl rode away from the McTavish Bookshop. Unless the glimmering moonlight had been playing tricks, Druridge was upset. There was no accounting for that, but there was also no dismissing the confident way he'd let himself into the shop. It had almost been as if he had a right to be there. As though the McTavish wench would welcome him.

And after all her airs and self-righteous rhetoric about helping the poor working class! Evidently she'd found a way to improve her own lot and had jumped at the chance.

The earl's whore. Not a pretty title, but depending upon Druridge's devotion, Rachel could change everything. An unexpected but bold move.

Cutberth definitely needed to hear about this.

Truman slammed his fist into the stable wall, scaring the horses. They nickered and whinnied in surprise, but he didn't care if he woke the stable master, the stable master's dogs and all the lads sleeping above.

She was still with him, damn it. After five miles of slow travel, he couldn't escape his desire for Rachel McTavish. He had left her standing in that humble bookshop, her eyes closed and her mouth slightly parted, waiting for his kiss, and he had managed to walk away. But he had regretted it the moment he climbed astride his horse—more with each passing mile. She did something to him, something he couldn't quite combat. He'd chosen to ignore her and move on. But that wasn't as easy as he'd expected it to be. Deep down, he believed that maybe, just maybe, a woman like Rachel would be the perfect antidote to his cynicism and doubt.

Shaking away the pain in his hand and willing away the ache in his loins, Truman wished he'd never met Rachel. He'd been caught in her spell ever since he'd seen her on that ladder—a bit of revenge for Jack, were he alive to enjoy it. After last night, Truman was more enchanted than ever. He remembered the feel of her arms around his neck, the way she'd gasped as he moved inside her. . . .

Ah, sweet torture. But she was just one more thing to steal his focus from where it needed to be: solving the mystery of Katherine's murder. Considering all that had transpired, Rachel would never have a kind thought for him.

It was better to forget her. Certainly he'd be able to, eventually.

The sound of hooves beating the damp earth and then clattering over the gravel of the drive echoed above the settling noises of the stable he'd just left. Truman stepped closer to the stone wall that separated the slaughtering house and chicken coop from the kitchens and waited for his cousin to shelter his horse. What kind of shape would Wythe be in tonight? Rough living and alcohol were taking a toll on his work at the mine, but he refused to believe he had a problem.

Because Truman expected Wythe to be drunk, again, he was surprised to watch his cousin make his way toward the house on sure feet.

"Another late night?" he asked, stepping into his path.

Wythe didn't seem startled. "Not as late as most," he said, barely breaking stride.

Truman fell in step beside him. "Did Elspeth close early?"

"Elspeth never closes," he said with a grin. "That's what I love about her. But you wouldn't know. You take your pleasure right here, eh, cousin?"

Truman refused to let Wythe bait him, especially when he believed that Wythe was to blame for last night. "Actually, I'm glad you mentioned that. Rachel claims your horse threw her. You wouldn't have any idea how that could have happened, would you?"

Wythe slanted a glance his way. "She must've been dreaming. I told you this morning I merely made her an offer—one she apparently couldn't refuse."

"That's what I thought." Truman smiled and clapped a hand on his shoulder. "I knew you wouldn't lie to me. Just like I know you will stay away from her in future . . . because we wouldn't want any trouble between cousins. Am I right?"

Wythe stopped and gaped at him, shocked by the veiled threat. But Truman wasn't about to back down. He wanted to make his point perfectly clear. Rachel might hate him, and he might want to keep his distance from her. But he would not allow anyone connected to him to hurt her ever again.

"Right," Wythe said, then strode quickly to the house, leaving Truman outside to have another smoke.

Unwilling to open her eyes until she absolutely couldn't hide from the day any longer, Rachel woke late. The financial picture she'd created after going through the books last night had not been encouraging. Her mother owed a traveling vendor almost twenty pounds, which might've been two hundred for all of Rachel's ability to pay. Rents for the cottage and the shop were overdue. And their cupboards were nearly bare. In order to satisfy her creditors and garner enough to survive, she would have to sell off a portion of her inventory, perhaps to a shop in London, which was probably the only place she'd find someone with sufficient funds. But even if she did that, she would be faced with the same situation next month, and the month after. The bookshop wasn't meeting its overhead. The place would be dismantled bit by bit and she'd soon be left with nothing. Or almost nothing. She'd have her teaching, of course, but the miners paid her in foodstuffs and handmade items. Such bartering provided a more comfortable existence, but would never be enough to support her and young Geordie.

How had her mother managed?

That was a question Rachel feared to ask, even herself. Jillian had started the shop with the backing of her rich father. Although she was illegitimate, he had eventually accepted her, paid for her schooling, even set her up in business. But the money had stopped when he died. From there, Jillian had kept the shop afloat by using the money Jack had received for supposedly setting the fire at Blackmoor Hall, which was long gone. What had she been doing since?

According to what Rachel had figured out last night, one mysterious payment came in each month that was not categorized as to its source. Without that, they would have lost the shop long ago.

With a groan, she pulled her quilts up over her head. For a moment she remembered the money she'd turned away, just yesterday, and wished she could lower her pride and her ideals enough to accept it. She could go to Blackmoor Hall this morning and apologize to the earl for her high-handed rejection....

But how would she ever be able to live with herself?

There had to be another way.

"Rach?" The front door slammed as Geordie came charging into the cottage. The smell of fresh-baked bread accompanied him, making Rachel's mouth water.

"Look! Mr. Sandler gave me some bread for shoveling off his walk." He sat on the corner of her bed, holding a golden brown loaf in his hands.

"It snowed this morning?"

"Aye. The skies are clear now, but it's near freezin'." He threw off his scarf, hat and gloves but left on his coat. The cottage was nearly as cold as outdoors. No fire had been lit this morning. Considering the dwindling woodpile in back, Rachel had no plans to heat the cottage until nightfall.

"Are you hungry?" he asked. "Do you want some of my—"

He stopped midsentence and frowned at her, worry clouding his former expression. "Are you sick, Rachel? What's wrong? You look so white."

Rachel summoned the energy to sit up and give him a bright smile. She was drawing on reserves she didn't know she possessed, but she prayed she could keep up appearances, for his sake. Even if she had to resort to working in the mine, she would find some way to care for him.

All roads in Creswell seemed to lead to the earl.

"I was out late, finishing the accounting," she said, "but it's time I get up. I need to open the shop. Would you like to help me?"

He nodded and tore off a chunk of bread to give her. "I'll shovel the walks."

Rachel gratefully accepted his offering. He was such a good boy. If only she could provide him with an education and the chance to be something besides a miner.

"Rachel!" Mrs. Tate blew in next, her face red, her movements agitated. She usually knocked, but today she was obviously too upset to mind such convention.

"What is it?" Mrs. Tate's married sons worked at the mine. For a moment, Rachel feared there'd been another accident. "Is it Rulon or Charles?"

Her neighbor's mouth opened and closed twice before any sound came out. "No, it's the laundress, Mrs. Miller. She said . . . she said that ye and the earl"—she flapped a hand in front of her face as though she might faint— "that the two of ye—"

A sick feeling began in the pit of Rachel's stomach, but she had the presence of mind to stop Mrs. Tate long enough to get her brother out of the cottage. "Geordie, would you be so good as to bring in some more wood?"

Hesitant, he looked from Mrs. Tate to Rachel and back again. "I don't want to do it now. I want to hear—"

"Geordie, please."

The gravity in her tone must have frightened him enough to get him to obey. Reluctantly, he pulled on his hat, scarf and gloves and trudged outside, taking his bread with him.

After the door banged shut, Rachel steeled her nerves and turned to Mrs. Tate, who was wringing her hands. "What about me and the earl?"

Rachel felt as if she was standing in front of a firing squad, waiting for the first crack of gunfire.

"They're sayin' . . . I mean it's all lies, of course, but oh, Rachel, I am so frightened for ye. The whole village is buzzing with the news, and they're not takin' it well. Mrs. Chauncery, down at the corner shop, wouldn't even serve me because of my connection with ye. An' I passed the blacksmith on the street. 'E wouldn't so much as return my greetin'."

"Tell me why. What are they saying?" Rachel knew it had something to do with her visit to Blackmoor Hall but hoped against hope that she was wrong.

"They are sayin' yer the earl's *mistress*," Mrs. Tate blurted, tears streaming down her face. "That ye're sellin' yerself now yer poor mum's gone. Only they're not usin' a word that's nearly so kind."

Rachel felt like Gilly had just kicked her in the head. The room started to swirl, and she nearly fell back onto her pillows before she was able to control the dizziness and the nausea. "Who started this rumor?" she whispered.

"I can't say for sure but word 'as it it was Roxy, down at Elspeth's."

Wythe. Rachel pictured the earl's cousin leering at her just before she stole his horse. Roxy wouldn't have made up such gossip. She had to have heard it from Wythe.

Damn him! He'd had his revenge. Wasn't what he'd done enough?

Throwing off the blankets, Rachel climbed to her feet. She had to let the villagers know the rumor was false, had to tell Mr. Cutberth and the miners she hadn't turned on them. They would hardly approve of her selling herself to anyone—no God-fearing citizen would—but the earl! They'd brand her a traitor and run her out of town. What could she do for poor Geordie then? It was the dead of winter, for heaven's sake!

"Where are you going?" Mrs. Tate demanded.

"To talk to Mrs. Chauncery and Mrs. Miller and the others."

"Don't bother with them. Go to the blacksmith's apprentice. 'E offered for ye once. Maybe there's still a soft spot in 'is 'eart. If ye can convince 'im that yer still untouched, per'aps 'e'll stand by ye an' 'elp convince the others."

Untouched. She was no longer untouched and couldn't sell the poor blacksmith's apprentice on such a lie. She wouldn't even try. It wasn't fair.

"I will speak to who I can," Rachel said. Certainly the villagers would believe her. She'd grown up with them. She'd helped in the struggle to unionize. She and her mother had taught some of the adults to read, and many of their children too. If she said she wasn't the earl's mistress, they had to believe her, didn't they?

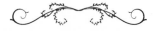

Rachel threw back her shoulders and lifted her chin as she made her way down the main street of Creswell. She had visited the laundress, the tailor, the shoemaker and the milliner, but the story had been the same with all of them. They'd stared through her as if she hadn't been standing in front of them, had refused to acknowledge her, no matter how many ways she pled her innocence. Which was difficult to do in the first place. Somewhere in her heart, she accepted partial responsibility for what had transpired at Blackmoor Hall.

But it *had* been an accident, she told herself. At least, it had stemmed from one. It wasn't something she'd entered into knowingly. And she hadn't accepted the earl's money when it was over.

She wasn't about to give up. Certainly someone would remember all her mother had done for the community and how much she herself had tried to give. Someone *had* to believe her.

The chimney sweep who traveled through the more sparsely populated counties passed her on the street, wearing his usual sooty hat. In stark contrast to how she'd been treated so far, he greeted her, but he couldn't do anything to reverse the tide of public opinion. He had to move on in a few days or weeks. Creswell didn't have enough chimneys to keep him busy for long.

At least his smile was heartening. Perhaps there were others like him who hadn't heard or didn't care.

Rachel's hopes in that regard fell a little more each time she encountered someone new. Almost everyone who had any influence in town cast her a disparaging look and stepped wide to avoid direct contact, as if she might contaminate them. She visited the baker who had given Geordie the bread that morning, but he treated her no more charitably than the others. Evidently word was spreading fast and emotions were running high. Even the baker's errand boy narrowed his eyes and spat at the ground as she passed.

By the time she decided to go directly to the source of the problem—Roxy at Elspeth's, and then, possibly, *probably*, Wythe Stanhope himself—hot tears burned behind her eyes.

Elspeth's was a ramshackle building on the back side of town, two wattle-and-daub houses and a converted shed, joined together. The street leading to its sagging porch was usually muddy, but today the ground was too frozen for mud. The ice and snow crunched beneath Rachel's boots as she cleared the small gate at the entrance to what had once been a garden but was now barren earth. The walks hadn't been cleared. They rarely were.

The smell of fried food and dirty linen assaulted Rachel's senses as she waited in the front foyer for the girl who'd answered the door to summon Roxy, but at least the room was warm. She felt like she'd been freezing for months. Sometimes she wondered if she'd ever be warm again.

"Madame Soward said not ter disturb Roxy. She's got ter work in a few 'ours," the girl announced, returning. "But Madame will see ye. Back 'ere."

Rachel followed her through the maze-like interior of the house. It had been partitioned off in several places to create more private rooms, but the thin walls did little to cloak the sounds of what went on inside. It was just after noon, and already Rachel could hear a rocking bed.

Quelling a shudder, she focused on the back of the slender girl she followed. Rachel had visited Elspeth's before, but always first thing in the morning. Most of the women were asleep then, the last of their customers just claiming their horses and heading home—like Wythe had been the morning she'd passed him.

Evidently business picked up much earlier than Rachel would have guessed.

"Rachel, how are you?" Elspeth glanced up from where she sat on a narrow settee as the girl led Rachel into a small parlor. She was wearing a red dress with a tight-fitting bodice that failed to give her a waist but succeeded in pushing her huge bosom up and almost over the top of a deep décolleté. She was heavily powdered and rouged, but nothing could camouflage the fact that she was getting older, well past her prime.

The room, gaudily decorated with purple velvet drapes, flocked wallpaper and purple upholstery, was far different from the small, brown study at the back of the house where they'd met before. A breakfast tray resided on the marble-topped table in front of Elspeth.

"I've been better," she admitted. "Have you heard?"

Elspeth considered her thoughtfully. "Please, come sit next to me and relax. You've made some powerful people angry."

"I am not sure I know why." Rachel perched on the edge of the seat closest to Elspeth and hoped sight of the food wouldn't make her stomach grumble.

She'd dashed off with nothing more than the crust of bread Geordie had given her for breakfast.

"Is that so?" Elspeth went and closed the door. When she turned she eyed Rachel from head to foot. "First, tell me why the miners would have reason to distrust you."

"I have no idea," Rachel said. "I have always done my best to help them. My father and brother were miners."

"But the earl believes your father had something to do with the fire, does he not?"

"That's no secret. The past few months, his solicitor, Mr. Lewis, and his butler, Mr. Linley, have been questioning everyone in town about my father."

"Ah, but the fact that your father was hired to start the fire is not so well known, is it?"

"How did you—?"

Her smile turned sly. "There is very little that goes on in Creswell that I do not know about."

"Then you know who hired him."

"Maybe, maybe not." She shrugged. "If I did, I wouldn't tell you."

"Why?"

"Life is not as simple as it seems, Rachel." She paused to straighten a porcelain poodle on a what-not shelf that hadn't been dusted for days, possibly weeks. "You've always had your nose in a book, filling your head with unrealistic expectations. You have zealously supported any cause you deem worthy, while innocently missing the subtler changes that have taken place here in our small village. If you are not careful you will find yourself in serious trouble."

"Are you trying to frighten me?" Rachel couldn't have been more surprised.

She chuckled. "I am trying to warn you not to get caught in the tug-of-war between the miners and the earl."

Rachel felt caught already. "But I have always been on the miners' side."

"Like your father before you. But where your loyalties really lie is unimportant. It is where they are *perceived* to lie that counts."

"What are you saying?"

"That some of the miners might harm you if they think you have become too sympathetic to the earl."

"*Harm* me?" Rachel couldn't believe her ears. "What could I do that would threaten anyone? I am just one person, and a woman at that."

"Never underestimate your power as a woman. The miners won't. That's exactly what has them nervous. But it isn't as complicated as all that. Someone set fire to the earl's manse and killed his wife. He is determined to get to the bottom of it. His digging is threatening the labor movement. If he finds out who the leaders are, he could quell the uprising before it happens. Many men would lose their jobs and all the ground that the unionizers have worked so hard to gain will be lost. It could take years to recover from such a blow."

This was sounding familiar. "You have been talking to Mr. Cutberth."

"Among others."

"He comes here?" Rachel found that rather ironic, after hearing him profess his love for his wife and children and all his lofty ideals.

"Oh, how innocent you are, Rachel." Elspeth shook her head, and Rachel imagined it was with some disgust.

"But there is more, isn't there?" Rachel asked. "I can't believe you care so much about the union."

"Only so far as it affects me. There is still a murderer on the loose, don't forget."

"Surely *that* doesn't affect you."

"It affects me in the same way it affects you."

Rachel watched Elspeth cross to the window. If her bearings were correct, the other woman was looking out on a narrow alley, one filled with trash, judging by the surrounding neighborhood.

"You know who did it," Rachel said. "You know who fired Blackmoor Hall."

Elspeth didn't answer right away. Finally, frowning, she said, "I have my suspicions, and my reasons for them."

"And you think *I* know something about that day, too, because of my father, and the money."

Elspeth looked back. "Isn't that what anyone would think who hears about the money?"

"The fire happened two years ago. If whoever set it is concerned about what I know, why haven't there been problems before?"

"Maybe there was reason to believe you would hold your tongue."

"And now, whoever it is, fears I will talk?"

"Have you given anyone reason to believe you might?"

Rachel wanted to scream. First Druridge and now Elspeth. How could she tell something she didn't know? "No!" she said, but all she could think about was her two treks to Blackmoor Hall. The earl appearing at her mother's funeral. Wythe telling everyone she and the earl were intimate.

No wonder the unionizers were worried. If the murderer was among them, they had more to fear than being sacked. They could be hung as accomplices.

The absurd thing was that everyone seemed to know more than she did.

"The union protects its own," Rachel said. "Is that what you are trying to tell me?"

"Now you've got it," Elspeth replied. "'Tis best to let sleeping dogs lie. That's the way I choose to think about it."

"I thought I was one of the miners, part of the community." Rachel heard the wistfulness in her own voice but didn't have it in her to hide the hurt.

Elspeth's expression softened. "Some lessons are harder than others. The good news is that you can still protect the miners and yourself, if you want."

Rachel waited for Elspeth to explain, but she didn't. "You're suggesting I do what Cutberth wants," she said, finally realizing what Elspeth had been getting at all along.

"Yes. Tell Druridge your father caused the fire. That would put an end to everything."

"Then Wythe would take back the lies he's spreading about me?"

Elspeth's painted eyebrows shot up. "Wythe?" she scoffed. "What does he have to do with anything?"

"Maybe nothing," Rachel admitted.

"Just do what Cutberth told you. That would go far enough toward proving your loyalty."

Perhaps it would, Rachel silently conceded. But something inside her rebelled at the idea of letting Cutberth or anyone else blackmail her into lying to the earl. To her, the end did not justify the means. Especially when, in her heart, misleading Druridge didn't feel noble or good.

It felt more like betrayal.

Chapter 8

Rachel shivered against a strong northern gale. The walk to Blackmoor Hall had taken longer than she'd expected because the wind kept pressing her back. Good thing she wasn't in a hurry. She'd closed the bookshop for the rest of the week. Lately so many of the great houses that used to order from her mother were getting their books from London, where they could choose from a much wider variety. Thanks to that and the recent damage to her reputation, not a single soul had stopped by, to browse or to buy, in several days—since she'd visited Elspeth. Even those with reading lessons had canceled.

She'd cleaned the cottage, lovingly tucked away her mother's possessions, and would have busied herself making stew or something else for supper—anything to avoid this errand—but the food was gone.

Huddling deeper in her cloak, Rachel remembered how her little brother had slowly eaten the thin gruel she'd given him at suppertime the night before. He'd left the table with a smile on his face, but she knew that smile lied, as did her own. They were both hungry, and she couldn't, *wouldn't*, let Geordie go without. She was all he had.

At last she reached the drive that wound up to the earl's imposing home. As she let herself through the tall, wrought iron gate, she wondered how she would be received. For all his taunts, the earl had not been happy at their last meeting. But that was before, when she'd still had some confidence and a great deal of pride. Since then, the unionizers had turned on her and stripped her of both. Now she was desperate—and desperation was an unkind bedfellow to pride.

When she sounded the brass knocker, Linley opened the door. She told him she had something of importance to discuss with the earl and, this time, she wasn't treated unkindly. He asked only if he could take her cloak. When she refused, he bowed before showing her into the same drawing room she'd seen before.

"It will be just a moment," he told her and disappeared.

Rachel faced the well-stoked fire in an attempt to absorb its heat. But when she heard the door open behind her, her fingers were every bit as cold as when she'd just arrived.

It was the earl. She could sense his presence even before she turned to see who it was. No servant could cause her stomach to flutter the way it did now, or bring visions of intimacy that turned her knees to jelly....

"Miss McTavish."

Squaring her shoulders, Rachel turned. She had been determined to look Druridge in the eye, but somehow she couldn't quite meet his probing gaze. "My lord."

He paused as he reached the rug, studying her. "Are you ill?"

She shook her head.

His eyebrows drew together as though he didn't quite believe her. Then he poked his head outside the room and ordered food and drink to be brought immediately.

Rachel nearly groaned aloud. She must look a sight to give her hunger away so easily. Shame caused her cheeks to burn despite the coldness in her limbs.

She turned back to the fire and stared at its orange flames, wishing, somehow, she were the log it consumed.

"Won't you sit down?" Druridge asked, suddenly beside her.

With a stiff nod, Rachel took the seat closest to the fire, but she couldn't keep her hands still. Her fingers plucked nervously at the fabric of her cloak as he sat opposite her.

"I am sorry to disturb you," she began. "I—" As closed and hard as she had always assumed him to be, the look on his face was almost hopeful. It nearly caused her to falter from her course, but only until she remembered Geordie. "I came because I have something to tell you."

"And I have something to tell you." He cleared his throat. "I owe you an apology, for the other night. I don't know what came over me. I am certainly not in the habit of paying for a woman's favors. Neither do I typically seduce young virgins."

"Perhaps it was an act of anger," she said, unsure how to classify what, exactly, had happened to transform the two of them into such passionate, if temporary, lovers. "We . . . we have not exactly been the best of friends."

"Is that what you think?" he asked softly. "That I was trying to hurt you?" She closed her eyes against the memory of his gentleness. "No."

"What I felt had nothing to do with anger, but I still owe you an apology, and perhaps an explanation—"

"Please, don't," she broke in. "It was Wythe's fault. I provoked him. Let's just forget it ever happened."

His mouth quirked to one side. "A truly generous response. Won't you at least allow me to make some sort of reparation?"

Reparation? How could he ever replace what he'd taken? She hoped he wasn't going to offer her money again. This time she feared she might take it, grab Geordie and run far away from Creswell. Far away from the earl and the miners.

If only she could run from herself.

"I am not that kind of woman," she said.

"I know."

There was a knock. At the earl's bidding, a servant Rachel didn't recognize carried in a tray very similar to the one Mrs. Poulson had delivered before. Rachel's gaze lingered on the clotted cream, scones, preserves and small sandwiches, but she didn't want to eat anything, not with Geordie hungry at home. Besides, she couldn't accept Druridge's hospitality and then purposely mislead him. . . .

"Won't you eat something?" he encouraged.

She forced her attention away from the tray, hoping he hadn't noticed her preoccupation with it. "No, thank you. I-I'm fine."

"You don't look well."

"I am."

"You have lost weight."

"I'm wearing a cloak. How can you possibly tell?"

"I can see it in your face."

"I've been . . . busy, working."

"Books are selling well, then?"

"Very well, yes. Business has never been better." She forced a bright smile.

He nodded. "I am glad to hear that. Some tea, perhaps?"

This time Rachel didn't refuse. Certainly there was nothing wrong with accepting something so minimal as a spot of tea. She took a sip of the warm brew and felt its bolstering effects within seconds.

"You have something to tell me," the earl reminded her when she finished and set her cup on the tray.

For her father's sake, even for the earl's sake, she winced at what she was about to do. But the miners had won. Or maybe it was the hunger caused by their withdrawal from her life. Regardless, she tried to find some peace in knowing she wouldn't tarnish her father's reputation for nothing. What she was doing here at Blackmoor Hall should, as Elspeth and Mr. Cutberth said, help the labor movement.

"Yes." She cleared her throat. "About the fire."

"You know more than you have shared?"

Rachel took a deep breath and launched into the lie she'd prepared for him, the one about finding her mother's diary and reading all about how her father set the blaze. She had thought about forging a diary and bringing it to him but hadn't been willing to carry the lie quite that far.

He listened without interrupting, showing no emotion beyond the rigid set of his shoulders. Then he asked one simple question. "Are you familiar with Pieter Bruegel?"

"I'm sorry?" she responded.

"Pieter Bruegel. Have you heard of him?"

At a complete loss, Rachel shook her head. She had just given the earl the answers he had been searching for, for two years, and instead of exhibiting any joy or relief, he brought up this Bruegel.

"He was the greatest Flemish painter of the sixteenth century," he explained.

"My education has centered on literature and poetry, my lord. I am afraid I know very little about art."

He smiled, but uncertainty flickered in the depths of his eyes. "I understand. Will you let me compensate you for your trouble in coming here today?"

Oh God, now he was going to try to reward her for the lies she had just told him. Her conscience bucked at the thought. "No, thank you." Rachel jumped to her feet. "I expect nothing."

"But you didn't have to come. At least let me send some flour and eggs and other foodstuffs to your cottage—"

"No!" What would the miners think if the earl started sending her barrels and crates? "I-I don't need anything," she amended.

He didn't look convinced, but in the face of her adamant refusal, he sketched a slight bow. "As you wish."

"Then I will be on my way." Rachel pulled her cloak tighter and turned to leave, but he caught her by the elbow. His fingers seemed to burn through the fabric of her cloak and dress, making her aware of him not as an earl, but as she knew him that one night, as a man.

"If you will wait here, I'll have the carriage brought around. There is no need for you to walk. In any case, I would like to show you something before you go."

She agreed to stay so he would release her, but as soon as he left the room she headed for the door. She had already done what the miners wanted her to do. She had no desire to see whatever it was Druridge planned to show her, and she certainly didn't want to ride in his carriage. She couldn't withstand his scrutiny a moment longer. Being in his company made it impossible to forget his strong hands on her body, his soft, firm lips at her temples, her neck, her breasts.

But just as she reached for the knob, the smell of the food caught her about the neck like a shepherd's crook, and she thought of Geordie. He was hungry. The earl would never miss a tart or two. The servants would clear the remains of the meal, possibly even throw them away.

The idea of waste proved unbearable. Grabbing as much as she could carry, Rachel hid the food under her cloak. Then she let herself out and ran most of the way home, feeling as much like a thief as if she'd stolen the earl's silver.

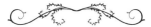

Truman stood in the empty drawing room, staring down at the tray.

"Here is the painting you requested, my lord," Linley said, coming in behind him. "I had it covered, but—" He fell silent when he realized that, besides them, the room was empty. "She's gone?"

Truman didn't answer. He went to gaze out the front window, but he could see no sign of Rachel.

"Shall I take the painting to her house?"

"No, don't bother."

"What is it?" Linley pressed.

"She took the food," Truman replied.

"Sorry, my lord?"

"Rachel. She's hungry." Truman felt his gut twist when he remembered how many times her eyes had cut to the tray. She had wanted it, needed it, but she had been too proud to eat it. She hated letting him see her weakness, and he hated the fact that her pride made it almost impossible for him to help her.

"I don't understand, my lord. Are you talking about Miss McTavish?"

"Yes." He turned his attention to his butler. Over the years he'd spent more time with Linley than his own parents and because of that the boundaries between them sometimes blurred. Their relationship felt more like father and son these days.

"She said she was doing fine, never better," he explained. "Yet there were dark circles beneath her eyes. And suddenly, out of nowhere, she tells me her father lit the fire that burned the hall and killed Katherine. Only she showed very little emotion when she said it. She seemed more frightened or agitated than anything else."

Linley's tufted eyebrows raised above his round spectacles. "So you asked her about the missing painting."

"No. I hadn't gotten that far yet. She had never even heard of Bruegel, so it seemed pointless. That was why I asked you to get *Peasant Wedding Feast*, to see if she would perhaps recognize Bruegel's style." He had just purchased the painting, which hadn't been part of his father's original collection. So far, they hadn't been able to locate any that were. But the more time passed, the more certain Truman became that his father's favorite, *Landscape with the Fall of Icarus*, was missing before the fire so much as scorched the walls.

"An excellent plan."

Truman shrugged. "It was worth a try, even though I doubt Jack set the fire or stole the paintings, at least on his own. If it were that simple, I would have figured it out months ago. But . . . why would Rachel lie?"

At first, he'd thought she'd been grasping for a way her conscience would allow her to accept money from him. She was obviously going without, which meant her brother couldn't be faring much better. But when she flatly refused everything he offered, again, he had to reconsider that assumption.

"Do you want me to do some more checking, my lord? Perhaps have her watched?"

Truman rubbed his face. "She is not to be bothered in any way. Just keep an eye on her cottage and make sure whomever you use has no obvious connection to me. Something about her whole confession didn't feel right." He had to reach the truth and, more and more, he believed Rachel was the key. But it was the food that troubled him at this moment. She was going hungry, and because she wouldn't accept anything from him, there wasn't a damn thing he could do about it.

Or was there?

He whirled to face his butler. "Linley, please have Mrs. Poulson send a ham, a turkey, eggs, flour, sugar, salt, nuts, wine and some fresh fruits and vegetables to the McTavish cottage. See that the food gets there as soon as possible. And tell whoever accompanies it that it's to be left to rot by the front door if Rachel won't accept it."

"Aye, my lord."

To hell with Rachel's bloody pride, Truman decided. He wasn't going to sit back and watch her starve.

Geordie was home alone when Rachel returned. She looked around the sparsely furnished cottage in surprise, then put the tarts and sandwiches she'd taken from Blackmoor Hall on the table. "Where is Mrs. Tate? She said she would keep an eye on you while I was gone."

"She'll be right back." He was turned away from her, his voice muffled as he worked to clean out the fireplace.

Rachel poured some water into a basin to wash her sticky hands. "Come clean off the soot," she said. "I brought you something to eat."

His eyes rounded when he saw the food. "How did you come by such fancy fare?"

Not wanting to think of her recent visit to Blackmoor Hall, or any of the ones before, Rachel made a show of drying her hands. "Don't worry about that. Just enjoy yourself."

She didn't have to tell him twice. Geordie washed his hands and face, then bellied up to the table and polished off two of the larger pastries before looking questioningly her way. "Have you eaten?" he asked politely. "Because I could stop now. I'm not that hungry."

Rachel smiled and took a seat opposite him. "I will halve the last one with you." If she didn't eat something, she'd faint. And she couldn't faint. She had to contact Mr. Cutberth and let him know she'd done what he'd asked her to do. Then maybe the rumors about her would die and everyone would go back to treating her like they always had.

"Where did Mrs. Tate go?" she asked.

"Don't know. We . . . we had a disagreement. She scolded me and cried and scolded me some more. Then she grabbed her cloak and hurried out just before you got back."

Rachel studied her young brother. "She rarely scolds you. What did you do?"

He shrugged, his face reddening.

"Geordie?"

Setting his portion of that third pastry down uneaten, he shoved away from the table and went back to cleaning the fireplace. The shovel clanged as he hung it on a hook. Then the bristles of the horsehair broom swished as he swept out the rest of the cinders. "I don't want to talk about it," he said. "You'll get angry too."

Foreboding flickered somewhere in the back of Rachel's mind. "I won't get angry."

At first she wasn't sure he'd heard her. But he finally set his tools aside and turned to face her. "I am going to apply at the mine."

His voice sounded older, more like their brother Tommy's had the year before he died. Already Geordie was beginning to grow up, and because of their mother's death, he was being forced to do it far too soon.

Rachel swallowed hard to alleviate the sudden dryness of her throat. "Surely you don't mean that, Geordie. You are only eight—"

"I will be nine soon. Mr. Clifton says I am plenty old enough. He said his own son started trapping at five."

"Mr. Clifton? What has he got to do with this?"

"I saw him outside the apothecary today. He told me I am the man of the house now and wanted to know when I would be starting at the pit."

Rachel's temper began to simmer. Clifton had no right putting the responsibility of their situation on Geordie's young shoulders. "He doesn't know what's best for us, Geordie. Next time you see him you can tell him you won't be starting at the mine *ever*."

Her brother's chin jutted out. "He used to be one of the best coal hewers at Stanhope & Co. He knows plenty—"

"He had to give up being a hewer because he couldn't see anymore. That is what working down in the pit does for a man, Geordie. It clogs his nose and lungs with dust and ruins his eyes."

"Well, he can see now. He's a fireman at the mine, isn't he? If not for him, who would check the safety of the workings before each shift begins?"

"I don't care who or what he is. That's not the point. The point is . . . " she struggled to keep her emotions in check " . . . the point is the pit is dark, dusty, filthy, stuffy and wet. You will work for more than twelve hours a day with sweating, stinking horses and perspiring men, and never see the sun. Surely you do not want to consign yourself to a life like that—"

"I have to do *something* to help you," he said, his eyes imploring. "You haven't been able to open the shop. The villagers are treating you like a leper."

He blushed, and Rachel feared he already understood far too much about what the villagers were saying, even at his tender age.

She glanced at the food left over from the meal they had just shared at the earl's expense and guiltily feared Geordie had guessed where it had come from. "I know the villagers are talking about me, but I haven't done anything to be ashamed of, Geordie." That was true, wasn't it? She hadn't been in her right mind. Surely she wasn't responsible for what had occurred in the earl's bed. But she had let him finish. . . . "You don't have to worry about that," she went on. "I am much older than you, and I can take care of us. You have to trust me."

But the cold nights, when she had tried to conserve the last of their wood and coal, and the small or nonexistent meals they had shared over the last few days had, no doubt, left an indelible impression on him, undermining his confidence in her.

"Mr. Clifton said I can earn enough to buy us the basics," he said. "And I won't be down in the mine, not at first. I will be at the pithead, working on the belts, sorting the rocks from the coal. Anyone can do that."

"I don't want you there!" Rachel nearly screamed the words, then regretted her burst of temper when Geordie looked like she'd struck him. Infusing some calm into her voice, she said, "I'm sorry, Geordie. I didn't mean to yell. It's just that, if you go to work in the mine, you will have no time to get an education. And if you don't get an education, you will always be a miner."

"Dad was a miner," he said defiantly. "So was Tommy."

Curling her hands into fists, Rachel closed her eyes. How could he possibly understand how easily he could get roped into a life of endless, back-breaking labor? A life rife with strikes and lockouts and short time? From week to week he'd never know what stoppages would be kept from his earnings. Depending upon the whim of Whythe Stanhope, who was steward over the mine, he could be overcharged for the tools, candles and powder he used underground. Fines could be imposed on him for unsatisfactory work. And if he ever chose to live in colliery housing, he could be fined for offences as trivial as keeping dogs, cows, pigs, donkeys—even pigeons! Rachel saw more for him in life than that, more for herself than worrying whether there would be another cave-in. . . .

"When you get older, we will talk about it," she said, hoping the idea of future compromise might mollify him.

"That's what Mrs. Tate said," he sulked.

"And she has the right of it. For now, letting you work at the mine is out of the question; do you understand? If anyone applies there, it will be me."

"But if we both—"

Mrs. Tate rushed in, interrupting their argument. With her was the blacksmith's apprentice. He took off his hat and wrung it in his hands, hovering just outside the door and going beet red when Rachel looked at him.

"Mr. Wilson, I am sorry. I wasn't expecting you." Rachel stood and brushed the crumbs from her dress. "Please come in."

"Mr. Wilson 'as somethin' 'e'd like to say to ye." Mrs. Tate held the door and waved the blacksmith's apprentice on through, then motioned for Geordie to join her on her way back out. "Come, lad. Let's go see what comfort we can give poor Gilly on this cold day an' let Mr. Wilson an' yer sister 'ave some privacy, aye?"

Geordie frowned but Rachel encouraged him with a nod. "We will only be a moment, Geordie. Then I will come find the two of you."

As they left, Rachel felt her palms grow moist. She had never been alone with James Wilson before and wasn't sure she wanted to be now. After what had been circulating in the village, he had to be wondering if she was really the whore and traitor the miners made her out to be.

His pained expression told her he was feeling as uncomfortable and embarrassed as she was. Taking courage from that, she broke the awkward silence. "I am afraid Mrs. Tate came to you without my knowledge. I apologize. Her heart is in the right place, but—"

"I've heard what they are sayin' about ye," he blurted, suddenly tightening his grip on his hat. "I don't believe it, of course."

"Thank you." Rachel's conscience stirred as, in her mind's eye, she saw the earl naked above her, limed in firelight. But she shoved the vision away.

"Mrs. Tate was wise to seek me out," he said. "I've 'ad my eye on ye for a long time, ever since ye were just a girl. Ye already know that, I imagine." He looked down at the tips of his boots, the walls of the cottage, anywhere but at her face. "I still care for ye an', if ye would accept me, I'd be willin' to marry ye, even now."

Rachel had to catch her jaw to keep it from hitting the floor. She had considered petitioning Mr. Wilson to stand by her as a friend, so someone would break ranks with the rest and possibly pave the way for her life to return to normal. But she had never dreamed he would offer to take her on as his wife, not after she rejected him once before.

"I cannot offer ye much, but it's more than ye got," he went on, evidently reading her stunned silence as reluctance. "I'll always take care of ye, and I'll take care of young Geordie, too, just like 'e was my own son." He blushed more furiously at the mention of a son, but blundered on, "I'll treat ye tenderly, Rachel. An' though I might not be so smart with letters, like ye are, I will do my best to learn. An' I will work 'ard an' not spend all my money on drink. Ye got my word on that."

The refusal that came instantly to Rachel's lips hovered there without making the leap into words. She couldn't turn him down again. Mr. Wilson was a humble, generous man, who obviously cared a great deal for her. She believed he would be a kind husband. He said he would take care of her *and* Geordie. She could certainly do worse....

"What do ye say, Rachel?" He came close, took her hand, and went down on one knee. "Will ye marry me?"

Love could grow from respect, couldn't it? She definitely respected James Wilson. She always had. And she would do anything to keep Geordie out of the mine.

Silently vowing to make him a good wife, she gazed into his earnest face. "Yes," she said, but the creak and groan of iron wheels on pavement sounded outside, drawing their attention to the front window where a wagon, loaded with food, pulled up to the fence. Its driver was one of the earl's servants.

No! Rachel couldn't move as she watched the man jump to the ground and approach the house. The power of his knock seemed to rattle the walls around her, yet she stood rooted to the same spot.

It was James who answered the door.

"Lord Druridge sends this with his compliments," the footman announced and rushed back to unload everything.

James shut the door and together they listened to the thud of the servant's feet hit the wooden steps of the porch, again and again, followed by the thump and scrape of whatever he carried.

"The earl sent it," James repeated. He sounded incredulous, as though he couldn't quite absorb the meaning of it.

Rachel cringed and had to turn away. She'd known the moment she'd seen the wagon who'd sent the food.

Behind her, she heard the blacksmith's apprentice draw a bolstering breath. "Tell me 'e's never touched ye," he said. "I'll believe ye, if ye just say the words."

Rachel squeezed her eyes shut. She wanted to tell him what he hoped to hear but couldn't. The food called her a liar before she even got started. Besides, Druridge *had* touched her. He'd made her giddy with his hands and his lips and his body. He'd taken her virginity and, heaven help her, she'd enjoyed it. Even now, just the thought of pressing her lips to his mouth left her warm and tingly and slightly breathless.

What kind of woman did that make her? Certainly not one who deserved to marry a decent man like James Wilson. What had she been thinking?

"Rachel," he pleaded. "Just tell me it's not what it looks like."

"I can't," she said, choking back a sob. "It wouldn't be fair to you. I'm sorry."

She didn't know how long she stood there, face averted, tears sliding down her cheeks, but the servant and the earl's wagon were gone when James spoke again.

"I'm sorry, too," he said and, with his head down and his hat still off, he left.

Chapter 9

The Fore-Overman's office was not far from the pithead of the mine. Rachel knew right where to find it. She'd often walked with her father to pick up his pay. When Tommy was alive, he had received his wages there too, at the hand of Mr. Tyndale, who had long handled all the labor issues at the mine. He was the one who'd sacked her father, but she didn't hold it against him. The order had come from above, from the earl himself. Tyndale had told Jack so at the time.

Knowing Mr. Tyndale would've kept her father on if possible made her feel slightly hopeful. It meant she'd be applying to someone likely to treat her well. If anyone would be fair, surely it would be the man who had so often winked and called her a "pretty little girl" when she was a child.

Despite the fact that she was expecting to meet a friendly face, she hesitated before entering the building. Mr. Tyndale's attitude could have changed toward her, given recent events. Not only that, but after tossing and turning the past three nights—ever since the blacksmith's apprentice had left her standing in the middle of her own kitchen feeling absolutely bereft—she was too fatigued to deal with such an emotional situation. Here she was, about to sue for work at the very place she'd sworn no one in her family would ever work again. That made her feel as if she was reneging on everything she believed.

But what else could she do? Word had spread that the earl had delivered an expensive amount of food, even wine, to her house, negating any relief she might've obtained by cooperating with Mr. Cutberth's demands. Even Cutberth seemed unable to believe she'd followed through, especially because the earl hadn't reacted to what she'd told him as Cutberth had ex-pected. Instead of accepting her at her word and blaming Jack for the fire, Druridge had sent Linley on another round of inquiries. Geordie had heard the earl's butler prattling about that Bruegel painter Druridge had asked her about—although she had no idea what a Flemish painter had to do with the fire. She might've been curious, except she had such pressing problems. She got the impression that Cutberth somehow blamed her for the way the earl had responded, as if she'd made him *more* suspicious instead of less. As a result, she was becoming acquainted with what it meant to wind up on Cutberth's bad side and no longer admired him.

You can't worry about Cutberth. Not now. Taking care of Geordie had to be her first priority. She didn't have a lot of time to adjust to the setbacks she'd experienced. Once the earl's food was gone, she would have no means to buy more. Unless she wanted her little brother to starve—unless she wanted to starve herself—she had to find a way to provide.

Throwing back her shoulders, she told herself her stint in the mine would be temporary, just until she could figure out a better solution, and opened the door.

At her unexpected intrusion, Mr. Tyndale glanced up from his over-size desk.

"Rachel!" The flame of his lamp threatened to gutter out, thanks to the sudden rush of outside air. He protected the opening at the top with one hand, then stood and gave her a welcoming smile.

That he didn't seem to hate her like all the others nearly brought tears to her eyes.

"Hello, Mr. Tyndale." Somehow she managed to talk despite the lump in her throat.

He walked around his desk and motioned to a chair. "Would you like to sit down?"

She'd worn her tattered cloak to help cut the biting cold. He held out a hand as she passed by—an offer to take it from her—but she was so chilled she didn't dare relinquish the garment. She also didn't want him to comment on her dramatic weight loss. "I will keep it, thank you."

With a slight nod, he moved back to his customary place. "What brings you out to the mine on this cold day?" he asked, obviously surprised that she would show up.

She blinked several times, trying to hold back tears. Her mouth felt so dry she wasn't sure she would be able to speak, but she managed a rather wobbly, "I was hoping that . . . I was hoping you might have a bit of work for me, Mr. Tyndale."

His eyes widened. "*Here*? You mean, *at the colliery*?"

She held her head high. In the West of Scotland, they'd quit hiring women in the coal mines in an effort to save those jobs for the men, but not here, not entirely. She knew of at least a handful of women who drew a paycheck from Stanhope & Co. "Yes, please. I-I will be a good worker. Do you . . . happen to have a position on the sorting belts, perhaps?"

He hesitated long enough that she clutched the fabric of her cloak. Would he turn her away? She feared that was the case, but he must've read her panic because he smiled again and seemed to change his mind.

"Of course. I am sure I can find room on the payroll for one more. But"—he leaned forward—"screeners make only a schilling or two per day. You realize that."

Rachel's heart sank. That was even less than she'd expected. Her father, as a hewer, had brought home as much as twenty schillings a week. Even Tommy had made fifteen. She would be working for a fraction of their wages, and that simply wouldn't be enough—not to pay the monthly rent *and* support her and Geordie.

She bit her lip. "Is-is housing included?"

He shook his head. "Not for a screener."

"Is there any binding money if I agree to stay for a year or more?"

"You don't want to commit yourself for so long. We don't need screeners enough at the moment to be offering binding money anyway."

"Then . . . maybe there's another position . . . something else you think I could do?"

Before he could reply, the door opened and Wythe Stanhope stepped inside. "What a miserable day," he grumbled.

He hadn't yet noticed her so he was probably remarking on the weather. When he looked up, he froze.

"Miss McTavish." He gave her a mocking bow. "What a shock to find you here."

Fear crept up her spine. The last time she'd come face to face with Wythe she'd felt compelled to escape him any way she could. He'd exacted a painful and lasting revenge. But, certainly, after all he had done he would be satisfied.

She forced herself to stand and curtsy. "Mr. Stanhope."

He studied her for a moment. "Are you, by any chance, seeking Lord Druridge?"

His allusion to her connection with the earl came off as a purposeful reminder of the night she'd lost her virginity—which was something he'd *caused* to happen.

"No, I-I am applying for work, sir."

He laughed softly. "Ah . . . I couldn't have asked for a more pleasant surprise. Perhaps today *isn't* so bad."

She remained silent.

"What has Mr. Tyndale arranged?" he asked.

The Fore-Overman began to straighten the items on his desk. "Actually, sir, I-I was thinking she would make a dependable screener."

He waved that suggestion away. "A job for children. You don't have very high expectations of Miss McTavish, Tyndale."

"Of course I do. She is very capable. But . . . anything else would put her down in the mine. *With the men*," he added to drive home his point.

"And why would that be so terrible? Certainly she's no better than her fellow villagers."

When Tyndale went red in the face, Rachel guessed he understood how the miners felt about her. Working with them in such dark, dank and close quarters would not be a pleasant experience, especially for her.

"I didn't say 'better,' sir."

"You did, Tyndale. In so many words."

Rachel's heart thumped against her chest. Why did Wythe hate her so much? He'd asked for what she'd done to him.

"So . . . you're suggesting she become a trapper?" Tyndale asked.

No. Rachel could've answered that herself. She was tall for a woman, too large to be a trapper. Only children sat in the small recesses behind the ventilation doors, pulling the ropes that would open the doors for the wagons to pass through. She couldn't drive the teams either. Her lack of experience with horses barred her from that. And she'd never have the physical strength to be a hewer. Only the toughest and most seasoned men faced the rock with pick and shovel.

Wythe folded his arms as his eyes ranged over her. "I think . . . a putter."

Tyndale came to his feet. "But, sir! Putters have to haul as much as two hundredweight. And the men in the shaft, they often remove their clothes in the summer when it's hot. The pit wouldn't be the best place for such a lovely—"

"Apparently you haven't heard the rumors I have, Mr. Tyndale," Wythe interrupted. "Putting her in the dark with a lot of sweaty, naked men is exactly where she would be most comfortable."

Rachel wanted to speak up, to defend her honor, but she couldn't. Gaining employment at Stanhope & Co. was her last hope of providing for Geordie.

"Sir, please." Tyndale tried again, but Wythe would have none of it.

"Do as I say, Tyndale, or you too will be looking for a job." With that he removed his gloves and walked into the next office.

Staring at a spot somewhere behind her, as if it was all he could do to hold his tongue, Tyndale slowly took his seat. "It's sorry I am," he murmured. "Surely you cannot accept such a position."

She could tell he wanted her to refuse, to take away Wythe's power. She wished she could. "How much does it pay?"

Two lines formed between his eyes. "It would be *grueling* work."

"How much, Mr. Tyndale?"

"Three shillings a score."

She lifted her chin. "So I could make as much as . . . what? Six shillings a day?"

"Possibly. Paired with strong hewers."

That was more than she would make all week as a screener. "I'll do it."

He shook his head. "Miss McTavish, if I could discourage you—"

She stood. "I appreciate your concern, but . . . I must cope with certain realities. When can I start?"

Tossing a frown at the office Wythe had disappeared into as if he didn't like his boss any more than she did, he said, "When would you like to start?"

"Would now be too soon?"

"Not if you're set on it," he said with a sigh.

She smiled to reassure him. "Thank you."

It had been a week since he'd seen her, and he still couldn't stop thinking about her. Truman pushed his palms into his eyes, but the vision of Rachel staring up at him in her bookshop remained. He could even smell the soft, clean scent of her skin, taste the sweet fullness of her lips—lips that had once opened for him, responded to him, just like the rest of her had. The night he found her in his bed she'd moaned at his touch, arched into him. It made his pulse race just thinking about it.

But memories of the village bookseller usually bothered him at night, when his bed was empty and cold and he shifted restlessly, wishing for dawn. He had no excuse for staring off into space in the middle of the day!

"Mrs. Poulson!" he snapped, irritated at his lack of self-control. He never should have bedded Rachel. He let his physical desires get the best of him and lost a small piece of his soul in the process. "Mrs. Poulson!"

"Aye, I'm here, m'lord." His housekeeper stepped into his study from just down the hall, where he had overheard her giving instructions to one of the maids.

"Send Linley for"—he checked his notes—"Mr. Bandoroff. Tell him I want to speak to the man straight away."

"Aye, m'lord." She dipped into a shallow curtsy and left, and it was nearly two hours before she reappeared.

"The gentleman you requested is waiting in the front parlor," she said. "Mr. Linley sent him ahead."

Truman scooted his chair back. "Ahead? Why? What is Linley doing?"

"Looking after some of your other concerns. His message indicated he will be back shortly."

"Fine." Truman gave up on the letter he'd been writing. Perhaps he should head to London and track down his own leads, he thought as he made his way to the winding staircase that led to the first floor. He was growing impatient with those he had hired to look for the paintings. If he were there, in the flesh, people would be more responsive, and things would happen more quickly.

And if he broke away from Blackmoor Hall for a time, perhaps he could forget his fascination with Rachel McTavish.

"M'lord." Mr. Bandoroff, a short, wiry man Truman had met once before, bowed deeply the moment he entered the room. His eyes were red-rimmed, his face covered with salt-and-pepper whiskers, and he smelled like fish.

Trying to ignore the unpleasant odor, Truman offered him a welcoming nod. "Thank you for coming."

"'Tis a pleasure, m'lord."

In an attempt to conceal the degree of his interest in what Mr. Bandoroff might say, Truman crossed to the window. "You make your living off the sea, is that correct?"

"Aye, sir. But I spent nearly twenty years in the mine before that."

A gentle flurry of snow had begun to fall since lunch. "As a hewer?"

"For the most part. Some days I would like to return. I miss the pay, I do. But the wife, she won't 'ear of me goin' back, which is why I'm willin' to pick up a little extra on the side, workin' for Mr. Linley."

Truman turned from the window. "I understand. But it has been ten days or more since Linley hired you to keep an eye on the McTavish cottage, and I have not received a report."

Bandoroff's eyes widened. "M'lord? Linley said to let 'im know if anythin' unusual 'appened, but it has been quiet as a graveyard. What with the shop closed down an' everybody treatin' Rachel like she's got the plague—"

"What?" When Truman stepped forward, Bandoroff moved back by an equal distance.

"Did I say somethin' wrong, m'lord?"

"The bookshop is closed?"

"Aye. I thought ye knew. Been closed for over a week."

"But why?"

Bandoroff's Adam's apple bobbed as he swallowed. He started to say something, then stopped and shrugged. "Ye got me."

The fisherman's body language told Truman he knew exactly why the shop had been closed. He was hesitant to state the reason, which could mean only one thing. "What does its closing have to do with me?"

"You, m'lord?"

"If you want to be paid, you will speak plainly."

"As you wish." He cleared his throat. "Ever since word got out that Rachel is yer . . . well, yer woman, if ye know what I mean, decent folks won't 'ave anythin' to do with 'er. I guess she closed up the shop because it wasn't doin' 'er any good to keep it open."

Truman had to tell himself to breathe. *God!* The villagers had turned on Rachel because of him? He remembered her sitting in his drawing room, saying that business had never been better, but even that was a lie. Why? Why had she come to him with some concocted story about her father when she should have been asking for his help? Demanding he take responsibility for what he had done?

Damn her bloody pride! And damn his own foolish thinking. He had taken Rachel's virginity and then simply walked away, as untouched as she had once accused him of being. Meanwhile, she was suffering the approbation of her friends and neighbors for what had happened that night. "And her little brother?" he asked numbly.

"'E stays with the neighbor while she works at the mine."

"It's true." Linley appeared at the door, a grim look on his face. "I just came from speaking to Mr. Tyndale."

Truman fought the violent emotions swirling inside him. He wanted to kill Wythe for not telling him that Rachel had come to the mine for work. There were other women there, sorting on the screening belts, but not a lot. Even if she were someone else, it would have been remarkable, something he should have mentioned.

Truman also wanted to get his hands on the person who had spread the news that Rachel was his doxy. They had ruined her reputation and cost her the shop. When he found out who was to blame, he would make them pay dearly. And if it was Wythe . . . heaven help him. "That will be all, Mr. Bandoroff," he said. "Linley will compensate you and show you out."

"Would ye like me to keep watchin' the cottage, m'lord? It has been awful quiet, like I said, what with Rachel in the pit all day. But ye never know. I would certainly be willin' to keep—"

"No. That will be all."

Truman listened to the hum of Linley's voice grow faint as he saw Bandoroff to the door. Leaning against the wall, he pinched the bridge of his nose while waiting for his butler to return.

"Tell me what happened," he said as soon as Linley reappeared.

The butler closed the door. "Everyone claims one of Elspeth's girls started the rumor."

"How could someone at Elspeth's have known what happened here, unless Wythe told them?"

"Wythe's not the only one who lives here, my lord. As you know, servants gossip something terrible."

Dropping his hands, Truman headed for the door. "Have Arthur ready my horse. I am going to the mine."

"My lord?"

"You heard me."

Linley's lips slanted into a frown. "She won't thank you for it, my lord. The more you interfere, the worse you make her look."

Truman whirled around, raising his voice at the aging butler for almost the first time in his life. "And if I don't? What would that make me? How can I live another day knowing men and women who aren't worthy to wipe the dust from her feet are ostracizing her, because of me? Because of one blind moment of lust and desperation? How can I eat each meal in luxury knowing she is going without for the sake of her young brother? Even there I am to blame! Had I not used Jacobsen to gain some ground with her, her mother might not have died."

"You don't know that."

"I know she was a virgin, Linley. I took something I can never give back. But I will not allow whoever is behind all of this to capitalize on it further."

Linley's face filled with worry. "What will you do?"

Truman didn't answer. His butler would think he was mad. Hell's fire, he probably *was* mad. But no matter how many times he tried to blame Wythe or someone else for Rachel's lot, he kept coming back to one irrefutable fact: They couldn't have ruined her without his help.

And now he was going to do the only thing he could to save her.

Chapter 10

Rachel's back ached from stooping as she moved through the narrow tunnels, and the muscles in her arms and legs quivered even when she stood still. After three days in the pit working in conjunction with four hewers—Greenley, Henderson, Thornick and Collingood—she wasn't yet accustomed to the physical demands of her job. As a putter she had to take empty tubs to those working at the coal face, then bring the full ones back to the "flats" or shaft bottom so the coal could be lifted to the surface.

Thanks to Wythe, who, on her second day, had moved her from the relatively comfortable place Tyndale had assigned her, she'd been working Number 14 Stall, an isolated area that traced a narrow seam of coal a quarter of a mile from the shaft bottom. She had been at her new location for nearly six hours, since before dawn, struggling to move wheeled containers that sometimes weighed as much as two hundred pounds. Damp with sweat, her skirts sodden from wading through stagnant pools she couldn't see in the dim light of her safety lamp, she could scarcely breathe amidst the foul odors that permeated the workings, which mostly came from men who relieved themselves without care or concern for the comfort of those around them.

"This ain't no tea party, Miss." The irritation in John Greenley's voice rained down on her like a rockslide. "Git ter work."

Rachel stretched her back as best she could, considering the tunnel wasn't tall enough to stand up in, and shoved off the wall. She needed a few minutes to gather her strength, but the hewers were paid by the amount of coal they extracted. Their object was always the same: to get as much work out of their putters as possible.

"Coming." She positioned an empty tub next to Greenley and took hold of the full one he had waiting for her.

"I got one what's ready for ye, too," Henderson barked, a few feet away.

Rachel acknowledged this with a weary nod before starting off. She pushed her tub across a dead level, followed by a slight rise, another short level, and then an abrupt fall. As usual, she fought to keep the heavy tub from getting away from her on the downhill. Every muscle felt pulled out, and her strength seemed to be running like sweat from her limbs.

When she reached the shaft bottom, where the coal was being loaded onto wagons, she grabbed her flask and swallowed a mouthful of tea, luke-warm but refreshing. Then she started dragging an empty tub back to Number 14.

A broad-shouldered fellow with Herculean biceps dipped his head when he saw her. They were both putters and had passed each other several times but had never spoken. Now he said, "After my first few days on this job, I thought I was dead."

At the moment, Rachel wished she were. If not for Geordie, she would have given up.

Or maybe not. Wythe wanted to break her. He was trying to punish her for rejecting him, or hitting him, or both. But he deserved a good knock to the head, and Rachel couldn't regret having delivered one. Maybe she was at his mercy now, but her body would grow accustomed to the labor. Somehow she would withstand it.

Sparing a grateful smile for her fellow putter, she summoned what energy she had left. "I suppose one gets used to it."

"Aye, but it takes time." He followed her partway back, pausing where the tunnel forked. "Look, if ye get behind, I'll catch ye up if I can."

"Thank you." That simple kindness, amid all the hours of crude language and jibes she had suffered so far, gave Rachel the emotional lift she needed. But as soon as he saw her, Greenley started in on her again, complaining about her slowness. Doing her best to bear his tirade in silence, she wrestled another tub around to get it moving.

"Yer placin' yer floor supports too far apart," Collingood charged Greenley. "If ye don't take care, yer goin' ter cause a cave-in!"

"Bugger you. I know what I'm doin'," Greenley mumbled.

Shaking his head in disgust, Collingood went back to using his shovel, but the exchange was enough to make Rachel glance uncertainly above her. Tommy had died in a cave-in. The thought of being buried beneath a thousand pounds of dirt and rock was enough to make the darkness seem more palpable, the passage narrower. Especially because she had no confidence in Greenley. Was he really setting the roof supports too far apart? He hadn't been a hewer more than a few months and had less experience than the seasoned Collingood—or Thornick and Henderson, for that matter. Even worse, he struck Rachel as a man who was long on confidence and short on brains.

"My father always used ter say pit work's more than 'ewing. Ye've got ter coax the coal along," Thornick shouted over the *thwack* of their picks.

"Ye 'ave ter know yer place like a mother knows 'er young 'uns," Henderson agreed, but neither man took up Collingood's argument.

Rachel opened her mouth to say something just as Greenley maneuvered his mammoth-size body around to glare her down. Even in the dimness, she could see the scowl etched on his flat face.

"Any reason yer standin' around like ye got all day?" he demanded.

"No, it's just that I . . . that I—" She noticed a pile of dirt and rock had tumbled down from the ceiling not five yards away and swallowed against the sudden dryness of her throat. "I agree with Collingood," she finished. "You might be setting the roof supports too far apart."

"Ye do, do ye?" He threw his pick to the ground and got to his feet, but the ceiling wouldn't allow him to rise much higher than a crouch. "Now why didn't I think ter ask ye before?"

Rachel wanted to fold her arms in front of her but, realizing it was a defensive posture, kept them at her sides. "I don't have much experience," she allowed, "but even I can see—"

"Oh, ye've got experience, all right," he broke in. "Ye spread yer legs for the earl quick enough, but if ye knew what ye were doin' even there ye wouldn't be down in this 'ell 'ole."

"You don't know what you're talking about," she said, but he wasn't listening.

"Still, I'm not opposed ter teachin' ye a thing or two about workin' on yer back—since ye already know everythin' about coal minin'. What do ye say, 'Enderson, Thornick? Should we teach this bitch a lesson?"

Rachel tried to retreat, but two steps backed her up against the wall. "I am not the earl's whore," she said, trying to keep the fear twisting her insides from revealing itself in her voice. "My brother died in a cave-in. I am merely trying to prevent a similar accident. We wouldn't want something like that to ever happen again."

"I'll tell ye what's goin' ter 'appen," he said. "I'm gonna throw up yer skirts. Then I'm gonna give my friend 'Enderson a turn."

"Leave 'er be," Collingood admonished. "You know what Cutberth said. We're not ter touch 'er. Go to Elspeth's tonight if ye want."

"Why spend my hard-earned money on those tired whores?" Greenley countered. "They aren't anythin' like the educated Miss McTavish, always so prim and proper and too good for a simple miner. Or even a besotted blacksmith's apprentice. I bet she's tighter than a drum. Besides, I'm not goin' ter 'urt 'er. I'm just gonna enjoy her as the earl did. 'E's no better'n us!"

"What about Cutberth?" Collingood asked, but he was glancing around as though sizing up the possibilities.

"We don't 'ave ter tell 'im, do we? If we all take a turn, we'll be in it together. What do ye say, 'Enderson, Thornick?"

Greenley's eager smile caused Rachel's panic to rise to a new level. "I'll scream," she threatened.

Henderson tossed his pick aside and crawled over to cut off her exit. "So what? Ye won't be heard above the shouts and shovels an' 'orses an' machinery. An' even if ye are, do ye really think someone's goin' to lose time comin' all the way out to Number 14 Stall ter investigate somethin' that could mean nothin' more than some scraped knuckles?"

He was right. Rachel knew it the moment he said the words. Providing her cries *were* heard, they'd probably be interpreted as a bump on the head or some smashed fingers or a million other minor accidents that happened all the time.

"Why not make it easy, Rachel?" Henderson suggested. "Give us what ye gave the almighty earl, an' we'll look after ye down 'ere."

"Ye need some allies," Greenley agreed. "We'll stand by ye as Henderson says, which is more'n Lord Druridge 'as done."

Only a full tub of coal stood between Rachel and the men. Behind her the passage narrowed into a crawl space that ended in fifteen feet or less. "If you touch me, I will go to him," she threatened. "I will tell Druridge, and he will sack you."

Greenley laughed. "Ye're not worth four good hewers to 'im. Besides, it'll be your word against ours, four upstanding citizens against a whore."

"Come on, Rachel, we're no fancy-smellin' earls, but there's no need ter turn yer nose up," Collingood added.

"The earl's twice the man you four could ever hope to be!" Rachel shoved the tub at them with all the strength she had left. It hit Collingood, still on his knees, in the chest and knocked him back.

Greenley jumped left but there was little room to maneuver in a tunnel less than five feet square. He suffered a glancing blow to the shoulder, which slammed him into Thornick and Henderson and took them all down.

Rachel tried to run past them, but someone caught her by the ankle. Using the walls to hold herself up, she wrenched her foot away and, in a flurry of panic, kicked Henderson in the chin as he was getting up. With a curse, he threw up an arm to protect himself, but by then Greenley had grabbed her skirts and was pulling her down.

A moment later, Rachel could feel the rock floor cutting into her spine as Collingood's face loomed above her.

"Do 'er now," he told Greenley, pinning her down with one hand and squeezing her breast with the other.

She screamed and squirmed but her efforts were futile. She couldn't hold off four strong men. "Help me! *Help!*"

"'Old her tighter!" Greenley's rough hands clawed at the insides of her thighs as he tried to force her legs apart. "I'm goin' ter show 'er what it feels like ter 'ave a real man, not some fancypants earl."

"You touch her or anything else that belongs to me, and I will kill you."

Druridge's voice was unmistakable. He stood not six feet away, with Wythe at his side.

Greenley, Collingood and the others released her and pressed back against the walls like cockroaches suddenly exposed to the light. Rachel tried to push her skirts down to cover her legs, but she was shaking so badly she couldn't manage the volume of material.

"We meant nothin' by it," Greenley said.

"We weren't really goin' to do anythin' but give 'er a good scare," Collingood chimed in.

"We thought ye'd already cast 'er aside. We wouldn't 'ave touched 'er if we thought ye still 'ad use for 'er, m'lord," Thornick added.

Fury and contempt flickered on the earl's face. "Get out," he said, stooping to wrap his cloak around Rachel. "Get out and don't come back."

"My lord—" Wythe's eyes darted between the hewers, the earl and Rachel. "These men have families to support."

"Then let them go home and explain to their wives and children how they lost their jobs trying to rape an innocent young woman."

"But how will they live?"

"If it were up to me, they wouldn't. Give their families some wages so they can survive until these men find other work, but I will not have them on my payroll another day."

Wythe's jaw clenched. "She is only a village wench, my lord. Some of these miners have worked for us for years. We arrived in time. There wasn't any harm done. Couldn't we leave them with a warning and be about our business?"

Truman pulled Rachel up beside him. "A warning?" he repeated. "Knowing what you knew, you should have put her anywhere but down here. Pray I don't throw you out with them. How is that for a warning?"

Wythe looked as if he would continue to argue. His eyes sparked with anger. But he bowed in acquiescence, pulled a pistol from his belt and waved it at Greenley and the others. "You heard him," he told the men. "Collect your things and get out."

The earl drew Rachel away with him. As they left, she felt the hatred of the four men hit her like slugs in her back.

"Bloody whore!" one shouted. "'E'll tire of ye before long, an' then where will ye be? *No one* will want *ye*."

"Good thing ole' Jack's gone," Greenley said, his words more effective despite the softness with which they were spoken. "'T would kill 'im to know ye've turned on yer own."

Rachel winced at the mention of her father and summoned the strength to stand on her own. If she left with him now, she'd be crossing an invisible line—the line to his side. Once she did that, there would be no going back.

But what else could she do? She couldn't stay. Wythe had been publicly humiliated and would punish her for being the cause of it. She knew him well enough to expect that much. And when word of what happened got out, there would only be more men to replace Greenley, Thornick and the others. She had alienated the miners and could no longer work safely among them.

Unable to continue to support her own weight, she slid down the wall to sit on the floor. What now? If not for the earl, those miners would have raped her. If not for the earl and what had already happened at Blackmoor Hall, they never would have tried.

Did she hate Druridge or admire him? Criticize him or give thanks?

"Please," she muttered, but she didn't know whom she petitioned for help: God, or the earl. She only knew that her situation had gone from bad to worse since the day he first appeared at her shop.

"Are you injured?" Druridge bent over her.

She shook her head. "I will make my own way out . . . in a moment. Th-thank you for your help. I am g-grateful. Or at least I'm sure I will be when I sort everything out."

He looked back at the men who were gathering their picks and shovels. "You have to choose, Rachel," he said. "And now is as good a time as any."

Something about the earl's voice made her look up, into his eyes. What did he want from her? What had brought him here? Why couldn't someone else have interfered, like the brawny putter who had offered to help her catch up? "Choose what?" she repeated dully.

"Me . . . or them."

Rachel watched the men shuffle past, Wythe and his enforcing pistol at their backs. They would tear her limb from limb, if they could. She couldn't help noticing their cutting glares and bunched muscles.

But Druridge was more dangerous still, because he made her heart twist and yearn for something that could never be.

"I will leave," she said. "Go somewhere far away. That must be the answer."

"What would you do in another village? Go back to work in a mine? You have three days' experience, sweet Rachel. You would make pennies, hardly enough to survive."

She shook her head. She had no solutions, only a young brother to care for. Somehow, some way . . .

"Come with me to Blackmoor Hall," he said.

Remembering how her skin had burned beneath his touch, Rachel caught her breath. It was almost as though she hadn't been alive until that night, as though his kiss had awakened her from a long slumber. If she let herself, she could fall in love with this man, and then where would she be?

Worse off than ever before.

"No. I will not be your whore."

"I am not asking you to be my whore," he said. "You will have a place among my servants. You will receive honest pay for honest work. And Geordie can pitch hay in the stables. The training would be good for him. Perhaps he could become a groom or a driver one day."

She said nothing. The offer was a generous one. Such jobs were not easy to come by. A steady stream of country girls traipsed to the manse, hoping for just such a position. And a job for Geordie too?

But going into service meant giving up the only life she had known. She would no longer be part of the village, no longer run the shop. Everything would change.

It had changed already, hadn't it? She was trying to hang on to something that wasn't really there.

"Certainly my offer is better than starving, or working here," he coaxed.

That was true, but what of her parents' wishes? Her mother wasn't yet two weeks cold and Rachel had already lost the shop. And what of her dead father and brother?

What of her *living* brother, another voice in her head replied. Shouldn't he matter more? She would never get rich sweeping out fireplaces and polishing furniture. But at least she and Geordie would have a roof over their heads and food to eat.

Druridge touched her arm. "The whole village has turned on you. The only place you will be safe is with me."

Weary beyond words, she rested her head against the rock wall. "I know."

"So you accept?"

She thought of Geordie, of how many things he needed that he would go without if she didn't agree, and nodded. "Yes. Thank you."

"Let's go," he said and helped her to her feet.

Chapter 11

As simple and safe as Lord Druridge had made it sound for her and Geordie to come to Blackmoor Hall, Rachel knew they'd face plenty of hardships. Maybe none so dire as starvation, but she could tell when he turned her and Geordie over to Mrs. Poulson that the housekeeper would not be kind. Poulson resented having them thrust upon her, resented the fact that Druridge had involved himself in household matters. Even though the housekeeper responded in a carefully modulated voice when they were introduced, her courteous mask fell away the moment Lord Druridge left them alone.

"So what am I supposed to do with the both of you?" The housekeeper fisted her hands on her hips and walked around her and Geordie as if they were mere vermin and she was tempted to call out the rat catcher. "You are both far too thin. You won't have the strength to work like I require. And yet you will need sustenance."

"Please, ma'am. I will do all you ask. I promise," Geordie said.

"Fortunately, *you* won't be my problem. Flora?" She addressed a scullery maid, who dropped the vegetables she was cutting and hurried over. "Yes, ma'am?"

"Take this one out to the stables and tell Mr. Grude to see to him." She narrowed her eyes as she glared at Geordie. "I don't want you in the house unless I have requested your company. Do you understand?"

He glanced at Rachel, obviously fearing that meant he would no longer be able to see her. Rachel wished she could reassure him but dared not speak up in front of the housekeeper.

"Yes, mum," he said, his face stoic but glum.

Rachel lifted her chin to show her determination. "And I am stronger than I look. I . . . I was a putter in the mine."

"And you lasted three whole days." She laughed in derision. "I have heard all about *your* abilities."

Ashamed and humiliated that Poulson would reference in front of Geordie the night she'd been with Lord Druridge, she lowered her eyes. "We will both do our part," she insisted.

"That you will. I plan to see to it."

Rachel's gaze trailed after her brother as Flora led Geordie out through the larder. When he twisted around to catch a final glimpse of her, she could tell he was scared and uncertain of this new world. She could only hope that the stable master would show more kindness than the housekeeper, because this arrangement was the best she could do for him.

"Come on, then," Poulson snapped. "You can't stand around all day. You've got work to do."

The contempt that gave those words such a sharp edge made Rachel uneasy, but she followed the housekeeper up the back stairs, which were reserved for the servants to come and go as quietly and unobtrusively as possible, to a drafty garret, where she was given a narrow bed in a row of narrow beds, presumably belonging to other maids. There was no fireplace, which meant nights would be cold. It was chilly now, despite Rachel's wool dress and shawl.

Surely she'd made the right decision. This had to be better than suffering the recriminations of the villagers and the indignities of working amongst the miners.

But already she missed her freedom, her own bed, the books she loved to read and sell—all that had been her life before. She had no idea what would become of those things. Lord Druridge had indicated they would discuss such matters later. She guessed her belongings would be sold to buy out her lease and Druridge would let both the shop and the house to someone else.

She hated the very thought of that—it signaled the end of the autonomy she prized so highly—but what could she do?

Nothing. For better or worse, she'd made her decision at the mine.

"Girl? Girl!"

With a blink, Rachel drew her attention to the housekeeper. "Yes, mum?"

"Stow your belongings in that before I give you a good smack." She pointed at a wardrobe against the wall. "Then return below stairs immediately."

Rachel had put in long hours at the bookshop, and at the mine, but she had a feeling her days here would be just as long and probably as grueling. Mrs. Poulson confirmed such when, in the kitchen, she handed Rachel a mop and a bucket and told her to remove all the rugs, beat them outside and scrub the floors—a job Rachel knew, with a house as vast as this one, would take her deep into the night, especially because she was getting such a late start.

"By day's end, mum?" she asked.

"By day's end."

Mrs. Poulson waited to see if she would balk at the sheer enormity of the task, but Rachel clamped her mouth shut. After dipping into a polite curtsy, she carried her mop and bucket to the family wing so that she could, hopefully, be finished there before Lord Druridge and Mr. Stanhope decided to retire.

Lord Druridge's bedroom brought back memories. Rachel held her breath as she entered, hoping those memories wouldn't crowd too close. But she had to breathe eventually, and when she did, the smell of the furniture polish, his clothes and a hint of pipe smoke brought it all back to her.

Her eyes shifted to the bed, even though she'd been trying to look elsewhere. She'd lost her virginity right *there*. Maybe she'd thought she was dreaming when it started, but she'd been aware of what she was doing by the end, and the mere audacity of her actions amazed her. No doubt he, and everyone else, would laugh at a poor village girl lusting after the great earl.

Soon, sweet Rachel, soon . . . Let me savor the taste and feel of you. . . .

Had he really spoken those words? Or was it a hallucination caused by the laudanum or whatever else Wythe had likely given her?

A noise in the hall jerked her out of her reverie. She had to hurry and get out of here. She'd chosen to start in this particular chamber so she wouldn't be anywhere close to it by the time night fell. But the door swung wider than she'd left it, and the earl walked in.

He seemed taken aback when he saw her. Obviously, he hadn't come to his room expecting to bump into her. She thought he might go about his business. She was only a cleaning maid, after all, and would soon blend into the background of his life. But he stopped and stared at her as if he wished he could read her thoughts.

Face burning, she ducked her head. "Excuse me, my lord. I-I will come back when you no longer have need of your chambers," she murmured and started to leave.

"Rachel."

Jittery and unsure, she turned back. The bed seemed so large, as if it were taking up all the space in the room. And *he* was taking up the oxygen. "Yes?"

"Will you be comfortable here at Blackmoor Hall?"

He seemed genuinely interested in hearing her answer, but she couldn't imagine why. He'd saved her from those men in the mine and put a roof over her head. He'd even taken in her brother. His conscience should be clear.

"Yes, my lord," she said and hurried away despite the fact that he might have wanted to ask her more.

Rachel didn't see the earl again for three weeks. Word had it he and his man, Linley, had left for London on business, and it must be true. Otherwise, she couldn't have avoided him. She didn't have the energy to do anything so calculated. She was up, blacking fireplaces by five, and didn't finish her work until eleven or later. She barely had time to eat—usually managed only two small meals a day. Rachel was certain the housekeeper was taking over where Wythe had left off. Poulson was trying to get her to quit so she could prove to Lord Druridge that he never should've hired her in the first place.

But Rachel had refused to let Wythe break her; she wouldn't let Poulson either. She dragged herself out of bed before dawn each morning and performed every chore assigned to her—and she did it without complaint. Unfortunately, she also did it without so much as a smile or a kind word from anyone else. The other maids didn't want to cross Mrs. Poulson. The housekeeper had made it very clear she found Rachel to be lacking in character and that her "moral corruption" might spread to others if they did not maintain a proper distance. So, isolated, hungry and tired, Rachel faced long, lonely days spent in an endless round of beating rugs and mattresses, spreading the carpets with damp tea leaves to remove the dust and sweeping and mopping and emptying chamber pots.

After what seemed like an eternity of Mrs. Poulson's unrelenting hatred, she might've succumbed to the despair that threatened, especially in her most tired moments. But Geordie was so happy. She didn't get to see him often, but the few brief encounters her job afforded her had convinced her that he was thriving under the tutelage of the stable master. Geordie claimed he was being treated like the man's own son and talked on and on of all he was learning and how much he loved the horses. When he slipped her a peppermint drop the stable master had given him and thanked her for bringing him to Blackmoor Hall, she couldn't let on that she was miserable. In her heart she knew she'd suffer *anything* to keep him in such a healthy situation. Even Mrs. Poulson's spite. And Wythe's occasional baiting. She'd bumped into Lord Druridge's cousin at least four times since she started in service. As expected, he was determined to continue his persecution. But so far she'd survived their encounters by ignoring the ugly things he said, which always revolved around her lost virtue, even though he was the one who'd deposited her in the earl's bed.

Late one night, when she dragged herself to the garret especially late, she found a book waiting for her—*The Complete Servant* by Sarah and Samuel Adams. No doubt Mrs. Poulson had left the tome on her pillow so that she could begin to cure her many shortcomings.

Barely able to lift her eyelids, she set the "rules" aside and crawled under the covers in her clothes. The housekeeper would surely chastise her for not taking a few minutes to undress and say her prayers. Such negligent behavior would be additional proof of her poor breeding. But the blanket she'd been given wasn't enough to keep her warm. She huddled beneath its thin covering, shivering while she listened to the soft breathing of the other girls, who'd gone to bed at least two hours earlier.

Each night it seemed harder to get warm. She'd lost too much weight. But the cold wasn't the worst of her worries. The cleaning solutions she used each day were so harsh they were destroying her hands. She feared the cracks that were starting to bleed would soon turn into open sores, and she didn't know how she'd continue to clean if that happened.

Would the stable master keep Geordie if she was turned out? Her little brother was all the family she had left. She couldn't bear the thought of being separated from him. If she was forced to leave, she might never see him again since she'd have to go to London or Manchester if she hoped to find work. Even then, her chances of securing a suitable position wouldn't be good. It was winter, and she'd arrive without so much as a letter of character. . . .

It'll get easier, she told herself. It had to. In ways, her work here was worse than what she'd endured at the mine because even her free time was spent beneath someone else's roof and without the slightest comfort.

Someone touched her shoulder. Startled and a little frightened by the unexpected contact, she twisted around to see who had crept up behind her. But she'd already extinguished her candle and it was far too dark to make out a face.

"Don't be frightened. 'Tis me."

Mary. Another one of the maids. Rachel recognized her distinctive Scottish accent.

"Is something wrong?" she whispered back.

"No. Scoot ye over."

"Excuse me?"

"Do ye want to get warm or not? Yer teeth are chatterin' so loud yer likely to wake the dead."

Rachel was miserable enough to accept any crumb of human kindness. But she knew what helping her could potentially cost Mary.

"Mrs. Poulson won't like it if . . . if you talk to me."

"Mrs. Poulson ain't here, is she?"

"The others—"

"Are asleep," she broke in. "Hurry. Scoot."

Afraid they'd both be penalized for this fraternization, Rachel reluctantly slid to one side. She didn't know this young woman, hadn't exchanged more than a few words with her over the past weeks. But when Mary got in and drew Rachel up against her, the instant relief brought tears to Rachel's eyes.

"It's okay," Mary whispered. "Sleep. That's what ye need."

The lump in Rachel's throat made it impossible for her to answer. She nodded. Then she lay there, thinking she probably wouldn't be able to sleep anyway. Her hands and her back hurt so terribly; it seemed like she ached everywhere. But before long she felt warm for the first time since she'd moved into the garret, and that was all it took. She drifted into a deep, dreamless sleep and was surprised in the morning to find Mary back in her own bed.

Hoping to offer her some form of thanks, Rachel took the rare and delicious peppermint drop that Geordie had passed along, which she'd been saving as a reminder of his love, from under the clothes in her chest. When she slipped it into Mary's hand, Mary shook her head as if she'd refuse the gift. But the other girls were rousing at that moment, and neither one of them dared let on that anything had changed.

Lord Druridge was back. Rachel felt the excitement amongst the servants and heard the buzz of their voices in the kitchen as she put the teakettle on to boil for Cook.

A few minutes later, she saw him stride into the manse, looking slightly haggard—cold and tired. He must have been traveling all night to arrive so early in the morning.

Linley trudged in behind him and went straight to his bed while the earl climbed the staircase and disappeared into his study, where he remained all day. Rachel knew he was there because once it grew dark, she kept checking for light under the door. She was supposed to dust the bookshelves and was afraid Mrs. Poulson would find fault with her if she didn't get it done, whether she'd had access to the room or not.

She went ahead with her other chores and kept returning, but it wasn't until everyone else had gone to bed that she finally found the door ajar. Eager to finish so that she, too, could seek her rest, she slipped inside before realizing her mistake. The earl had not retired. He was standing in front of the fireplace, one hand on the mantel as he gazed into the flames.

At the sound of her entrance, he turned and ran a hand through his hair, which fell long and loose about his face. "Rachel."

"I apologize for the intrusion, my lord. I thought . . . I will come back." She pivoted, but he stopped her.

"No, it's getting too late to put you off any longer. Go ahead and take care of whatever you have to do."

While he was there with her?

Because he had told her to go about her business, she did, but she could feel his eyes following her every move.

"Am I . . . bothering you, my lord?"

His face creased into a disapproving frown. "You look thinner than when I saw you last. Are you not getting enough to eat?"

"I am fine, my lord."

"And Geordie?"

She couldn't resist the smile that tugged at her lips when she thought of her last visit with her brother. "He is very happy. I owe you my gratitude for that."

It was easily the most effusive thing she'd ever said to him, but he didn't return her smile. "Gratitude," he mumbled, as if it was an odd word for her to use.

"Yes, my lord."

"So . . . you like it here?"

She hesitated as she searched for the right words. "It is a . . . wonderful place for Geordie."

"You like it about as much as facing a lynch mob, eh?" He chuckled dryly. "Enough said. Do you play chess, Rachel?"

Her eyes followed his to a table situated to one side of the fireplace. "*Sir?*"

"Chess. Surely, educated as you are, you know the game."

"Of course. I-I have a real fondness for it."

"As do I." Straightening, he motioned toward the seat closest to the fire. "Perhaps you will indulge me."

She blinked at him. "You want me to play? *Tonight?*"

"If you would be so kind."

But . . . what if Mrs. Poulson found her ensconced in the earl's study with him?

She checked over her shoulder as if the housekeeper might already be watching from the door. "Mrs. Poulson would most assuredly *not* approve."

"As if I give a fig about Mrs. Poulson's approval."

He didn't have to care; he didn't work for her. Rachel almost said as much. But she was afraid that complaining would only make matters worse. If she couldn't succeed in his household, maybe he would be left with no choice but to sack her. She couldn't see one reason he wouldn't.

He pulled out the chair. "If you please."

She didn't see how she could refuse him. So she put her feather duster aside, smoothed her uniform and took the seat he proffered.

"The first move will be yours," he announced. "Or"—he seemed to consider—"maybe I should give you three or four."

"You are so confident you can beat me?"

That she would question his assumption caused him to arch his eyebrows, as if it was inconceivable for him to think anything else. "I fear I can do it quite handily, but I am hoping for a challenge, a true diversion."

Rachel had played many hours of chess with her mother during the long winter evenings when her father worked at the mine. Even Geordie knew how to play and was quite good. "Then I shall do my best to provide one."

Intent on that, Rachel slid her pawn forward, but she hadn't yet retracted her hand when he grabbed hold of it.

"What is *this?*"

When she winced at the pain his grip caused, he let go. "Nothing," she said. "Your move."

"Nothing?"

"They will heal. It's the . . . the lye and other chemicals I clean with."

She slipped her hands under the table. They were unsightly, apparently *too* unsightly for his view. Except for that one night in his bed, when she'd felt him touching her, he kept a glove on at all times to hide the damage the fire did. He had it on even now. If she hadn't been so caught up in his odd request to give him a game she would've known better than to let him see.

"I have yet to notice another maid's hands so cracked and sore."

"I apologize. We don't have to play." She started to stand, but he got up and insisted she remain in her seat.

"Wait here." He headed for the door.

"My lord, please. Say nothing to Mrs. Poulson." Rachel couldn't believe she'd uttered those words. She had no right to tell him what to do. But she could not afford to make Mrs. Poulson hate her any worse. "It will not help me," she added more quietly.

"It absolutely will." He ground out each word as if it were a separate sentence. He simply could not imagine that Mrs. Poulson would disobey him. But he had no idea the many petty reprisals the housekeeper would have in store. Rachel was so convinced that whatever he was about to do would prove her eventual ruin that she nearly fled. It was the thought that she'd never see Geordie again that stopped her—the same thought that had stopped her all along.

Her palms were sweating by the time the earl returned with Mrs. Poulson in tow. Although the housekeeper carried a tray of bread, cheese, nuts and apples, which she brought in and set on the desk, she'd obviously been in bed and was not pleased to have been summoned from sleep.

"What is it she's told you, my lord?" she demanded as she turned to face Rachel. "It must be a lie. She has been nothing but trouble since she arrived—always up to the devil's mischief."

"I find it difficult to believe that she has been up to much of anything other than scrubbing night and day." He strode over and held Rachel's hands out as proof.

Mrs. Poulson's lips pursed. "Such is the nature of the job."

"It's barbaric."

"She must be allergic to the soap," she said, trying a different tack. "I have barely had her do a thing since you brought her to me."

"Which was why she was waiting for me to retire so that she could dust in here at"—he glanced at the clock—"midnight?"

Mrs. Poulson sent Rachel a withering glance. "Perhaps she was looking to achieve more than the completion of her chores."

His jaw hardened. "If she wants that, she knows where my bed is."

Rachel was embarrassed by his response, but she was glad he hadn't let the housekeeper get the best of him when she resorted to *that* reminder.

"She never even mentioned that her hands were sore!" Poulson said. "I would have adjusted her duties if only I had known."

It was far more likely she would've gloated, but Rachel kept her mouth shut.

"Well, now you know," the earl said. "She will not be required to scrub anything until her hands have completely healed. Do you understand? No"—he shook his head, then pointed a finger at Mrs. Poulson as if she had better mark his words—"she will not be required to do any work that requires the kinds of chemicals that cause this ever again. Do I make myself clear?"

"Surely your favoritism extends too far, my lord. How will she be of any use to me? To this house?"

At first he didn't seem to know how he wanted to answer. Rachel was afraid he'd decide there really was no use for her. She couldn't go back to the shop; no one frequented it anymore. She couldn't return to the mine. And now she couldn't work as a maid?

At best Rachel felt she could expect him to offer her a few extra pounds and a reference so she could go elsewhere. But then his gaze landed on the chess set. "I require a chess partner. Nightly. It will be her job to entertain me."

Mrs. Poulson's nostrils flared with disapproval. "Might I caution you, my lord, that such an arrangement would be unseemly for a man of your station?"

"I doubt others could think any worse of me than to believe I murdered my wife, Mrs. Poulson. And Rachel's reputation is already ruined. You alluded to that fact yourself—indelicately, I might add—so I can do no more damage there."

"I was concerned about . . . that other matter."

"What other matter?" he asked.

"Concerning the Duke of Pembroke."

"I'm sure you were."

"It's true! We *both* know what is at stake, my lord. I care only for your ultimate well-being."

Rachel could scarcely breathe as she listened. What were they talking about? From the look on the housekeeper's face, the "matter" she'd mentioned was serious, even ominous, but the earl didn't address whatever it was.

"Please have her moved into Lady Katherine's chambers immediately. She will be sleeping there from now on."

At this, Rachel almost objected herself. She could not trust such benevolence. How long would Lord Druridge be able to tolerate such an arrangement—a *maid* living in his late wife's chambers?

"My lord—" she started, but he angled his head to indicate the game.

"Let us continue, Rachel," he said. "Mrs. Poulson, you are excused."

Chapter 12

The tick of the clock seemed overly loud. "Surely you didn't mean it," Rachel murmured, breaking the silence that had fallen in the wake of Poulson's departure.

Instead of returning to the game, as he'd indicated, Lord Druridge had gone to the brandy decanter and poured himself a drink. She could see the starkness of his visage as he stared out the window. "I wouldn't have said it if I didn't mean it."

It was a simple, imperious answer. He wasn't used to having his commands questioned. But this was madness. "Lord Druridge, I cannot take Lady Katherine's quarters. Imagine how far word of this . . . odd arrangement will spread."

"Let people wag their tongues." When he turned, there was a hint of defiance in his demeanor. "It wasn't as if I didn't try a more *circumspect* arrangement." He lifted his glass. "I trusted you to the care of my staff, and look at you. After only three weeks, I return from London to find you about to faint from hunger and fatigue."

"While *you* have come back so very well rested?"

His eyes narrowed at the tartness of her words. "You speak frankly."

"I am who I am. Putting a uniform on me doesn't change that."

"Apparently not. Anyway, I sleep when I can."

"Will you sleep any better by having me next door?" She had made it clear she would not be his whore, and he had said he didn't expect it. Was he breaking that promise? Why else would he put her in Katherine's room?

"Perhaps I will," he said.

"And what do you anticipate in return for your generosity?"

"Nothing you won't be able to freely give."

"There will be a door adjoining our bedrooms," she pointed out. "I've cleaned this entire wing many times and know all the rooms well."

"That door you may keep locked as you see fit."

Had she heard him correctly? "Then what will my duties include?"

"You will spend your days however you like."

"Not without work. Surely you jest."

"If it pleases me to make your life easier, I will. You read, don't you? I have an extensive library. You can spend your days in there. Or hold classes for the household staff, if you want, teach them as you've taught the miners. Other than that . . . you must know how to do some sort of needlework. Isn't that what ladies do in their free time?"

"But"—she floundered for words—"how long do you see something like this working?"

"Until your hands have healed and better arrangements can be made."

"I see." So it was temporary. That eased her mind somewhat, but there was still the other matter Poulson had referenced, something to do with the Duke of Pembroke. Rachel couldn't even begin to guess what that was about, and yet it worried her. "I appreciate your generosity, my lord, but you really *must* put me in a more modest room."

"Where? In the other wing of the house, where you will be alone? Or back with the servants who will resent you too much to show you the least bit of kindness? Or maybe you meant this wing, but closer to Wythe?"

She saw his point. None of those choices sounded appealing. Fortunately, he didn't wait for her response.

"I am done with finding you in dire straits, Rachel. It is better to keep you close."

"But putting me in Katherine's rooms will . . . " She let her words drop off because she couldn't think of an inoffensive way to say what was on her mind.

"You're suddenly unwilling to speak up?" He slanted her a look with his sarcasm that said he could hardly believe it.

She drew a deep breath. "It will seem to confirm to everyone who has wondered . . . that your wife never meant too . . . much to you, my lord."

"I can't say she did, not toward the end." His shoulders lifted in a shrug. "Maybe not even toward the middle. It wasn't long after we were married that I realized I could never love her."

Sometimes he was too honest for his own good. "I wouldn't admit that to anyone else, my lord."

"But my secrets are safe with you? Someone who believes I fired Blackmoor Hall? Someone who hates me more than my usual assortment of enemies?"

"I don't . . ." She wanted to say "hate you," but was afraid such an admission might reveal just how much her feelings had changed. "I don't think you fired Blackmoor Hall."

A wry smile twisted his lips. "Is that so? And what evidence has brought you to my side?"

"I didn't know what kind of man you were when I made that accusation, only what I had heard others say."

"Those 'others' included your parents—reliable sources, wouldn't you say?"

"Perhaps they were equally misguided. But, be that as it may, we do have to deal with certain realities. We *both* have enemies, my lord."

"Now that my enemies are your enemies, you mean."

"To be honest, I am more worried about your friends."

He arched an eyebrow at her. "My *friends?*"

"If you make my life *too* easy, Mr. Stanhope and Mrs. Poulson will be waiting for their revenge. And when you are ready to cast me off, they will have it."

He tossed back the rest of his drink. "I will take you to London and put you in service there, if need be. Until then, you will fall under my protection. In return, I ask for only one thing."

She swallowed hard. Could she deny him *anything*? She was completely at his mercy. "And that is?"

"That you meet me here whenever I request your company."

"To divert you by playing chess."

With a slight bow he said, "If you prove to be a worthy opponent, yes."

She motioned to the chess set. "Then allow me to prove myself up to the task."

Although he insisted she eat before they could start the game in earnest, once he was satisfied she couldn't take another bite, he settled himself across from her.

The game lasted two hours and was one of the most difficult Rachel had ever played. When he took her queen, she was sure she would lose. He was a far better player than her mother had been and wiggled out of every trap. But she got lucky and managed to corner his king.

"Checkmate," she said with a huge rush of relief.

He scowled as if he couldn't believe what he saw, but then he started to chuckle. "Ah, even here you thwart me."

"My lord?"

"I deserved the beating for being so arrogant. You are a credit to woman-kind, Rachel—bright and refreshing."

She moved the pieces back into their starting places. "Perhaps you would like me to beat you again, since it obviously pleases you?"

She was teasing. She could tell he understood that, and yet he grew serious.

"There is one thing that would please me more."

Unable to tear her eyes away from his, she curled her nails into her already tender palms. "And that is . . . ?"

"Did you know it was me, Rachel?"

He was talking about that night in his bed. She could tell by the level of his intensity. No doubt it would ease his conscience to hear the truth, but she couldn't reveal that she'd recognized him without also revealing that she'd wanted him as badly as he'd thought.

"I was . . . drugged or something," she mumbled.

His gaze remained steady on hers. "That isn't what I asked you. You wanted me to remove my glove. You wanted to feel both my hands on you with nothing in between. No one else would wear a glove while making love to a woman. I only left it on because—"

At last she managed to look away and wished she could hide her face too. "I know why you left it on. But I don't find your hand nearly so repulsive as you seem to think I will."

"You still haven't answered my question."

"I *didn't* know it was you."

"Despite the glove."

"Despite the glove. I had no idea where I was."

"Then I take full responsibility." He stood. "It's late. We are done for the night. Enjoy your new sleeping quarters."

That he had accepted her words as the truth reminded her of what he'd said in the bookshop the night he appeared out of nowhere, and that stung her conscience. His opinion had been far more accurate when he mocked her: *You would never willingly give yourself to* me, *not for money, not for anything. . . . I am your nemesis.*

She'd believed he was her nemesis. Even now, she had the feeling he could all too easily destroy her if she wasn't smart. The yearning she felt whenever he drew near—it wasn't safe, which was why she left the subject as it stood and headed for the door.

But after only a few steps, she turned back. She couldn't lie to him any longer, even if such honesty left her vulnerable. From the beginning, he'd acknowledged his part in what had occurred; maybe it was time she did the same.

"I knew it was you the moment you touched me," she admitted and left.

Truman was drinking too much. He hoped it would dull his mind and slow the racing of his heart to the point that he would be able to sleep. But that seemed unlikely, given Rachel's parting words.

Linley was right. He should find her another position, with a master who would be kind. He could check on her periodically, make it possible for Geordie to see her now and then. Keeping her here where she was perfectly accessible to him threatened everything he'd just achieved in London. If he couldn't find the missing Bruegel paintings, he had to accept the Duke of Pembroke's offer. Without the duke's support, the Abbotts would triumph, and he would be tried for murder.

So *why* was he tempting fate?

Because he couldn't bring himself to do otherwise. Maybe Rachel was stubborn, opinionated and steeped in the philosophies of her class, but she soothed his beleaguered soul like no one else.

I knew it was you the moment you touched me. That potent admission made his body ache with desire—desire that had to go unfulfilled. He would not cost Rachel any more of her self-respect.

At least he had the small revenge of knowing that Katherine had to be turning over in her grave. She'd always wanted to drive him to distraction, hated that she couldn't enslave him as she did her other men. That he was consumed with desire for someone else, someone she would consider far inferior, would have driven her mad, if she were around to see it.

He offered her portrait a taunting smile. "Our newest servant is taking your rooms, love. She is asleep in your bed this very instant." He held the last of his drink high. "And heaven help me if I wouldn't trade a fortune to join her there."

Someone was looming over her. Rachel almost screamed before she realized it was Lord Druridge. She was no longer in the utilitarian garret with the other maids. She was asleep in his late wife's bed, which was far bigger and more comfortable than any place she'd slept before.

"My lord? Is something wrong?" Oddly, she wasn't frightened. Once she knew who it was, she scooted into a sitting position.

He carried a lamp, which he set on her bedside table. He didn't seem as steady as usual. She got the impression that maybe he'd had too much to drink. The scent of brandy clung to him, as did the scent of the outdoors, even though he'd come to her room through his own. She could see the light of his fire through the open doorway.

"What good does it do to lock my door if you have the key?" she asked.

He didn't answer the question. "I found what you need," he told her.

"What I *need?*"

"The horse salve. This is what I used after the fire. It helps a great deal. I had to wake William Grude, but he knew right where it was."

This couldn't have waited until morning? When did this man sleep? "You went out in the cold for the sake of . . . of my hands?"

"Let me see them."

Dutifully, she allowed him to apply the thick salve, which brought instant relief—not from the pain but from the dryness and cracking.

"You're not wearing your glove," she said.

"It's dark."

"I can feel the difference."

He instantly withdrew. "You can apply the ointment yourself, I'm sure."

She knew she shouldn't, but she reached out to capture that particular hand before he could go. She couldn't help wanting to feel, once again, the flesh that had been damaged, to soothe any residual pain, to become familiar with such an irregularity. This was a part of him he shared with no one. She liked that aspect, liked the intimacy of touching what he wouldn't trust just anyone to touch.

She stared up at him, trying to see him more clearly in the darkness as her fingers explored the damage. He seemed unsure, hesitant, as though he was anxious to pull away rather than expose himself where he was most vulnerable. But she'd been telling the truth. His scars didn't bother her. On the contrary, they brought back memories of their night together, when he removed his glove and touched her with the hand that was unique to him.

"Such terrible damage. It *can't* please you." He tried to get her to take his other hand instead, but she wanted to minister to the one she held, to let him know that, somehow, it was just as beautiful to her as the rest of him. "It does please me," she insisted. "Letting me touch you in this way involves an element of trust."

"Trust?" He sounded like he'd almost choked on the word. "I'm not someone you should trust, Rachel," he warned, but their hands slid together, smearing the ointment, making their skin slick and sensitive. She got the impression he wanted more. *Something* held him fast and, since she could scarcely breathe, it wasn't difficult to imagine what that might be.

"My lord . . . ," she whispered. She wanted him to slide his hands up her arms, to pull off her nightgown and smooth that ointment all over her body, but he stepped out of reach and put the salve on the table by her bed. "Make sure you put more on in the morning."

"I will," she promised and he took his lamp and left.

Suddenly bereft in a way she'd never felt bereft before, Rachel curled up on one side and stared at the light under the crack of his door until her pulse slowed and she finally nodded off.

When she woke, it was late morning, but she was still tired. She felt like she could sleep all day—except there was an argument going on next door.

"In Katherine's bed?"

"Why not? Last I checked she no longer needed it."

"But, my lord, how do you expect her family to respond?"

It was Linley and the earl. Rachel easily recognized their voices.

"It's none of their business."

"You can't be serious. News of this will spread like wildfire. She is a mere servant, after all. What are you going to do next, hire her a lady's maid?"

"No. No doubt that would make her extremely uncomfortable. In any case, she is not a servant. At least, she wasn't until *I* employed her."

Throwing back the covers, Rachel got out of bed and crept closer.

"She is a pauper still the same," Linley argued.

"She owns the village bookshop. There is plenty of respect in honest industry."

"You think making her your paramour will go over any better because of the shop?"

"She is *not* my paramour."

"Then what is she?"

"My . . . ward."

"She is of age, Truman. And you have bedded her."

"Considering Wythe's culpability in her deflowering, I am shocked you would bring it up."

"You know how I feel about your cousin. But that is beside the point. I care about you, am merely trying to remind you what having her so close will mean. Whether you are in actuality lovers, others will assume you are. In this case, it is the perception that counts."

"I don't care what the Abbotts 'perceive.' I will not let them sit in judgment of me. Had they been honest about Katherine's character and temperament, I never would have married her."

"Then what of the Duke of Pembroke? I saw how he treated you, heard what he had to say. It may gall you to be in such a position—and rightfully so—but you are in dire need of his support. Surely you care about *his* opinion."

From what Rachel could tell, the earl didn't answer. It was Linley who continued.

"If you don't marry his daughter you will be ruined, my lord. He will abandon your cause and the Abbotts will soon have full sway. Do you want to find yourself at the end of a hangman's noose?"

Rachel winced at the thought of the earl going to the gallows but refused to consider why his marrying upset her just as much. He was still young, needed to produce an heir. And it sounded as if he had the opportunity to make a favorable match. She should be happy for him.

"I refuse to allow whether I swing from the gallows to hinge on where Rachel sleeps."

"You may not have a choice. Maybe you would have more leeway if you were your old self. But people are wondering about you as it is. You are up all hours of the night. You come and go like a shade. You no longer maintain the relationships that used to be important to you. You should hear the rumors that are circulating in London and elsewhere—"

"And have been circulating for two years," the earl broke in. "Rachel is not the cause of that. Forget what people are saying!"

"I can't. And neither can you. Forgive me for speaking so plainly, but any odd behavior makes you look guilty."

Rachel gasped that Linley would be so bold, but the earl didn't react in anger. He sounded almost . . . philosophical.

"It wasn't Katherine's death that changed me. It was marrying her in the first place. You, of all people, should know that. Certainly you remember how miserable I was, how hard I tried to love her and how bitterly I failed. Anyway, I may not be the man I started out to be, but I will prove my innocence all the same."

"Just marry the duke's daughter, my lord. Then you can put the past behind you and, one hopes, forget."

"I *can't* forget, Linley. Not until I prove my innocence."

"It has been two years and *still* no one knows how the fire broke out."

"Someone knows," the earl insisted. "Maybe even Rachel."

Rachel covered her mouth and stumbled back, away from the door. *She didn't know. She'd told him as much.*

But Elspeth might.

The same maid who had helped her get warm that last miserable night in the garret knocked on the door shortly after noon. She was carrying a tray of food. Rachel guessed the earl had requested it, once again making her grateful for his generosity. She wasn't sure what would've happened had she been forced to go in search of sustenance. She definitely didn't want to run into Mrs. Poulson. She wasn't sure of her new place at Blackmoor Hall. Should she try to teach the staff to read, as Lord Druridge had suggested?

Mrs. Poulson would definitely not like that. But would she tolerate it? Or would she find some way to quash it?

"Gaw, look at ye sittin' in this fine room as if ye own it!" Mary said.

Rachel had donned the wool dress she'd been wearing when she first arrived at Blackmoor Hall. Thankfully, Mrs. Poulson or someone else had piled her belongings on Katherine's bed last night so she didn't have to wear her uniform. "It's beautiful in here, isn't it?"

"Aye, but I've seen the room before. It's a poor lass bein' treated like a queen I can't fathom." She lowered her voice. "Is he a kind bedfellow?"

Rachel felt herself flush. The exchange they'd had in the wee hours made her feel guilty. They'd only touched hands but it had felt like so much more. "He didn't come to me." Except to put salve on her hands. She was still amazed by the fact that he'd gone out in the cold in order to gain the remedy, but she didn't mention it.

Mary's eyebrows shot up. "Why not?"

"I don't know what his intentions are," she admitted.

"But ye've been together before. I 'eard all about it. Caused quite an uproar below stairs, it did."

There wasn't any point in denying what'd happened. All of Creswell knew of that night. "We were together *once*," she admitted. "But . . . I wasn't in my right mind."

"And if he pays ye a visit, ye'll be out of yer mind again," she said with a laugh. "So be prepared. A man of 'is age and station doesn't install a maid in the lady's quarters for nothin'. 'E obviously wants more."

Everyone else had to be thinking the same thing. Even Geordie would hear of her new living arrangements. But there wasn't anything Rachel could do to stop the servants from talking. And she had little choice but to stay where she was. She couldn't go back into the ranks of service—not here with Mrs. Poulson. She'd barely survived her last stint.

She knotted her hands in her lap. "He claims he does not expect that."

"Oh, 'e expects it," Mary said. "An' 'e's got a right with what 'e's doin' for ye. E's a fine figure of a man, regardless. I don't blame ye for liftin' yer skirts. I'd do it, too, if only 'e'd ask." She put the tray on a table and started to go out, but Rachel pulled her back.

"Stay for a few minutes. There is plenty here for the both of us."

Mary hesitated as if she wasn't convinced she could trust the invitation, but when Rachel gestured again, she smiled a conspirator's smile and closed the door.

Rachel pulled the tray close, and they ate everything on it as if they hadn't seen food in weeks. There *had* been far too little of it.

"I 'ave never been so full in my life. I'm guessin' that was intended for the earl hisself," Mary said, rubbing her stomach in satisfaction.

"It's nice, how the other half lives," Rachel murmured.

"Aye, but whatever ye do, don't get used to it." Mary stood and indicated the elaborate trappings surrounding them. "This won't last, and it'll break yer bloody 'eart if ye expect it to. Soon ye'll be back in the garret with me, or some other garret."

"I know," Rachel said, sobering.

Mary seemed to realize she'd just cast a pall over everything, because she smiled again and gave Rachel a quick hug. "But that doesn't mean ye can't enjoy it while it lasts, eh? And that goes for what the earl's got 'tween 'is legs."

When Rachel covered her mouth, Mary laughed at her scandalized reaction, grabbed the tray and twitched her bottom as she sauntered out.

"Good luck with Mrs. Poulson," Rachel whispered after her. But she wasn't really thinking about the housekeeper. She was remembering that night in the earl's bed, how eager she'd been to join their two bodies, how she'd ached for the completion he promised. There'd been that terrible flash of pain, which had almost mucked it up, but . . . if he came to her again, would letting him have his way be more enjoyable now that she was no longer a virgin?

Chapter 13

Mrs. Poulson knocked shortly after lunch. Rachel had just bathed and dressed. At the moment, thanks to the earl, the housekeeper could do little to hurt her, but Rachel worried she might attempt to make Geordie's life miserable.

The older woman frowned in obvious contempt as her gaze traveled down Rachel's body. "You are finally awake, I see."

Rachel said nothing as Mrs. Poulson pushed past her.

Once inside, the housekeeper stood in the center of the room and surveyed her surroundings. "You don't deserve all this."

"Did you come for a reason?" she asked.

That she would dare respond with a bit of ice in her own voice caused Mrs. Poulson's eyes to narrow. "Do not think you will be here long. He will toss you out as soon as he is finished using you. And then where will you be?"

"I will no longer be working for you. We can both agree on that," she countered.

"Once he turns you out, maybe you will be more grateful for honest work. Starvation will humble the most uppity of maids."

The venom in those words made Rachel shake her head in wonder. "What have I done to make you hate me so?"

She sniffed. "You don't know your place."

Could this stem back to the night she'd appeared at Blackmoor Hall, frantic because her mother was dying? Did it bother Mrs. Poulson so much that the earl had overridden her authority when she tried to turn Rachel out?

It was no use trying to talk to such a person. Rachel had never met anyone so spiteful. "What is it you want?" she asked.

"Mr. Cardiff, the dressmaker, is here. Lord Druridge had him summoned from the village."

Rachel stepped back. "And what does that have to do with me?"

"Apparently you are to have one of Lady Katherine's gowns." She'd spoken as if the words tasted bitter on her tongue.

"But there is a needlewoman on staff who is probably capable of making the alterations."

"Which is what I told him." She tilted her head back and glared down her blade-like nose. "You must have done your part last night to make him want to be so generous."

Rachel could have argued that she hadn't done anything immoral. But why bother? Mrs. Poulson would assume the worst no matter what. And with the thoughts going through her head lately, Rachel wasn't sure she was innocent enough to expect anything different. She was beginning to feel as if she might be willing to sacrifice her virtue—to sacrifice almost anything—to be part of his life.

"Where is Mr. Cardiff?" she asked.

"In the drawing room. He has asked that you bring your choice of gowns from Lady Katherine's wardrobe down with you," she said and stalked out.

She was to pick out a *gown*? That would only make the other servants more jealous than they probably were. They would all feel as if she were putting on airs. And the villagers . . .

Dropping onto the bed, Rachel wondered how to handle this latest development. If she was to entertain the earl at his bidding, he likely wanted her to be robed in something that reminded him less of her station. But she would always be a poor village girl, and there was no getting around that.

A soft knock sounded and Mary poked her head in before Rachel could even stir. "Did ye 'ear? The dressmaker is in the parlor, and 'e's waitin' for *Mistress Rachel!* I 'eard 'im tell Mrs. Poulson so!"

"I know. Poulson just left, but . . . what am I to do?"

"What do ye mean? Ye pick yer favorite, of course." She dragged Rachel into the dressing room and opened the armoire. "'Ave ye ever seen more fancy gowns than these?"

Rachel felt so out of place she almost couldn't bring herself to *touch*

Katherine's clothing, let alone select something that would be altered to fit *her*. "I am happy with my own plain clothes."

"Get what you can," Mary admonished. "Ye can sell 'is gifts later, if ye 'ave need." She pulled a beautiful green velvet frock from the armoire and held it against Rachel. "See what this one does for yer eyes? I bet ye'll look even prettier in it than the former mistress did."

Rachel caught Mary's arm. "You knew her? Lady Katherine?"

"Not as well as Rosie did. Rosie was her lady's maid. She went to the Abbotts after the fire, but ye didn't 'ave to be close to get an inkling of what Lady Katherine was like."

"So? Tell me about her."

Obviously afraid she might be caught loafing, Mary peeked into the other room. "She was spoiled and haughty, threw a tantrum every time somethin' didn't go 'er way, she did. I don't know of a single servant who liked her. She'd get especially spiteful when she was bored, and she grew bored any time the master wasn't around because 'e was the person she loved to torment most."

"Would you say he cared a great deal for her?" Rachel knew what Lord Druridge had told her, but she was curious to hear how the servants perceived their relationship.

Mary shrugged. "Och, what does love matter? It was an arranged marriage, a calculated match."

"Weren't they ever tender with each other?"

Mary's expression changed. "Ye canna fall in love with 'im, Rachel. Ye need to listen to me."

Mary had already warned her once. "I won't. I just . . . I saw Katherine occasionally on the streets of Creswell. She was *so* beautiful."

"On the outside, maybe." She left the dress in Rachel's hands. "Ye'd better not keep Mr. Cardiff waitin'."

Rachel rubbed the rich fabric against her cheek. "I should choose this one? You're sure?" She'd probably never have the chance to own something so fine again.

"Aye, I'm sure."

With a smile of thanks, she carried the dress downstairs.

The earl didn't summon her for chess that night or the next. Rachel was beginning to believe she might already have lost his favor. She heard him come and go late at night, but he never entered her room or invited her to his. She had no communication with him at all except a brief note in which he said he hoped she was making herself at home on the estate. Mary delivered the note. She delivered everything, including food, water for bathing and even the green gown when it was ready.

Other than those visits, Rachel was alone or visiting with Geordie. She walked with her brother in the gardens or along the cliffs, or ventured to the library down the hall on her own, which contained a more extensive collection of books than her bookshop.

By the third day of her new situation, she was feeling stronger, better rested and more satisfied, but she was growing anxious for some way to get back to town. She had a message for Elspeth, but she had no idea how she would get it into Elspeth's hands. Although Wythe went to the brothel regularly, she knew better than to trust him with it, or to beg a ride. He frightened her far more than the obdurate Mrs. Poulson, although she did all she could to avoid them both. Once when she was sitting next to the window in the library, using the sunlight pouring through the panes to read Lord Byron's *Don Juan*, a book her mother had always considered too scandalous for her, she heard Wythe in the hall outside and ducked beneath the desk lest he enter and find her there.

Fortunately, he hadn't intruded on her as she feared he might, but she listened for him always.

On Friday, instead of a tray of food for her evening meal, Mary brought a note from Lord Druridge.

Please join me for dinner this evening.

She stared up at her new friend. "Does he mean *in the dining hall?*"

Mary seemed equally awestruck. "Aye. Mrs. Poulson already 'ad me set another place, so that's exactly what 'e means. I'm to 'elp ye dress."

"But I feel like such an imposter!"

"At least ye're more likable than Lady Katherine ever was."

They laughed, but Rachel was no longer laughing when she walked downstairs. She was too nervous, especially when she saw that Lord Druridge was already seated. What would he think of her in his late wife's dress?

She wasn't even sure he'd recognize it. She'd had the dressmaker remove the pretentious frills and bows. Now a much simpler design, it had a wide neck that showed her shoulders, a fitted bodice and full sleeves with a wide skirt that fell to her ankles, where a few inches of her stockings showed above the kid leather slippers that had arrived with the dress. For the first time since she could remember, she was wearing three petticoats in addition to her corset.

Lord Druridge stood when she entered the room. "Good evening."

She dipped into a curtsy. "Good evening to you, my lord." Feeling self-conscious and shy beneath his regard, she smiled—until Wythe strode into the room. Then she no longer wanted to be there.

"Ah, we have company tonight. And doesn't she look ravishing." He bowed but she could tell he wasn't pleased to have her present. "Cousin, I commend you on your eye for beauty. But I must warn you. If the house help are forced to serve her, they might beat her from the door as soon as you're not looking."

Druridge's gaze turned flinty. "And why would they do that?"

"Because they are green with envy. You are not merely offering Rachel a few baubles for her favors; you are treating her like a respected *lady*. Pray she does not forget her place or she might wind up more of an outcast than ever before."

"Sit down and hold your tongue," he said.

Wythe smiled as if the earl had been joking, but Rachel could feel the tension in his body. He resented his cousin's authority even more than he resented her being at Blackmoor Hall. Maybe he felt as if she was driving a wedge between them. Regardless, the current situation didn't sit well with him.

"It makes a nice illusion, anyway," he said. When this drew another sharp glance from Lord Druridge, Wythe ate in silence.

The earl's eyes flicked to Rachel every few seconds, but she couldn't tell what he was thinking. Had Wythe's disapproval made him regret inviting her to dinner? Was he wondering what he would do with her now that she was no longer a servant?

When the meal ended, she stood and curtsied again. "Thank you for supper, my lord."

She was halfway to the stairs before he said, "I believe you owe me another game of chess, Rachel."

"Tonight, my lord?"

"Unless you are too tired."

"No." She wasn't tired. She was self-conscious and uncomfortable and unsure where her life was going. She also felt weak in the knees whenever she looked at him, and that scared her more than anything.

"Why did you invite me to dine with you and Mr. Stanhope?"

Truman watched Rachel carefully as he massaged his gloved left hand. In damp weather, it often pained him, had never been the same since the fire. "I'd like you to be comfortable here at Blackmoor Hall, and that means we need to make certain adjustments."

"But you knew your cousin would feel insulted to be forced to dine with someone of my low station."

He shrugged. "My cousin is as much a guest in my house as you are. He has no right to object."

She crossed to the window. "Mrs. Poulson has even less right, and yet she is just as displeased."

He could see her solemn reflection in the glass. Forever stoic, she seemed willing to brave anything for the sake of her brother. He'd never encountered such unselfishness.

Maybe that was what drew him to her. It was unlike anything he'd ever known from Katherine.

He got up to pour himself a drink. "Mrs. Poulson is not a pleasant individual generally, but my parents thought her presence might ease Wythe's transition, seeing as he lost both father and mother in so short a time."

"She was already familiar to him?"

"She has worked for Wythe's family since he was a babe. Whenever I am tempted to sack her, I remind myself that it would be cruel to deprive my cousin of a servant he values so highly, especially because she is, despite her other faults, efficient." Not only that but the memory of his cousin struggling to get him out of the house before he could burn to death bound him to behave in certain ways, despite all the disappointment and suspicion that complicated their relationship.

"You are far more generous than most lords."

"And what do you know of any other lords, Rachel? Any other *men*, for that matter?" He lowered his voice. "From what I remember, you've known only me."

She flushed at his words. "I am not likely to forget that."

He tossed back his drink. "Unfortunately, neither am I."

"Because you now feel obligated to take care of me?"

The fact that she would hate being an unwelcome burden brought the truth to his lips. "Because I crave more of the same."

At this admission, her mouth dropped open in surprise, but it was better that she feel empowered than he. He had every other advantage. "I-I inquired as to what you expected," she said. "You haven't asked me to pay you a visit."

"No, and I won't. I will keep my word, because I wouldn't want you to 'pay' me anything. I would be a liar, however, if I said I don't dream of you coming to me on your own."

Her eyebrows drew together, marring an otherwise smooth forehead. "You left my room the other night, when you brought the salve."

"I don't want your gratitude to be . . . a compelling force."

"Why me?"

His voice grew husky. "Are you *that* unaware of your beauty?"

"I am aware that there are plenty of other women—from high-born ladies to servants to village girls—and that you can have your pick of the lot."

"So I keep telling myself." He only wished the promise of "other women" was enough to distract him. "Shall we play?"

She made no move toward the chess set. "I heard your argument with Linley the other morning."

He'd gotten too worked up, allowed the conversation to get out of hand three days ago. But he'd never had Linley oppose him so stubbornly. "I apologize. Please don't let anything we said worry you."

"Even if Mr. Linley is right?"

"About . . . ?"

"Angering Lady Katherine's parents."

Leaning one hip on the edge of his desk, he took a sip of brandy. "You mean *further* angering them?"

"You should send me off to . . . to London, as you mentioned once before."

Even though he feared what might become of her? Even though it was the thought of her that brought him his only happiness? "Is that what you want, Rachel?"

She began to pace. "I would hate to leave Geordie, but—"

Setting his glass aside, he came up behind her. "Then why suggest it? Are you so eager to avoid *me*?"

She didn't turn to face him, but she didn't step out of reach. "If it means you will escape the gallows, yes."

Unable to resist, he brought her around and caught her face in his hands. "Don't tell me you are starting to like me, Rachel. I am the village monster, remember?"

Her cold fingers circled his wrists, although he could only feel it on the one that was ungloved. "*Someone* has to fear for your safety, my lord. It's not as if you take much care to look out for yourself."

Wythe accused him of not caring whether he lived or died. He often wondered if that was true. As Linley so often pointed out, he hadn't been the same since the fire. The long, lonely nights wore on him, the constant soul-searching, the despair of ever finding the answers he craved.

But when Rachel was around he felt new again. That was why he couldn't bring himself to part with her.

"I have rarely been denied. I fear it has made me no better than Wythe." Touching her was a mistake. Such close contact turned his blood to fire in his veins, making it difficult to let go. But he did—and put some distance between them. "Do you like the gown?"

She peered down at herself. "It is by far the loveliest thing I have ever owned."

Thanks to the difference in their respective heights, he had a generous view of her bare shoulders and cleavage. Perhaps she wasn't as curvaceous as was fashionable. Her life had been too difficult. But he thought she looked better in that dress than Katherine ever had. And her delight in such simple things brought a little of the innocence back into his own life. "Enjoy it. I will treat you well while I can."

"Meaning what? You will send me away once you marry?"

"I will have no choice."

Her voice softened. "Will that happen soon?"

"Most likely." Given his precarious circumstances, it was a small miracle that the Duke of Pembroke was willing to help. He'd be a fool to let the opportunity slip through his grasp. Although he continued to proclaim his innocence, he hadn't found any hint or trace of the paintings he believed were missing, and that shook his faith, made him wonder if he'd dreamed up the absence of *Landscape with the Fall of Icarus* to absolve himself from the guilt that plagued him.

Maybe he deserved to swing. Part of him would be grateful to put a decisive end to the matter. But duty got in the way even there. If he was hanged, who would look after Blackmoor Hall? Should he die without a son, the entire estate would pass to Wythe, and his cousin showed no aptitude for running his own life, let alone managing so much land, money and servants. Wythe could barely fulfill his duties as steward of the mine.

"Wythe would not make a proper lord," she murmured as if she were reading his mind.

"Wythe cares more for drinking and whoring than anything else," he agreed. "I would be letting down every Stanhope who came before me if I allowed Blackmoor Hall to pass to him."

"Then you must do everything in your power to avoid it."

But that meant he should be doing everything in his power to avoid *her*, because the more time he spent with Rachel, the less inclined he was to notice another woman.

Rachel was so sure it was the storm that disturbed her sleep, she almost rolled over and drifted off again. Rain slashed the windows and wind howled through the eaves but, despite the intense weather, she heard a far more subtle sound: a key, turning in the lock on her door.

At first, she thought the earl was coming in. He'd been awake when she left the study. But she couldn't figure out why he'd be entering from the hall. She almost called out his name, but a sense of foreboding snatched her words away. She didn't even have the chance to sit up before the hinges on the door whined.

Mouth dry, pulse racing, she blinked repeatedly, trying to make out the shape of her intruder. She wanted to believe it was Mary coming to avoid the dampness of the attic. But when a bolt of lightning zigzagged across the sky outside her window, she realized who her visitor was.

"Wythe?" she whispered.

He moved more quickly once he realized she was awake and knew he was there. "What you're trying to do will never work," he whispered harshly.

"I don't know what you're talking about." He was drunk again. She could smell the alcohol on him, remembered how he'd treated her that night she'd been coming up the road from Creswell. She hoped this wouldn't be a repeat performance.

"You think you can pretend to be a *lady*? That some coalminer's daughter can keep company with the Stanhopes?"

She drew the covers up under her chin. "You have no business here. Get out."

"Or what?" he taunted. "You'll call my cousin? Do you realize how easy it would be for me to break your neck? I could throw your body into the ocean and tell my dear cousin that you ran away in the night."

"Except I wouldn't believe you." The earl's voice shot through the darkness. It came from the far corner of the room, but Rachel couldn't see him.

"My lord?" she said.

"Go back to sleep, Rachel," he replied. "You have nothing to fear. I will walk Wythe to his own room. It appears that drink has gotten the best of his judgment once again."

At first Wythe seemed too stunned to speak. But he soon rallied. "You are making a mistake, Truman. She's a poor village girl, not worth what she will cost you."

"I will be the judge of that."

"But you're not thinking with the correct part of your anatomy. She will lead you right to the noose!" he responded and stormed out.

Rachel jumped when the door slammed, but only because she was on edge, not because she was still frightened.

"My lord?" she whispered to make sure *he* hadn't left too.

"I'm here."

"How did you know he would come?"

"I didn't," he said. "That's what worries me."

Before she could say more, the door opened and closed between their rooms and he was gone.

The next morning Rachel was almost sure she'd dreamt that incident in the night. She couldn't believe Wythe would threaten her *life*, whether he was drunk or not. She also couldn't believe that the earl had been in her bedroom. How long had he been sitting there? And why?

She planned to ask him the next time they were alone, but he didn't send for her that night or the next. He and Wythe seemed to be gone, possibly overnight. She listened for his return, especially late, when she typically heard him next door, but there was only the usual movements of the servants.

When the earl did reappear, his cousin wasn't with him—a fact that seemed of particular interest to Mrs. Poulson.

From where Rachel hovered at the top of the stairs, just out of sight, she heard the housekeeper ask after Mr. Stanhope. She also heard the earl reply that he was lodging with the Fore-Overman at Cosgrove House until he could bring his drinking under control.

"*You put your cousin out?*" the housekeeper asked in shock.

"I made it clear that his behavior needs to change," he responded and handed his coat to one of the footman.

"For *her* sake?"

Rachel didn't have to guess who Mrs. Poulson meant; she knew she was the subject of that question.

"For *his* sake," the earl replied and started up the stairs.

Rachel waited until he reached her. Then she stepped forward.

When he noticed her, he paused. "Let me see your hands," he said without preamble.

She held them out for his inspection.

"Better. Already. You are looking healthier every day."

"Thank you, my lord. But . . ."

His eyebrows slid up when she didn't finish.

"I do not want to be a problem for you."

A rare smile broke across his face as he fingered a lock of her hair. "*Be* a problem? Dear Rachel, you feel like the antidote."

Their eyes met for a second but then he pulled away. "If you will excuse me, I have a commitment in town and must change."

As soon as the earl left, Rachel pulled on a heavy cloak, slipped out the back and walked to town. It took over an hour to get there, which meant it would also take considerable time to get back. But she was desperate to accomplish two things: She wanted to pay Elspeth a visit, and she wanted to go to her former home and pick up the ledgers. Before her mother died, she'd seen for herself that the bookshop hadn't been making a profit. She'd been over and over the accounts. It was that one extra payment each month that had sustained them. So who'd been helping Jillian—and why? *Had she been receiving hush money?* Is that what that one payment had been?

If Rachel could determine that, maybe she could also learn enough about the mystery of Katherine's death to prove Lord Druridge wasn't responsible. She didn't want to do anything that might besmirch the memory of her dear mother, which was why she'd let the matter go until now. It was easier not to think about it, or to assume that mysterious income had no correlation to the fire. But if her parents had done something wrong, she didn't want to perpetuate their mistake. The memory of that argument between Lord Druridge and Mr. Linley had been wearing on her. She couldn't ignore what she'd discovered, not if it might stop an innocent man from being hanged.

Her errands were simple. She hoped they'd also be quick because she felt a deep sense of foreboding when she reached the edge of town. Other than her former neighbor, Mrs. Tate, she had no friends in Creswell. She hated the thought that she might run into the blacksmith's apprentice. Lord knew how much his opinion of her must've changed. She didn't want to see Mr. Cutberth either. Or anyone else. She no longer trusted them, and they no longer trusted her. When she'd proclaimed her innocence mere weeks ago, no one would believe her. Imagine what the villagers thought now, after hearing she'd been installed in the room adjoining Lord Druridge's. Her most recent accommodations would seem to suggest that they'd been right about her.

For all she knew, even Mrs. Tate had turned on her. Considering what the poor woman had probably been told, Rachel couldn't blame her.

Keeping her hood up and her head down, she blew out the lantern that had guided her steps so far. Any household facing the main thoroughfare had to put out a lamp from dark until eleven, so she no longer needed her own. She preferred to conserve her oil and stick to the shadows. Although it was dark, it wasn't late. She could easily encounter someone she'd rather avoid if she wasn't careful.

She could smell chimney smoke and food cooking, see light gleaming around the shutters of even those cottages that were off Creswell Proper, but as she made her way to her former home, the streets were, thankfully, quiet.

The shop had been locked with a heavy padlock and chain, and someone—the earl's solicitor?—had posted a notice that trespassers would be prosecuted. The sight of it looking so forbidding reminded her of how drastically her life had changed in the past month. But there was no time to dwell on her losses. At least Geordie was in an enviable situation.

Voices rose on the night air, coming from down the street. It sounded as if two men were walking her way, so she ducked into the alley. She had to go around to the house anyway.

The small, wooden cottage where she'd grown up was as dark and empty as the bookshop. The memory of returning, so recently, to find her mother dead made Rachel's breath catch as she stepped into the garden, but she pushed the pain aside. She'd come here for a reason; she couldn't think too much or she'd get nowhere.

She had the key out of her pocket, ready to open the front door, when she realized that a key wouldn't be necessary. The door wasn't latched, let alone locked. But that wasn't how she'd left it. The day the earl rescued her from the mine, he'd brought her home to pack a bag and collect her brother. She'd locked both the house and the shop. . . .

A prickle of unease crept up her spine. Someone had been here since. Was it Mrs. Tate on some innocent errand? Or was it a thief? Had someone stolen their simple furnishings, and what had been left of their candles and coal?

That was hard to believe of the high-minded people who'd turned on her. But she supposed anything was possible. Maybe her former friends thought she owed them whatever was left.

The door creaked as she pushed it wide. "Hello?"

She heard nothing in response. *No one's here*, she told herself—and yet she hesitated, too nervous and unsettled to go farther. She feared what she might find, but she'd stowed the ledgers under the loose floorboards in the bedroom. If she didn't get them now, maybe she never would.

Inside it was even darker than outside, but she didn't want to go to the time or trouble of relighting her lamp. She left it at the entry so she could grab it as she left and slipped into the main room. She should have been able to navigate such a familiar place with ease, but it no longer felt familiar. The smell—cold and damp without a fire for so long—wasn't even the same. She bumped into several objects that weren't where they were supposed to be before she managed to reach a window and open the shutters.

The moonlight that filtered through made it possible to see why she'd been having difficulty. *Nothing* was where it was supposed to be. The entire place had been ransacked.

Why? From what she could tell, nothing had been stolen—except, maybe, the ledgers. She'd hidden them in the bedroom, but she had no idea how thoroughly it had been searched, whether or not someone had found those loose floorboards.

Careful not to trip, she made her way to where she and her family had slept and opened the shutters in that room too. Someone had scattered and overturned everything here as well. Obviously whoever it was had gone through the whole house.

What had they been looking for?

She feared it was what she'd come to claim herself. Perhaps she'd been right to return. Perhaps the ledgers held some clue as to who had fired Blackmoor Hall—or at least could offer the earl proof that he hadn't done it himself.

The floorboards hadn't been disturbed, but her chest tightened in spite of that.

"What have I gotten myself into?" she murmured as she pried them up. She couldn't see inside the hole, but when she reached in, she felt the telltale bindings and let her breath go. "Thank God."

She was just climbing to her feet when she heard someone at the front door. A moment later, she saw a light. Whoever it was had a candle. She didn't want to be caught with the ledgers for fear they'd be taken from her, but there was no time to put them back.

Chapter 14

"Mrs. Tate! What are you doing here?"

Her neighbor nearly fainted. "Good Lord, child. Ye gave this old woman a start, that ye did. Why ye sneakin' around in the dark? An' where's Geordie?"

Rachel tucked the ledgers under her arm. "He's at Blackmoor Hall. Fortunately, he loves it there."

"And you? Do you like it too?"

For the most part, she did. She just wasn't as optimistic about the path it had put her on. "It keeps a roof over my head."

Eyes alight with curiosity, her neighbor's gaze shifted from the hole in the floor to what Rachel was carrying. "What ye got there?"

"Ledgers, for the shop. I . . . I shouldn't have left them behind. I need them to create the financial statements necessary to sell the business."

"Someone else is goin' ter come in an' run the shop?"

Feeling guilty for the lie, she gave a noncommittal shrug. "I hope so. If not, I'll have to sell the inventory, and the earl will have to lease the building to someone else."

"Ye've seen this." She lifted her candle higher and motioned around them. "Of course."

"They ransacked the shop too. Did a lot more damage there."

Rachel hated the thought of that. The shop had been her sanctuary for so many years, maybe even more so than this house, considering all the faraway places she'd visited via the books she'd read there. "How? There's a sturdy lock on the door. I saw it."

"On both doors," she volunteered. "They broke a window."

"When?"

"Only a day or two after ye left—as soon as they knew ye were gone. I tried to keep an eye on the place, but the buggers came at night. One morning, I noticed that the door was busted and walked in to find the damage." She heaved a sigh. "I would've sent word of it, but I didn't want to put any more on yer poor shoulders, not when there was nothin' that could be done. Do ye have any idea what they were lookin' for?"

"I can only guess it was Collingood, Thornick, Greenley and Henderson bent on revenge. The miners aren't very happy with me, as you know—those four in particular."

"I 'eard there was a misunderstandin' in the mine."

Rachel didn't correct her, didn't tell her that "misunderstanding" was clearly an attack. It wouldn't change anything. Why split her loyalties?

"An' what's 'appening with you must be a misunderstandin', too," she was saying. "That's what I keep tellin' myself—and them. I've told my own sons not to believe a single word. I've known ye since ye were born; ye've always been a good girl."

Homesick for the way things used to be, Rachel smiled. "Thank you for that."

A pained expression settled on her round face. "It's *not* true, is it? What they say about . . . about you and Lord Druridge?"

Rachel wished she could deny it, but she couldn't. Maybe she wasn't technically the earl's mistress, but she had been compromised, and ever since then her thoughts, where he was concerned, had been impure—far from what an innocent maid should be daydreaming about. "Yes."

"I can . . . I can understand a young girl gettin' bowled over by the attentions of such a . . . a remarkable man. But ye know 'e'll set ye aside eventually, Rachel. Ye 'ave to know that."

Everyone felt inclined to warn her. Warnings weren't necessary, however. No one understood the perils of her situation better than she did. "I do know, Mrs. Tate. But nothing has been simple since Mum died."

"Child, ye can come live with me if—"

"And have the whole village turn on you too? No. I won't hear of it. Geordie has a good position. I'll remain grateful for that and fare as best I can." Feeling pressure to reach Elspeth's so she could begin the long walk to her new home, she shifted the ledgers so she could give her neighbor a hug. "Thank you for all you have done for me and my family. Someday I hope to repay you. But for now . . . I must go."

She started to slip past, but Mrs. Tate caught her arm. "There's one more thing."

Rachel waited.

"I can't tell ye who did this. Like I said, I didn't find it until the followin' mornin'. But Rulon, my oldest, mentioned something curious to me."

"Curious?"

"Involving the earl's cousin and Jonas Cutberth. You know Jonas—"

"I do," she said, although she wished she didn't. He could've stood up for her, could've minimized the negative reaction that had essentially expelled her from her home, from all of Creswell. Instead, he'd treated her with as much disdain as anyone else, acted as if she'd never done anything for the miners or their cause. "What was so curious?"

"He thinks they're up to something . . . *secretive*, says they've been acting strange of late."

The edges of the books cut into her bicep, she gripped them so tightly. "In what way?"

"They're always having private conversations, he said, ones where they clam up as soon as they realize someone else is around."

What could that be about?

Rachel had no idea, but this was further proof that she should be leary of Cutberth. "Thank you," she said, her smile tight, and stepped out.

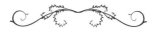

Elspeth refused to see Rachel, refused to so much as accept her letter. Rachel was so shocked that she could only gape at the girl who came to the small antechamber at the back door to give her word. She might've expected such a snub from any of the other villagers, but Elspeth? How could Elspeth judge her?

"Did she say why?" she asked as she stared at the envelope that had been thrust back into her hands.

The girl wouldn't quite meet her gaze. "I'm afraid she's very busy."

"But I said I'd wait—or return at a more convenient time."

"She doesn't want ye to wait. And she doesn't want ye to come back. She doesn't want ye 'ere at all."

"But if she'd only read my letter—"

"I told ye. She doesn't want that either."

"I see." It couldn't have been stated more clearly. Elspeth had joined the rest of Creswell and turned her back on Rachel.

With a nod, Rachel lit her lamp before recovering the ledgers she'd set aside.

Although impatient for her to be gone, the girl waited to see her off and, after glancing over one shoulder as if she feared someone might come upon them from inside the house at that moment, shoved another note into her hand.

"What's—" Rachel started, but the girl pressed a finger to her lips to indicate silence and opened the door for her to go.

Obviously, Rachel was to leave without a second's delay—and without another word.

Slipping the note into her pocket, she hugged the books against her body to help ward off the cold and started the long trek back.

She walked for at least a mile and didn't stop until she felt quite alone on the deserted road. Then she put down the lamp and the ledgers, opened the sealed envelope and read Elspeth's hastily scrawled message.

I do not have the answers you seek. Please stay away.

Elspeth wouldn't have been able to write a single word of that if Rachel hadn't taught her how. And now Elspeth was treating her like a pariah? It hardly seemed fair. But the fact that the town Madame, who had acted so knowledgeable and self-assured during Rachel's last visit, was now frightened told Rachel *something* had shifted since she'd gone to Blackmoor Hall. Elspeth felt threatened, or felt as if she would be threatened if it became known that she'd had any contact with Rachel.

Why? And of whom was Elspeth frightened?

A loud rumble caused her to scramble to retrieve what she'd left in the middle of the road. Fearing she might meet up with a dangerous stranger— or, worse, *Wythe*—she was about to duck into the woods. But when she looked behind, she saw that it was a fancy coach, no doubt the earl's, and simply stepped aside so she wouldn't be run down.

When the driver didn't slow the horses, Rachel assumed that Lord Druridge hadn't noticed her. Or, if he had seen her light, he didn't recognize who was carrying it. As the conveyance disappeared around the bend ahead, she almost wished she had made some attempt to gain his lordship's attention. The books were growing heavy; she was cold and had miles yet to walk.

Fortunately, she didn't have to regret her lack of action for very long. It was only a moment later when she heard the driver call out and could tell from the noise that he was bringing the carriage to a halt.

Lord Druridge opened the door as soon as she came around the bend. "Rachel? Is that you?"

"Aye, my lord." Relieved to have trusted company, she hurried to catch up.

"What are you doing out here alone? You must know it isn't safe."

Harnesses jingling, the horses stamped the ground. The driver seemed just as eager to continue. No doubt he was cold. But he said nothing.

"I had errands in the village, my lord." She didn't need to see Lord Druridge's face clearly to know he was scowling.

"I don't like the idea of you going to Creswell during the day, much less at night. Especially alone. Why didn't you alert me to your need?"

Because she hadn't been sure how much she wanted to tell him about the ledgers and Elspeth. Neither provided a great deal of hope, and yet . . . there were odd inconsistencies. "I didn't want to trouble you."

"I could've at least provided you with a horse. Get in, out of the cold."

At this, the driver scrambled down, took the ledgers and blew out her lantern for her while the earl extended his hand to help her up.

"You needed . . . *books?*" he asked when the driver handed them inside.

"They are the ledgers for the bookshop."

The conveyance swayed as Timothy climbed up and clucked to the horses. Then they jerked forward.

"Are you very disappointed about losing the shop?" the earl asked when they were underway.

"I am disappointed. But I don't blame *you* for what happened. There have been a lot of forces at play." Ironically enough with the exception of Mrs. Tate and possibly Mary, the earl had proven himself to be her only friend. "I'm grateful for how you have helped Geordie. He is better off than before."

"I wish the same could be said for you," he muttered. "I would offer to buy the business, Rachel, to hire you to run the bookshop for me, but I fear you will not be safe working in Creswell."

The possibility of returning to the familiar made her want to argue that she'd be fine. What if she could reclaim her independence? Managing the bookshop would be comfortable, and it would put an end to the constant temptation she faced when she was in such close proximity to him.

But she knew, after how she'd been received at Elspeth's, he was right. The miners were not ready to forgive her and would not welcome her back just yet—if ever.

So what was to become of her? She couldn't stay at Blackmoor Hall forever. As soon as the earl married, maybe even before, she would have to find a new home.

"I can't go back." She smiled when she said this, but it wasn't easy. The betrayal of the villagers stung, especially after how she'd tried to help them.

"What would you like to do with the inventory?" he asked. "I have had the place locked up, but I am not sure there is any point in letting it sit forever. I can't say when the climate in Creswell might change."

She could see the gleam of his eyes beneath his top hat. He was watching her as closely as he could in the dark. But she was grateful he couldn't see everything—like the tears that suddenly welled up. "There's not much inventory left, at least inventory that hasn't been destroyed."

He leaned forward. "What are you talking about?"

A lone tear rolled down her cheek, but she didn't wipe it for fear he'd notice. When she'd left the house, she'd surveyed the damage at the shop. "Someone broke a window, went in and spoiled everything. They broke open the door and did the same at my house."

Reaching across the distance between them, he clasped her gloved hands in his. "I'm sorry."

"It seems like *everything* has changed since my mother died. Those I called friends are now enemies. And those I called enemies . . ."

"Are now friends," he finished. "That is true. I will do all I can to figure out who is responsible for the damage and bring them to justice."

If she told him what she knew, she'd be taking yet another step away from her past, away from the person she used to be, and well she knew it. But that former Rachel seemed to be long gone anyway. If he was her friend, she was also his. "I think whoever it was might have had something to do with the fire, my lord."

"Because . . . ?"

"I believe I know what they were after."

"*What?*"

She felt his hands tighten on hers and wanted to remove her gloves so she could touch him, *really* touch him as she had when he brought the ointment. But she dared not be so forward.

Withdrawing instead, she lifted the ledgers she'd placed on the seat beside her and set them in his lap. "These."

"What are you saying?"

His manner reminded her of the earl as she used to view him. Haughty. Austere. But she knew it was the depth of his passion for this subject that put such an edge to his voice and she was no longer put off by that passion. "You have questioned my mother's finances."

"Yes."

"These ledgers prove the bookshop was not making enough of a profit to support us and hadn't for some time."

"So there *had* to be money coming in from somewhere else."

"There was a payment each month that is currently unaccounted for." She didn't want to believe her mother had any culpability in Katherine's murder, even if that culpability extended only so far as helping to cover it up, but she had to acknowledge the possibility. Considering the way Jillian had felt about Lord Druridge, she probably believed her actions were justified.

"Your mother might've been on the payroll of those who fired Blackmoor Hall," he said. "But you don't know who was paying her?"

"Although I have my suspicions, I can't say with any certainty."

"Whom do you suspect, dear Rachel?"

This was getting more difficult by the moment. Was she going to tell Lord Druridge about Mr. Cutberth and the union? If she brought up the clerk's name, the rest would come out as soon as the earl took a closer look at his bookkeeper. And what if Cutberth had nothing to do with the fire and really was worried about how Lord Druridge's efforts might interfere with meeting the miners' demands? She didn't want to erode what little power they'd gained. Their lives were hard enough.

But the earl was being blamed for something he didn't do and while the possibility of catching the real culprit existed, she had to tell all she knew.

"Mr. Cutberth has shown considerable interest in your affairs, my lord."

He straightened. "My *clerk*?"

"Yes."

"Do you think he was acting alone?"

"There could be others," she conceded. "Mrs. Tate just told me that her son believes Cutberth and your cousin are involved in something together."

"What makes him believe that?"

"He claims the two have been acting secretive."

"That could mean nothing. That could be mine business."

"I'm just relaying what she told me. But even if Wythe wasn't involved, wasn't somehow in it all along with Cutberth, I still doubt Cutberth would have acted alone. He's very quick-witted. He wouldn't be the type to set the fire himself."

"From what I know of Mr. Cutberth, I would have to agree with you there."

"I could be entirely wrong about him, my lord. I want you to understand that."

"Then why do you suspect him?"

"He has said some things that have made me wonder." She lowered her voice. "And this much I can be certain of: He is no friend of yours."

The earl massaged his left hand. "He pretends to be."

"Of course." He'd pretended to be her friend too when he was trying to enlist her help. "You provide his paycheck."

"I would never have taken Cutberth for a Judas."

"He can be convincing."

There was a slight pause. "I didn't realize you knew him."

"Creswell isn't that large, my lord. I know most people, especially those associated with the mine, seeing as my father and older brother both worked there for a number of years."

"I guess it makes sense, in one way. Cutberth would've known your father, would've been aware of his problems—that he was disgruntled and eager for revenge."

She smoothed her skirt. "He would have, yes."

"And if Jack were caught, a promise to care for his family might convince him to take the fall. If he escaped, he would have every reason to carry the secret to his grave."

"I have . . . considered that," she said. "As well as this: If he refused, Mr. Cutberth would know other men who might be willing to take his place."

His breath misted in the cold air, looking like smoke in the moonlight. "Did you ever see him at your house?"

"He was a familiar figure," she admitted. "But he didn't come only to see my father." She cleared her throat. Did she now also admit her own involvement? How could she not? "He was usually there to see me."

"Mr. Cutberth is married. He wasn't—"

"No." Now that she'd come this far, it was all she could do not to squirm in discomfort, because there was no going back. "We . . . we were working together."

"How? When? He didn't help run the bookshop."

"No." Gathering her courage, she blurted out what she'd been holding back. She couldn't point a finger at Mr. Cutberth without accepting responsibility for her own role as adversary to the earl's best interests. "We were trying to organize the miners into a union, my lord."

The silence that met this admission made Rachel feel as if the temperature had dropped twenty degrees.

"I see," he said at length.

She wondered if she'd upset him. "My brother died in a cave-in," she said softly. "My father died of miner's lung. Surely you can understand why I might act in such a fashion."

When he didn't respond, she wished she hadn't felt obligated to be quite so honest. But she couldn't work for and against both sides and continue to look herself in the mirror.

"Is that all you've got to tell me?" he asked.

"Yes, except . . . Elspeth might know more—a lot more."

He'd turned his head to look out at the dark night, but at this, his attention shifted to her. "I have questioned Elspeth on a number of occasions. She has assured me she knows nothing."

"She once indicated the opposite to me, my lord, but that could've been mere posturing. Tonight when I tried to see her, she refused to give me an audience. She wouldn't even accept a letter." She handed him the note she'd written, begging Elspeth to come forward for the sake of saving an innocent man.

"You've become too closely associated with me."

When she said nothing, they lapsed into silence for the duration of the ride. The reminder of their different lives and different roles had cast a pall across their time together. In the face of that, they could no longer pretend to have found common ground.

Once they arrived at the manse, Linley met them at the door.

"Hello, my lord. I trust you had a . . . rewarding evening."

Lord Druridge scarcely answered. He certainly said nothing that gave away where he'd been. He'd given no indication while they were on the road either. But Rachel couldn't help wondering. Unless he was traveling to London or somewhere else, he didn't go out much at night. Of all the earl's estates, Blackmoor Hall was the most remote but seemed to be the one he preferred.

"Miss Rachel, how good to see you."

Linley's smile eased some of her misgivings. After what she'd revealed, the earl was treating her politely but distantly. She didn't get the impression he was angry at her, just doing his best to cope with the stark realities of what he was up against.

She relinquished her cloak into the butler's care because he offered to take it and she thought it would be impolite to refuse. But she was painfully aware of the fact that she had no right to be treated like a member of the gentry. That she could see Mrs. Poulson standing off to one side, watching, made her especially self-conscious.

"Goodnight, Mr. Linley." She dipped into a curtsy for Lord Druridge. "Goodnight, my lord. I-I'm sorry if I've . . . displeased you."

"Rachel."

When the earl called her name, she hadn't quite reached the stairs. "Yes?"

"I have something I want to show you."

The imperious note was back in his voice. She welcomed it because she hated the thought that, with her confession, she might've lost some of his respect or his regard. "What is that, my lord?"

"You'll see. It's in the far wing. If you will do me the favor of accompanying me there."

He didn't act as if she had much of a choice. "Of course."

The earl squeezed Linley's shoulder. "You look spent," he murmured. "I suggest you retire."

"I'm afraid I'm not as young as I used to be," the butler joked.

"Get some rest."

There was genuine affection in this exchange, making it plain that Lord Druridge cared a great deal for Linley.

"As you wish, my lord."

Catching Rachel's eye, the earl gestured to the stairs. "Shall we?"

She followed him to his study, where he lit the lamp he carried with them to the farthest reaches of the manse. They entered a wing that had been closed off and passed room after room, none of which had been occupied for some time. Many weren't even furnished. Others were draped.

"There used to be so much in this part of the house," he commented as they walked. "The cradle, from when I was a child—*all* my childhood belongings, really. Family heirlooms. Gifts and keepsakes from centuries back. Extra furniture."

"The fire took it."

A muscle moved in his cheek. "Yes. The wind carried the flames to this wing. It was the one that was most damaged."

The corridor stretched far beyond the reach of the lamp. She'd never even been asked to clean here. As far as she knew, no one visited this part of the house. "So what are you taking me to see?"

"Do you remember me telling you about the painter Pieter Bruegel?"

Wishing she'd kept her cloak on, she rubbed her arms. "Yes, although I still don't understand his relevance to the past."

"I asked you why Cutberth might want to fire Blackmoor Hall."

"Yes, and I had no answer."

"*This* might be the answer," he said and stopped at a door with a double lock.

Rachel had never seen a Pieter Bruegel painting, so she could shed no new light on the situation. But once Lord Druridge told her about his father's collection and how it might've been stolen—the fire set to hide the theft—she felt new hope. If the earl could prove the paintings hadn't been destroyed in the fire, he could clear his name *and* his conscience. And the scenario he presented sounded plausible. The amount of money to be gained from the sale of such rare art would provide Cutberth—or anyone else—with plenty of incentive.

Maybe the union organizer wasn't the selfless individual he'd always portrayed himself to be. Maybe he'd been hoping to get rich off Truman Stanhope and had carefully planned out the method he would use. It seemed more likely that Cutberth would be responsible than Wythe, since Wythe had saved Truman's life despite the fact that he had so much to gain from his death.

But when Lord Druridge told her he'd already been looking for several weeks and hadn't found anything, her hope dwindled again. Without at least one of the paintings, he had nothing solid to rely on, no evidence to protect him should his late wife's family gain the upper hand—only a vague memory, and even he didn't seem convinced that memory was reliable.

"So you will marry the duke's daughter," she said as matter-of-factly as possible. "If that doesn't save you from criminal prosecution, it will at least buy more time."

He stared down at the letter she'd given him in the carriage, what she'd written to Elspeth, pleading on his behalf. "Is that what you want me to do?"

It was the *last* thing she wanted. But what else could she say? She would never encourage him to risk the noose. Besides, as much as she preferred to ignore it, the odd feeling from the carriage persisted, despite what she'd read in his letter. "I understand the plight of my class; you understand the plight of yours."

"Meaning . . . ?"

"I have worked to create a union among the miners, something that is in the best interest of who I am and who I know and love. You will marry strategically, for the same reasons. We were born into separate worlds, you and I."

"But do we have to remain in those worlds?" He put down the lamp and the letter and gripped her shoulders as if he'd shake the answer he wanted out of her. But she wasn't even sure what that answer would be. What if she were to tell him she'd fallen in love with him? That she thought of him constantly?

"Is there no place to meet in the middle?" he asked. "The colliery doesn't mean everything to me. Must that stand between us?"

When his gaze dipped to her mouth, Rachel's pulse spiked. Would he kiss her? She wanted him to. But there was too much at stake. If she really cared about him, she would insist he do what was best and safest. "Not without a great deal of sacrifice, my lord. And I fear it would be *your* sacrifice far more than it would be mine."

His jaw hardened. "Only because you have already paid the price."

"We have nothing to mourn. A person in your position and a person in mine . . . we wouldn't have a chance, regardless." Forcing herself to step away, Rachel took another look at *Peasant Wedding Feast.* "I hope you can find what's missing."

When she glanced back at him, a sad smile curved his lips. "I fear, if I lose you, I never will."

Chapter 15

Once he saw Rachel to her room, Truman went to his study, where he sat at his desk and attempted to pen a letter. The account books she'd given him sat at his elbow. He planned to go through them and see what he could find. But he'd had a meeting earlier in the evening, at a tavern outside of Newcastle, where the duke's solicitor had given him an ultimatum. He needed to respond to that first.

But what would he say? He'd been mulling that over almost the whole ride back to Blackmoor Hall and still he had no answer.

"M'lord?"

Startled by the intrusion, he glanced up. With his head in his hands, he'd been so deep in thought he hadn't heard the door. "Linley. I thought you'd gone to bed. What are you doing?"

"I couldn't rest until I'd had the chance to speak to you."

Truman rubbed his face. "Of course. I should've realized you'd be worried."

Once the workday was through, Linley had taken to using a cane. An old wound, from when he'd been thrown from a horse as a child, kept acting up. Leaning more heavily on it than usual, he came farther inside and closed the door. "Did you meet him?"

"I did."

"What did he say?"

The terseness of the letter that'd arrived two days ago, requesting the meeting, had prepared Truman. His time with the duke's man of business hadn't lasted long, but it had been every bit as tense as Truman had anticipated. "It was as we thought."

"His Grace has heard about Rachel."

"Yes. The gossips wasted no time."

"We knew they wouldn't. They never do." Linley's cane hit the hardwood floor until the rug swallowed the sound.

"He finds it an embarrassment, of course."

"That comes as no surprise, but"—Linley's expression grew pained—"is it enough of an embarrassment that he has rescinded his offer?"

"Not yet. He has given me a choice."

"Find another situation for Rachel or forget about marrying Lady Penelope."

"Yes." Truman pushed away from his desk so he could stretch his legs.

The pitch of his butler's voice shifted to one of entreaty. "My lord, I realize you have endured a great deal—"

Truman lifted a hand to silence him. "Don't patronize me, Linley. I can't bear it, least of all from you."

"Then I shall speak bluntly."

"Why not? You usually do."

They both chuckled.

"Your welfare means a great deal to me," Linley admitted. "In my old age, it is almost all I care about."

"Then say what's on your mind, old friend."

"Don't do anything to risk the wedding. Think of all you stand to lose if the duke withdraws his patronage."

It wasn't what *he* stood to lose that bothered Truman. It was the thought of disappointing his parents, as well as all the other Stanhopes who'd come before him. It was *failing*. Somehow, that was worse than death. "I will take your advice into consideration."

"You can't hope to arrange a more favorable match, my lord. No one else—at least no one who holds such power—would even consider . . . "

When his words fell off, Truman finished for him. "Marrying his daughter off to a man suspected of murdering his first wife?"

"That's stating it even more bluntly than I would have, but . . . yes."

Truman trimmed the lamp on his desk. "The duke's man of business stated it similarly."

"Did he? And what did you say in response?"

"I held my temper, in case you're wondering." Even though it galled him to have anyone, even a duke, attempt to tell him what to do. He had more land and other holdings than the Duke of Pembroke, had never had to worry about anyone's "patronage" before. Were it not for Katherine, he could take his pick of brides.

"A wise decision."

"His man is awaiting my response at the tavern right now."

"He will carry it back?"

"Yes."

Linley indicated the blank sheet of paper on his blotter. "What will you tell the duke, then?"

Truman knew what he had to say but couldn't seem to make the commitment, couldn't bring himself to send Rachel elsewhere. "It's not that I find Lady Penelope too objectionable."

Linley propped his hands on his cane. "She's nothing like Lady Katherine. A small consolation, perhaps, but there is that."

"Yes, there is that." Penelope didn't come off as spoiled and vindictive. But she didn't possess Rachel's keen mind, strong values, or fighting spirit, either. "She almost has the opposite problem," Truman grumbled, stretching the muscles in his back. "She's *so* blasé I wonder if she isn't a bit daft."

Linley didn't like that statement, probably because he didn't want to acknowledge the truth of it. "I wouldn't go quite so far, my lord."

Truman rolled his eyes. "Of course not. You want me to make the match. But *something* has to be wrong with her. Otherwise, His Grace would have promised her to someone else, someone who isn't in the midst of such scandal."

"Maybe not. His Grace was a good friend of your father's. He has always been partial to you."

Which is why Truman felt an added obligation. He wanted to remain true to his legacy. To do as his parents would wish. To fulfill what he'd always perceived as his destiny.

He'd just never expected his heart to put up such a fight. "I know."

"At least you like Penelope's family."

"There's little question I prefer them to the Abbotts." Truman studied Katherine's portrait. "Linley?"

His butler followed his gaze. "Yes?"

"Could you imagine Jonas Cutberth having anything to do with the fire?"

"*Jonas?* I hope not. I've always held him in high regard. He's been the clerk for Stanhope & Co. for . . . more than a decade."

"And, according to my steward, he's very efficient."

"Not that the same could be said for your steward."

Truman allowed himself a wry smile. Linley rarely spoke ill of anyone, but he had little good to say about Wythe. "Which is why I appointed him steward over the mine instead of any of my other holdings. At least having him close means I can keep an eye on him."

"A wise choice on your part, I must say."

"But be that as it may . . . could you see either man being tempted into a plot to steal rare paintings?"

"You're asking about Wythe, too?"

Until now, Truman had been careful not to mention his doubts about his cousin to anybody, including his beloved butler. He had no proof to back up his suspicion, no reason to cause Linley to dislike Wythe any more than he already did. But he needed to voice his concerns to someone, needed to hear whether he was losing his mind. "Yes."

"Cutberth has the brains to be able to mastermind such an elaborate plan, but I can't imagine he has the heart for it."

"And Wythe?"

He sighed. "I would say the opposite is true for Wythe, my lord."

This time, Truman laughed out loud. "We seem to be of the same mind."

Linley used his cane to help heave the bulk of his weight forward. "Why do you ask? Has someone suggested that either man might be responsible for Katherine's death?"

"Rachel did." And Truman thought there might be something in the account books to support it.

He pursed his lips. "So she knows details of the fire, after all."

"Largely that Cutberth is no friend to me. He's secretly been trying to form a union at the mine."

Linley rocked back. "Not Cutberth. He makes a fine living. Why would he sow seeds of contention?"

"Empathy would probably be the noblest of the reasons I could name. Gaining power and influence among his peers would be the least."

"But you can't discount the possibility."

"No."

He managed, with some difficulty, to get to his feet. "How does Rachel know his business?"

She'd supported him, worked with him and admitted as much. But Truman was too protective of her to mention it. "He's been to her house."

"On union business?"

"Yes. I'm sure her father was more than willing to join his efforts."

"That hardly seems loyal of Mr. Cutberth, my lord." Linley came forward. "What are you going to do?"

"What I've been planning to do for some time. I'll increase wages across the board—for everyone except Cutberth. I can't bring myself to reward his duplicity, not when I already pay him more than he'd be making anywhere else."

"Are you sure you want to give in that easily? Won't that set a bad precedent?"

"It's a bad precedent that I want to be fair? I don't see how. The price of coal is up. I was already thinking about instituting a profit-sharing program. I talked to Wythe about it months ago."

Linley grimaced. "I can guess what he had to say. He told you that you don't know the character of the men. That if you give them more money, they'll just spend it on drink. Am I right?"

"He didn't like the idea, but I will make sure he understands I am no longer leaving the matter in his hands."

Linley adjusted his jacket. "One thing . . . what happens when the price of coal goes down? How do you take that money away once you've given it?"

"It won't be a decision I make. There will simply be less profit to share, and Cutberth's own records will attest to that. I don't run the market."

"More's the pity." He nodded in satisfaction. "I doubt anyone could quarrel with such an offer. There will be no reason to fight for what they're already getting. And they'll continue to produce or there will be no extra income for anyone."

"That's the way I see it."

"It's brilliant. A model I hope others will copy." He cleared his throat. "But if you will allow me to return to what you told me a moment ago."

Truman dipped his head.

"What was it that made Rachel connect Cutberth to what happened here two years ago?"

Truman showed him the ledgers and explained what Rachel had told him, including what she'd said about Elspeth.

"Good luck getting anything out of *her*," Linley said.

"Maybe Wythe can do it."

"If only we could trust Wythe."

"If only we could find one of those damn paintings!"

Linley tapped the desk. "We'll have plenty of time to look once you write that letter. I wouldn't want the duke's emissary to leave without it."

"You want me to marry *another* woman I don't love."

"You have to marry someone, my lord, someone with a proper lineage and connections. You need an heir."

But no matter whom he married, he'd never be able to forget the bookseller's daughter. No woman had ever stirred his blood the way she did. He wished she was waiting in his bed right now. "And Rachel? Would you have me send her to a city where she knows no one?"

"I like her, my lord. I do. But she would be as out of place in your world as you would be in hers."

Truman groaned in frustration. "This bit about worlds again."

"Excuse me?"

"Never mind. Just make some inquiries, Linley. Help me find the perfect place for her."

"I will."

"Thank you."

His butler hesitated at the door. "You could always subsidize her income, you know—if it would make you feel better."

Truman pictured Rachel's face, the intensity of her expression when she told him he would have to sacrifice too much to be with her. "I will happily provide for her—if only she will allow it."

"She wouldn't have to know it was coming from you."

"Rachel is not so easily fooled." He smiled at how handily she could beat him at chess and how clever she was generally.

"What kind of position should I seek for her?" Linley asked, his hand on the knob.

"One where it appears as if she's earning as much as she makes."

"So you've made your decision."

What good would it do anyone if he died in ignominy?

"I have an entire dynasty to protect. Did I ever really have a choice?" he replied and dipped his pen in ink.

Rachel could sense the earl's presence. He was in her room, over near the window, where he'd been the night Wythe paid her a visit.

Pushing her heavy eyelids up, she searched that corner, trying to make out his general shape, but there was no moon tonight. She could see nothing.

"My lord?" she whispered.

"I've disturbed you," he said. "I'm sorry."

Now that she was awake, she could smell a hint of the tobacco he smoked in his pipe. That must've been what gave his presence away, because he'd made no sound. "Is something wrong?"

"No, go back to sleep." He started to leave as if he regretted ever coming in, but she called him back.

"Wait."

He turned. "Yes?"

"Something's changed. I can tell. What is it?"

"I searched the ledgers, Rachel. There is nothing in there that will benefit me, just the tantalizing clue of that extra payment."

"At least we have proof of that." She hesitated. "Is that all?"

"No. I just wrote a letter to the Duke of Pembroke."

"Making the commitment?"

"Yes."

There was conviction in his voice she hadn't heard there before.

She hated the thought of him being with anyone else, and yet she couldn't fault him for taking the prudent course, the course she felt he should take. "When?"

"We haven't set a date. The duke has demanded that I make other arrangements for you first."

She squeezed her forehead. She'd known this was coming but . . . so soon? "I see." She swallowed hard. "Will I be taking Geordie with me?"

"If you wish. I would never attempt to deprive you of your brother, of anything," he added.

"How long do we have before—"

"Maybe a fortnight, just enough time to make inquiries."

"You're thinking I should go to London?"

"That would probably provide you with the most opportunity."

She tried to imagine herself in a bustling metropolis and couldn't. She'd heard and read about London but had never been there. She hadn't been much farther than Newcastle. "I would rather Geordie stay here if . . . if at all possible. He's only just settled in, and he likes it so much." She forced a smile even though he couldn't see it. "Where else will he find a mentor like Mr. Grude?"

"Then I will respect your wishes, of course. And I will take care of him—I promise you that."

She allowed her smile to fade. "Thank you."

He spoke again once he was standing in the threshold of the door between their rooms. "I wish. . . ."

"Yes?"

"I wish things could be different, Rachel."

It wasn't easy to withstand the ache in her chest. She would never meet anyone else like him—and would measure every man against him. "That's enough for me."

"If only wishing were enough for me," he said and left.

Rachel lay awake, listening to the noises she heard next door. The floor creaked. Something clanged as if the earl had thrown it. After an hour or so everything went quiet, but at that point Rachel couldn't remain in bed any longer. They had a fortnight, maybe three weeks, at most. She had to be with him while she could.

Truman had just gone to bed when he heard the door open. He knew it was Rachel. The sound hadn't come from the hall. He waited, wondering what she would do. Part of him hoped she'd change her mind and return to her own bed without engaging him—because if she'd come for the reason he guessed, he wouldn't be able to refuse her.

"My lord?"

"Rachel . . ." He told himself to send her back to her room while he could think straight, but the only thing he got out was her name.

"The last time we were together, I . . . I wasn't as aware of what was happening as I wish I would've been."

He could hardly hear above the racket of his heart. "You realize what you're saying."

"You can't offer me anything. I accept that. I just . . . I don't want that single memory to be the only one I take with me."

"If only I had the strength to make myself tell you to leave. This isn't fair to you."

"There's no way to preserve my honor when the rest of the world thinks we're lovers already."

"*You* know better. That's what counts."

"I'm not sure it does, not if I'm spreading my legs for you every night in my dreams," she said and her nightdress hit the floor with a soft *poof*.

Chapter 16

Truman knew he was only making their eventual parting more painful, but he couldn't deny himself this one night. Not when she wanted him as badly as he wanted her. Not when she was standing at his bedside already naked.

"I can barely breathe," she murmured as he reached for her.

He groaned as her bare skin came into contact with his. "I'm almost afraid to believe this is real," he responded and dipped his head to kiss her.

Her lips were warm and pliable. He could tell, as he had before, that she had little experience with men. There was nothing practiced or calculated about her actions. But he was pretty sure that was what he loved most: her emotional honesty, her lack of artifice. Katherine had behaved as if she were putting on a performance and expected him to be grateful for the sacrifice and effort it required. She'd never really seemed to *feel* anything.

Rachel was just the opposite.

"You taste like heaven," he told her. "How I have longed to be with you like this, to feel welcome to touch you, to taste you."

Her fingers slipped into his hair. She seemed eager to explore him, even the parts he wouldn't expect her to be particularly interested in at the moment.

"I've heard it said that a pious woman, a good woman, is not supposed to enjoy what goes on between a man and a woman," she said, kissing his brow, his cheeks, anything she could reach.

He was too wrapped up to do much talking, but this succeeded in gaining his attention. "Who told you that?" he murmured against her lips when they found his mouth.

"My mother."

That didn't say much about her father, but he didn't point it out. "Do you believe it?"

Closing her eyes, she rubbed her cheek against his, driving him mad with the satiny feel of her skin and clean, sweet smell of her. "I don't know. But if it is true, I'm more like Elspeth's girls than I once thought."

He couldn't help smiling at her words, at her innocent attempts to become familiar with his body as her hands moved over his chest before circling around to his back.

"You like this?" He ran a hand down over her breast, cupping it in his palm.

Her tongue quickly wet her lips. "Too much. More than I should. I'm lost," she finished simply.

With a laugh he buried his face in her neck. "No more lost than I am, dear Rachel. You have me so excited I fear I will embarrass myself."

She caught his face between her hands. "How?"

He laughed again. "I hope you don't have to find out, but just touching you here"—his finger touched the tip of one nipple—"and here"—his other hand slid down her stomach toward her core, where he wanted to touch her most—"makes me tremble with need."

Her teeth nipped at his bottom lip. "Your heart is racing, my lord. Like mine."

"Probably faster," he conceded, meeting her tongue with his own as he took her mouth the way he intended to take her body.

She gasped as his fingers finally found the most sensitive part of her. "The compulsion to feel you inside me is"—she had to take a breath—"overwhelming."

Kissing her even deeper, he slid a finger into the warmth that awaited him. When she gasped and arched as if she'd take more, take all of him, he feared he'd lose control.

"Ah, Rachel, you have created such desperate urgency." He felt like a schoolboy, not a man who'd been married and even fathered a child.

She held his hand in place as if she feared he might remove it. "I love you," she said. "I think I have loved you since you walked into my shop that day."

Those words sucked the air out of him, made him realize that he couldn't take what he was about to take. He had no right. She was giving everything—her body, her heart—and he was sending her away within a fortnight.

"Dear God," he muttered and dropped onto the mattress beside her.

"What is it?" She sounded confused. "What's wrong?"

He lifted his head so he could see her in what was left of the firelight. "I can't go on. There is no honor in this. What if you were to get pregnant?"

"I don't know. We-we would each do our part? You would pay for the child. And-and I would raise him?" She slid her small hand around his erection, causing every muscle to tighten in need.

He stopped her before she drove him beyond his ability to resist. "*Where? I could never let you go to London knowing you were carrying my child. Yet I couldn't expect my wife to tolerate having you here, knowing that I will probably never want her as I want you."

She froze for several seconds, then pulled out of his grasp. "I'm sorry. I shouldn't have come." Yanking the bedsheet up to hide her nudity, she leaned up, probably to search for her nightdress. But he tugged that thin covering back down. "No, let me look at you," he said. "Let me memorize every detail."

He'd said he was only going to look, but he couldn't help touching her too. As he ran his hands over her soft skin, her eyes grew heavy lidded, her lips parted and her nipples grew taut.

Unwilling to leave her so aroused, he nudged her knees apart and began to kiss every place that he'd touched.

"My lord, what are you doing?" She was obviously shocked, but he'd expected that reaction. He heard her catch her breath as he moved lower, and once he found what he was looking for, she anchored her hands in his hair as if she could scarcely let go. "Oh my!"

"There are ways to . . . minimize the risk," he explained, closing his eyes and nuzzling her as he took in the musky scent.

"But . . . it's unnatural, is it not?" she whispered. "Surely I'll go to hell."

"After what you've been through, I doubt a benevolent God could begrudge you this small pleasure," he said and hooked his arms beneath her knees so that she wouldn't wiggle away before he could show her what she'd been missing.

Rachel had never felt more wanton. Not only was she moaning and writhing, thanks to the earl's ministrations, she couldn't help crying out as he brought her to the very pinnacle of pleasure. But that moment was unlike anything she had ever known! And even though, in some dark recess of her mind, she feared she might be embarrassed by her behavior later, he seemed to enjoy her lack of control. He seemed to encourage it, to *thrive* on it.

"Again," he breathed, almost before the spasms could subside, and she felt the warmth of his mouth and the pressure of that suction drawing the pleasure back, carrying her higher. This time he seemed more possessive than before. He claimed her as if he had every right, as if she belonged to him, and sent her spiraling right back into ecstasy. But as good as it was, she craved more than what he was giving her, wanted him to join with her.

Drowning in both need and sensation, she gasped his name and that seemed to snap his restraint. With a growl, he covered her as if he would have her, as if he could no longer deny himself, *whatever* the cost. Sliding his hands beneath her again, he tilted her hips up to receive him—was only a fraction of an inch away from pushing inside her—when he cursed and buried his face in her neck instead.

"Do it," she urged as her hands gripped his buttocks. "Now."

He answered with a groan of frustration. "I can't." The words sounded harsh in her ear but she understood the purity of the intent behind them. "I will not let you take such a risk, not when I can't give you more than . . . than this."

Knowing what it cost him to make such a sacrifice, she clung to him until the intensity of the moment subsided. Then she thought she should leave. She guessed it might make his recovery easier. But every time she tried to get up, he pulled her back into the warmth of his bed and his embrace and told her not to go quite yet.

"You'll only drive yourself mad," she told him, but eventually the tension in his body eased, and he fell so deeply asleep she didn't want to move for fear she would disturb him.

She could have nodded off too. She'd been up most of the night. But she didn't want to waste one second of their time together. Knowing she might never have this opportunity again, she was far happier watching him sleep.

She must've succumbed to exhaustion at some point, however, because the next thing she knew it was morning, and the sun seemed especially bright. When she felt the earl stir, she couldn't help wondering how he was going to react to what they'd done—and what they hadn't done. But she never got the chance to find out. Someone startled them both by banging on the door.

"My lord, Mr. Linley asked me to bring you word that he has fetched Mr. Tyndale from the mine, as you required. They are in the parlor."

Cringing at the sound of the housekeeper's voice, Rachel dared not move for fear she'd give her presence away.

The earl seemed far less fearful, of course. He rubbed his face and yawned before opening his eyes. "Thank you for alerting me," he said. "I'll be right down."

When Mrs. Poulson's steps faded, Rachel hopped out of bed. "I'm sorry. I-I fell asleep."

He watched her pull on her nightdress and head to her own room.

"You will sleep in my bed from now on," he told her before she could reach the door.

She gaped at him. "Don't you think that will be . . . tempting fate?"

His gaze felt like a caress when it fell to her breasts, and that caused a corresponding tingle.

"I will have as much of you as I can—while I can," he said simply.

Her body grew warm, as if he were already touching her. "Yes, my lord."

"And if I choose to give you gifts, to . . . do what I can, you will take what I offer, regardless of the cost."

She felt her face heat as he got up, completely naked, in front of her. A respectable woman would glance away, but she'd grown brazen overnight. Remembering every kiss, every touch, she made no effort to hide the admiration or the longing that had brought her to his bed in the first place. "Don't bother giving me expensive baubles, my lord. You are the only thing that matters to me," she told him and fled.

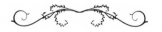

After being singularly devoted to finding Katherine's killer for the past two years, unable to think of anything else, Truman couldn't concentrate on his conversation with Mr. Tyndale. Maybe he'd been dealing with the mystery for too long, had begun to despair of *ever* finding the answers he sought, but his heart wasn't into yet another interview, even after what Rachel had told him about Wythe and Cutberth acting "secretive." That could be nothing, so what would he find that he hadn't found already? He'd followed up on so many false leads—and this one didn't seem to hold much promise. Maybe Cutberth had played him false by trying to start a union behind his back, but that didn't make him a thief. If he'd sold the Bruegel paintings, where was the money? Why was he still working at the mine?

Linley, sensing his distraction and probably attributing it to his having just got out of bed, took the lead, which allowed Truman to stand off to one side and gaze out the window as his mind wandered back to what had so recently transpired in his bedroom.

I love you. I think I've loved you since that day in the shop.

He'd made a mistake allowing Rachel into his bed last night. After what she'd been through, of course she felt like she loved him. He was the only stable thing in her world right now. He should never have given those emotions a physical aspect, should never have taken advantage of her innocence.

But she created such hunger in him. Even now, he felt a certain amount of frustration that he hadn't been able to completely possess her since that one brief encounter—when her virginity had come as such a shock. He couldn't give her up too soon, *wouldn't* give her up.

"I-I haven't noticed anything strange, Mr. Linley," Tyndale said. "Mr. Wythe seems quite satisfied with Mr. Cutberth's work."

Mention of his cousin finally drew Truman's attention to the conversation, especially when Linley, looking somewhat ill at ease, cleared his throat. "I'm not asking how Mr. Stanhope feels about Mr. Cutberth," Linley explained. "I'm asking what *you* think."

"*Me?* But I'm just the Fore-Overman. Surely the steward would be better able to assess Mr. Cutberth's performance, given he deals with him on a more regular basis."

"You work out of the same office, do you not?" Linley asked.

He twisted his hat in his lap. "Yes, sir."

"I would say you have had more than enough opportunity to observe how he behaves, who he talks to, when he comes and goes."

"Indeed, but . . ." Tyndale's words dwindled off as he glanced toward the door.

Giving up his vigil at the window, Truman turned and stepped closer to him. "Is something wrong, Mr. Tyndale?"

"No! No, of course not."

"I assure you that we are quite alone. As you know, Wythe is now living with you."

"I wasn't expecting to see Mr. Stanhope."

"Who then? You seem concerned that you might be overheard."

He adjusted his waistcoat. "Not really, sir. I just . . . I wondered if Mrs. Poulson was about. That's all."

"My housekeeper."

"Yes. She visits us quite regularly, you know."

"I see. And she carries tales of what's going on at Blackmoor Hall, does she?"

When he didn't answer, Truman knew it was true. He should've been able to guess she would. Mrs. Poulson had always been devoted to Wythe, had been supremely unhappy when he'd had Wythe move to Cosgrove House.

It made Truman uneasy to have such a high-level servant so devoutly loyal to someone else. He would like to be able to rely on his own staff. But Wythe *had* saved his life. Truman couldn't be thankless enough to sack Poulson.

Mr. Tyndale lowered his voice. "They seem to be . . . *close*."

"Indeed." Truman gestured toward the door. "Mr. Linley, would you please find Mrs. Poulson and keep her occupied while I have a word with Mr. Tyndale?"

"Certainly." Linley nodded to the Fore-Overman before he left.

"Now you can rest assured," Truman said once the door was closed. "Tell me, has my housekeeper done something to upset you?"

"No."

"Mr. Tyndale?"

"She has a sharp tongue, my lord."

It was easy to tell the Fore-Overman didn't appreciate being in his current position. "Meaning?"

"She has quite a bit to say about Miss McTavish."

"And you find that . . . offensive?"

"I've always had a soft spot for Rachel," he admitted. "I knew her father, of course. He was rough around the edges. I'll give you that. But he wasn't always so bad, not before life got the best of him. In the end I felt sorry for him. And I feel even sorrier for his daughter. The poor girl has had a hard life."

That was a lot of words for a man like Tyndale. "Yet you assigned her to Number 14 Stall when she applied to you for work."

"Mr. Stanhope may have indicated that was my doing, but it wasn't. I would never have put her in the mine with the men."

"Did you try to persuade my cousin to do otherwise?"

He sat up taller. "Indeed I did. I don't want to risk my job by saying anything . . . unflattering about Mr. Stanhope, but the truth is the truth."

"Nothing you say here will risk your job, Mr. Tyndale. I commend you for trying to protect Miss McTavish."

"Thank you, my lord." He seemed slightly mollified. "As I have indicated, I care about the girl. I can't help but take exception to what Mrs. Poulson has to say about her."

"But Mrs. Poulson is no real threat to Rachel."

"Make no mistake, she wants her gone and plans to throw her out as soon as . . . as soon as . . ." He couldn't quite spit out the rest.

"I tire of her?"

He flushed. "Those were her words, yes. But no matter what folks think of Miss McTavish, what *you* may think of her, I can't hold her accountable for the decisions she's made since her mum died. When it comes to taking care of Geordie, she'd do anything. I-I saw that firsthand when she came to my office to sue for work."

Truman liked Tyndale, respected him. "Don't worry about Miss McTavish. I will take care of her."

He sniffed, obviously surprised by the commitment. "Thank you. Truly. I am grateful for any help you can give her."

"Back to Cutberth, then."

From what Truman could tell, Tyndale didn't completely relax, but he came off a little more confident.

"Has he been derelict in his duty, my lord?"

"Not quite in the way you might think. I've heard he's trying to start up a union. Is that true?"

Tyndale seemed shocked. "I couldn't say, my lord. But other than you, and Mr. Stanhope, I fear I would be the last person he'd include in such plans."

"So all seems as it's always been at the colliery?"

"At the colliery, yes. But"—he paused before continuing—"there have been some surprising developments in Mr. Cutberth's personal life."

"What kind of developments?"

Again Tyndale jerked on the bottom of his waistcoat. He was attempting to straighten it, but he was too overweight to make it lie flat. "You haven't heard?"

"I have no idea what you're talking about."

"Mrs. Cutberth came to the office last week, almost in hysterics. She had a pack of letters she claimed she found hidden amongst his belongings."

"And what did those letters signify?"

"They must've been love letters of some sort because she accused him of . . . of being unfaithful."

While he couldn't admire a man who would betray his wife, Truman hardly felt as though he was in a position to judge, given that he was currently embroiled in a less-than-ideal situation himself. But he had never broken his marriage vows. At least he could say that. "Something gossipmongers would find interesting," he said. "But what does Mr. Cutberth's personal life have to do with me?"

Mr. Tyndale clasped his hands together. "That's where it gets interesting, my lord. I couldn't help hearing the name she screamed at him."

"What name was that?"

"Jillian McTavish."

Truman took the seat closest to his Fore-Overman. "You can't mean *Rachel's* mother."

"That's exactly who I mean."

Jillian had always been pretty—almost as pretty as her daughter. Many had marveled that she'd wound up with Jack. Someone like Cutberth would've been a much better fit, except for the age difference. "She must've been eight or ten years older than Cutberth," Truman said.

The Fore-Overman sighed. "Apparently that did not deter them."

While he sat at dinner with Rachel, Truman wrestled with whether or not to tell her what Tyndale had shared about her mother. It was only hearsay, after all. Maybe he should keep his mouth shut and pray she never learned of it. She deserved to take her good memories of her mother with her to London, didn't she?

On the other hand, this could explain the extra income she'd noticed. Maybe Cutberth had been using Rachel's mother to convince Jack to set the fire, and she wound up blackmailing him when the affair ended. Or it was possible he'd really loved her and had been giving her money to help.

"You're quiet this evening, my lord." Rachel paused, fork in hand, to look up at him.

She was on his left. He'd had the dressmaker send another gown, this one burgundy and made from Rachel's own measurements. It had arrived this afternoon and looked even more attractive on her than the one he'd allowed her to take from Katherine's wardrobe.

"I'm not good company today. I apologize."

"Is something wrong?"

He cradled his wine glass in his hand. "I'm concerned about the future."

"Shouldn't your marriage resolve at least some of that concern?"

"I wasn't talking about *my* future." He was tempted to set her up in a house in London, where he could visit whenever he liked. But he'd never been an adulterer and knew he wouldn't be able to respect himself if he became one. His wife would deserve better than that. Rachel too. At the very least she deserved marriage to a man who could live with her and openly love her. A man who would be a full-time father to her children.

She toyed with her cheese soufflé.

"You seem distracted yourself," he observed.

"Maybe I am."

"Is there any particular reason?"

"I'm curious, I suppose."

"About . . . ?"

Giving up the pretense of eating, she put down her spoon. "Lady Penelope. What is she like?"

He pictured the duke's buxom daughter. "She has dark hair and eyes. Although she's not quite as tall as you, she's larger overall."

"Do you find her attractive?"

He covered her hand with his own. "Don't make it worse, Rachel—for either of us."

"I was just wondering if you could see yourself being able to love her."

No. He didn't see that at all, but he couldn't say so without denigrating his future wife. "Maybe that will come with time."

"Have you learned any more about . . . ?" She fell silent as Linley came in to clear the plates in preparation for their next course.

"About . . . ?" he prompted when his butler was gone.

"Jonas Cutberth?"

"Not much. And I'm not sure it will do me any good to keep digging."

"Because . . . ?"

"If Cutberth is responsible for the fire, *why* would he set it?"

"You showed me the reason last night."

"But the more I think about it the more preposterous that seems. He is still working at the mine. If he had money, wouldn't he take his family and move elsewhere?"

"Maybe he hasn't sold the paintings. Maybe he's been unable to sell them or is waiting until he feels it will be safer to try."

That was a definite possibility, especially for a novice like Cutberth. "Where would he store them?"

"They could be anywhere."

Linley entered again. Only he didn't carry food; he carried an envelope. "My lord?"

Truman relinquished his drink in anticipation. "What is it?"

"This just arrived."

The note bore the seal of the Duke of Pembroke. "*Another* missive?" he muttered.

Linley frowned and didn't respond, but Truman knew what he was thinking. The man Truman had met with last night could not have had time to return to London with his answer. So maybe the duke had changed his mind and didn't want to move forward with the wedding regardless of how he had responded to the ultimatum.

Truman wasn't sure if that would make him happy . . . or sad. He craved an excuse to turn his back on what he felt he must do. But any relief would be short lived when the Abbotts made their next move and he had no way to counter it. He couldn't abide the thought that he would be the one to bring shame on the Stanhope name.

Rachel watched with quiet consternation as he broke the seal and read the note.

"Good God," he muttered.

"Is it as I fear?" Linley asked.

"No, but it's almost as bad." He tossed the note aside. "The duke has decided to bring Penelope for a visit."

The color drained from Linley's face. "*When?*"

"He's already on his way."

Chapter 17

It was late but Rachel was fighting sleep. She feared this might be her last night with Lord Druridge and didn't want to waste a second of it. The uncertainty of travel made it difficult to guess when the duke and his daughter might arrive. Would it be tomorrow? The next day?

"What are you thinking about?" the earl murmured.

"I should leave at dawn," she admitted.

He stiffened beside her. They were lying naked in each other's arms because he'd insisted that she join him in bed, but they'd barely kissed. That letter at dinner had changed everything, had made the end so imminent. "Where would you go, Rachel?" he asked. "Linley hasn't had the time he needs to make proper arrangements."

"Why should I wait for Linley, my lord?"

"Don't call me 'my lord,' anymore," he said with a grimace. "I think we're on an intimate enough basis that you could use my first name, don't you?"

"You are 'my lord' to me, and you need to stay 'my lord.' I-I am not your responsibility, and I don't want to get in the way of you reestablishing your happiness."

His arms tightened around her. "Don't talk like that. I would only worry about you if you left."

"But it would be far better if I were not here when your guests arrive. You can't argue with that."

"They already know about you."

"Now you're being stubborn. That's all the more reason I should go. They will, no doubt, be watching you closely."

His fingers slipped through her hair. "Don't talk about leaving until I know where you're going and feel comfortable with it. Don't even *think* about it."

"What's our other option? Shall I remove myself to the far wing while Lady Penelope is here? Hide there with *Peasant Wedding Feast* until she and her father leave?"

"This is a big enough house that we can make sure your paths do not cross."

"And afterwards, would we simply take up where we left off? I could never feel good about that, and I know you couldn't either."

He sighed. "Bear with me, sweet Rachel. I have to be certain I've got the right situation for you."

"That could take weeks, my lord. In the meantime, I refuse to get in the way."

"Stop," he growled, growing impatient. "I won't hear any more of this."

The fire popped and crackled but brought little comfort. Rachel felt cold in spite of its heat. "I'm sorry, my lord, but I'm leaving in the morning."

Assuming they'd only argue if she stayed with him tonight, she tried to get out of bed, but he stopped her.

"I don't think I can give you up," he said and kissed her fingertips, her arm, her neck.

The lethargy that'd gripped them since dinner burned off like fog beneath a hot sun. Suddenly they were touching and tasting each other as if they might never have another chance.

Maybe they couldn't have forever, but they could have this one night.

It would be her good-bye, Rachel decided and let go of all restraint. "One more memory," she whispered.

He didn't like the finality of that any more than what she'd said before. Briefly he pulled back to scowl at her so she'd know it, but she brought his mouth back to hers, kissing him with all the pent-up longing she knew she'd feel the moment she left him, and he seemed incapable of further protest. His tongue was too busy mating with hers; his hands were too busy making her shake with desire.

"I need you," he whispered hoarsely. "I've never needed a woman like I need you."

She needed him too. She wanted him to take her hard and fast. Even that wouldn't be decisive enough to change their situation, but the defiance of it appealed to her. Then she wouldn't have to fear that this moment might be stolen from her, too. She could feel the firmness of his shaft against her belly and knew he was ready. With the way her body clenched with anticipation, she knew she was just as ready.

For a moment, he seemed willing to forget all that had held him back before. He rolled her beneath him and spread her legs. But when he cursed and shifted as though he would bring her to completion some other way, she wrapped her legs around his hips and whispered, "Truman?"

He seemed pleased that she'd used his given name. "Yes?"

"Just once. Let me feel you inside me this once."

Truman knew better than to concede. He told himself she didn't realize what she was asking for. A baby was no small burden for a woman alone. But she insisted that it wasn't her fertile time of the month. And he planned to make sure she had everything she needed, regardless. That gave him just enough excuse to take the risk.

Allowing himself to succumb to the compulsion that drove him, he eased himself inside her. Thanks to Wythe, he'd made love to Rachel once before, but under much different circumstances. He knew her now, cared for her, and that made such a difference.

"Are you okay?" he asked. Katherine had claimed to be a virgin when they married, but he doubted she'd been truthful about that. Because she used sex as a weapon, or an incentive, he had a hard time believing she hadn't manipulated other men with certain . . . opportunities. She'd definitely used her sexuality indiscriminately *after* they were married.

But Rachel was different. Since this was only her second time—with him or any man—and the first hadn't gone as well as he'd hoped, he wanted to make sure she was comfortable before he continued.

"I'm fine," she told him. "Better than fine. I want to be joined like this forever."

He couldn't resist a powerful thrust. "Then tell me you'll stay, or I'll stop."

When she hesitated, he started to withdraw, but she clutched his shoulders. "I'll stay."

Relief as well as pleasure flooded through him as he began to move in earnest. They weren't down to good-bye quite yet. But knowing they would be soon made every moment precious—every touch, every gasp, every whispered endearment.

Rachel's body seemed made for his. She quickly caught on to the rhythm, lifting her hips to meet each thrust, but she didn't close her eyes. She watched him with such intensity that he was staring into her eyes when she gasped and shuddered, and then it was impossible to make himself withdraw. He wanted this too, wanted to let go inside her.

Just once, he said to himself. *Just once*, and felt the pleasure overcome him.

"Don't leave me quite yet," he said afterwards, making sure she wouldn't as he shifted, exhausted, to one side. But when he woke up, she was no longer in his bed. She wasn't in her room. She wasn't anywhere to be found in the house. And the few belongings she'd brought with her when she came to Blackmoor Hall were gone.

Rachel had nowhere to go except Mrs. Tate's. She didn't want to be a burden on anyone, especially someone she loved like her dear neighbor, but now that she knew she'd never be returning to the home she'd grown up in, there was no need to try to preserve the belongings that were left. If she could sell the furniture and books that hadn't been destroyed, she could pay Mrs. Tate for food and maybe retain a small amount for her upcoming travel expenses. Linley had caught her when she was leaving, just before she went to say good-bye to her brother, and assured her that he was working on the arrangements. It wasn't as if she had to hang on indefinitely. She also had her wages from when she'd worked as a servant to carry her through. That didn't amount to a lot, given she'd been a maid for slightly less than a month, but it enabled her to leave the earl's estate with her head held high instead of lingering like some desperate, greedy beggar, hoping to live off his largesse.

She wasn't in Creswell long, however, before word spread that she was back. She wasn't sure how everyone figured it out. Maybe the servants at Blackmoor Hall had gossiped to certain vendors who returned to the village with the news, but several people came by, including one of the hewers she'd worked with—Mr. Greenley. Mrs. Tate turned him and all the others away. Rachel had no idea if Greenley had come to apologize or berate her but she didn't want to find out.

By nightfall, even Mr. Linley came knocking. Rachel could hear him ask to speak with her, could hear him say the earl had sent him to ask her back, but she refused to come to the door. There was nothing he could do to convince her to return to Blackmoor Hall. She loved the earl too much to give the duke any reason to withdraw the offer that would protect him from prosecution.

"Ye won't say a word to 'im?" Mrs. Tate asked, her voice low since there were only two rooms in her house, and the door and Mr. Linley wasn't that far away.

Rachel shook her head. "I'm sorry. I can't."

"But 'e's adamant that 'e speak with ye. 'E says 'e shouldn't 'ave let ye go this mornin'."

"I heard." She couldn't allow herself to be tempted. Now that it was growing dark, she missed the earl—missed Truman—more than ever.

Once Linley left, Rachel went to bed feeling cold and lonely and cast adrift on a mighty ocean of change.

London will be a good place for me, she told herself. She couldn't imagine she'd like it, but at least she would have a clean slate. She wasn't important enough that her reputation would follow her. She hoped. The fact that her only reference would come from Blackmoor Hall concerned her. She didn't want to be the notorious maid who'd had an affair with the notorious earl. Would she be better off striking out on her own?

Mrs. Tate's voice rose in the darkness, from where she was sleeping in the other bed. Apparently she'd been tossing too much and had given away her inability to sleep. "When ye came, I thought . . . I thought 'e was done with ye. But it didn't sound that way when 'is butler showed up. Why'd ye leave?"

"I didn't want to lose sight of who I really am," she said.

"Won't you miss Geordie?"

She already did. Those few minutes she'd spent saying good-bye had been so difficult. But she wouldn't drag her brother away, not into such uncertainty. "Sometimes those we love are better off without us."

That was absolutely the case for Truman.

"I thought it would be more discreet to send you, but I should've gone myself." Truman stood in the parlor where he'd first received Rachel when she appeared the night her mother was dying.

Linley hobbled closer, once again using his cane. "Maybe she has a point, my lord."

He tossed the brass poker he'd just used to stir up the fire against its holder, but in his frustration he missed, and it knocked over a table. "And what point is that, Linley?"

Surprised by this uncharacteristic display of temper, his butler remained silent.

Mrs. Poulson ducked her head in to see what had caused the racket. Truman shooed her out by saying it was a clumsy mistake and she could right things later.

"You have no answer?" he demanded of Linley once Poulson was gone.

"Not one that will please you, my lord."

Pressing on his temples to ease the headache that had started earlier, he strode to the fireplace and gazed into the flames. "What will become of her?"

"She will stay with her neighbor until I can find her a position in London."

"Will she be safe there? I don't want her mistreated."

"I believe she's in good hands. And having her out of the house is far better for you, given that His Grace and Lady Penelope will be here any day. Miss McTavish has done you a great favor."

He clenched his jaw at the thought that she wouldn't be with him tonight. It had taken him so long to find the contentment he felt in her arms. "I didn't ask for this favor."

"Which is why I am so impressed."

"I'm glad *someone's* happy." He was weary of the mystery he'd lived with for two years. Weary of Katherine and the toll she continued to take. Weary of the constant battle. He just wanted to be left alone to rebuild his life. And he wanted Rachel to be part of it. If only he had a better option than the one he felt forced to take—but he wouldn't have a better option unless he could find at least one of those damn paintings.

"If you were Mr. Cutberth, and you'd stolen a Bruegel or two, where would you hide them?" he asked, abruptly changing the subject.

Linley puffed out his cheeks as he considered his answer, seemingly glad they could get back to business as usual. "Somewhere safe, of course. Somewhere I could get to them when I was ready. And somewhere they wouldn't be connected to me, if they were discovered in the interim."

"So not at your house."

"I would think not, my lord."

"I agree. But what other safe place would a man like Cutberth have?"

"The colliery. Possibly."

"*My* colliery?"

"Parts of it have been closed off. There are so many tunnels—it's a maze. And those who work there know its intricacies far better than you."

"Perhaps I'll ask Cutberth's wife about his activities."

"I can't imagine he told her he was going to steal your paintings."

"He might have. They could be in it together. And if not, who would be more likely to notice something odd about his behavior?"

"There is that, I guess. And considering what Mr. Tyndale told you, she might be eager for revenge."

"Such betrayal isn't easily forgiven." He would know, wouldn't he? Of course, he might've had a chance at forgiveness if Katherine had been the least bit penitent. *Her* affairs had had nothing to do with love—only torment.

"If we go to Cutberth's wife, she might tell him. And if he realizes you suspect him he could take evasive action," Linley said.

"I'm counting on the fact that she will tell him. And I'm hoping the knowledge that I suspect him will frighten him into making a mistake."

"What if he panics and destroys the paintings?"

Whether it would be wiser to wait or not, Truman was running out of patience. "It's a gamble, but I have to make my move sometime."

Linley shuffled closer. "Is this about Rachel, my lord?"

"It's about freedom," he said. "At last."

"Back already?"

Startled, Rachel dropped the broom she'd been using. She'd come to the bookshop to pack up what was left of her family's belongings and clean the building so the earl could lease it after she was gone. But first she'd boarded up the window that'd been broken and locked the doors. She hadn't expected—or wanted—to be interrupted.

"How did you get in here?" she asked.

Jonas Cutberth dangled a key in front of her face.

"Who gave you that?"

"Let's not worry about such details. I'm here now. That's what matters."

"Then my question is why—*why* are you here? Don't you have to be at the mine?"

"I'm on my way there."

"You're late for work, by my guess."

"This shouldn't take long. I just want to know how much you told Lord Druridge before he tossed you aside. Because he did toss you aside, didn't he? I can't imagine you'd be standing here in your old rags if he was still anxious to dip his wick." He *tsk*-ed at her "fallen" state and then laughed. "At least you got to pretend to be important for a few weeks. I just hope that fleeting moment was worth losing all your friends *and* your dignity."

Rachel couldn't help but wince at the image he painted of her. She wanted to tell him the situation hadn't been as he represented it. She'd only gone to Lord Druridge's bed because she loved him. She hadn't even taken the dresses he'd given her when she left.

But why bother? She'd only look more foolish for allowing herself to fall in love with a man who was as far above her as the moon and the stars.

"I told him everything," she admitted and was actually relieved to say it. She'd hated feeling as if she were breaking a confidence, if only because of the respect she used to have for Cutberth.

His taunting smile disappeared as quickly as if she'd wiped it away with a rag. "I hope to God you're just trying to make me angry."

A chill went through her. This was a side of him she'd only begun to see since her mother died. But she couldn't lie. For her own dignity—and for the sake of those miners who were simply looking to improve their terrible lot by banding together—she felt she had to tell the truth. Maybe it was time everyone did. "The earl knows about the union, Mr. Cutberth, if that's what you're asking."

He grabbed her arm. "Does he know *I'm* behind it?"

"Ouch!" She tried to wiggle away, but his fingers dug in deeper.

"*Does he?*" he demanded, giving her a shake.

"Yes!" she cried. "Let go of—"

Rachel didn't have time to finish her sentence, didn't even have a chance to brace for the slap that left her ears ringing. She stood, stunned and even slightly disoriented after he hit her, while he continued to rail. "You little bitch! Do you know what you've done? Do you know what a disappointment you would be to your dear mother, if she were here to see how far you've fallen?"

Strengthened by her own anger, Rachel jerked away. "How dare you bring my mother into this! You have no right to even mention her name!"

"That shows how much you know."

"What are you talking about?"

"Forget it. If you've cost me my job, you'll be sorry. Do you hear? I won't allow some stupid whore to destroy what I've worked so hard to accomplish."

Rachel wished Mrs. Tate or someone else would interrupt. Her cheek was stinging, her stomach was upset—and she feared Cutberth wasn't finished with her yet. "And what is it, exactly, that you've worked so hard to accomplish? Is it what you've always told me you wanted? Better conditions and better pay for the miners? Or a way to make yourself rich?"

This seemed to take him aback. "What are you talking about?"

She wanted to mention the paintings but dared not give away the fact that the earl had found a thread he could possibly use to unravel the whole mystery, in case Cutberth could somehow counter him. "What were you looking for when you broke in here? What were you looking for when you broke into my home?"

His eyes narrowed. "Wouldn't you like to know."

She arched her eyebrows. "Was it the ledgers?"

He froze. "Where are they?"

"Where did the money come from, Mr. Cutberth?"

He tried to grab her again, but she managed to put a table between them.

"Give them to me before I wring your neck!" he said.

"Threatening me won't do you any good. I couldn't turn them over even if I wanted to. I left them at Blackmoor Hall."

Putting a hand to his chest, he briefly closed his eyes and shook his head. "You have no idea of the damage you're doing."

"Feel free to explain so that I *will* understand."

"Why would I bother? After the past several months, you're the last person I trust," he said and stormed out.

Once she felt confident that he wasn't coming back, Rachel stumbled over to a chair so she could sit down. Her cheek hurt from when he'd hit her, and her legs felt like rubber, but she was more excited than upset. He'd all but admitted to breaking into her house and the shop, admitted that he'd been searching for the ledger books. That meant he knew something about the money.

She had to get word to Lord Druridge. But how? After what'd just happened, she dared not traverse the five miles to Blackmoor Hall. She'd be far too vulnerable. For all she knew, Cutberth would follow her and toss her over the cliff.

Truman passed a long, miserable night. He tried to convince himself not to let Rachel's absence bother him, but it was no good. Blackmoor Hall had never seemed so empty.

He walked around in her room, even felt the fabric of the dresses she'd left behind, and wished she'd waited. His guests hadn't arrived and could still be another day or two.

Grateful when the sun finally rose, he dressed with the intention of visiting Mrs. Cutberth at her home. By the time he arrived, her husband would be at work, giving him an opportunity to speak to her without him. But Wythe showed up, catching him before he could go anywhere.

"I need to talk to you," he said.

"You're not supposed to even be here."

"This is important."

Wythe had been upset ever since Truman insisted he move to Cosgrove House. They'd barely spoken since, which made Truman feel conflicted. His mother's dying wish was that he be good to his cousin. And this was the same cousin who'd subsequently rescued him from certain death—all the more reason to honor those wishes. But he wasn't ready to let Wythe back into his good graces. Although he'd spent years trying to take the high road where his cousin was concerned, he was consistently disappointed in Wythe. How he'd treated Rachel was just one reason. Truman wasn't ready to have his cousin return to Blackmoor Hall. He didn't want to be apologizing for Wythe's drinking and inelegant behavior when the duke and Lady Penelope were here.

So if Wythe had come to plead his case, Truman was hardly eager to listen. He'd heard it all before. How Wythe hadn't known what he was saying when he threatened Rachel. How he never would have entered her room if he'd had his wits about him. How he wouldn't have really hurt her, regardless. But Wythe started up the stairs toward the study, presumably because he wanted to speak in private, before Truman could demand he leave.

Truman cursed the delay this would cause—but he followed. He figured he might as well listen before His Grace and Lady Penelope arrived.

"What is it?" he asked as he closed the door.

Wythe turned to face him. "There's something happening at the mine."

This sounded ominous. Wythe usually pretended to have the colliery well in hand. "Nothing serious, I hope."

"It feels serious."

Truman swallowed a sigh. Didn't he have enough problems for one winter? "I'm listening."

Wythe's eyes were red-rimmed and his face pale but at least he was sober.

"There's been a shift in sentiment among the workers. It was subtle at first, but Cutberth tells me—"

"Cutberth," Truman broke in.

"Yes."

"That's where you're getting your information?"

Wythe spread out his hands. "Why not? He's always been reliable in the past."

"Tyndale's the Fore-Overman. Why aren't you listening to him?"

"Cutberth seems closer to the men."

Thanks to Rachel, Truman now knew why that might be the case. "When did you last speak to him?"

"I just came from the offices."

Rachel had mentioned that Wythe and Cutberth were being secretive, but Truman wasn't sure how much importance to attach to that. Because of their work at the mine, they had a lot of things to talk about that they may not want the miners to overhear. It could be nothing more than that. "Go on . . ."

"He claims that many of the miners are upset with you over Ra-Miss McTavish. They're talking about doing something to defend her honor."

"Defend her honor!" Truman couldn't believe it. "*I* was the one who had to defend her from *them*. They didn't care a fig about her honor, or even her safety, when they were trying to drag her to the ground so they could throw up her skirts."

"That was four men, Truman. Not all of them. And you're the only one who's actually bedded her. Hence the problem. I wish you would have left her to me instead of bringing her here. I could've used her as a sorter at the mine until they would accept her again."

"You could have made her a sorter to begin with and didn't."

"I regret that. I truly do."

If only Truman could believe him. . . . "You have never had any love for Rachel."

"I don't like her arrogance. She thinks she's smarter than everyone else."

"Because she is," he said.

A muscle moved in Wythe's cheek. "Be that as it may, now that you're involved with her, they're complaining about it. They're saying it's not enough that you can have every woman in your own class? You have to ruin Rachel?"

"I hope I don't need to remind you that Rachel would never have been ruined if you hadn't—"

He held up a hand. "I realize that. It was a mistake, one I'm not likely to forget since you publicly embarrassed me by banishing me from the house."

"You earned that and more."

"I may not be thrilled that you've taken up with a-a"—he seemed to note the warning look Truman gave him because he made an effort to curtail his comments—"woman so far beneath you, but I am still your cousin."

"Then prove you have my best interests at heart."

His eyes flashed with anger. "What do you think I'm doing here? I'm try-ing to warn you that this thing with Rachel is getting out of hand—in more ways than one. From what I can tell, you've grown besotted with her. You've certainly put her interests above mine. And now the villagers feel as if they have to defend one of their own. They're saying you drove her father to the grave, then you took advantage of his pretty, defenseless daughter."

Truman moved to his desk and picked up a paperweight, which he tossed from hand to hand. "And what do you think they're going to do about it?"

"Who knows? Maybe they'll set another fire, and maybe next time I won't be around to drag you out."

"I see." The irony of Wythe being his savior never ceased to amaze Tru-man. "And did Cutberth tell you why he would be privy to the sentiment of the miners?"

Wythe remained agitated but stopped pacing. "What did you say?"

"Did he tell you that, as our loyal employee, he has secretly been working to start up a union?"

His cousin's jaw dropped. "What? No! You can't be serious."

"I assure you I am. As steward, you didn't notice *anything*?"

"Nothing, I swear it!"

Of course he'd be oblivious. He had his head in a bottle most of the time. And Truman had been just as preoccupied since the fire. The miners could have held union meetings on his own property at the beginning of each shift for all he knew.

"Now that you are aware, has Cutberth ever acted . . . oddly, in your opinion?"

"Never." Wythe scowled. "Are you sure you have your facts straight?"

Truman put down the paperweight. "I doubt Rachel would lie about something like that."

"How would *she* know what Cutberth is doing, Truman? Maybe she's just trying to cast suspicion on anyone except her own family—"

"Even if her father set the fire, someone else paid him," Truman said. "I don't know a lot, but I know that the McTavishes came into some money after the fire. And they've been receiving additional payments ever since."

"From whom?"

"Cutberth, for all we know. Maybe he even embezzled that money from Stanhope & Co."

"Cutberth can't be involved. What reason would he have to murder Katherine? Whoever killed her had to have come from London. It was probably someone she played false, maybe even the father of her unborn babe."

Truman no longer believed her killer had come all the way from London—not since he'd learned about the money Jack McTavish had received to fire the manse. "No, the killer is here in Creswell."

"It's not Cutberth," Wythe responded. "Cutberth wouldn't hurt anyone—wouldn't risk his job, his family."

"Cutberth hasn't been as careful about his job and family as you'd like to believe, dear cousin."

"What does that mean?"

"Besides his union activities?" Maybe Truman should show him, see what his response might be. There might be a bit of truth to be gleaned from doing that. "I was heading out to speak with his wife. Why don't you join me?"

Chapter 18

Jonas's wife didn't look anything like Truman remembered her. He'd seen her at a company picnic two summers ago but she'd aged so much since then he doubted he would've recognized her if she hadn't been standing in her own doorway.

"Mrs. Cutberth?"

Her eyes narrowed in suspicion. There was no question she recognized *him*. But, of course, he expected to be recognized. He generally was. "Yes?"

"I wonder if you might spare my cousin and me a moment of your time."

A baby cried in the house behind her. She barked an order for one of her older daughters to take the child into the other room so they could hear. "My husband isn't home, my lord," she responded when she turned back.

"I assumed he'd be at the mine. It's you I'd like to speak to."

She hesitated. "But I'm sure he'd rather deal with you himself."

"I'm not here to make trouble. I just have a few questions."

"Mum, who is it?" A skinny, dark-haired girl of about twelve came to stand at her elbow. The moment she saw who it was at the door, she covered her mouth and her eyes went wide. "Lord Druridge!"

"At your service." He bowed. "And you are . . . ?"

"Sarah, the eldest." A wide smile spread across her face. "Wait till Papa hears about this. Would you like to come in?" She nudged her mother. "Mum, you must let them in. You wouldn't want the earl and his cousin to be left standing in the cold."

Shamed into remembering her manners, Mrs. Cutberth stepped back. "Of course. Please, come in."

Truman blocked Wythe from entering and lowered his voice even though Sarah had rushed back into the house to straighten up for their visit and wasn't paying close attention. "No, thank you. This matter is best handled in private."

She pressed her lips together and wrung her hands. "So . . . where would you like to go?"

"Maybe we could take a walk. It's chilly but not stormy."

Her chest lifted as she drew a deep breath, but she didn't refuse. She grabbed a cloak from a hook by the door and threw it around her shoulders. "Sarah, I'll be back in a few minutes. Watch your siblings."

"*What?*" Sarah cried. "They're leaving? But I've just about got the house ready."

Truman couldn't help smiling that she would be so disappointed. "Perhaps you'll forgive us if I send over some juicy oranges when I get back to Blackmoor Hall?"

She clapped her hands. "Oranges are my favorite!"

"Oranges!" came the echo from her younger siblings.

"You owe them nothing," his cousin muttered. "Especially if what you believe about Cutberth is true."

Truman ignored him. Mrs. Cutberth was already pulling the door closed.

"Whatever you want, my lord, I can't help you. I know nothing about the fire. I've said so before—to your man, Linley—who's questioned almost everyone in the village."

"This isn't about the fire."

Her glance shifted to Wythe before returning to him. "Please tell me my husband hasn't done something at the mine to get you angry. He would never intentionally cause a problem."

"Would he intentionally start a union—while on my payroll?" Truman asked.

He expected her to deny it, but she sighed in resignation. "Rachel told you. Jonas was afraid she would."

"You knew all along? About the union?"

"Of course I did. I warned him that he'd be jeopardizing his own family if he got caught, but he wouldn't listen. He feels so strongly about . . . about the men. Please try to understand."

Truman studied her, surprised by the sincerity of her defense. She obviously admired her husband a great deal, despite his infidelity—which was what he had to ask her about next. "From what I hear, he feels just as strongly about the men's wives. Or at least he did about Jack's wife."

The color drained from her face. "I had no business taking those letters down to the office, my lord. I wouldn't have, if I'd given myself some time to calm down."

"What did your husband have to say about them?"

Tears sprang up but she blinked them back. "He's sorry, terribly sorry. He made a mistake."

"And you've forgiven him?"

"It's not so hard when you know the circumstances. He's always felt sorry for the McTavishes, ever since their first son was caught in that cave-in. After Jack died, he stopped in every now and then to help chop wood and that sort of thing."

Truman hated the memory of the accident that had killed Rachel's brother. He felt the sadness as much as anyone. But short of closing the mine, he couldn't stop all the accidents, no matter how many safety measures he imposed. And if he closed the colliery, how would most of Creswell survive? "I see. Can I read those letters?"

"No, Jonas burned every last one of them."

That was unfortunate, but Truman could understand why he would. "Did your husband help Jillian financially too?"

"He did," she said. "Every month. It's our Christian duty to assist widows and orphans." Her voice thickened as she fought more tears. "I didn't know, of course, until I found the letters, that he'd been helping a bit *too* much, but I wasn't opposed to giving her what she needed to survive."

Truman had had a terrible time forgiving Katherine, but she'd never asked for his forgiveness. Not sincerely. She'd made a game of manipulating his emotions. And she hadn't gotten caught up with just one lover. She'd willfully betrayed him whenever the opportunity presented itself. "How could he afford to help for so long?"

"It was only about six months. She had a bit put by before that."

"Do you know where her savings came from?"

"No."

"And the monthly payments? Six months would be quite a burden."

"He told me he put together a fund. Several of those who were better off contributed."

With a scowl, Wythe broke into the conversation. "Why haven't I heard of this . . . *fund*?"

"*I* hadn't even heard of it, Mr. Stanhope," she said. "It was union business. No one was supposed to talk about it."

"You contributed personally, I suppose?" Truman asked.

She toed a rock. "Yes. We gave as much as we could. There was a time when Jack was making good money that he helped us. We were new here and Jonas hadn't yet found work. I doubt we could've gotten by without him. So I can hardly feel bad about doing a kind deed for his widow. I just wish . . . I wish it had ended there."

"*Jack* helped the two of you?" The disbelief in Wythe's voice revealed *his* opinion of Rachel's father, which came as no surprise since it mirrored Truman's own.

"Did you thank him the way Jillian McTavish thanked your husband?" Wythe asked.

"Please forgive my cousin." Truman spoke before she could respond— but she lifted her chin and answered in spite of his attempt to spare her the humiliation.

"It might seem strange to you, Mr. Stanhope. But my husband is a good man. He has his faults, like anyone else. Caring too much is one of them. Trying to save the world when he'd be better off leaving it alone is another. Jillian was lonely, and she was beautiful." Her gaze lowered along with her voice. "Far more beautiful than I."

"That depends on how you define beauty," Truman said. "I personally find loyalty at least as attractive as a pretty face."

It took her a moment to realize he'd paid her a compliment. When she caught on, she gave him a quick, shy smile. "Thank you, my lord. But I'm well aware of the vast difference between Jillian and me in that regard. If you don't remember her, Rachel's the spitting image of her. That should give you some idea of what my husband was up against."

She'd chosen a good way to make her point. Rachel was all he could think about. "How much did your husband give the McTavishes each month?" he asked, hoping to match the amount with that mysterious entry in the bookshop's ledgers.

"I never asked." She glanced around as if concerned as to who might see them. "I don't care to talk about Jonas when he's not here. Could we perhaps wait—?"

"You're doing a fair job of possibly saving your husband's job," Truman told her. "Could he do any better at convincing me?"

"I doubt it," she said with a skeptical laugh. "I fear the passion he feels for his many causes would only make matters worse."

Truman smiled. "I appreciate your honesty."

"I know you can't be pleased with my husband's choices where the union is concerned, my lord. Where Jillian McTavish is concerned, either. God knows *I* find that one difficult." She pulled her shawl tighter. "But I can admire what he was trying to do. And I hope you will at least *try* to understand why he has made some of the choices he has."

Was Cutberth a visionary? A hero to the poor working class, as his wife portrayed him? Or was he a simple crook? "Have you ever heard of Pieter Bruegel, Mrs. Cutberth?"

"Of course."

Her response made Truman catch his breath. He'd never expected her to admit to knowing of Mr. Bruegel. He'd merely wanted to witness her expression when he mentioned the artist's name, to see if he could ascertain some familiarity. He was looking for Wythe's reaction too. But he could ascertain no sudden nervousness.

"Your father had an extensive collection of his paintings that was lost in the fire," she said. "My husband has mentioned it many times. He says losing such rare art is as much a tragedy as the rest of it. Why do you ask?"

"Because at least one of those paintings *wasn't* lost in the fire."

It was her turn to be surprised. Wythe was shocked too. His cousin's gaze locked onto him as if he'd just bolted it there.

"*Landscape with the Fall of Icarus* went missing before the fire ever broke out," Truman told her.

"Why is this the first *I've* heard of it?" The pique in Wythe's voice suggested he was offended, and Truman couldn't blame him. Their relationship had all but disintegrated the past six months—ever since he started searching for Katherine's killer a little closer to home.

"*Why* did they go missing? How?" Mrs. Cutberth asked.

He could address Wythe's reaction once they left; he answered the clerk's wife. "That's what I intend to find out."

"You weren't going to tell me about the paintings?" Wythe asked after Mrs. Cutberth went inside and they climbed astride their horses.

Truman glanced behind him. The place where Rachel was staying wasn't far, just a few blocks closer to the center of town. He wanted to check on her, see how she was faring. But he had Wythe with him. And he'd purposely upset him to see what might come of it.

"I didn't think you'd be interested," he responded.

"In something that might help you solve the mystery of Katherine's death? When I know it's been eating you up inside?"

"The Abbotts are growing angrier by the day," he explained. "I need to provide them with some answers, and I need to do it soon."

"Then we will. Because you didn't set that fire. No matter how angry you were, you would never destroy Blackmoor Hall. You love it too much. That old place is in your blood."

Truman wished he found that monologue convincing, that he could believe his cousin was as innocent and supportive as he pretended to be. "I hope you're right. But I can't help wondering . . . where were you when the fire broke out, Wythe?"

"I've told you. I was on a ride."

"Alone."

"Yes, alone! I didn't do it." Wythe pulled his horse to a stop, causing Truman to slow up if he didn't want to leave him behind. "If I wanted what you've got, I would've let you burn."

Truman winced. Blaming Wythe didn't make sense, and yet he couldn't conquer that terrible doubt. "I'm sorry. I know you haven't received the gratitude you probably deserve. But if it makes you feel any better, I've grown suspicious of *everyone*."

"Except the forever devoted Linley."

"Is Mrs. Poulson any less devoted?"

Wythe didn't answer the question, but he came up alongside Truman. "How can I convince you?" he asked. "How can I *finally* prove myself and make things right between us?"

He seemed intent, sincere. "You could find *Landscape with the Fall of Icarus*," Truman said.

The gelding Wythe rode snorted and swished its tail. "Haven't you tried?"

"I have men searching, in England and abroad, but they've been doing so for more than a month—all to no avail. Which makes me wonder—have I gotten ahead of whoever took them?"

"Ahead?"

"Maybe they're still here. Maybe they haven't gone to market."

"After *two years*?"

His cousin's skepticism was more convincing than he'd expected it to be. "The culprit could be lying low, waiting for the perfect opportunity. It's even possible he didn't mean to kill Katherine. She should've been in church with everyone else but wasn't feeling well that day. No one would've known except the servants."

"I remember. But where could the paintings be?"

"Anywhere." Truman recalled his conversation with Linley. "Even at the mine."

"It would be too dangerous to leave something of such value there."

Truman had been of the same opinion, but Linley had made a good argument. "Not if they were well protected—and well hidden."

"But even if I happen to find them—say, in some tunnel that's no longer used—that won't necessarily tell us who put them there."

Exactly the point Truman had hoped Wythe would grasp. He wanted his cousin to feel safe returning the paintings, even if he was the one who'd taken them. "But it *would* prove my innocence. I was in London that whole week and returned just before the fire broke out. I would not have had the opportunity to secret them away between the time my driver saw me go in and you carried me out."

"That's true." Wythe nibbled on his lip as he considered Truman's words. "And they had to have gone missing sometime that day, otherwise the servants would've noticed them gone."

If his memory served correctly and *Landscape with the Fall of Icarus* was really missing when he argued with Katherine. He couldn't help but acknowledge, at least to himself, that he could be leading Wythe on a wild goose chase.

"Yes, which means, if we find the paintings, the Abbotts will have to back off." Maybe then they'd launch their own investigation instead of trying to persuade the authorities to press charges against him.

"Even if they refuse, no one of any import will listen to them at that point."

"It's the shred of proof I need."

"Then I'll head to the mine right now."

The bridle jingled as Truman's horse threw its head, but Truman easily reined in. "Get all those at the mine to aid in the search—and offer a significant reward."

Wythe adjusted his hat to cut the sun's glare. "How much of a reward?"

"A thousand pounds, no questions asked."

"Any miner I know would betray his own mother for that much money." Wythe brought his horse around so he could lower his voice. "This might solve that other problem too—the one I came to speak to you about earlier. You realize that."

"The miners' thirst for vengeance against me?"

"Yes. If they could be convinced that you aren't the murderer the worst agitators claim you to be, it might assuage their anger over Jack and Rachel. Especially Jack, since they would have to admit that he might have been the one who fired the manse instead of you."

Truman nodded to acknowledge the truth of that statement. "See that they are made aware of the possibilities."

Wythe gave him a mock salute. Then he kicked his horse's flanks and veered left, leaving Truman sitting in his saddle, watching. He wanted to believe the excitement he'd seen in Wythe's face was genuine. But he couldn't help thinking that his cousin might merely be using this as the opportunity Truman had intended it to be.

"Godspeed, cousin," he murmured, and then, without Wythe to give him pause, he turned around and headed to Mrs. Tate's.

Chapter 19

"Rachel?"

Rachel was lying down with a wet rag on her forehead when she heard Mrs. Tate call for her. She'd awakened with the worst headache she'd ever known. "Yes?"

"Someone's here to see you."

A tremor of foreboding caused her head to pound even more. Was Cutberth paying her another visit? Or was it Greenley again? "Who is it?"

"Lord Druridge."

The earl. Just his name made Rachel's heart yearn. She didn't want to let him see her like this, while she wasn't feeling well. But she figured this might be her only opportunity to tell him it was Cutberth who'd been searching for the ledgers. "I'm coming."

After tossing the rag into the bowl on the table beside her, she got up and did what she could to tidy her appearance. But there was no way to cover the blood vessel Cutberth's ring had broken when he struck her. The swelling near her eye wasn't so bad anymore but the area had turned bright purple.

She let her hair down in hopes that might cover it. What she had to tell Lord Druridge would be incendiary enough. She didn't want to start an all-out war between him and the miners.

"My Lord?" Her breath caught as she came around the corner and saw him standing at the door so tall and erect.

"There you are." He smiled as though he was relieved to see her, but his eyes honed in on her injury almost immediately and that smile disappeared. "What happened to you?"

"It's nothing. I'll grab my cloak so we can take a walk. I . . . I need to tell you something."

Mrs. Tate offered to go down to the church, where several of the older ladies were sewing a quilt for an upcoming wedding, but Rachel wouldn't hear of it. "No, you already decided it was too cold for you today. I wouldn't think of putting you out of your own house. We're fine."

The earl watched her step outside, his expression grim; her injury had upset him. "Have you had something to eat? There's a tavern halfway to Newcastle. I could take you there."

"Have your visitors arrived?"

"Not yet."

"There's no need to go to so much time and trouble. We can talk here, at my cottage. Then you can go back, just in case they arrive."

He said nothing as she led him next door—not until she let him in and he saw the destruction. Then he cursed. She'd cleaned the shop yesterday but hadn't yet made it to the house. Cutberth's visit had set her back, made her afraid to be alone, even when she was so close to Mrs. Tate. Her proximity to her neighbor hadn't helped yesterday.

"I wish I knew who did this," he ground out.

She shot him a glance. "I can tell you."

He stripped off his gloves. "Who?"

The scars on his hand didn't bother her. They never really had. She wanted to slip into his arms. It'd only been a day and a night since they'd been together but she had missed him terribly. She couldn't imagine what it would be like in London, knowing she'd probably never see him again. "Jonas Cutberth."

His eyes narrowed. "That name seems to be coming up a great deal."

"He was looking for the ledgers, which means he must know something about that mysterious monthly payment I discovered."

"He does. He started helping your mother as soon as the money your father received to fire Blackmoor Hall ran out."

"*Helping* her?" Instinctively her fingers sought out the place where Cutberth had struck her. She'd been thinking such bad thoughts about the mine clerk. Were they—at least somewhat—unwarranted?

The earl didn't answer her question. He stepped closer and touched the bruise himself. "What happened here?"

She didn't want this to become any more about her than it already was. She only had to stay another couple of weeks. It was better to leave matters as they stood, with Cutberth feeling as if he'd exacted a bit of revenge for her defection. "I ran into something yesterday, at the shop."

"What?"

Her mind grappled for a plausible scenario. "The . . . door."

He lifted her chin. "If someone hurt you . . ."

She cleared her throat so that she could speak more stridently. "No. Of course not. Don't worry."

"I *do* worry." His gaze dropped to her mouth and he stole a kiss before stepping away. "About Cutberth . . ."

"Yes. Cutberth." When the earl was around she could hardly think straight. "Why would he ever help my mother?"

His expression showed concern. "They were having an affair, Rachel. I didn't want to burden you with this news, didn't think you'd believe it even if I did, but I confirmed it with Mrs. Cutberth just this morning."

She struggled to take that in and to find some credibility in it, but it wasn't easy. Wouldn't she have seen some indication of inappropriate behavior had her mother been sleeping with *Jonas Cutberth*?

"You're right—I can't believe it," she said.

"I get the impression he's admitted it, at least to his wife."

"So the payments have nothing to do with the fire?"

"It doesn't seem that way. He probably wanted the ledgers because he was afraid evidence of those payments would reveal the affair."

"But if his wife already knew . . ."

"She found out this week, after . . ." he motioned around them ". . . all this. Mr. Tyndale was at the office when she showed up with several letters they'd written to each other. Jonas must've found them here or at the shop and taken them home."

"Why wouldn't he simply destroy them?"

"Sentimental value? I don't know, but they're gone now. Jonas burned them the day she confronted him."

Rachel couldn't see Cutberth with Jillian. The thought that they might be lovers had never even crossed her mind. "He was helping my mother because he *loved* her?"

"That's what Mrs. Cutberth indicated."

She thought back through all their many encounters. "But he came here quite often. I never got the slightest inkling that he was involved with my mother." Had she been blinded by her own romantic fantasies? By the hope that he found something worthy in *her*, since she was so taken with *him*?

No! Feeling the way she did toward him would've made her *more* sensitive to how he dealt with other women, rather than less. "That can't be true, my lord."

"It's difficult—"

"No more difficult than what I believe to have happened," she broke in.

"And that is . . . ?"

"It was hush money."

"Blackmail?"

She couldn't imagine her mother blackmailing anyone. "Maybe not blackmail exactly. Perhaps an *incentive* to remain quiet, offered rather than extorted."

"And Mrs. Cutberth was in on the whole thing?"

"She could be protecting her husband."

"Subjecting herself to such humiliation wouldn't be easy."

He was sensitive to it because he'd been through it. He couldn't imagine anyone lying about such matters. But Rachel could see where they might view that as the lesser of two evils. "Is she standing by him?"

A cynical smile curved the earl's lips. "Yes."

"It's only been a few days. That's not very long to come to terms with something so painful."

"And to think I liked her."

Rachel righted a chair that had been tossed on its side. "Jonas couldn't find those ledgers, so he had to cover for what they revealed."

The earl massaged his hand, as he so often did. "Why? I've been through them carefully. There's nothing in the ledgers that indicates the money came from him."

"*He* doesn't know that. My mother could've kept far more meticulous re-cords, even left an explanation."

"No wonder he searched your house and shop." He scooted the broken shards of a bowl into a pile with his feet. "There's this, too: He's aware of the paintings, as well as what they're worth. I asked his wife about them this morning, and she readily admitted a familiarity."

Rachel used her broom to sweep the glass away. "Are you going to have him arrested?"

"Not yet. But I will have him sacked, especially if he's the one who struck you."

She brought her head up. "How'd you know?"

"You had to have learned he did this somehow. I'm guessing he paid you a visit."

"Yes."

"If he ever touches you again, I'll kill him. He needs to understand that."

"Don't ever court trouble on my account." When she met his eyes, she saw steely determination and that made her fear for his safety. "Truman, please."

"*Now* you'll use my first name?"

"You have to listen to me. The miners will not tolerate much more."

"I can take care of myself."

"Against how many?"

"As many as want to precede me to the gallows."

She flinched. "Don't talk about the gallows."

When he saw how worried she was, his expression softened. "I saw Geordie in the stables this morning," he said. "He's sad you left."

She felt a pang of longing for her brother. "I said good-bye, but . . . give him my love, will you?"

"Of course." He glanced around the house. "I'm sorry about this."

"I know."

In a sudden, brisk movement, he stepped toward her and took her hands. "Come back with me to Blackmoor Hall, Rachel—at least until I can get you situated in London. You want to be with me. I know you do."

She stared at their joined hands instead of searching his face. She knew if she saw the same longing she felt, her willpower would crumble. It was even harder to deny him than it was herself. "And if His Grace and Lady Penelope arrive before that can happen?"

"They are aware of the situation. They understand I have to make arrangements before . . . before I can move on."

She finally met his gaze again. "I can't go back with you."

Scowling, he released her. "Why not?"

"Because I wouldn't be able to stay out of your bed."

"I wouldn't want or expect you to."

"I would expect it of myself. Don't you see?"

"No. I don't see. I don't have to see. I simply demand it!"

That autocratic statement should have put her off. It would have, at one time. But she knew him now, knew he was wrestling with the same demons she was—desire, frustration, loneliness. Only he was far more used to getting what he wanted.

"I'm no longer one of your servants, my lord. You cannot order me about. And I can't go back to your bed. You've already agreed to marry Lady Penelope. We must remember her and . . . and be kind."

"But if we find the paintings I will be free of suspicion."

"Does that mean you won't marry her? You'll break the betrothal?"

"Yes!"

"Why? It won't change the fact that I'm a-a shopkeeper's daughter. A poor village girl. An unsuitable wife for an earl."

"Then for God's sake be my mistress!" he growled.

"It's a sad reflection on my state of mind that I'm tempted by that offer," she said with a bitter laugh.

"It won't be so bad. You'll want for nothing, I swear it."

"Your money is the last thing I'm after. And such an arrangement would destroy your marriage, make certain it never had a chance."

"The last thing I need is *you* trying to save me for another woman!"

"What choice do I have?" she argued. "How long do you think you'd be happy in such a situation? How long would it be before you began to regret being with me? In the end, you'd hate me for making you into the kind of man you never wanted to be."

"I could *never* hate you."

"Do you think I don't understand who you really are?"

He lifted a hand. "Stop painting me as more noble than I am. I can't be that noble if I'm asking. At least we'd be together. What matters more than that?"

"Duty and honor, because I know you were raised to prize those things above all else." She gripped his forearm. "You told me you were loyal to Katherine."

"That is of no account."

"It signifies a great deal. You didn't love her. You didn't even respect her. Yet you remained true. You can't become someone other than who you are, my lord, at least not for very long."

He jerked away. "Don't tell me that. I've never wanted anyone as badly as I want you," he said and stalked out.

Dammit! Rachel did things to him no other woman could. It didn't matter what he did—if he tried to put her out of his life or draw her back in—there was no way to win. He couldn't find any peace where she was concerned. He could only ache with want.

He was on the edge of town when he saw his own carriage.

As soon as Timothy spotted him, he pulled the conveyance to a stop and Linley stuck his head out.

"There you are, my lord."

"What is it?" He hoped they'd found the paintings—but he knew in his heart that wasn't it. Linley's next words confirmed it.

"The duke and his daughter have arrived. I wanted to make you aware as soon as possible."

Truman pressed a finger and thumb to his forehead. He was in no mood to be diverted. He had yet to deal with Cutberth. He also wanted to oversee the search at the mine.

But Cutberth wasn't going anywhere. And, reward or not, there was a good chance the paintings would never be found. He couldn't go off on a whim when his best chance at salvaging all he had, including his good name, was waiting for him at Blackmoor Hall.

"Thank you, Mr. Linley."

"Would you like to tie your horse behind and ride back, my lord?"

"No, this will be quicker," he said and urged his horse into a gallop.

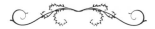

Mrs. Tate was working in the kitchen when Rachel returned. "What did Lord Druridge want?"

Rachel wasn't willing to share too much of their conversation. She knew Mrs. Tate loved her, but her neighbor was defensive of her to a fault and might repeat some of what she heard in an attempt to change the villagers' minds about her. "To tell me he's made inquiries about a position in London."

Her neighbor frowned. "I hate to see ye leave. With yer mum gone and yer brother out at Blackmoor Hall, it's gettin' mighty lonely 'ere in this 'ouse."

She had her two sons, but they were married, worked long hours and lived across town. She saw them and their families every Sunday, but it was Rachel's family that had given her daily company and purpose. "I'll miss you. But it will be better for me to start over somewhere else." It *had* to be better. She didn't see how her prospects could get any worse.

"I suppose he saw your injury."

Mrs. Tate had been angry over that since Rachel returned from the shop yesterday with her face red and swollen. "How could he miss it? Cutberth must've hit me just right for it to look so bad." He'd hit her hard, too—hard enough to rattle her teeth—but she was trying to calm the troubled waters, not make them worse.

"What kind of cad strikes a woman? I wish yer dad was still around. 'E'd take care of Cutberth."

With a smile for the love her protective anger proved, Rachel decided to ask Mrs. Tate about Jillian and the earl's mine clerk. "He would indeed. Especially if he heard what I just did."

She put down the knife she'd been using to cut up a chicken. "Which was ...?"

"Mrs. Cutberth claims that her husband had an affair with my mother."

Mrs. Tate blinked several times before she could find words. "Gah! Jillian never even liked 'im. 'E made her nervous, comin' 'round the 'ouse, spendin' so much time with you. She didn't want ye to get caught up in what 'e was doin', didn't want 'im to lead ye into trouble—an' she saw 'im as trouble, I assure ye. An agitator—that's what she called him."

Mrs. Tate would know. She'd spent long hours with Jillian in that final week, caring for her while Rachel worked. They'd had nothing to do but talk, at least when Jillian was lucid. "Did she *tell* you that?"

"Several times. She'd ask me almost every day if 'e'd been by."

He'd stopped in at the shop quite often. Her mother didn't know about those visits and neither would Mrs. Tate. But had he also been secretly visiting Jillian?

It didn't seem plausible.

"Mum agreed with the need for a union," she said.

"That could be true," Mrs. Tate responded. "Most of us 'ere in the village agree. But she didn't want ye to 'ave any part in the fight."

"I understood why at the time. She'd had enough of the mine and everything connected to it and wanted it out of our lives. But now I wonder how she could feel that way when Mr. Cutberth was helping to pay the bills." Rachel wasn't convinced he and her mother had ever slept together, but she had to believe he was the one who'd given them the money, or he wouldn't have been so interested in finding the ledgers.

"Maybe it wasn't Cutberth who was 'elping," Mrs. Tate said.

Rachel didn't give this much credence. "Mrs. Cutberth admitted as much to Lord Druridge."

"It could be that they're both protectin' someone."

This was an interesting thought. "Such as whom?"

After drying her hands on a towel, she sat at the kitchen table. "Once, when yer mother was tossin' an' turnin' with fever, she was arguin' with the earl's own cousin, she was. I 'eard 'is name clear as a bell. 'Wythe,' she said, 'you'll protect my children when I'm gone. Promise me you'll protect my children.' I wasn't sure what business she'd 'ave with Mr. Stanhope, or why she might be on a first-name basis with 'im. But I knew it was none of *my* business, so I said nothin'. I figured it was the delirium talkin'." She gazed across the room, eyes unfocused, as if reliving the incident. "But after 'earing such rubbish about 'er and Cutberth ... I wonder."

Rachel had never heard her mother speak of Wythe in any particularly passionate way. It was always the earl. "Stay away from him," Jillian had told her, over and over. Had Mrs. Tate witnessed the nonsensical ramblings of a very sick woman? Or was there some meaning behind them? "Did Mr. Stanhope ever come to the house when I wasn't there?"

"Not that I remember." Mrs. Tate smoothed her apron. "The only place 'e bothers to go 'ere in the village is the brothel. An' 'e goes there so often they should rent 'im a room."

That had to be at least part of the reason Elspeth felt she could claim to know so much about the goings-on at Blackmoor Hall and the colliery. Was it also why she'd refused to see Rachel? Was she afraid of what Wythe would do if he thought she might share his secrets?

As far as Rachel was concerned, that was a strong possibility. *She* was certainly frightened of the earl's cousin.

But if Elspeth really did know something that could help Lord Druridge, and Rachel could get her to talk, maybe it wouldn't be so all-important to find those missing paintings.

Chapter 20

Lady Penelope smiled whenever he looked at her, but Truman couldn't help feeling as if her eyes were a bit . . . vacant. She was so placid, so quiet, which added to the feeling that her mind was somewhere else. Her father carried the conversation at dinner. He even spoke for her whenever Truman tried to draw her out.

Richard Mayberry, the Duke of Pembroke, sat on his right, across from Penelope, and had a booming voice for such a small man. He barely came up to Truman's shoulder and was often bedridden with gout, but when he could get around he carried himself like a king. "I thought we might see Wythe for dinner," he said, "but I suppose what I've heard is true."

Truman had just lifted his wine glass. He paused before drinking. "That depends. What have you heard, Your Grace?"

"That he is no longer staying at Blackmoor Hall."

"Yes. We've had some . . . difficulty at the mine. I felt it would be in my best interest to have my steward stationed closer—for the time being."

"So you had him move in with your Fore-Overman because of unrest at the mine?"

Truman ignored the skepticism in his voice. "More or less, Your Grace."

The duke frowned when Truman wasn't more forthcoming. It wasn't any of His Grace's business where Wythe was staying, but Truman could understand why he would be interested. The duke had been digging for information on Rachel ever since he arrived. While Lady Penelope was dressing for dinner, he'd admitted he was vastly curious about "the Creswell shopkeeper" who had caught Truman's eye. This latest question told him the rumors circulating about her included some account of Wythe's banishment.

The duke stuffed another bite of roast duck into his mouth. "What kind of difficulties are you facing at the mine?"

Truman barely refrained from exchanging a glance with Linley, who entered the room with their dessert. "The usual struggle, Your Grace, over pay and benefits."

"Miners are a bunch of greedy buggers, aren't they?"

Since he'd always made the lion's share of the income from the colliery, Truman wasn't sure he could call the miners greedy, but the last thing he wanted was an argument with the duke. He was already anxious, waiting to hear some word from his cousin regarding whether his offer of a reward would recover the paintings. "Greedy or justified, they are trying to create a union to force my hand."

He made a face. "Good Lord, you have to quash that immediately. Make sure they understand if they don't want to work, you'll find others who do. Once they start to go hungry, they'll change their minds, I assure you."

"Fortunately, there should be enough common ground to avoid a starve out."

"Excuse me?"

The duke didn't seem to have detected the sarcasm in Truman's voice. Truman made more of an effort to eradicate it as he explained. "The price of coal is up. I don't see any reason we can't all benefit."

"You're going to give in to their demands?"

"As far as I see fit. I need workers; they need work. A fair trade should solve both problems."

The duke washed the rest of his meal down with a swallow of wine as Linley took his plate. "They're paid by what they produce, are they not? What could be more fair than that?"

Truman knew this conversation could not be interesting to Lady Penelope, but her father didn't seem to care. He didn't seem to consider her any more than he would a potted plant. But, again, Truman got the impression.

"Some of the stronger hewers do quite well during their most productive years," he explained. "But it's a difficult life, which makes it incumbent upon me, as the colliery owner, to insure that everyone gets what he needs."

The duke arranged what he'd bumped of his silverware as if he couldn't bear to see any of it out of alignment. "You sound quite liberal, Truman. You shock me. These are grown men. And you already pay prevailing rates, do you not?"

"I do."

"Then, if they aren't making enough, let them work harder. You're not running a charity."

Truman clenched his teeth so he wouldn't say what rose to his lips. He didn't feel the need to make others suffer, especially men who had women and children depending on them. He possessed far more than what one person needed.

But he had to remember that the duke wasn't only criticizing his labor relations. His Grace obviously assumed that to have gotten involved with Rachel, Truman must be too "liberal" with the lower classes on a more general basis. His attitude toward the miners' demands was just further proof of it.

"A union could be very damaging to your interests," His Grace pointed out. "If you allow the miners too much power, you will be sorry."

"I don't particularly like being sorry, which is why I plan to fight the union immediately and with the most reliable of tactics."

The duke took another swallow of his claret. "And those are . . . ?"

"To make sure the men feel as if they have no need of one."

"What's a union?" Lady Penelope surprised Truman by speaking up. Apparently she'd tuned in to the conversation. The fact that she didn't know what a union was seemed slightly odd, but she had lived a very sheltered and traditional life—and maybe he was judging her against the exceptionally well-read and intelligent Rachel.

Whether she should have known the term or not, he would've been happy to explain, except her father didn't give him the chance.

"Leave the business to us, dear," he said. "You don't need to trouble your pretty head about any of it."

"Yes, Father. Of course you're right." She smiled and fell silent again but Truman got the impression the duke had embarrassed her, which was probably why she quit eating and started doing a lot more drinking.

"You've had enough spirits for one evening," His Grace snapped when Linley came to refill her glass for the third time.

Truman thought he saw anger flash in her eyes, but it disappeared so quickly he assumed he must've been mistaken. With a nod of acquiescence, she slid her glass to the top of her plate. "The long journey has made me excessively thirsty."

Eager to see if he might enjoy speaking to her any more than her father, Truman shifted to face her. "Did you see anything interesting during the ride?"

"It was long and grueling," the duke piped up. "You know what travel is like. You've gone between here and London often enough."

Truman said nothing; neither did Lady Penelope. The duke didn't seem to care that he'd interrupted before she could answer a question that had been posed directly to her.

"Shall we talk about the wedding?" His Grace asked.

That was the last subject Truman wanted to discuss, but if settling those details would bring on the conclusion of their visit, he was willing to make the sacrifice. He'd known he wasn't looking forward to seeing them, but he hadn't realized just how much he'd hate every minute of their stay. The past four hours had required more self-control than any four hours previous. Maybe it was because he resented the way the duke seemed so ready to capitalize on his misfortune.

Or was he really trying to help? To support the son of an old friend, as he said?

Regardless, Truman kept seeing Rachel in his mind's eye, kept wishing she were here instead of them. Her presence made even monumental concerns seem light. His current company made every minute feel like another step toward the gallows. Maybe it was a different type of gallows than the wooden platform in London, but he hardly thought he'd be "saved" if he went along with the duke's wishes. Saved from one type of misery only to become well-acquainted with another, perhaps.

"I'd like a June wedding," the duke said.

It was already late February. "That soon?" Truman asked.

"June leaves enough time for preparations to be made, if we start immediately, so why wait? You both have reason to take your vows as soon as possible."

"We are all aware of *my* current predicament," Truman said. "But why would Lady Penelope have any reason to hurry?"

He would've directed this question to her, but he knew she would defer to her father.

The duke's face reddened as if he'd spoken without thinking. "She doesn't have any reason to hurry, exactly. She just doesn't have any reason to wait."

Truman got the impression he'd meant what he said the first time. "You have no qualms about promising your daughter to a man who is in the midst of such a terrible scandal? I can't imagine many men, especially men of position, who would want to tie their daughter to such a poor wretch."

The duke made a negating gesture with one hand. "A woman who betrays her husband deserves whatever she gets."

This was hardly a testimonial to his innocence. Shocked that His Grace could be so practical and uncaring, Truman slid his chair back, but before he could respond, Lady Penelope spoke up.

"What my father meant to say is that I am dutiful and obedient and will give you no cause to become angry."

"She knows what's at stake," the duke chimed in. "She wouldn't be stupid enough to provoke you."

Truman lost his appetite. As hard as it was to believe, it seemed the Duke of Pembroke didn't really care whether he'd murdered Katherine.

He glanced at Lady Penelope. Twin spots of color rode high on her cheeks, but Truman got the feeling it wasn't embarrassment that had put them there—not this time. "You have nothing to fear," he told her. "I *didn't* kill my wife, and I hope, within another week or so, to prove it."

"What makes you think anything new will turn up?" the duke asked.

As Truman explained about the paintings, His Grace listened without interrupting.

"I hope you find them," he said when Truman had finished, but Lady Penelope suddenly piped up again—this time to contradict her father.

"Actually, I'm not sure Daddy would want that," she said with a sly smile. "Then you'd have no reason to go through with the wedding."

His Grace shot his daughter a sharp look, and that was enough to shut her up. Sobering instantly, she dropped her gaze to her plate. "Please excuse my interruption," she mumbled.

"The wine has gone to her head," the duke explained. "Obviously, joining our two families would be advantageous regardless of whether those paintings are found. I'm merely trying to help the son of a dear friend. You couldn't do any better than Penelope."

Then why the rush? What was so wrong with Lady Penelope that she couldn't make an advantageous match with any one of a dozen or more eligible suitors? She was the daughter of a duke! "Of course," Truman said. "I appreciate your generosity. Your daughter is a rare jewel."

"She will certainly do more for you than that poor village girl," the duke said as if he'd held his true feelings back as long as he could.

For Lady Penelope's sake, Truman smiled, but no one could do more for him than Rachel. "Shall we adjourn to the drawing room so the servants can finish clearing the table?"

The girl who answered the back door at Elspeth's told Rachel essentially the same thing she'd been told before. Elspeth wouldn't see her—no need to come back. She was clear and frank, maybe even a little angry that Rachel had returned. But Rachel wasn't about to leave without achieving an audience.

She pretended to accept her dismissal, but as soon as the girl went inside, she slipped in behind her and found her own way to the room she'd visited previously. Before she could knock to see if Elspeth was there, however, the sound of Elspeth's voice confirmed that she was.

"Is she gone?" she asked.

"Yes, ma'am," came the reply from the girl Rachel had just spoken to.

The door stood open a few inches. Rachel felt a nervous flutter in her stomach as she stepped up to the crack and peered inside. Elspeth and the girl who'd answered the door seemed to be alone, but Rachel couldn't be certain. She could see only a portion of the room.

"What does she want?" the girl asked. "Why does she keep comin' back?"

"What she wants and what she's going to get will be two different things if she's not careful," Elspeth replied.

"What do ye mean by that, mum?"

"It's none of your business, Milly." She flicked her hand to shoo the girl off. "Go get me something to eat—and clean up for your shift. I'm hoping for a busy night. I don't want you looking like an old sow."

The girl hung her head like a berated child. "Of course not."

Rachel stepped to one side as "Milly" came out. She could avoid a collision, but she couldn't avoid being seen.

"*What are ye doin' in 'ere?*" the girl cried. "*I told ye to go!*"

There didn't seem to be any point in responding. It was obvious enough that she hadn't listened. Throwing the door wide, Rachel circumvented the prostitute and walked in.

Elspeth had heard the commotion and was halfway across the room. "Rachel!"

"Yes, it's me."

"Ye need to go. Now."

"Why? Is there some reason we're no longer friends, Madame Soward?"

She rolled her eyes. "Ah, innocent to the last. We were never friends, *Miss* McTavish. We all 'ave our best interests to look out for, after all."

Maybe she *was* too innocent, because Elspeth's words stung. "That's what I can't figure. Why is it suddenly in *your* best interest to keep your distance?"

"Because I want to stay alive. And if *ye* want the same, ye'll listen to me an' get your arse out of 'ere."

She sounded seriously frightened. "Who are you afraid of? Cutberth? Wythe? Or someone else?"

"Men talk when they drink and screw, Rachel. I know more secrets than ye could ever imagine, and that puts me in a very bad position. If ye give anythin' away to the earl, *I'm* the one who'll get blamed. Ye mark my words."

"Maybe you'd be better off going to him yourself. Tell him what you know. Do the right thing. Then ask for his protection. He's a good man—"

She made a sound of disbelief. "As if an earl would 'ave anythin' to do with me. Unlike you, I know my place in life."

"But—"

"Don't argue with me. It would only be a matter of time before 'e threw me out on the streets. 'E can't protect me indefinitely. Look at you! 'E got in-volved just long enough to ruin ye."

"I know you won't believe this but I left Blackmoor Hall of my own accord."

"Ye should never 'ave sided with 'im to begin with, should never 'ave betrayed your own kind."

"That statement just shows how little you really know. If you'd let me explain—"

"I already know more than I want to," she broke in.

"Do you?" Rachel challenged. "Do you know that Cutberth and my mother had an affair during the six months prior to her death? Is that one of your secrets?"

This succeeded in surprising her. Rachel could tell by the look on her face.

"That's ridiculous," she responded. "What are ye talkin' about?"

"There's proof."

"What kind of proof?"

"Mrs. Cutberth found some letters they exchanged."

She shook her head. "So *that's* how he handled it."

"What do you mean? Who is *he*?"

"Just get out," she said and Rachel knew she'd be sorry if she didn't. Whatever thin bond had once existed between her and Elspeth had been sev-ered by doubt, fear and expediency.

Truman heard a soft knock, but it was well after midnight. Assuming it was a maid wanting to bank the fire, he didn't bother putting on a shirt. He an-swered the door in his trousers and robe.

It *was* one of his servants—Susanna, the maid he'd assigned to Lady Penelope for the duration of her visit—but she wasn't alone. The duke's daughter was with her, dressed in a filmy nightgown, from what he could tell, thanks to the gap in her satin wrap.

"Is something wrong?" he asked.

Lady Penelope answered. "I hoped we might have a few minutes to . . . talk."

Curious as to the reason she would choose to approach him in the middle of the night—and assuming it was because she didn't want her father to know—he nodded to Susanna that it was okay to leave Lady Penelope where she was. Then he stepped aside.

The duke's daughter smiled nervously as she moved past him.

"Would you like a drink?" he asked.

"Please."

She sounded almost desperate in her eagerness. He'd noticed her pre-occupation with alcohol earlier—as well as her father's disapproval of how much she drank—but he poured her a brandy to be polite. He wanted to learn why the duke was so anxious to have them marry and thought she might tell him.

"Thank you." She wouldn't meet his gaze when he handed her the glass.

"What did you come to talk about?"

After downing the brandy as if it were water, she set the glass aside, turned and slipped off her robe.

The nightgown was more than filmy—it was transparent.

"Lady Penelope, I highly doubt your father would approve of this, and I would never abuse his trust." He bent to retrieve the wrap she'd let fall to the floor, but she stopped him.

"You're not serious."

"I am. I have nothing but respect for you and your father and would never—"

She threw back her head and laughed, which caused him to fall silent. "Who do you think sent me here?" she asked.

Truman straightened. "Your *father* told you to offer yourself to me like this?"

"Why not? We *are* betrothed. That's all that matters to him."

The alarm bells that had been going off in Truman's head earlier rang loud and clear. "If all goes as planned, we will be married in June. Why are you here before we even have the chance to get acquainted?"

She lifted her chin. "You don't want me?"

He couldn't say that he did. She was attractive enough. It was Rachel that stood in the way. He feared she'd ruined him for all other women. His pulse quickened the moment he thought of her lying beneath him—but Lady Penelope stood all but naked in front of him and he felt nothing except the urge to cover her up and preserve her dignity. "I am trying to behave in as honorable a fashion as I can."

She shrugged. "Or you're getting your fill from your little trollop."

"Don't call her that." The words came out before he could stifle them, but they didn't evoke the response he expected.

Her eyebrows arched. "Your quick defense of her does you credit. So she means something to you."

He sighed. "She means a great deal."

"Which is probably why my father sent me. He's not stupid. He knows I must compare favorably, or we could lose you yet."

"What I don't understand is why your father is so set on this match."

She helped herself to more of his brandy. "A woman isn't worth anything unless she has a husband and children."

"There are other men."

"What would you say if I told you I don't want *any* man?"

"You'd rather be single for the rest of your life?"

She held up her glass and laughed. "I didn't say that."

"What am I missing?"

"I've been compromised, Truman, and my father is terrified that word will get out."

This time when he reached for her wrap, she let him retrieve it. She even accepted it and put it on. "You're in love with someone else," he said.

"Yes. And given that you are, too, maybe you can have some compassion for me."

Was he in love with Rachel? So far he'd refused to name what he felt, re-fused to tell Rachel because it would be selfish to give her false hope. He couldn't put his own wants and desires over his duty, wouldn't be able to respect himself if he did. But he couldn't deny that he felt far more for her than he had any other woman. "Who is your lover?"

"I won't name her."

He grabbed her arm. "*Her?*"

Her eyes lowered to his hand, but she didn't try to shake him off, and she didn't correct him. That was when he finally understood what was driving the duke. His Grace wanted to make a match for his daughter and send her off into the middle of nowhere before news of her sexual persuasion could come out. *That* was what the duke deemed a fair trade for saving Truman's neck.

"Was he not going to tell me you'd prefer to have a woman in your bed?"

"Of course. He wouldn't risk having you find out after the wedding and petition for an annulment on those grounds. He plans to tell you tomorrow."

"Once you've proven that you won't deny me my marital rights."

"You catch on quickly. His name and support will give you the protection you need to avoid prosecution for Katherine's death—no proof required. And I will give you an heir, regardless of what gender I prefer in my bed."

"Marriage lasts a long time. What of your happiness? What of mine?"

She gave a bitter snort. "We each have a family name to protect."

But at what cost?

"What will you do now that you know?" she asked.

"I will do what I was going to do anyway," he replied.

"And that is . . . ?"

"Tell your father I can't marry you."

The glass slipped from her hands but she didn't even flinch when it hit the floor. He got the feeling she was too intoxicated to react abruptly to much of anything. Maybe she'd thought alcohol would help her get through the night. "But you must," she whispered.

"I made the mistake of marrying for the wrong reasons once," he said. "I can't do it again."

"But you could hang! The Abbotts will not go away simply because you want them to. If only you knew how determined they are."

"I'm fully aware of what's at stake."

"You're *that* certain you'll be able to prove your innocence?"

"I'm not certain at all."

"Then you're willing to go to the gallows for this . . . shopkeeper?"

He drew a deep breath as he considered the question, but the truth was finally clear—at least in one regard. "If need be. Like you said, I'm in love with her."

"At least you have half a chance of being together," she said and swept from the room.

"Penelope."

When she turned, there were tears streaking down her face.

"I wish you the best."

She touched his arm. "Maybe I could've been married to you."

"I'm sorry that's not an option. But I don't think it ever really was."

"Then fight for her," she whispered. "Do everything you can to be together. Do it for those of us who are battling far more than a class barrier."

Chapter 21

The duke wasn't happy when he left. He said Truman was foolish to turn away such an advantageous alliance. But Truman couldn't do anything else. Maybe he was risking his neck, literally, but if he married Lady Penelope he'd be miserable every day of his life—and not because he didn't like her. He liked her a lot more than he'd thought he would. He just couldn't betray his own heart.

"You turned him down."

Truman glanced over at Linley. His butler stood at attention beside him on the drive as the duke's coach pulled away from the manse.

"Yes."

"And if we are unable to find the paintings?"

Truman knew his disapproval stemmed from concern. "I'm taking a gamble."

"One I fear you might regret."

"Never," he said. "I will take what comes but I won't imprison myself in another loveless marriage. Have William saddle my horse."

"Are you going to the colliery?"

"I'm going to the village to get Rachel and bring her home where she belongs."

Linley gave him an odd smile.

"What?" Truman said, surprised by his sudden softening.

"Now I know that you have found exactly what you've always wanted."

He thought of what Rachel had said when they argued yesterday: *How long would it be before you began to regret being with me?*

How could he convince her that he'd *never* regret it?

She could be so stubborn. . . .

"The question is whether or not she'll believe me."

Rachel had locked the doors when she first arrived for fear Cutberth would show up again, but that gave her little security. If he had a key to the shop, he could easily have a key to her house. How had he gained possession of it?

She supposed if he really had been having an affair with her mother, Jillian could've given it to him. But Wythe could've provided it, too. Since the earl owned both buildings, he had a master, and Wythe was his steward. She couldn't imagine he'd have trouble gaining access to any of the earl's properties.

She stopped sweeping. What had she been thinking? Cutberth couldn't have been the one to break into the bookshop. Why would anyone risk discovery by shattering a window if he could get in an easier way?

Before she could even attempt to solve that riddle, a knock drew her attention to the door and her earlier trepidation reasserted itself. She set the broom aside, hoping it was Mrs. Tate bringing nuncheon and not one of the hewers who'd sworn vengeance on her head. Cutberth, either.

The knock came again—brisk and insistent—before she could reach the door. "Rachel? Open up! Are you in there?"

It was the earl. A wave of relief washed over her, powerful enough that she had to put a hand on the wall to steady herself, but she wasn't about to let him in. She wanted to see him too badly—knew, after another lonely night, and with only a series of lonely nights stretching indefinitely into the future to look forward to—that she wouldn't be able to resist whatever he offered, no matter how unfair it would be to his betrothed.

"Go back to Blackmoor Hall," she called. "Go marry the duke's daughter."

"I can't," he said. "I sent them back to London today."

She couldn't believe her ears. "They were here?"

"They arrived yesterday, just after we talked. And now they're gone."

"What did you tell them?"

"I broke the engagement, Rachel." He rattled the knob. "Open the door."

Weak with the longing she'd been holding at bay, she closed her eyes and slid down the wall to the floor. Now she really wouldn't be able to deny him—or herself. "All the more reason you should leave."

"I'm *not* leaving," he responded. "Not without you."

His certainty and determination gave her a brief flash of hope. "Did they find the paintings, then?" In some small corner of her mind, she'd held out hope that he'd be able to clear his name, that he'd come for her. Was this that dream, coming true?

She caught her breath as she awaited his answer.

"Not yet."

"Have they searched the whole mine?"

There was a pause before he answered. "I'm afraid so. I received word just before I came here."

Tears sprang to her eyes. "Then I won't listen to you. Write the duke. Apologize and beg him to forgive you. I won't let the Abbotts gain any greater advantage, won't let you risk your life, not when marrying Lady Penelope could save you."

"That's my decision, not yours," he said.

Suddenly enraged that he'd hold out something she wanted so desperately but couldn't take, she got to her feet and opened the door. She intended to send him packing—and in no uncertain terms so that he would never return—but he forced the door out of her grasp as soon as he had the chance.

"Rachel, listen to me."

"I won't. I can't. The best thing I can do, probably for both of us, is stay away—"

"Even if I can't live without you?"

This brought tears to her eyes. "Don't make it any harder. You said that to me once."

He caught her arm. "Look at me."

"No. I mean it. Go." She tried to wrench away, but he wouldn't let her. He brought her up against his chest.

"Stop fighting," he murmured in her ear.

"But you're ready for Bedlam if you think we have *any* chance—"

One hand fisted in her hair as he cut off her words with a kiss. The way he held her made it impossible for her to escape. She remained determined to finish her sentence in spite of that, but not for long. Once his arms tightened, the longing she'd been battling since she left took control.

Parting her lips and meeting his tongue with her own triggered an onslaught of emotion. He seemed to sense her need, seemed to feel plenty of his own and responded by kicking the door shut and carrying her into the bedroom.

"That's it, sweet Rachel," he murmured as he put her on the bed. "Trust me. I will always take care of you."

Not if they hung him. But she wouldn't think of that, couldn't even bear the thought of it. The familiar smell of him—horses and cold weather and sandalwood soap—evoked the most intimate of memories, making her burn to feel his skin against hers yet again.

"We are making a mistake," she warned. The further in love she let herself fall, the harder it would be to recover. In this moment, she doubted she would *ever* get over him. She feared she'd die a lonely spinster, completely devoted to the only man she'd ever loved—and the one man only a fool would believe she could ever really have.

But she couldn't resist such overwhelming desire, couldn't even think straight while his lips were moving down her neck and his hands were sliding up her skirt.

"We are from separate worlds." She wasn't sure why she went back to that tired argument. To make him see reason? To remind herself?

Regardless, he was having none of it.

"Then it's time for our separate worlds to become one," he told her. "Marry me. I want you to be my wife, by my side no matter what happens."

This *had* to be a dream—but if it were, Rachel didn't want to wake up.

They didn't take time to remove more clothing than they had to before he thrust inside her. She moaned as she arched back, reveling in that distinctly full sensation she'd known only with him. Truman was here with her now in the most intimate of ways. Maybe they were cheating the world and would pay later, but there was some sort of victory in the here and now, in the celebration of their feelings.

"You will be mine," he said with a powerful thrust. "Regardless of where or how you were born, you are *meant* to be mine."

She gripped his shoulders as she stared up at him. "Do you love me?"

"Would I risk everything for a woman I didn't?" he asked.

Worry stole some of the enjoyment from her. "I fear you will regret it."

His lips touched hers, briefly, tenderly. "I could *never* regret loving you."

They fell silent after that as the tension grew. There was no reason to talk. The way he made love to her was different this time. It was far more desperate and hurried now that they'd almost lost each other, but there was as much commitment in his actions as in his words. When she reached climax, he smiled but didn't even attempt to withdraw. He gave an animalistic growl, as if he were laying claim, closed his eyes and let go, willingly spilling his seed inside her.

Because Rachel had wanted to finish cleaning—it was her way of saying good-bye to the house she'd lived in with her family and to the memories it contained—the earl had gone on ahead, saying he'd send his carriage back later. And Timothy had arrived not long after to collect her and her meager belongings.

"Yer really goin' back to 'im?" Mrs. Tate asked, scarcely able to believe it.

Rachel couldn't believe it either, but she nodded.

"I wish ye the best, child. I've always wished ye the best."

"I know. Thank you for your unfailing kindness." She hugged Mrs. Tate as if that one brief embrace would have to sustain her for a long while. What lay ahead wouldn't be easy. She could already guess that Mrs. Poulson wouldn't welcome her in her new role. Nor would Wythe. Even Mary, her maid friend, and the kind butler, Mr. Linley, would be shocked and skeptical. *Everybody* would think the earl had lost his mind. She'd be treated as if she wasn't good enough for him—and he'd be treated as if he was a fool for wanting *her* when he could marry into one of the greatest families in all of England.

If she were Mrs. Poulson, Mr. Linley, or any of the other servants or villagers, she'd probably feel the same way. An earl simply didn't marry a poor miner's daughter.

But Truman seemed convinced that he wanted her to be with him. And he'd insisted, before he left, that she rely on what *he* said and not anyone else.

Overcome with a sudden panic, she almost couldn't bring herself to climb into the earl's carriage, however—especially when a few of the other neighbors came out to stare at the peculiar sight of the earl's coach sitting in front of Mrs. Tate's humble abode.

"Miss McTavish? May I offer you my assistance?" One of the earl's footmen held the door while Timothy, the driver, remained in the box on top.

Taking the hand the footman offered her, Rachel forced a smile and let him help her inside. But she'd never felt more self-conscious of her low position in life.

"Are you all settled, mum?"

"Yes, thank you," she replied and he climbed on back before Timothy cracked the whip and they started off.

Rachel rode with her hands clasped tightly in her lap. The first time she'd been inside this carriage was the snowy night she'd brought the doctor. So much had changed since then. Was she wrong for agreeing to marry the earl? She didn't want him to have to cope with the social stigma they would face, but he seemed singularly determined.

Despite the strength of his commitment, when they approached the gates, she almost cried out for Timothy to take her back. She was in love with the earl, but maybe that was precisely the reason she should run away and never speak to him again.

"Timothy?" she called.

He didn't stop. They started up the drive before he spoke above the grating of the carriage wheels.

"Yes, Miss McTavish?"

It wasn't easy to get any words out with her heart in her throat. She pressed a hand to her chest in an effort to settle her pulse, but before she could insist he return her to the village, she saw Geordie running toward them.

"I'll get out here," she said.

Geordie threw himself into her arms as soon as she alighted. "I am *so* glad you're back, Rachel. I hated thinking I wouldn't get to see you as often."

Rachel gazed up at the manse. It looked more imposing now than it ever had before. And she was to be mistress of it? "I'm glad to be back, Geordie."

"The earl has asked Mrs. Poulson to make us some meat pies and savory pudding. He said I can have the afternoon off and the two of us can eat in the parlor and be together as long as we like. Isn't that nice of him, Rachel? Mum and Dad never cared for him, but he seems like a kind fellow to me."

"He *is* a kind fellow, Geordie." Knowing the earl had provided her with this opportunity so she could tell her brother about their betrothal before he heard the news from someone else, she smiled. "Did he also tell you we are to be married?"

His eyes went round. "*You?* Marrying the *earl?*"

She frowned as she stared down at her very practical and not particularly nice wool dress. She hardly looked the part. "He asked me today."

It took her brother a moment to absorb it. "Do you think he was teasing?" he asked at length.

Only those few minutes when they were making love made it feel real. She knew Truman hadn't been teasing about anything then. "He seemed serious at the time."

She expected her brother to react with the same shock and skepticism she anticipated from everyone else. But a broad smile curved his lips, and he seemed completely in earnest when he said, "Then he's a smart fellow, too."

Grateful for this single token of confidence, Rachel mussed his hair and stepped aside as the carriage rolled past them. "Thank you for that, little brother. God knows how much I needed it."

"Shall we go eat?"

The thought of confronting Poulson so soon wasn't appealing. She decided she'd rather put it off—until she became more accustomed to the idea of being Lady Druridge. "No. I want to enjoy the outdoors. Would you mind if we went for a walk along the cliffs instead?" They'd developed a few favorite spots. She wanted to go back to them.

"Not at all. We could always bring the meat pies."

"You wouldn't be too cold?"

"Cold! It's warm compared to what it's been these past weeks, almost like summer."

"Good." Again she felt that reluctance to face Mrs. Poulson. Doing so would wreck her fragile excitement. "Run in and get the food."

"You want *me* to get it?"

She chuckled. "If you're brave enough to manage the earl's housekeeper."

"I'm brave enough," he boasted. "Mr. Grude tells me I'm not to let her bother me one bit. He says some people are naturally unlikable and they'll get what's coming to them eventually."

"That sounds like good advice." Rachel grinned as she watched him hurry inside. She didn't think the air was quite as warm as he did, but she could manage until the sun went down, thanks to her cloak.

She stood staring at Blackmoor Hall as she waited. Who would've thought this would ever become her home?

"I've got it," Geordie called as soon as he came back out. Sure enough, he carried a hamper.

"That's a good lad!" she said. "It has certainly been an interesting winter, hasn't it?"

"A hard winter," he said. "I wish Mum was around to hear you're marrying the earl." His tone was a trifle awestruck.

She slipped her arm through his as they walked around to the back. "I don't think she'd like it, do you?"

"Look how good he's been to us. She was wrong about him, Rachel."

"I think so too," she said.

Chapter 22

"*What* did you say?" Wythe addressed a flushed Mr. Tyndale, who'd hurried out to meet him as he slid off his horse.

"Your cousin is going to marry Rachel McTavish!"

The boredom he'd been feeling after spending so many hours in the mine evaporated. "That can't be true."

"It is." Tyndale was obviously pleased. He acted as if Rachel had had the last laugh and he was glad of it. He'd never really cared for Wythe, and Wythe knew it. They came to loggerheads at the colliery all the time. Although the Fore-Overman never dared to expressly disagree—he was far too circumspect for that—Wythe could feel his disapproval and was determined to be free of it. Soon.

"How do you know?"

"I just came from the village. They are saying he broke his betrothal to Lady Penelope and proposed to Rachel. The news is everywhere."

Tyndale's excitement irritated Wythe. He couldn't wait to wreck it. "That pleases you, Tyndale?"

"It does, sir. I have always been partial to Rachel. It is wonderful to see her come out on top for a change."

"So you're happy the earl will hang?"

The smile dropped off his face. "Excuse me, sir?"

"That's what will happen if he marries Rachel. He will go to the gallows. It is just a matter of time."

His mouth opened and closed twice before any words came out. "It's not as serious as all that, is it? The earl is . . . well, he's an earl. They won't hang a member of the aristocracy, not without solid proof."

"The Abbotts are powerful too, Mr. Tyndale."

"I would never want anything to happen to Lord Druridge," he said. "I have always respected him."

"Then you will agree that he is making a terrible mistake. It would be a mistake to marry someone like Rachel even if he wasn't facing murder charges. She might be beautiful, but a lot of women are beautiful—and they all look the same in the dark."

"He is obviously in love," Tyndale responded, instantly defensive.

"Ah, yes, love." Wythe rolled his eyes. "Is this why you were looking for me? To share the *wonderful* news?"

"I'm sorry—what did you say?"

The old goat was upset now, enough that his mind had been almost instantly diverted.

"I ran into Cutberth as I was leaving the mine. He said you were looking for me earlier."

Tyndale yanked on the bottom of his waistcoat. Given how his buttons strained, it was a miracle they held fast. "Yes, I-I was. But everyone thought you'd left."

"I hadn't finished searching."

"You were *in* the mine? But we finished looking for the paintings this morning."

He had only been sitting around, draining his flask in an abandoned tunnel, but no one would know that. "I had to check Number 15 stall."

The look that came over the Fore-Overman's face was gratifying. Tyndale had regarded the earl with that expression many times, but never Wythe. Part of Wythe wished he deserved the veneration, but he wasn't one to quibble over details. He had realized long ago that he couldn't compete with his far-more-noble cousin.

"You went into 15?" Tyndale breathed. "But that could've cost you your life. We decided it was too unstable."

"As I said, the earl's life is at stake." Wythe brushed some of the coal dust from his clothes. "We couldn't ask any of the men to take such a risk, but I felt like we had to be sure."

"That is very brave of you," he said. "And? Did you find anything?"

"No. Which makes this news about Rachel far worse than it might have been, does it not?" He sighed. "If the earl isn't careful, that woman will prove his ruin."

A frown tugged at Tyndale's lips—but he made an attempt to rally. "I think Katherine's already got that well in hand, don't you? You explained to me earlier that without at least one of those paintings, Lord Druridge can't prove his innocence. That has nothing to do with Rachel."

"It does when you consider that marrying Lady Penelope would have provided him with a certain amount of protection." Wythe handed the reins of his horse to the groom who approached. The stable at Cosgrove House was not nearly as large or well staffed as the one at Blackmoor Hall. He was tired of the inconvenience, tired of being cast into outer darkness like a child who'd lost favor. But he didn't think his situation would remain what it was for much longer. "As soon as I change, I will go over to see if I can talk some sense into him."

"Poor Rachel. I hate to see her hurt, but . . . I now understand why this is so important." Tyndale fidgeted with his waistcoat again. "It is admirable of you to do what you can, Mr. Stanhope—all the more so because of the situation."

Wythe paused, purposely playing dumb. "What situation, Mr. Tyndale?"

He shifted uncomfortably. He knew, had to know, it was indelicate of him to mention it, but he finally came out with the explanation Wythe had requested. "Well, the obvious, sir. If the earl dies before he can sire an heir, you will inherit everything."

"If I wanted my cousin dead, I would've let him burn," Wythe said with the dramatic flourish he'd come to enjoy and strode to the house. Maybe he hadn't done many things right in his life, but he was glad he had troubled himself that day. Had Truman died in the fire, Wythe would have taken the blame. No one else had as much to gain from his death.

But everything was going to work out in the end.

He started to whistle when he thought of what the Abbotts would be able to do. Let his cousin marry Rachel. Let the bitch think she was going to get everything she'd ever wanted. Her happiness wouldn't last. Soon, she would watch her beloved die on the scaffold at Newgate and the title and Stanhope fortune would pass to him. Then he'd dump her and her brat of a brother out on their arses without so much as a halfpenny—unless he decided to make her his paramour for turning her nose up at him before.

Maybe that would teach her to respect her betters.

Truman found Cutberth at the office. Although Tyndale and everyone else had gone home for the day, a lamp burned on the clerk's desk and he was bent over his bookwork, looking for all the world like the most diligent of employees.

"My lord," he said quietly when Truman walked in.

"I see you received my message."

He didn't seem surprised that Truman had requested a meeting. Truman hadn't expected him to be. Word had spread about his betrothal to Rachel. Cutberth had to have guessed she would tell him about their encounter at the shop.

"I am just finishing up," he said. "All the excitement yesterday when we were searching for the Bruegel paintings set me back, and I wanted"—he cleared his throat—"I wanted to bring the books current before turning them over to my replacement."

"Then you know why I am here."

"I do."

Truman stopped at the edge of the desk and picked up a vase, obviously made by a child. "It's unfortunate, really. You have a nice family. I hate the thought that they might suffer because of your actions."

"I knew I was taking a risk." He shoved his shoulders back. "But I believed in what I was doing. I still believe in it and will continue to organize the men as long as they will pay me enough so that I can keep a roof over my family's heads."

Truman put down the vase. "I appreciate your newfound honesty, so I will be honest with you. That might prove difficult. They may not see any point in hiring you once I announce my new profit-sharing plan. But I understand you must do what you must do."

He seemed shaken, as if he had been pushing against an immovable object that had suddenly given way. "Profit-sharing plan?"

"Wythe will provide the details in the next few days. Since you are no longer an employee of Stanhope & Co., I won't go into it with you, but I do want you to understand that I am not letting you go because of the union, even though you had no business marshaling forces to oppose me while on my payroll and pretending to have my best interests at heart."

Looking chastened, Cutberth cleared his throat. "I didn't plan to continue after—"

Truman lifted a hand to indicate he had no interest in his excuses. "I am not letting you go because I suspect you were involved in the fire that caused my wife's death, either."

At this he jumped to his feet. "My lord, no. You can lay the union at my feet, but I had nothing to do with the fire, and I don't know who did, as I have always said."

"Forgive me for pointing out that your credibility isn't quite what it used to be." He forced a pained smile. "Regardless, I wouldn't have taken your job on suspicion alone. I would have waited until I had proof."

"You will never have proof, because I didn't do it. I swear!"

"Then why did you lie about your relationship with Mrs. McTavish in order to explain away the payments she received?"

He didn't attempt to deny it. "To protect the union, of course. That money came from a fund I created to help the widows and orphans of miners who die on the job. That is why I got so upset when Rachel admitted she told you about my efforts. I feared it would cost me my livelihood *and* destroy everything I'd accomplished so far. It has already scared away many of those who were interested in contributing to that fund and creating other, similar schemes for those who work at Stanhope & Co."

Truman leaned forward, bringing his nose very close to Cutberth's. "So you *struck* her?"

Cutberth seemed to realize that *this* was the part that angered him most. "I-I shouldn't have," he said. "I cannot explain what came over me. I was . . . out of sorts, enraged. I felt as if she had ruined so many good things by reaching for a man who was—who *is*—too far above her."

"How did you get the key to her shop?"

Cutberth's nostrils flared and he could no longer meet Truman's eyes. "Wythe has a master set to all your holdings. I went through his office when he wasn't around."

Of course. And it probably wasn't too difficult to find. Wythe wasn't as diligent as he should be about anything. There was even the possibility that he'd given Cutberth the key.

"What about the lie you told about her mother? You didn't care about the humiliation that might cause her? You didn't care about the humiliation that might cause your own wife?"

"I felt it was . . . for a good cause, my lord. I *had* to protect the union."

"It's a miracle your wife will speak to you, let alone live with you. Maybe she will leave now that you no longer have a job."

"I admit I let myself get carried away. I am sorry about that. I truly am."

"You should be," he said. "Don't *ever* come near Rachel again. Not for any reason. Do you understand?"

"Yes, of course."

"You will have a month's wages. I suggest you use it wisely." He turned to go, but Cutberth spoke before he could reach the door.

"My lord?"

"Yes?"

"If one of the miners set that fire, I would probably know about it. Although I couldn't say this before, no one is closer to them than I am. Have you considered . . . ?" He stopped, obviously unsure whether he should continue.

"Go on."

"I hate to cast doubt on anyone, but . . ."

Again Truman had to prod him. "Out with it, man!"

His chest lifted as he drew a deep breath. "Have you considered any of the servants?"

Truman narrowed his eyes. "All the servants were in church, Mr. Cutberth."

"Except Mrs. Poulson."

That was true. She'd left the day before to visit a sick aunt. But his housekeeper would have no reason to murder Katherine. On the contrary, Truman was convinced she had secretly gained some sort of satisfaction from watching his wife play her manipulative games. Why would she want to get rid of her? "And what would be her motive?"

"To protect you from scandal."

Truman had to laugh. "That's hardly something that would motivate Mrs. Poulson to murder."

"Someone else in your household then."

"I have told you all the rest of the servants, barring Mrs. Poulson, as you have just pointed out, were in church."

"That doesn't mean they didn't hire someone to do it."

"I have already learned that it was a group of miners who approached Jack." Truman didn't want to give up on that. Nothing he had found had led him to believe it could be a member of his domestic staff.

"Can you be sure that's accurate? You asked the miners what they'd heard, and they'd heard that Jack was offered some money. Maybe they only assumed it was from other miners. In their minds, that is who would logically approach him. But it could have been anyone, even a woman."

"Except Mrs. Poulson would have no reason to set fire to Blackmoor Hall. How would a mere servant come by the money to give Jack McTavish, anyway?"

"Mr. Linley makes a good salary."

Truman walked back to his desk. "You think my *butler* stole those paintings and set the fire to cover his tracks?"

"No, I think maybe your butler wanted Katherine dead. He could have taken the paintings for a variety of reasons—to sell them, to salvage them, to throw off an investigation."

Linley was the only person Truman knew who'd loved those paintings as much as his father did. He had mourned their loss far more than Katherine's life. Linley had hated Katherine, was convinced she would be the ruin of the

Stanhope dynasty he had spent so many years serving and protecting. He definitely wanted her gone. But he would never *kill* her.

"It has to be someone else," he insisted.

"It's not one of the miners, my lord."

"*What* are you getting at?"

"It's someone who lived at Blackmoor Hall. Maybe even your cousin."

Cutberth was growing bold now that he had nothing to lose. Although Truman suspected Wythe and had for several months—ever since he'd come to the conclusion that no one from London had traveled all the way to Creswell with murderous intent—he was still a member of the family. Truman would not humiliate him by sharing his suspicions with just anyone. "Have some respect. My cousin rescued me; it couldn't be him."

"*Someone* had to have fathered her child," he said. "And I don't think it was a miner or a servant. Do you?"

The thought had certainly crossed Truman's mind before. But Wythe was a Stanhope. He had *some* boundaries, didn't he?

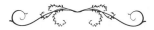

It felt strange to be back at Blackmoor Hall—and even stranger to hold yet another position in the household. Rachel had come here as the lowest of the maids. She'd graduated to something rather awkward and undefined as the earl's chess partner. And now she was the earl's betrothed. She knew it had to be as difficult for his staff as it was for her to make the appropriate adjustments, but so far they had treated her better than expected, and that included Mrs. Poulson. The housekeeper had greeted Rachel politely, even dipped into a curtsy when Truman lined up the staff and told them they were to accept her as their new mistress. There had been some shocked faces, of course—maybe even some hidden resentment, especially when he had stated, in no uncertain terms, that she had the authority to sack anyone who proved the least disagreeable—but no one stepped up when he asked if they would rather leave their post than serve her.

Although Truman had privately suggested that, for her sake, it might be wise to start over with a whole new staff—other than Mr. Linley and

Mrs. Poulson, of course—she had asked him to give the servants time to acclimate. As long as Mrs. Poulson continued to be civil, Rachel thought they would manage. After all, she and Mr. Linley set the tone for the whole household.

Following that meeting Rachel was feeling optimistic, especially when Mary winked at her as they all filed out. She had one friend. She had the earl and her brother and, possibly, Mr. Linley, even though his determination to expose her father had once made him her enemy. That was a start. After the dread she had felt going before the staff, she relaxed, to a degree, and enjoyed a delicious dinner with Truman. But that pleasant interlude proved all too brief when he left right after to seek out Cutberth. Rachel had tried to talk him into waiting until morning, but the bruise on her cheek bothered him so greatly he'd been intent on having a word with his clerk as soon as possible. He didn't like that he hadn't been able to deal with the issue since the duke and his daughter had arrived and didn't want to let it go any longer.

"Mum?"

Rachel glanced up from the book she had been using to distract herself while she waited for Truman. Susanna was standing just inside the doorway of the library.

"Yes?"

"Mr. Stanhope is 'ere. 'E asked me to let ye know that 'e'd like a word with ye."

Wythe. Rachel barely refrained from wrinkling her nose. She didn't want to see him, was still afraid of him. Other than a few vague references, she hadn't told Truman how he had behaved that night on the road to Blackmoor Hall. She figured she would give him, like the servants, a chance to accept her. He was the earl's cousin, after all. She wouldn't come between them if she could avoid it. But that didn't mean she was excited to spend any time alone with him and, as far as she could tell, the earl had not yet returned.

"Shall I tell 'im ye'll be down, Mistress Rachel?" Susanna prodded when she hesitated.

Rachel was about to put him off. But then she changed her mind. Maybe if she told him she would never divulge exactly what he had said to her that night—that she would credit it all to drink—he would be equally willing to put the past behind them.

With that in mind, she told Susanna to tell him she would be just a moment. Then, when she had gathered her courage for whatever might ensue, she abandoned her book and started for the stairs.

He turned from the fire when he heard her come in. "There you are."

She smiled politely. "Hello, Mr. Stanhope."

"Now that we are to be cousins, you don't feel as if you can use my first name?"

"I feared doing so might seem overly familiar, considering the changes have been so recent."

"How can you and I be too familiar?" he said with a laugh. "I have seen you naked, have I not?"

She stiffened at the reminder but worked to keep her smile in place. "I prefer that we forget that night. I thought perhaps you might agree."

"I do. I absolutely agree. Although forgetting it will do little if you have already told Truman what I said . . . what I wanted."

"I haven't elaborated. He knows only that you deposited me in his bed without my express permission. I prefer to spare him the ugly details, given that you are his family and he cares so much about you."

He smiled but somehow Wythe's smiles never reached his eyes. "You are as generous as you are beautiful. What a lucky man Truman is."

She got the impression he was being sarcastic. Obviously, a poor miner's daughter was no real prize for an earl, but she wasn't willing to abandon her attempt to make peace quite yet. She saw nothing to be gained by barging into Truman's life and upsetting the balance; she was already self-conscious about what he would have to deal with, due to their decision to wed. "Thank you for your kind words. As you may know, Truman is out this evening. But he should be back shortly. Is there anything I can do for you in the meantime?"

He chuckled.

"What is it?" she asked.

"It just might be possible."

"To . . . ?"

"Make a lady out of you. You certainly sound high and mighty."

She had done what she could to dress the part, had chosen the burgundy dress Truman had bought her for this evening, but Wythe made her feel as if she was standing there in her wool dress. "I hope to sound polite and friendly. If that is high and mighty, I apologize."

"You won't even fight with me?"

"Are you *trying* to vex me?"

"Getting a rise out of you would be more interesting, and probably more honest, than this, but . . . you are determined and I won't provoke you." He looked her up and down. "So . . . what? Are you planning to step into my cousin's life without making a ripple?"

"If I can."

"And what will you do when they summon him to court?"

She curled her fingernails into her palms as she battled the fear his words evoked. "I hope the paintings will be found, and he won't be summoned to court. I am sure you hope the same."

Wythe's expression made his true feelings difficult to determine, but his words were what she would expect them to be. "Of course. But I'm not sure you should depend on finding those paintings."

"Because . . . ?"

"We have already been through the mine. Where else can they be?"

"They could be anywhere." She stepped closer. "Elspeth's, for instance."

"The whorehouse!"

If he thought his blatant use of the word might make her wince, he was wrong. She hadn't been sheltered like the ladies of the gentry. "Why not?" she responded. "Elspeth could be storing them in her attic or cellar."

A muscle moved in his cheek. "You will find nothing at Elspeth's."

She arched her eyebrows. "How do you know if you've never looked?"

"Because she would have told me if she was hiding paintings that could prove my cousin innocent of Katherine's murder."

"You are *such* great friends?"

"We are very great friends indeed."

She clapped. "Wonderful."

His face reflected his confusion. "Excuse me?"

"Then she won't mind letting Truman search tomorrow. *You* can arrange it."

He opened his mouth as if he would refuse but seemed to think better of it. "I will talk to her when I go there tonight."

Would he? What would he do when he got there? That was what she intended to find out. "I know Truman would appreciate it. I will tell him you might save him yet again."

His nostrils flared with dislike despite her acknowledgment of his heroism, but he gave her a bow nonetheless. "Mistress Rachel."

"Goodnight, Wythe," she said.

Chapter 23

As soon as the earl's cousin left, Rachel sent for Mr. Linley. She would have gone to Truman instead, but he wasn't yet home, and she didn't want to let his cousin get too far ahead of them.

"Yes, Mistress Rachel?"

She looked up from the settee as the butler entered. "Mr. Linley, thank you for coming."

"Of course. I am at your service. Always."

The devotion in that statement filled her with gratitude. There were times when it felt as if she and the earl would have to stand against the world. "I appreciate that. I do. But the favor I am about to ask is a bit out of the ordinary. I dare put it to you only because I am confident of your great love for Lord Druridge."

He dipped his head. "You can depend on me, my lady."

The ending to that statement took her aback. "You don't have to address me that way, Mr. Linley. We both know I am not a *true* lady, and I am not one to put on airs."

"You certainly act the part. And you will soon be the wife of an earl. I am more than happy to give you the respect due your new station in life."

She dipped her head to acknowledge his kindness. "That is truly generous of you. I hope the rest of the staff can accept me too, so we can all get on . . . comfortably."

"Considering they will make the adjustment or work elsewhere, I do believe they won't find it *too* difficult."

He acted as if she had every right to expect their full cooperation. "I appreciate you trying to ease my concerns," she said, "but I would hate for it to come to that."

"I will see to the servants. Never you fear." He used his cane as he came closer. "Now, this favor you wanted. What can I do for you?"

She was nervous to tell him. She was acting on instinct alone and had no real justification for what she was about to propose. "As I mentioned, you might find this a bit odd, but Lord Druridge isn't here and I don't want to miss what I feel could be important in proving him innocent of Katherine's murder."

"I will do anything, especially anything you deem important."

In spite of that, she braced for his reaction. "I would like you to follow Mr. Stanhope this evening."

He lowered his voice. "You mean . . . *secretly*?"

Rachel hated to reveal her distrust of the earl's own cousin. But he had given her such an odd feeling a moment ago when she suggested he make arrangements for a search of the brothel. And she knew Elspeth had information, which had most likely come from Wythe. In her mind, it was entirely conceivable that, if the paintings were still in Creswell, she was hiding them in a locked attic or cellar. "Yes, secretly," she confirmed. "I want to know where he goes and what he does." Since Wythe knew her intentions were to search the brothel, he might try to move the paintings, if they were there in the first place. She planned to be ready for him if he did.

He propped both hands on top of his cane. "How do you feel this might prove his lordship's innocence, my lady?"

"I believe Elspeth's will be one of Mr. Stanhope's stops."

His thick eyebrows shot up. "Knowing Wythe, it will probably be his *only* stop. But I am rather certain we already know what he does there."

Chuckling, she came to her feet. "Perhaps tonight will be different. I have asked him to secure Elspeth's agreement so that we can search the brothel tomorrow and—"

"Excuse me, my lady. But you did say *brothel*?"

"I am afraid so, Mr. Linley." Most decent folks wouldn't go anywhere near a house of ill repute. She understood that. He probably wondered who would perform the search even if Wythe made it possible. No God-fearing

Christian woman would want her husband in such a place. They couldn't use the footmen or stable lads for fear of corrupting them, and the maids were out of the question. Just darkening the doorstep of a brothel could ruin a young girl. But Rachel was determined. She would do it herself, if need be. She had taken the risk of associating with Elspeth before. Whatever happened, they couldn't leave it to Wythe. If they did, they might as well not search at all. "Those paintings have to be somewhere, Mr. Linley."

Two deep grooves formed between his eyes. "What makes you think they might be *there*?"

"Elspeth knows something about the fire. I am convinced of it."

"She claims she doesn't. I have spoken to her many times."

"I have spoken to her too. Although she once led me to believe she could name those who approached my father, she has since clammed up. I wonder why—what, specifically, she is afraid of. . . ."

"She would certainly have reason to fear if she has the paintings."

"*If* Wythe took them in the first place, he had to have somewhere to put them."

"The earl has offered a significant reward for their recovery. I would expect someone like Elspeth to come forward and claim it."

"Unless she is afraid she won't live long enough to enjoy the money."

"You're not suggesting Wythe would . . . *kill* her?"

It wasn't an accusation she enjoyed making. She was probably crossing all kinds of lines when it came to the "hero" who had pulled Truman from the fire. But she had to do everything in her power to clear the earl's name. And the Wythe she knew was capable of anything. *I could throw your body into the ocean and tell my dear cousin that you ran away in the night.* Although he had later recanted those words and claimed he hadn't been serious, they had felt *quite* serious at the time. "Someone killed Katherine, did they not?"

"Indeed. Thank you for relying on me to handle this for you. I will take the matter from here."

She felt a flicker of concern. "Are you sure you are up to going out this late? I know you must be tired. Maybe there is someone you trust—"

"Not with this. But never you worry. I am more than capable, my lady."

She breathed a sigh of relief. He was no longer a young man, but she didn't feel as if she had anyone else to turn to. "Thank you, Mr. Linley. I—"

The floor creaked in the entry, causing Rachel to fall silent.

Was someone there?

A shadow fell against the single door that stood open. She wouldn't have noticed if she hadn't heard that creak, but now that she had focused her attention that way, it looked to be in the shape of a person . . . .

"Hello?" she called. "Who is it?"

The shadow vanished as whoever cast it darted away, but Rachel managed to get out of the room quickly enough to see a flash of fabric—the hem of a skirt—disappear around the far corner.

Was it the housekeeper?

Rachel couldn't be certain. She hurried to the steps leading to the kitchen and servants' hall, but they were empty.

"Mrs. Poulson?" she called down, just in case.

There was no answer.

Wythe took a long swig from the flask in his pocket as he paced in his room at Cosgrove House. He had hated few women as much as he hated Rachel. He had managed to endure the conceit of his aristocratic relations—he had put up with being treated as the "lesser" cousin his whole life—but he could not endure a mere miner's daughter acting as if *she* was better than him, too. How dare the earl pretend as if he could take a common villager into his bed and make her into anything he wanted, including his wife, when he hadn't even tried to demand that his own cousin be treated with the proper respect. And how dare that woman assume she had a right to all she had been offered. Rachel wasn't the mistress of Blackmoor Hall quite yet. Truman hadn't even been home, yet she had dared step up and take over for him.

Wythe thought about the many things he had planned for Miss McTavish after the earl was hanged. She would be sorry then, he told himself.

Planning his revenge helped ease his anger but did nothing to solve the problem at hand. He had to get the paintings out of Elspeth's right away, before the earl could organize a search. If they were found, he would lose everything he was about to inherit. There was even a chance he would be hanged instead of his cousin.

But how would he get them out? He couldn't carry them on horseback, couldn't even ask for a wagon this late—not without good reason. And where would he put the paintings once he rescued them from the brothel?

He took another pull from his flask. *The mine.* He would put them in the mine. No one would look there because it had already been searched. He could hide them in Number 15 stall, where everyone was too afraid to go, until he could sell them.

But he wasn't sure moving them would warrant the risk or the effort. They were worth a great deal, but things had changed. When he wound up with everything Truman had, he wouldn't miss the money from the Bruegels, so they were no longer important.

What had been unthinkable just a few days before now seemed like his best option. He should destroy them. Immediately. That way they could never come between him and the future that was within his grasp. He wouldn't have to secret them out of the brothel in order to do it. He would merely have to chop them in pieces and burn them in the grate.

"Mr. Stanhope?"

Tyndale. The old windbag was calling up to him from below. What did he want now?

"What is it?" he snapped.

"You have a visitor."

He refilled his flask. "Who?"

"Mrs. Poulson."

Good. The only person he could trust. He needed to talk to her.

He poked his head out of his room so that Tyndale could easily hear him. "Send her up."

The rotund Fore-Overman gaped at him from the bottom of the stairs. "You want her to come to your *bedroom*, sir?"

Yes. He definitely wanted that. He wasn't about to let Tyndale overhear a word they said. And he wasn't about to go out in the rain to avoid that. "If you are afraid it might compromise her reputation, Mr. Tyndale, please don't worry. Knowing you to be an honorable man, I trust you will not tell a soul."

He straightened his waistcoat. He fidgeted with that thing so often, Wythe wondered why he bothered wearing one—or why he didn't get one that fit properly. "I would *never* create gossip, Mr. Stanhope."

"You see? We have nothing to fear. Send her up."

"*Now?*" he stalled as if he were trying to think of another argument against it.

"Of course now. There is no point in keeping her waiting. And rest assured that I will not act the least bit inappropriate with the housekeeper of Blackmoor Hall." He wouldn't sleep with her if she were the last woman on earth—and there was good reason for that.

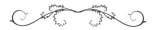

Linley hung back in the trees surrounding Cosgrove House. He had been fairly certain that Mrs. Poulson had overheard him speaking with Rachel, that she might know what they had planned. So he had been waiting to see if she would come along and, sure enough, she had. She'd hurried down the path as if her life had depended on reaching Wythe as soon as possible.

He watched her pass. Then he watched her knock at the door and go in.

"Are you telling him what I think you are telling him?" he murmured to himself. She had to be. Why else had she come out in this inclement weather? She hadn't even bothered to be discreet about it. That is what concerned him. She knew he would be watching—had heard as much when she'd been hovering outside the drawing room—yet that didn't stop her.

Was it because Rachel had stumbled upon the truth? Were those paintings at Elspeth Soward's? And did Mrs. Poulson know it?

The earl should have sacked her long ago, Linley thought. She had been a thorn in everyone's side since she came to Blackmoor Hall. But Druridge wouldn't put her out. Every time the subject came up, he would reference a promise made to his parents and excuse her loyalty to Wythe by saying she had been his wet nurse.

Evidently that had created a strong bond indeed, if she was going to risk her position at Blackmoor Hall to help him.

"What should I do about you?" Having her involved complicated everything. Maybe he wouldn't wait and follow Wythe. What was the point? If he had been warned, he would do nothing that could get him in any trouble.

Linley shifted in his saddle to ease the pain in his bad leg. He would go straight to Elspeth's and demand to search, he decided—get to her before Wythe could.

But first . . . he wanted to speak with Mrs. Poulson.

He waited until Blackmoor Hall's housekeeper came out and intercepted her as soon as she started down the path. "What did you tell him?" he demanded.

She lifted her hand to her heart as if he had startled her, but he could tell she felt no real surprise. She'd expected him to be watching; she just hadn't expected him to confront her.

"I wanted a word with Mr. Stanhope."

"About . . . ?"

"Cook makes a special dish he likes. He asked if I could bring it tomorrow. I was letting him know that she has been unable to locate one of the ingredients."

"And what dish is that?" he asked.

There was a long silence. But she eventually came up with an answer. "Kidney pie."

"Which requires the simplest of ingredients."

"Providing one remembers to order the kidney from the butcher."

"Surely Cook could do that tomorrow morning?"

"I'm afraid she will be far too busy. Now that Lord Druridge is betrothed, she wants to focus on impressing our new mistress."

Linley moved the reins of his horse to the other hand and nudged his horse forward. "Ah, Rachel. You like her so."

"I don't have to like her to serve her, Mr. Linley."

"No, you don't. But you do have to be employed at Blackmoor Hall."

A wary look entered her eyes. "You're not planning to get me sacked for trying to give Mr. Stanhope word of his favorite dish. . . ."

"No, I am planning to get you sacked for betrayal."

She lifted her chin as if she was ready for the challenge his words presented. "The earl will never go along with it. He promised his poor mum he'd look after Wythe, and Wythe loves me. Maybe it would be different if you could prove something against me, but you can't."

"We will see about that."

He could have offered her a ride home. The rain was falling fast. But she was already soaked through and he had no interest in sparing her any discomfort. Besides, he was heading in the opposite direction.

"Good evening, Mrs. Poulson," he said and started off.

He had once heard Elspeth talk of retiring.

He would offer her the chance to do it somewhere much warmer than Creswell.

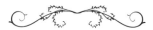

The rain had turned into a constant drizzle. Rachel kept one eye on the weather and the other on the clock as it grew later and later. Lord Druridge had not returned. Anxious to see him, she had been waiting in the drawing room so she would be sure to hear him when he came in, but the passing hours had turned to an agony of worry. It was nearly one o'clock. She couldn't imagine what could be keeping him so late.

Had his meeting with Cutberth not gone well? Had the clerk reacted violently or prevailed upon some of his most trusted miner friends to jump the earl on his way home?

At the very least, Collingood, Greenley, Thornick and Henderson would be eager for a chance to express their unhappiness and dislike. . . .

She wished she could seek out Mr. Linley and ask him to create a search party. But he had left shortly after their talk in the parlor and hadn't come back either. She didn't know who, other than Mrs. Poulson, would have the authority to take over for him. And there was no way she wanted to include the housekeeper.

The only ally she had left was her brother, and he was, no doubt, blissfully unaware that she was pacing the floor while he slept. She couldn't even *talk* to him without heading out into the cold and barging into the dormitory-style room above the stable. A lady would *never* intrude on the privacy of those men and boys, but . . . the earl's life could be at risk.

Should she send Geordie out to find Truman? Or would that only put her brother in danger too?

He was too young to go out alone, and he wouldn't be any good to the earl if the earl was hurt—wouldn't know what to do. She would have to go herself. No one else would be as determined to find Truman or save him, if necessary. She couldn't bear to stand around another second anyway, not when she was imagining such terrible things.

After retrieving one of the earl's cloaks—it was heavier and warmer than her own—she lit a lamp she could carry to the stables. She had to wake one of the grooms to saddle a horse; the tack was locked up. But since she wasn't after Geordie specifically, she could just bang on the door until someone answered.

As she passed the drawing room where she had spent the evening, she remembered the shadow she had seen earlier. Was it Poulson who had been standing at the door, listening in?

If so, and if she had carried what she'd heard to Wythe, there was no telling what was going on in the rainy dark. But Rachel was determined to find out and to offer her betrothed whatever assistance he needed.

Rachel was soaked by the time she reached the mine. She hadn't seen anyone along the way, and the place seemed deserted. She confirmed that the offices were empty when she slid off her horse and peered in through the windows. There was no lamp burning, even in the main office. She banged on the door and called out, but she couldn't get in.

"*Truman, where are you?*" she cried. Tears burned behind her eyes as she turned in a slow circle, searching for the earl's horse or some other sign that he had been here. Had the meeting taken place?

Logic suggested he had made it this far. If there were going to be trouble, it would most likely occur *after* his confrontation with Cutberth rather than before. Given how hard Cutberth had struck *her*, she could easily see him losing his temper. Had he become enraged at the prospect of being sacked and pulled out a pistol?

"God, no," she whispered. "Please, no."

So what should she do now? She had no idea where the earl might have gone. Elspeth's was the only place where people might be up this time of night, but he wouldn't go there. Something or someone had to be keeping him or he would have returned home.

She bit her lip, wondering if she should have gone to Creswell in search of Linley. Had she brought him, she wouldn't be alone. But finding the earl's butler would have taken at least an hour, if she could find him at all, and she hadn't been willing to take the time. Wythe would have been on her way, if he was at Cosgrove House, but just remembering the chilling, vacant quality she had noticed in his eyes made her shiver.

She would go to Cutberth's house, she decided. That was her only real option. She would ask if he'd met with the earl and, if so, what time they had parted. She needed a starting place, needed to figure out who had seen him last. But as she led her horse to the mounting block, her eyes landed on the gate that secured the pithead. There was something different about it, something that . . .

She froze when she realized what it was. Usually after hours the gate was locked to stop people from getting hurt or from disturbing, even sabotaging, the machinery.

It wasn't locked tonight.

Chapter 24

As Rachel gazed into the shaft, she couldn't see so much as a hint of light. For all intents and purposes, the mine looked as abandoned as she would have expected to find it in the dead of night. But someone had unhooked the machine that was used to lift and lower the cage so that it could be manually manipulated. And, when she listened carefully, she could hear the faintest echo of voices.

Was it Cutberth? Had he and some of the men taken the earl into the mine? Did they plan to kill him there so they could easily drag his body off to an abandoned tunnel where it might never be found?

She knew at least some of those who had been pushing for the formation of a union would find poetic justice in burying the earl in his own mine. She could easily imagine Thornick, Collingood and the other hewers who had attacked her smiling as they went back to work once Wythe inherited Stanhope & Co.

She couldn't let it go that far. She had to stop whatever was happening *now*. But how?

The thought of going into the mine, with its foul-smelling tunnels, throat-clogging coal dust, urine-filled puddles and bad memories made fear rise up like a monster inside her. It was so dark and close in there. And she would have to carry a light, which would announce her presence to anyone who happened to see it.

But they would know only that someone was coming. They wouldn't be able to tell who it was—or that wasn't a man. Maybe seeing her light would be enough to scare them away, make them run. Maybe then they would leave the earl as he was.

She just hoped he wasn't too bad off already.

Whether she got lucky enough to save him or not, she had to do *something,* and she had to do it fast. If the men she could hear in the mine were planning murder, the earl would be dead before she could bring help. Whoever was down there couldn't allow themselves to be found inside the mine come morning, and it was inching closer and closer to dawn.

Bringing the cage up so she could use it was much harder than she had anticipated, however. It was possible to lower oneself down—she had seen plenty of men do it—but she had never had to do it herself. Just lifting the metal contraption to the surface proved difficult. She tried to pace herself with a pull, a deep breath, a pull and a deep breath. But the strain caused her arms to shake, and the squeal of the rusted pulleys stretched her nerves taut. Whoever was down there had to be able to hear the noise.

Would they be waiting for her when she reached the bottom?

Once she saw the glimmer of the moon hit the cage, she breathed a sigh of relief that she had managed thus far and hesitated to listen again.

All had gone quiet. Were they in a panic? Would they soon come rushing toward the entrance?

She held her breath and almost collapsed in relief when the same steady hum rose to her ears. Whoever had been talking was still talking. Nothing had changed. But she couldn't take a regular lantern into the mine, not with the firedamp down there, or she could cause an explosion. She would need a Davy lamp, and she would need a weapon—a pick, if she couldn't find anything else. That meant she had to figure out a way to break into the supply shed behind the main office.

Fortunately, that wasn't as hard as she'd anticipated. There were several picks lying around, together with shovels and other tools. They were old and rusted—nothing anyone cared much about—but she was able to use one of the better picks to smash open the door so she could get a safety lamp and some oil.

Her heart felt like it was trying to escape her chest as she hurried back to the cage. Putting the pick and the light at her feet so she could use both hands, she slowly and painstakingly lowered herself down. She refused to imagine what she might encounter when she got there. It took all of her concentration not to let the coarse rope slide through her hands so she wouldn't go crashing to the bottom.

"I'm coming," she whispered over and over to herself.

Because of the darkness, she had no way of estimating when she would reach the flats. Thanks to that, she landed with a solid thud, but at least it wasn't as bad as it could have been had she been going any faster.

The smell, so familiar from when she had worked here, curdled her blood. She hated this place, feared it like no other. Tommy had died here. She couldn't say if he had been killed quickly or had to suffer for several days, because it had taken a week to dig out the bodies of the five who had died. She didn't want to face the same end. She would rather die any other way.

But she couldn't bear the thought of Truman being harmed. So, as quietly as possible, she climbed out, got the pick and the light and began to follow the sound.

The men weren't far. She had known that going in. If they were very deep she would never have been able to hear them, wouldn't have known they were even here. She decided to be grateful for that one small thing—that she wouldn't have to go into the nether regions of the mine, where it was less ventilated and far more dangerous.

It was only a few seconds later that she could pick out distinct voices from the steady drone of earlier. Fortunately, the men were just past where the tunnel curved to the right—at the loading dock—so her light didn't give her away.

She had expected to recognize Cutberth's voice as the dominant one. He had been asked to meet the earl at the office and was the most recent person to lose his job, so it made sense. But as Rachel crept closer to where the tunnel turned, she recognized *Wythe's* voice and stopped.

What was *he* doing here? She'd assumed he had gone to Elspeth's. Had he been there and back? Did that mean Mr. Linley had found him—or not?

It didn't appear that he had. None of the men had brought their horses. Maybe that was how Wythe had slipped away from the butler.

"Like Thornick just said, we been loyal to ye. We 'aven't told a soul what we know."

A fresh wave of chills went through Rachel, and these had nothing to do with the cold. Collingood was speaking. She easily recognized his voice. So . . . Wythe was with Collingood and Thornick? Had they formed an alliance? Was that part of the reason he had assigned her to Number 14 Stall? So he could better keep her under his thumb?

No wonder he had been so reluctant to sack those men. *She is only a village wench, my lord. Some of these miners have worked for us for years. We arrived in time. There wasn't any harm done. Couldn't we leave them with a warning and be about our business?*

"But ye 'aven't paid us a farthin' for months." Thornick's voice broke into her thoughts. "Ye got us to come all the way out 'ere in the middle of the bleedin' night, thinkin' ye 'ad some coin for us at last, and all we're gettin' is more bloody excuses!"

"I couldn't meet you in town. I was afraid I would be followed. It took long enough making sure I could safely come out this direction."

"A waste of effort, if ye ask me. Yer all talk."

That was Henderson, Rachel realized. So he was here too.

"You have to give me more time," Wythe responded.

"Time? 'Ow do ye expect us to survive? 'Tis not like we're workin' these days!" Henderson snapped.

"That wasn't *my* doing," Wythe told him. "You have only yourselves to blame for that."

"But we should be able to fall back on yer promises. We've done our part."

That was Greenley chiming in. All four of the hewers she had worked with were here.

"Have you?" Wythe challenged. "The earl knows that someone tried to hire Jack McTavish to fire the manse. That is what made him turn his attention to Creswell and this colliery, and none of us has been able to breathe since. I wouldn't have to fear being followed if one of you hadn't talked. So it's your own fault you're no longer getting paid."

"Easy for ye ter say," Thornick grumbled.

"Yer cousin 'as more money than 'e knows what to do with," Greenley said. "Surely ye can figure out a way to get us what we need."

"You received a month's worth of wages."

"An' it's been over a month," Thornick complained. "'Ow long did ye expect the money to last? We got families to feed. Bills to pay."

"I guess you should have thought of that before you tried to rape Rachel McTavish."

"Ye said we could 'ave whatever fun with 'er we wanted," Thornick said, obviously appalled by Wythe's comment.

"That's true," Henderson concurred. "Ye even said to make it rough. That there would be a *bonus* in it if we would."

"Or 'ave ye forgotten?" Greenley asked.

"That didn't include *rape*," Wythe replied.

"It didn't *ex*clude it, either." Collingood again. "Just 'ave Cutberth pay a friend of ours for a little more than he actually hews, an' 'e'll slip us the difference. Problem solved."

"Except that Tyndale keeps too close a watch on the mine's productivity. Cutberth would never do it anyway. He's scrupulous about that sort of thing. You know him and his bloody ideals. He will risk his job to start a union, but he won't steal a halfpenny, even from a man who's rich as a king."

"Cutberth's a man of integrity," Henderson said.

"Don't act like he's some kind of hero," Wythe snapped. "If he knew you were the ones who approached Jack, he would turn you in so fast your heads would spin."

Henderson didn't let that deter him. He jumped in to defend Cutberth again. "Because he's an 'onest man. We all know that, an' we respect 'im for it."

"Honest or not, he had better watch himself," Wythe said. "When I am earl, I won't tolerate any secret meetings. And there will be no profit-sharing, either."

"Profit-sharing?"

The rocks were beginning to cut into Rachel's back, she was pressing into them so hard. The earl wasn't here. She should go. But she was learning so much, so much she could take back to him, providing Cutberth hadn't killed him. *They* thought Cutberth admirable; she was no longer so sure.

"Forget it, for now," Wythe said.

"Sounds as if ye're plannin' to take over soon," Greenley said.

"It won't be long." The earl's cousin sounded supremely confident.

"It will if ye don't start payin' up," Thornick said. "Ye 'ave three days. Then we go to Druridge."

From what Rachel could tell, Wythe didn't seem the least bit frightened. "It won't do you any good. By now those paintings have been destroyed. I sent someone over to do it hours ago. He won't have the proof necessary to save his own neck, regardless of what you say."

"Our testimony will count for somethin'!" Greenley said.

"It will show you are out to get me—the man who sacked you. Nothing more."

Rachel had heard enough. She needed to get out before they decided to leave and discovered her listening in.

She had just started for the lift, however, when the arguing got worse. Wythe shouted that he refused to let anyone threaten him. Then she heard two gunshots, fired in rapid succession followed by an exclamation of surprise and some groaning, cursing and scuffling.

Covering her mouth to keep from screaming, she started to run. But once she reached the lift, she was so shaken she couldn't climb into it. She fell on her first attempt. She managed to get in on the second, but she feared she was making entirely too much noise. Surely Wythe had heard the crash of her lantern when she fell.

She didn't want him to know anyone else had been in the mine, but she didn't have time to gather what she had brought.

It doesn't matter. Go. She had to reach the surface. *Fast.*

Footsteps pounded toward her. Apparently, he *had* heard. She grabbed the rope attached to the pulley but was so filled with panic, she couldn't lift the cage, didn't have the strength for it.

A light appeared as someone rounded the corner, and she heard a shout: "Stop right there!"

It was Wythe. She had no idea what had happened to the others, but they didn't seem to be coming.

Were they dead? She feared they were and knew this mine would be her grave too, if she couldn't haul herself up.

Staring at the darkness above her as if she could fly toward it, she yanked on the rope. It took all of her willpower and every last ounce of energy, but the bucket began to rise, inch by inch.

"Come on," she muttered, straining for all she was worth. She managed to lift herself another few feet and some more once again. But she wasn't going nearly fast enough. Wythe reached the rope system she was using before she could get all the way to the top, and he began pulling her back down.

Truman sat on his horse, side by side with his butler, staring up at the brothel. Although they were gone now, the paintings had been there. He was sure of it. According to the girl who had let them in and allowed them to search, Elspeth had removed four large, rectangular objects from the attic two days ago. They had been loaded onto an old wagon and taken somewhere—she didn't know where. Then, shortly after supper, Elspeth had packed her bags and left.

"For good?" he'd asked.

"She told me I could 'ave the brothel, my lord."

He had no idea what Madame Soward had planned. But at least he had encountered some evidence that the Bruegels had existed after the fire. That alone made Truman feel as if a huge weight had been lifted off his shoulders. The mysterious objects she had removed, together with his memories, made him feel confident if they hanged him for Katherine's murder, they would be hanging an innocent man. He wasn't the one who had hurt her. He wasn't guilty of starting the fire, even in his rage. He had merely shown up at the wrong time, and he had nearly lost his life, just as she had.

If not for Wythe, he would have died. So . . . who had started the fire?

"We had better hurry, my lord," Linley said. Truman had encountered his butler while following Cutberth to the village after their meeting at the mine. He had wanted to see what the sacked clerk might do, wanted to make sure he wouldn't visit some of the miners on his way home and stir up trouble. But just as he approached the outskirts of the village, riding well behind his quarry so he wouldn't tip him off, he had found Linley plodding along the same road. And once he'd heard what his butler was about, he had eagerly accompanied him to the brothel, where they had searched every room—whether they interrupted what was going on inside them or not. Fortunately, it had been a slow night for business.

They had gone into the cellar and attic, too, and found the spot where something had been stored that was now gone.

"If we start off right away, maybe we can find Elspeth," Linley said.

Truman finally turned away. He too wanted to go after Madame Soward, but it wasn't realistic to think they would be able to find her tonight. She could be almost anywhere and, at this hour, she was probably holed up somewhere asleep, not out on the road. It wasn't safe for a woman to travel at night, especially with such expensive cargo. Not only that but Mr. Linley wasn't looking well. The many hours on horseback and the lack of rest had been hard on him. Truman needed to get him to the manse, where he could recover.

"Madame Soward has had plenty of time to make sure those paintings are in a safe place," he said. "What would we do even if we found her?"

Linley acted surprised that he would ask. "We'd talk some sense into her. Offer her money in exchange for the paintings, more than she could get if she sold them."

"I'm sure she has already heard about the reward. If she were interested, she would have come forward."

"I'm guessing she's scared of whomever asked her to store them in the first place. Maybe she's only recently become aware of exactly what they are and what they mean. We could offer her protection, too."

"And we will, if we have the opportunity."

"What do you think she will do next?" Linley asked.

"I have no idea," he replied, "but I know what *we* are going to do. I'm taking you home. You should not be keeping such hours at your age, and with your bad leg."

"I'm fine, my lord. At last we have the break we have been praying for. We cannot let Elspeth slip through our fingers."

Truman had to smile at his willingness to continue what would likely be a futile search. He was so exhausted he could hardly stay astride his horse and yet he wanted to go after Elspeth? And to think Mr. Cutberth had suggested that maybe Linley had been behind the fire! "We will do what we can come morning. I should get back to Rachel. This is her first night at Blackmoor Hall since she left Mrs. Tate's. I don't want to worry her."

"Then I'll send out a group to search for Elspeth at first light."

"We will hire anyone with the time to look and have them search all the way to Newcastle. Surely she won't be able to get far. Not with those paintings."

"I hope that's the case," Linley said with a sigh.

They rode the rest of the way in silence, too tired to speak, especially over the distance that sometimes separated their animals. Truman couldn't wait to drop into bed. For once maybe he could sleep without the nightmares that had plagued him for the past two years. What he had found out tonight hadn't solved *all* his problems, but it should be enough to put his worst fear at ease: the fear that he might not be the man he'd always wanted to be, always thought he was.

What would it be like to sleep peacefully, with Rachel at his side, every night?

He was excited to find out. But when he hurried up the stairs and let himself into his room, he found his bed undisturbed. Her bed was the same. Her belongings were all there, but he couldn't find her anywhere in the house.

It wasn't until he went out to the stable to see if Geordie knew anything that he was told, by a sleepy stable boy, that she had taken a horse.

"She said you 'adn't come home and she was goin' out ter look for ye, my lord. I told her I'd go in 'er stead, I did, but she would 'ave none of it. She told me she would be back soon. An' off she went."

Truman grabbed his arm. "When? When did she go?"

The boy screwed up his face. "I was pretty sleepy so I can't be certain, my lord, but ... musta been a couple 'ours ago."

Once he learned that, he got a sick feeling in the pit of his stomach. She had to have gone to the mine, where he was meeting Cutberth. But why hadn't she come back?

Chapter 25

Rachel was no match for Wythe's strength. No matter how hard she pulled, the bucket went down. It didn't happen quickly. It was a battle. But it was a battle she was guaranteed to lose. How would she save herself once he forced her all the way to the bottom? At that point he'd be able to do anything to her, anything he wanted. No one would know where she was. She would be stranded in the mine with him, and once he hid her body, there wouldn't even be anything to suggest what had happened to her.

She thought of the earl and her fear for his safety. Had Wythe murdered him? She had heard him shoot at least one of the miners—very likely two—and was pretty sure he had killed the rest. He'd lured them here under false pretenses and then he had attempted to silence them for good. Maybe some were merely hurt, but she knew Wythe couldn't leave them alive. They would tell everything they knew.

She heard no noise coming from the loading dock. Did that mean he had a knife or some other weapon, in addition to the pistol he had already discharged? Only two shots had rung out.

Help me. Lend me strength, she prayed silently. She hadn't spoken, hadn't cried out. She didn't want the earl's cousin to know she was a woman. If he realized that he would also realize that he possessed easily twice her strength and, with such added confidence, he would reel her in that much faster.

Her muscles burned as she struggled. But the rope kept slipping through her grasp, tearing the skin on her hands with its abrasive, hoary fibers until the pain became excruciating.

If only she had a weapon. If only she had the pick she'd dropped on the ground with her Davy lamp—

Suddenly she realized that she did, possibly, have *one* weapon. She had gravity, didn't she? If she acted at the right moment, the cage itself could harm him. It was made of steel. It would be traveling fast. And he was standing right underneath her. That left her vulnerable to injury too, but with any luck, she would hurt him worse than she would hurt herself. Maybe she would even knock him out.

Given so many variables, there was only a slim chance that her plan would be successful. But she had no better option. Gritting her teeth against the pain, she clung stubbornly to the rope, even managed to stop her descent for a few seconds. This angered him enough that he yanked that much harder, and she let go.

The exhilaration of free fall lifted her stomach as she dropped at least fifteen feet in a fraction of a second. She heard Wythe gasp in surprise. But he must've moved, at least a little, because when she hit him it was more of a glancing blow. The force didn't knock him out, as she had hoped, but it did make him stumble and fall. At least it sounded that way.

She banged her shoulder on impact and, as the cage swung wildly away from him, tumbled onto the hard-packed earth. Maybe she had been in *too* much of a hurry to escape the confines of that metal bucket, but she knew if he grabbed her while she was still inside it, there would be nothing she could do to gain her freedom.

"Bloody hell!" he swore as he staggered to his feet.

The energy behind that curse gave her hope that he was suffering at least as much as she was. She could feel the sticky wetness of her own blood. But what scrapes and bruises she had sustained would be the least of her problems if she couldn't rally quickly enough.

Get the pick, she reminded herself as she struggled to shake off the effects of that bone-jarring collision.

Fortunately, she could see the outline of that tool in the dim glow of her Davy lamp, which was still burning—and dove for it.

Wythe seemed to comprehend her intent about the same time she got her brain working well enough to execute such action. He tried to kick the handle out of her reach, but he hadn't quite recovered from having the lift fly out of the darkness to nearly flatten him. He only managed to kick some dirt in her eyes before falling again, but that made it almost impossible to see.

Grabbing two handfuls of dirt herself, she threw them in *his* face before grabbing hold of the pick. But once she had it, she could hardly lift it. How had it gotten so blasted heavy in the last fifteen minutes?

"Get back, or I will put this through your skull," she warned as he found his feet, cursing and spitting and wiping dirt from his eyes.

Her eyes were watering, too, which helped clean away the grainy particles, but she had to blink rapidly in order to keep him in focus.

"Rachel, what luck," he said. "I was merely planning to turn you out when I become earl, but I can't promise such leniency now. I'm afraid *this* ending will be far more permanent."

It wasn't only the dirt in her eyes that made it difficult to see. The light from the lamp didn't carry far. When he'd come barreling out of the tunnel to stop her from escaping, he hadn't been carrying any light with him. There was just the single lamp, so they stood mostly in shadow.

Fleetingly, Rachel considered running for her life. Her heart was pounding so hard she could barely breathe, and her arms felt as if every muscle had been wrung out, like water from a damp cloth. She doubted she could make much of a stand. She wanted to believe she could somehow evade him long enough to hide until the miners arrived for work. But he was cutting her off from the section of the mine that contained all the tunnels. There wasn't much at her back, except a couple of storage rooms. She wouldn't last long heading in *that* direction.

"You killed the others," she whispered, still barely able to comprehend what she had heard earlier and the fact that none of those men—none of *four*—had come out to see what was going on.

He didn't argue. "How did you find me?" he asked instead. "I wasn't followed. I made certain of it."

Linley should've been there. . . .

"I came in search of Truman," she said. "What did you do to him?" Fearful of what she might hear next, she swallowed hard. "Did you and Cutberth kill him at the office and toss his body down here?"

"Why would we bother? The Abbotts will see to him soon enough. Why not let it be someone else's doing?"

He edged around the small clearing, trying to get close enough to gain some advantage over her. She maintained her distance, stepping to the left every time he took a step to the right. It gave her hope that he would eventually move out of the path she longed to take. "If you wanted him dead, why didn't you let him burn?" she asked.

"Ah, the question that has nearly driven him mad." He laughed as if he took great pleasure in knowing how deeply conflicted Truman had been. "Two years ago I was still trying to curry his favor. I wanted him to approve of me at last. A childish hope, when I think of it. Anyway, I would have taken the blame. No one else had any reason to murder him. Then I would be heading to the gallows myself, which would make it quite difficult to enjoy my inheritance."

Her hands were growing sweaty on the handle of the pick. He was obviously trying to decide how he would disarm her; she could see the way he studied her. "Then . . . where is he?"

"How should I know?" he responded. "Maybe the Abbotts decided they were tired of waiting for the slow wheels of justice and decided to dispatch him to the next world straightaway."

She shook her head. "I don't think it had anything to do with the Abbotts. But I wouldn't put it past Cutberth."

"Cutberth doesn't have the nerve for murder."

He crouched slightly as if he was getting ready to spring. She needed to stall, keep him talking. "He's got the nerve to risk his job by starting a union!"

When he stepped more directly into the light, she could see that he had a knife. "A bunch of hot air. A way to gain favor among the men."

"Stay back," she breathed.

"Or what?" he taunted with a threatening jab.

"Or you will be the one who gets 'dispatched' next."

He chuckled softly. "You think you can kill me, Rachel? *With a pick?* As soon as you take your first swing, you're dead."

"Then I had better make that swing count."

The determination in her voice seemed to convince him that she intended to do all she could. "You have no chance," he said.

He was right. If only she had more time. Dawn had to be near. It seemed like an eternity since she had left Blackmoor House. "So you were sitting back the whole time, laughing while Truman searched for the person who tried to hire my father? You were behind it? *You* killed Katherine?"

His lips curved into a self-satisfied smile. "No, I merely impregnated her. We had quite the debauched affair, the two of us," he bragged. "I had her in the earl's own bed while he was traveling. She came to me even when he was home." His voice grew husky. "She said I was big as a horse. Does that excite you, Rachel?"

"It makes me want to vomit. How could you, or anyone else, murder their unborn child, not to mention the mother of that child?"

His face grew hard. "You're not listening. I told you, *I* didn't kill her! Why would I? As far as I'm concerned, it would have been a grand joke to watch the earl raise my bastard."

"Until he found out that you were the child's father. And you know Katherine would have told him eventually. From what I have learned, she couldn't possess such a powerful weapon and not use it—against you both."

"Sadly, that's exactly why Mrs. Poulson said she had to die. She wouldn't let Katherine destroy me."

"And the paintings? Did she steal those, too?"

"No, that was me. I didn't see why they shouldn't be salvaged."

"But you weren't expecting Lord Druridge to arrive."

"That was terrible timing, really." He sounded quite wistful. "You should have seen Mrs. Poulson's face," he added with a laugh that indicated he was as out of touch with what he should be feeling as ever. "We thought we were done for—until he rushed straight to Katherine, oblivious of everything except his rage. Of course, the smoke was barely discernable at that moment. For once, fate was on my side and not his. And now Truman will hang for her murder, and I will spend the rest of my days with a title and more money than I know what to do with. How's that for a reversal?" He gestured with the hand that held the knife. "*Everyone* will scrape and bow as I walk by."

"So Mrs. Poulson set the fire? She's the one who tried to hire my father?"

He crouched lower. "She hired Greenley and the boys to do it for her, but that was a mistake. It left us vulnerable and essentially got them killed."

The path was almost clear. If only he would shift a bit more to the right. "I don't understand. *Why?* Why would *she* kill Katherine?"

"She wants me to inherit the title as much as I do."

"You won't get it," she said, in no uncertain terms.

"What's to stop me?"

He had finally moved far enough.

"Me," she said and threw the pick as hard as she could.

She saw the whites of his eyes as they flared wide. He hadn't expected her to make such a bold move, hadn't seen it coming. Instinctively he dropped the knife so he could protect himself, but the pick hit him far more solidly than the lift and knocked him down again. He got up as fast as he could, but she grabbed the Davy lamp, blew out the flame and made a run for it.

When Rachel reached the place where Wythe had been meeting with the hewers of Number 14 Stall, she could see their bodies lying on the ground. Their blood, looking like black ink in the dim light of the two Davy lamps that had been left behind, seeped into the ground.

Such a gruesome sight made it far too easy to imagine what would happen to her if Wythe managed to catch her.

It wasn't a pleasant thought that she would be alone in the dark with four dead bodies *and* their killer, but she had to extinguish the lamps. If he was going to have light with which to come after her, she wanted him to have to go back to the surface to get it. It would buy her some time, at least.

"You bitch!" he screamed. The sound echoed off the walls, making it difficult to tell if he was coming after her. The extreme darkness made it feel as if the mine had swallowed her whole. She hadn't spent enough time as a putter to feel comfortable navigating the many tunnels without light. She had assumed she would be able to remember the various footpaths, but that wasn't remotely realistic.

Keeping one hand on the wall so she would know approximately where she was in relation to what was around her, she moved as fast as she could.

She wished she could break into a full run and put some real distance between them. But there were too many dangers in the mine for that—low ceilings, sudden drop-offs, machinery, turns. She could only hope she was walking at least as fast as he was.

When the ground gave way, she yelped in surprise. She half expected to fall to her death—but it was just a puddle. Still, she turned her ankle, which caused some pain, and the stinking, fetid water soaked through her shoes, making her even more miserable. Lord knew what was in it, but the real problem was that she had given her location away.

"You think you're getting out of here alive?" he asked.

Fear nearly choked her. He was *right* on her trail—and he spoke low, as if he knew it.

God help me. Covering her mouth to keep from making any sound, even when she dared breathe, she felt for a crevice, slipped into the first one she could find and tried to make herself small. He would be batting the air, hoping to make contact.

She prayed he would pass her by so she could double back.

Chapter 26

Wythe had never been angrier in his life. Everything he wanted was *so* close he could taste it. Now that Collingood, Greenley, Thornick and Henderson could never reveal what they knew, only Rachel stood between him and the title, between him and the admiration and power he had always craved. *He would* be the one riding through the streets of Creswell in the earl's coach. *He would* be the one hiring a steward to run the mine. *He would* be the one traveling to London with an entourage of servants to cater to his every whim instead of being a burden, someone who was only tolerated, a mere hanger-on.

Maybe he would even take up residence in Town part of the year.

But first he had to silence the stubborn, overly ambitious wench who threatened it all. And he had to dispose of the four bodies lying on the loading dock. The miners would arrive for work in two hours or less. If the earl wasn't lying hurt or dead somewhere, as the bitch seemed to think, he could show up sooner.

"You're making a mistake," he called out.

He paused to listen, but there was no response. Could she even hear him? Or had she slipped too far away?

"Rachel?" He wished he hadn't sent Mrs. Poulson to destroy the paintings. He needed someone to block the entrance of the mine so that Rachel couldn't escape while he took those corpses to Number 15 stall. They would be safe there until he could bury them, if only for the chance to load them into a wagon.

But even if he had the opportunity, it wouldn't be as easy as it could have been. Thanks to Rachel, he didn't have a lamp.

What was he going to do? He could spend hours down here searching in the dark and never find her. Even if he went to the surface and brought back a Davy—and locked the lift up at the top so she couldn't get out while he was gone—he could search any number of tunnels before finding her. It was possible that she could elude him indefinitely.

That meant he had to do something else, something with a better chance of success.

"You have a choice," he yelled. "Come out, or I will blow up the mine."

He thought he heard a slight whimper, but there was water dripping not far away, and that made it difficult to tell. "It must be a frightening prospect for you. Your brother died in a cave-in." He made a clicking sound. "What a terrible way to go. Straining to breathe. Unable to get air. Depending on how much damage my explosion causes, you could go the same way. I have heard it can take several minutes to suffocate. Imagine the panic." He lightened his voice. "Or, if you're lucky, you could be blown to bits. Either way doesn't matter to me, as long as you're dead in the end."

Had his gruesome description of her death caused a response?

Not that he could tell. There was just the water, continuing to drip. *Plink. Plink. Plink . . .*

"Rachel?"

Something scrabbled past him. He reached out, hoping to grab her, but it was just a rat or some other noxious animal. *Damn it.* If only he could get his hands around her slim neck.

"Come on, Rachel. Don't make this any harder than it has to be. I don't want to destroy the mine but you are giving me no choice. Think of how many lives *that* will impact."

He felt his way along the wall, sliding his foot out at the same time to make sure he didn't miss her on the other side. "You deserve what you are about to get, you know that?" he finally bit out. "And it won't hurt me one bit to lose the mine. Not really. You might not be aware of this, but Truman has so many other holdings. Maybe this will be for the best. When they find Thornick, Collingood, Henderson and Greenley in pieces, they won't know they died before the blast. They will assume they brought you down here for a little revenge."

He was starting to get excited about his newest idea. Could she see how perfect it was?

"Do you hear that, Rachel?" he said, hoping to reiterate. "Everyone will think Collingood and the others dragged you down here. Maybe you fought back and got a little reckless with the lamp and . . . *pow!* . . . firedamp did the rest."

The more he spoke, the more convinced he became that he had hit upon the ideal solution. Losing some of what he would inherit was better than losing everything. An explosion would solve all his problems at once. Then he could hurry home and pretend he'd had nothing to do with it.

Pivoting abruptly, he felt his way to the cage and started hoisting himself up. The black powder, used for blasting new tunnels, was locked up.

But, as steward, he happened to know right where Tyndale kept the key.

Wythe was rolling a keg of gunpowder around the corner of the office toward the pithead when a horse bearing a rider stepped out of the shadows. Shocked to find that he had company, he almost let the slope of the ground carry the keg away from him.

"What are *you* doing here?" Cutberth asked, his horse rearing up at the sudden encounter.

Wythe wasn't happy to see the clerk, but at least it wasn't the earl. "I could ask you the same thing. Isn't it a little early for you to be starting your day?"

"I'm not starting my day. I'm looking for Thornick."

The knowledge that Thornick lay in the mine, dead, made Wythe begin to sweat. "I would imagine he is in bed this time of night."

"Apparently not. His wife came to my house thirty minutes or so ago, frantic because he hasn't come home."

Wythe managed a shrug while keeping one hand on the powder barrel. "I haven't seen him. You might try Elspeth's."

The rain had stopped but Cutberth's hat was still dripping. He removed it long enough to fling off the water. "He told her he was coming here. For a union meeting. That's why she sought me out."

The smell of wet horse made Wythe wish he had his own animal. He had left it in the stables at Cosgrove House so he could move without alerting anyone, but he feared that would prove to be a mistake. He felt *so* immobile.

Putting a knee on the barrel, he straightened. "*This* is where you have been holding your meetings? At my own bloody mine?" He laughed as if he could appreciate the irony, but promised himself he wouldn't let that go on in the future.

Instead of laughing with him, Cutberth gave him a funny look. "Don't you mean the *earl's* mine?"

"Of course. Didn't I say that?" He tried not to glance toward the pithead, even though he was *desperate* to get back there before Rachel could do anything else to thwart him. "Anyway, you might find Thornick at Elspeth's, like I said. The poor bloke had to tell his wife *something* in order to get out of the house, didn't he?" He grinned as if that had to be the answer and hoped Cutberth would accept it. But the clerk didn't leave. He lowered his gaze to the keg.

"Planning on doing some blasting?"

"When the men arrive. I couldn't sleep so I thought I would come over and get ready for the day."

Cutberth's horse neighed and pranced to one side as if it was tired of standing in the same spot, but Cutberth brought it around again. "That's a bit out of the ordinary, isn't it? For you to get involved in this type of work?"

Wythe propped his hands on his hips and jutted his chin forward. "What are you saying?" He used a tone that suggested Cutberth had no right to question him, that he had no right to judge his actions no matter what they might be. He would soon be the Earl of Druridge and he expected people to remember that. But the clerk didn't back off as he always had in the past.

"I'm saying that's a bit out of the ordinary." His voice was firm.

When their gazes locked, Wythe cursed silently to himself. Cutberth knew something wasn't right, and that created yet *another* complication.

But there was still hope. The explosion Wythe had planned could take two lives as easily as one. He just had to get Cutberth into the mine.

"Not necessarily. Not if you knew what I was up to. Come on, I will show you. You can give me a hand."

Cutberth shook the water off his hat again. "A hand with . . . what?"

"Getting this into the pit. I will hook up the machine on the lift, and you can lower me down. It will make it much easier. This thing weighs a ton."

"I'm afraid you're on your own with that, Mr. Stanhope," he said. "I'm going to keep looking for Thornick."

Wythe stood the barrel on its end so it could no longer roll. He had his knife in his belt. He wanted to use it, but it wouldn't do him any good to try unless he could get Cutberth to climb down off that damned horse. "If you value your position here, you will take a minute and help me," he said.

An odd smile curved Cutberth's lips.

"What is it?" He was trying to act no differently than usual, but the stress he was feeling added an unwanted quaver to his voice.

"I guess you haven't heard the news. I spoke to your cousin earlier. I no longer have a job here to protect," he said and galloped away.

Wythe didn't have the means to go after him, not without his own animal. So what now? What was he going to do about Cutberth? The ex-clerk was no friend of the earl's. Or Rachel's, either. But he would know exactly what happened as soon as Thornick and the others were discovered in the rubble.

Damn it! He couldn't set off an explosion, not now that Cutberth had seen him with gunpowder.

He would have to find Rachel and kill her the hard way, he decided, and then bury *all* the bodies. As long as the corpses were never discovered, no one would know he had been involved.

If only he could get hold of that little whore before daybreak. Everything hinged on timing.

Dear God, his hands were shaking. He needed something to calm his nerves.

He withdrew his flask, only to find that it was empty. How could he have forgotten? He'd drunk the whole thing while waiting for Thornick, Collingood, Henderson and Greenley.

Truman urged his horse into a faster clip. It wasn't safe to travel at a full run, not at night. But he had to find Rachel as soon as possible. There were too many people, people like Cutberth, who blamed her instead of themselves for their recent turn of bad luck.

What if she had fallen into the hands of the sacked clerk? Or the hewers who had attacked her that day he took her from the mine?

"My lord! You go on. I will catch up when I can," Linley called.

Truman couldn't wait for him. He had to find the woman he loved. All the things that had once seemed so important to him were nothing in comparison to her.

"Go back," he called. "Wait at the manse." He had tried talking Linley into staying in the first place. His butler was too old to help with something like this. He had done enough for one night, anyway. But he'd insisted. "Two is better than one," he'd said.

Truman appreciated the devotion, but with Rachel's safety in jeopardy, he had to stay focused, had to act quickly.

He leaned over to avoid the tree branches that swatted at him as his horse charged down the familiar path to the colliery. Cosgrove House came up on his right. It seemed as quiet and dark as he would expect it to be so early in the morning, but he was still tempted to stop there. The memory of Wythe telling Rachel, "I could throw your body into the ocean," kept playing in his head. If his cousin had *anything* to do with why Rachel hadn't come home—anything at all—the forbearance Truman had shown him over the years would be gone in an instant. The promise he'd made his parents would mean nothing. Neither would the fact that Wythe had once saved his life. He was carrying his pistols and wouldn't hesitate to use them.

It seemed to take longer than usual to reach the office, despite his breakneck speed. He was relieved when he finally charged into the clearing. But he found everything as he had seen it last night.

Except that there was a keg of gunpowder sitting out.

He got off his horse to investigate. Black powder was expensive, and it could be dangerous. It was not to be left out in the open.

The locker where they stored the gunpowder was closed but the key had been left in the lock. Another storage shed close by, this one full of tools and Davy lamps, had been broken into quite forcibly and the door stood ajar.

What had happened here? As far as he could tell, no one was about. But *someone* had been here. Who? And did the state of those storage closets and the gunpowder keg have anything to do with Rachel going missing?

He couldn't see how. Maybe the damage had happened earlier, before he met with Cutberth. Or immediately after. Cutberth could have done it in anger. . . .

"Rachel?" he called.

There was no answer.

"Rachel!" Where could she be? His imagination suggested many places, but none eased his fears. "I don't want to live without you," he murmured. Especially now, when he'd finally allowed himself to hope, to believe, he could have her forever.

Just in case she could have gone into the mine—or been dragged there— he walked down to the pithead. But the gate was locked and all seemed quiet. Should he search the mine, despite that? He was tempted, just to be sure he had covered every possibility. If Cutberth could get the key to Rachel's shop from Wythe's office, he could certainly come by the key to the pithead after working in the office for so long. But searching the tunnels would take forever. The time would be better spent heading to the village so he could check on Cutberth, Thornick, Greenley and the others. He would wake the whole damn village if he had to.

He hurried back to his horse, but almost as soon as he climbed into the saddle, he heard the approach of someone else, also on horseback.

Unsure of who or what he might face, he pulled out one of the pistols he had brought from the house as Cutberth entered the clearing. "What are you doing here?"

His ex-clerk reined in a few feet away. "Where is he?"

"Where is who?"

When Truman let his pistol be seen, Cutberth stiffened. "What do you plan to do with that, m'lord?"

"Anything I have to in order to find Rachel. What have you done with her?"

His eyebrows shot up. "Nothing! I haven't even seen her."

"She went out looking for me and hasn't come back."

He lifted his hands. "I swear to you. If she is gone it has nothing to do with me. I am not here to start trouble. I was merely hoping for another word with your cousin."

Truman squinted through the darkness, trying to ascertain his expression and decide whether he was telling the truth. "Why would you expect Wythe to be here?"

"Because this is where he was not more than half an hour ago." He pointed at the powder keg. "He was wrestling that toward the pit."

His cousin was the one who had gotten out the gunpowder? Surely this couldn't be true. "What could he have wanted powder for?" Truman asked.

"That's what I came back to find out. Something isn't right, my lord. Thornick, Collingood, Henderson and Greenley are all missing."

This news made Truman sick to his stomach. "Then *they've* got Rachel." He couldn't think of another explanation, but Cutberth didn't seem convinced.

"I don't think so. If they were planning to harm her, they could have done it when she came back to the village. It's not as if Mrs. Tate could have stopped them. Greenley told me he stopped by there to apologize, but she wouldn't receive him."

Truman frowned as he looked around. Was Cutberth really searching for Wythe?

"Thornick's wife claims he was coming here to attend a union meeting," he said. "The other wives say the same about their husbands. But I haven't called a meeting. And Wythe, when I saw him, was behaving strangely. He was sweating, despite the cold. And he wanted me to help him get that powder into the mine and seemed overly upset when I wouldn't."

"Why would he want to get powder into the mine in the middle of the night?" Truman asked.

"He wouldn't say."

If Cutberth could be believed, Rachel, Thornick, Collingood, Henderson, Greenley *and* Wythe had all been out tonight. Why? "He must have left," Truman said. "All is quiet now. And the pit is locked."

A strange expression came over Cutberth's face. "That's it. That's where they're at."

"What are you talking about?"

"The pit wasn't locked when I was here before."

As soon as Wythe hauled himself out of the mine, Rachel had run to the lift, hoping to find a way out herself. But it was no use. He had made it so that she couldn't bring the cage back down.

She had retrieved the pick, even though she knew it could do nothing to protect her from an explosion, and waited—scared and shaky—in the dark. She'd been sure she wasn't long for this earth, couldn't imagine how she would survive what Wythe had in store for her. She had just decided that she would rather be killed by the blast than any cave-in it might cause, that she would stand right out in the open and wait for it.

But then . . . there had been no explosion. She'd heard Wythe above her, cursing to himself as he climbed into the lift. He'd been upset, newly frustrated. She could tell that but nothing more. Had he changed his mind about igniting a blast?

She'd thought so. But that didn't make her safe. A flicker of light had suggested he was bringing a lamp. At that point she'd faced a very difficult decision. Did she grab the ropes to try to stop his descent? Would she be physically capable of holding him off that way? Or did she hide to the right, hoping he would go left, where they had been before?

There weren't many places to conceal herself on the right. That was the reason she hadn't chosen it before. But left took her ever deeper into the bowels of the mine, meaning he could cut her off from the lift indefinitely. And now that he had a lamp, she would have no way of slipping past him unseen. The tunnels were too narrow. She would have to stay well in front of him even though *he* could travel much faster.

In the end, she had chosen to run left. Her other options were more of a gamble. She had to go with the odds, use as much time as possible. She was hoping that the miners would arrive before Wythe could find her.

If they didn't . . . at least she had a weapon.

She had been trying to out-distance him ever since, had been dodging him and his bloody light. She kept praying he would choose the wrong tunnel. Although she couldn't see the various openings, she knew there were more turns than the ones she was taking. But any noise gave her away, and she couldn't move fast without noise. She was just thinking she should have tried to stop the lift instead when another twisted ankle brought her to her knees.

Gasping in pain, she watched the edge of his light draw closer. Heard his footsteps. Heard him say, "You are only making this harder on yourself, Rachel. I will kill you quickly if you quit running. If you don't . . . heaven help you."

He meant it. He was beyond angry. He was probably desperate, too—as desperate as she was.

If only she could figure out a way to get him to move beyond her.

But how?

Drawing a bolstering breath, she limped around the next bend and flattened herself against the wall. She was out of options. She had to swing her pick. But once she did that, there would be no second chances.

Either she would survive, or he would.

"Rachel?"

He was coming, drawing so close she dared not breathe. Tears slipped down her cheeks as she waited, and her lips moved in silent prayer. *Please . . . please . . .*

Suddenly the light fell over her. She heard his excited intake of breath, saw the knife—and, feeling as vulnerable and exposed as she had ever felt in her life, swung the pick.

She caught him with a fairly solid blow, solid enough to knock the lamp out of his hands and send him reeling. And that gave her time to swing again.

It was the second blow that did the most damage. The sharp metal end lodged in his chest so deeply she couldn't pull it out.

He seemed as surprised as she was. He stared down at himself in horror, until the pain and the realization of what she had done enraged him even more. Cursing, and swinging at her with one hand, he yanked the pick out with the other and tossed it away. Then he lunged for her.

She tried to run, but it was no use. Her sprained ankles could no longer support her weight. Terror overwhelmed her as he caught hold of her hair. And, almost immediately, his hands circled her neck.

Rachel could feel his extreme hatred as he squeezed—squeezed until she couldn't fight anymore. Then everything went dim, as if the light he'd dropped had gone out.

Chapter 27

It was obvious as soon as Truman reached the flats that someone had been in the mine. A broken Davy lamp lay on its side near the lift. Around the corner, in the loading area, there were more broken lights—and four bodies. Using his own lamp to see who they were, he glanced up at Jonas Cutberth, who had accompanied him into the mine.

"'Tis Thornick and the others," he said.

Cutberth knelt to confirm it. "Two have been shot. The others stabbed."

"I can't believe Wythe has done this," Truman said.

"Who else could it be?"

Truman supposed that Cutberth could have done it himself and used the excuse that Wythe had been here to get him into the mine. But he had been holding one of Truman's pistols since they entered the cage. If he meant him any harm, Truman would've found out before now. "But why would he kill these men?"

"Maybe they knew something they shouldn't."

Truman rued the day his parents had been kind enough to take Wythe in. "He will hang for this."

"We have to catch him first," Cutberth responded.

With a sigh, Truman lifted his light to see a few feet down each of the tunnels that branched off from here. With four men murdered, he was so afraid of what he might find he could hardly move. Did Wythe have Rachel? Or had he killed her, too?

"You take the tunnel heading to Number 8. I will go this other direction, to Number 10," he told Cutberth.

With a muttered curse against Wythe, the ex-clerk left his dead friends.

Truman stood as he hurried past. "And Cutberth?"

His lamp cast shadows on his face as he turned. "Yes, my lord?"

"Be careful. He is obviously not right in the head."

"You be careful, too. I would guess you are more of a target than I am. He won't get any bloody title from me—pardon my language."

"Maybe not." Truman nudged Thornick's foot. "But he will kill anyone who gets in his way."

Cutberth indicated the pistol Truman had given him. "I'll shoot if I have to."

As Cutberth ran off, Truman pulled out the other pistol, which he'd slid into his waistband for the ride down. "Rachel?" he called. "Rachel, answer me!"

There was no response.

"Wythe, if you hurt her, you have no idea what I will do to you. You will never inherit a halfpenny. Do you understand? But if you give up and bring her to me, I will do whatever I can to help you."

He paused to listen, but only his own voice bounced back to him. He couldn't even hear Cutberth now that the man had hurried down the other tunnel.

"Rachel?" It felt hopeless, but he kept calling to her as he searched. He felt as if he had been everywhere before the miners started to arrive for work. Then they all searched. They were so angry over the deaths of Thornick, Greenley, Collingood and Henderson that he didn't have to offer them any incentive to take the task seriously. But it wasn't until an hour later that word finally reached him: She had been found.

He wanted to ask if she was alive, but he didn't dare. He had already seen too much loss in his life, knew he couldn't bear the answer if it was no.

"Take me to her," he said instead.

Rachel lay on the damp ground, tossed to one side like a used rag. She was shivering and covered in something damp and sticky. She didn't know if it was the grime of the mine or if it was blood. Twice she had tried to call out but couldn't seem to find her voice. Or maybe she had managed it, because she'd drawn someone's attention. Cutberth was nearby. She might have been afraid of him, but he was being careful not to spook her. He called out that he had found her, then remained crouched to one side, keeping his distance because every time he tried to touch her she gave a frightened cry.

"Rachel, thank God! Are you badly hurt?" The earl came rushing toward her, his voice filled with fear. She was so relieved to see him she couldn't even speak. He was alive. They were *both* alive.

But where was Wythe? She wanted to get up and look around, to prepare for another assault, if there might be one coming, but she didn't seem to have her usual strength. Her fingers sought her throat, where she could remember *his* hands . . . squeezing the life out of her.

"Truman," she managed to croak. "I thought I might never see you again."

He dropped down beside her and wiped the tears that streaked down her face. "I'm here, Rachel. I'm here with you. And I won't ever leave you again. Tell me you will survive."

"I think—I think I will be fine."

"What happened?" His voice was as gentle as a caress when he pulled her into his arms.

"I'm not . . . certain," she admitted. "I-I thought my life was over. I thought he was going to kill me. And then . . . I heard footsteps. Men hurrying past me, calling my name. I was afraid I was dreaming, that if I dared answer he would come back."

"My poor Rachel," he said. "He can't harm you now. I'm here. And I will never let him or anyone else harm you ever again."

It was difficult to swallow. Her throat hurt too badly. But she was grateful for the pain. It was the only thing that convinced her that this moment in his arms might be real, that the earl was with her again, after all.

"Is he still here in the mine?" Cutberth asked.

Her memories were too foggy to be able to answer that. "I've tried to piece it together," she managed to say. "I slid my hands out in search of him, but he didn't seem to be lying close by."

"Over here," someone shouted. "I've found Mr. Stanhope."

Cutberth went to see. Truman looked over but he didn't relinquish his hold on her. "Is he alive?" he asked.

"No, my lord. I think he bled out. He's got a chest injury. It looks like he tried to get up, maybe to stagger out, but . . . he didn't make it far. He's lying in a pool of his own blood."

"Get a wagon and take him to the surface," the earl said. Then he pressed his lips to Rachel's forehead. "Thank God I found you," he whispered and carried her to the cage.

"It's over," he promised and soon they were out of the mine and squinting against a beautiful, clear dawn. "It's all over."

When Rachel opened her eyes, she saw a large painting propped up near her bed. She studied it for a second, wondering why it was there and why it looked so familiar. And then she realized. It was *Landscape with the Fall of Icarus*! With a small gasp, she tried to sit up, but Truman was there, and he gently pushed her back.

"Not so fast," he cautioned. "Dr. Jacobsen *just* left. He said you are to take it easy for several days yet."

"But you found it!" She studied the farmer and the plow and the ship he'd told her about. It was beautiful. "You found the Bruegel you were looking for."

"I found *all* of the missing paintings. Well, they were recovered," he corrected. "As soon as Madame Soward learned that Wythe was dead, she came out of hiding and contacted Mr. Linley, eager to trade them for the reward."

"When was this?"

"Yesterday."

"But . . ." She remembered nothing about that. "Where was I?"

"In a laudanum-induced sleep. Jacobsen said you would recover more quickly if you gave your body a chance to get some rest before facing the emotional trauma of what you experienced."

But she didn't feel upset. She felt . . . free. Surely he did too, now that the demons that had nearly destroyed him were gone—those within and without. She smiled as she gazed at the painting. "You were right all along."

Something else occurred to her, something she wanted to tell him. "My lord . . ."

"Rachel, call me Truman, please," he said with a laugh.

She closed her eyes at the pleasure it gave her when he rubbed her cheek with the back of his hand. It was such a tender gesture.

"If you are going to be my wife, you will need to get used to it," he chided her.

"I like the sound of that, of being your wife."

He smoothed the hair off her face. "I like the sound of it too."

"But . . . what of Mrs. Poulson? You know she had a hand in the fire, in Katherine's death."

"I do. But we don't have to worry about her. Not anymore."

"Is she . . . gone?" Rachel asked.

He sat on the edge of her bed. "Yes. Gone for good."

"What happened?"

"As soon as she heard that Wythe was dead, she"—he cleared his throat—"let's just say she fell into despair."

"I have never seen a servant love someone she has served as much as Mrs. Poulson loved Wythe," she marveled.

"He wasn't just someone she served, Rachel."

There was something . . . odd about his tone. "What do you mean?"

"She was his mother."

Rachel felt her mouth drop open. "But . . . how?"

"All too easily, I'm afraid. Apparently his father dallied with the servants as often as he did."

"The woman who was supposed to be his mother hid that from the world?"

"From everyone, even my parents."

"Why would she be willing to do that?"

"She was unable to give him a son herself. Maybe she felt it was her duty to accept Wythe because of that. I don't know. But I didn't find out about the relationship until she learned of his death. Then she fell to the floor, weeping uncontrollably and rocking back and forth, moaning, 'My son, my son, what have they done to you?'"

Rachel winced. She wasn't sure if it was for the sight Mrs. Poulson must've made or the pain she must've felt. Rachel had no love for the housekeeper, but losing a son was a terrible thing. She knew because her own mother had suffered so badly when Tommy died. "Could she have meant that metaphorically?"

"No. It makes too much sense, now that I know. Why she was his wet nurse. Why she followed him everywhere. Why she was so devoted."

"Katherine was carrying Wythe's babe." That was it. That was what Rachel had wanted to tell her betrothed. But she was still so weak and tired. "Mrs. Poulson killed her for fear she'd tell."

He grimaced. "Yes. I know that, too. She didn't stay crumpled in a heap of grief for long. She soon grew angry. She told me about the baby, said I wasn't man enough to father a child, that Wythe never should've saved me, that I wasn't anything compared to him, that he deserved the title." He waved a hand. "You get the idea."

Rachel had a headache. She adjusted the pillows to give her more support. "It's a wonder she didn't try to kill me, too, before I could bear you an heir. It felt like she hated me enough."

"I'm afraid she might've tried. That's why I'm glad she's gone."

"What happened to her in the end?"

"She ran out of the house and, before anyone could stop her, jumped off the cliff to the rocks below."

Horrified, Rachel covered her mouth. "No . . ."

"I'm afraid so," he said.

"We will both forget," she promised. "We won't think of it again. Her or Wythe."

His gaze shifted to the Bruegel. "It's sort of eerie that this particular painting is what unraveled the mystery, don't you think?"

"Why?" she asked.

"You know who Icarus was." His fingers moved over hers as he talked.

"Someone from Greek mythology?"

"Yes, a very ambitious fellow. He wanted to fly. So his father made him a set of wings with feathers secured by wax."

It seemed as if she had read the story before, but she couldn't remember it. "Did those wings work?"

"They did. But he got too ambitious for his own good and would not heed his father's warnings. He decided he would fly all the way to the sun."

"And the heat melted the wax." It was coming back to her now.

"That's right. He fell into the sea and drowned." He pointed to the painting. "These are his legs here, just below the ship. As you can tell, he didn't get very far."

"Wythe tried to fly too close to the sun," she murmured. It was such a fitting description for what had happened, how ambition had taken hold and caused his downfall.

"At least he got a lot further than Icarus," Truman responded.

"He wanted your title so badly—and all that went with it, my love. The admiration, the respect, the money."

Truman's handsome face looked pensive. "If he had only waited, he might have inherited it all."

"No." She smiled as she placed his hand on her stomach. "You will one day have a son to inherit it all."

He bent to kiss her lips. "And the farmer continued to plough."

"What does that mean?" she asked.

"It's an old Flemish proverb that goes with the painting. It means life will go on."

"It will do more than go on, Truman. We will be happy, won't we?"

His hand cupped her cheek. "It makes me feel guilty to say it, but I am already happy. *You* make me happy. That's all I need."

EPILOGUE

Rachel snuggled closer to the warmth of her husband's body. They had been married for six months, but having him in her bed never grew old. She enjoyed hearing his steady breathing, relished the feel of his bare skin sliding against hers as he moved in the night. She had tried telling him it was unseemly for them to sleep without clothes every night, but he wouldn't hear of letting that change, and she had only been teasing him anyway. She never felt so content as when she was lying naked in his arms.

A knock sounded at the door. "Uncle Truman? Are you coming?"

It was Geordie. He had taken Wythe's old room. Although he insisted on being able to continue to work in the stables, he had let them talk him into moving into the house. "Hello? Are you up?"

Truman stirred. "Coming!" he called. Then he grumbled, "Is it morning already?"

"I'm afraid so," Rachel said with a laugh.

"Um . . ." He pressed his lips to her temple. "Too bad. That means I have to leave you."

"It's nice of you to take Geordie to the colliery. To teach him how to manage your assets."

"If he is to be steward there someday, he might as well learn while he is young."

"He would gladly go anywhere with you."

"He is a good boy. I love having him accompany me. And I can't think of a better person to understand the needs of the miners."

She felt as if, by having suggested he groom Geordie to take over the running of Stanhope & Co., she was doing her part for Tommy, her father and the other miners. She didn't want to abandon their cause or forget her roots, and Truman had proved so understanding about that.

"Uncle Truman? Are you sure you're getting up?" Geordie asked.

Rachel could hear the eagerness in his voice and knew Truman could too. Her little brother idolized her husband, tried to emulate everything he did. "I promise. I will be right there."

"I'll have the horses ready."

The floor creaked as he hurried away.

"He has been so happy since we came here," Rachel murmured. "I owe you for that."

"And what about you?" Leaning up on one elbow, he stared down at her, suddenly serious. "Are you happy, my love?"

She smiled as she gazed into his handsome face, into those amber-colored eyes that had once frightened her so badly. "I couldn't be happier."

His hand slid over the swell of her abdomen—evidence that their baby was growing fast. "I can't believe I almost tried to live without you."

"You don't mind being married to a poor village shopkeeper? You don't mind that your son will be the offspring of a *commoner*?"

He kissed her extended belly. "There is nothing common about you," he said. "There isn't another woman on earth I would want to be the mother of my child. You are so much more than I ever dared hope for."

She slipped her fingers through his thick hair. "I could never love anyone more."

"That's what I wanted to hear." He pecked her lips. "I had better go. I don't want to keep my brother waiting."

Reluctantly she let him slide out of bed and, while he dressed, she enjoyed the view. But as he started to leave, she shifted her attention to *Landscape With the Fall of Icarus*, which they had hung in their room.

"What are you thinking?" he asked, following her gaze.

She pursed her lips. "Of the fire, everything. It seems like such a distant memory now."

"It was all worth it," he said.

She studied him. "You can't mean that. You endured so much."

His eyes met hers. "But without my particular past, I never would have found you."

ABOUT THE AUTHOR

Micah Kandros

When Brenda Novak caught her daycare provider drugging her young children with cough medicine to get them to sleep all day while she was away at work, she quit her job as a loan officer to stay home with them. She felt she could no longer trust others with their care. But she still had to find some way to make a living. That was when she picked up one of her favorite books. She was looking for a brief escape from the stress and worry—and found the inspiration to become a novelist.

Since her first sale to HarperCollins in 1998 (*Of Noble Birth*), Brenda has written nearly fifty books in a variety of genres. Now a *New York Times* and *USA Today* best-selling author, she still juggles her writing career with the demands of her large family and interests such as cycling, traveling and reading. A three-time Rita nominee, Brenda has won many awards for her books, including The National Reader's Choice, The Bookseller's Best, The Book Buyer's Best and The Holt Medallion. She also runs an annual online auction for diabetes research every May at www.brendanovak.com (her youngest son suffers from this disease). To date, she's raised over $2 million.